Mariah Stewart is the *New York Times* and *USA Today* bestselling author of twenty-six novels and three novellas and has been featured in the *Wall Street Journal*. She is a finalist in romantic suspense and the recipient of the Award of Excellence for contemporary romance, a RIO Award for excellence in women's fiction, and a Reviewers Choice Award from *Romantic Times Magazine*.

By Mariah Stewart:

Mercy Street

Cry Mercy

Acts of Mercy

Coming Home

Home Again

Almost Home

Hometown Girl

Home for the Summer

The Long Way Home

The LONG WAY HOME

MARIAH STEWART

piatkus

PIATKUS

First published in Great Britain in 2013 by Piatkus,
an imprint of Little, Brown Book Group

A CIP catalogue record for this book
is available from the British Library.

ISBN 978-0-349-40141-6

Typeset in Bembo by M Rules
Printed and bound in Great Britain by
Clays Ltd, St Ives plc

Papers used by Piatkus are from well-managed forests
and other responsible sources.

MIX
Paper from
responsible sources
FSC® C104740

Piatkus
An imprint of
Little, Brown Book Group
100 Victoria Embankment
London EC4Y 0DY

An Hachette UK Company
www.hachette.co.uk

www.piatkus.co.uk

For Chery Griffin.
She knows why –

Diary ~

*When I was young and impatient and would say things like
"I wish Christmas would hurry and get here!" or "I wish I
were twelve already"—or fifteen, or eighteen, whatever the
perceived magic age was at the time — Mother would always
say, "Don't wish your life away. Time passes quickly
enough." Another of her favorite expressions was "The older
you get, the faster time flies." The truth of the latter has been
made clearer to me with each passing year.*

*It seems that only last week or so, my daughter was
planning that first big wedding at the inn last winter, and now
here we are, a year later, Halloween behind us and
Thanksgiving only weeks away. I blinked, and we went from
talking about Lucy coming home for the summer to staring
down the barrel of winter all over again.*

*Another of Mother's favorite expressions was "Be careful
what you wish for." On my last birthday, I made two wishes:
I wished that my two wandering children would come home—
come home and stay home. Well, half of that wish has come
true with Lucy coming back . . . and joy! Making plans to
marry Clay, just like I always knew she would do. Now if I
could only wish Ford home as easily, I'd be the happiest
woman on earth. Oh, I know I should count my blessings—
and I do, every day. But with Ford involved in . . . well, who
knows where he is or what he's doing? Certainly not I. People
ask me what UN Peacekeepers actually do, and sometimes
I'm not even sure myself. I know he's somewhere in Africa.
He said if he told me exactly where, I'd worry too much and
he'd rather not lie if he didn't have to, and that he's safe where*

1

he is, so I shouldn't be anxious. But really. What kind of mother would I be if I didn't worry after hearing that?

Exactly.

Sometimes I ache so much to have him home—to have all three of my babes safely under this roof with me. Even though they're adults, they're still my babes, and I still worry and fret over all of them.

Lucy thought she'd be having a wedding of her own this fall, but since word has spread that she's the new event planner at the inn, business has gone through the roof and she hasn't had time to plan her own wedding. She's so good at what she does, transforming the inn into something different for every happy couple. I don't know where she gets her ideas from. I just hope she saves something wonderful for herself!

Anyway, it's nice to head into another holiday season. Lately, though, I've been sensing that something's coming, something that's about to change our world here in St. Dennis— not in a significant way, but a change nonetheless, and I can't quite get a handle on it, but I think I'll know it when I see it.

I suppose I could consult the next world and see what my spirit friends have to say—Alice _always_ has something to say—but on the other hand, since the change doesn't feel like a threat, perhaps it might be more fun to just wait and see what comes our way!

~ Grace ~

Chapter 1

SO *this is St. Dennis.*

Ellis Chapman drove slowly along Charles Street—slowly enough to earn her a few short polite beeps from the cars following her. At the top of the street, where she'd turned off the highway, there'd been an old farmhouse and an orchard on the left side of the road, and woods on the right. Where the farmland ended, a residential area began with a long block of lovely old homes set on nice lawns surrounded by old shade, mostly maples and oaks. The fallen leaves had blanketed many of those nice lawns with yellow and red and brown, all just waiting to be raked into irresistible piles into which the neighborhood children would surely jump.

The commercial district crept up gradually: it took a moment for Ellis to realize that the clapboard houses she'd passed were actually a restaurant, an antiques dealer, a bookstore, a gift shop, a children's clothing store, and a candy store. The heart of the district had a handful of storefronts. There was a cupcake bakery, a women's clothing store, another restaurant with an upscale look about it, a coffee shop, a flower shop, and a small newsstand that apparently sold beverages, judging by its name, Sips.

3

Nice, she thought as she drove along. *All the basics, but with a slightly trendy touch.*

She continued on through the town, past a sign announcing a marina, yet another restaurant, and an ice-cream parlor.

Looks like the people around here like to eat.

"Works for me," she murmured.

The drive from Massachusetts had taken longer than she'd anticipated, though she was still almost thirty minutes early for her appointment. She made a left turn and drove around the block. Once back onto Charles Street, she made a second pass through town, trying to decide how best to assuage her hunger. There was no time for a meal, but coffee and maybe a quick snack would be welcome. She parked across the street from the coffee shop—the sign read CUPPACHINO in a stylized script—and headed down against the wind, dodged the midafternoon traffic to cross to the other side.

She pushed open the coffee shop's red door and rubbed her hands together to warm them while she glanced around for an empty table. She was just about to head for one when a little wave from the teenage boy at the counter caught her eye.

"I can take your order here," he told her. He went on to explain, "We're counter service only."

"Oh. Well . . . " She squinted to read the handwritten menu on the chalkboard behind him.

"Take your time. No hurry."

"I'd like a large regular coffee with whole milk." She paused to survey the edibles. She really shouldn't indulge, she told herself, right before she heard herself say, "And one of the vanilla cupcakes with the pink frosting."

"Excellent choice." The boy nodded his approval and poured her coffee into an oversize blue mug. "Cream and sweeteners are over on the cart there behind you."

"Oh," she said for the second time, and turned to locate the station.

She paid for the coffee and the cupcake and took both to a table that sat off by itself next to the wall, then carried the mug to the cart, where she added milk and a packet of raw sugar. She sat, sipped, and took a bite from the cupcake.

Bliss.

It was excellent, with tiny bits of strawberries in both the frosting and the cake. The coffee was equally good, and she sighed. If St. Dennis had nothing else to recommend it, at least there was great coffee and baked goods to be had.

The door opened and three chattering women entered the shop and went directly to the counter, where they were served coffee in mugs from what appeared to be a special shelf along the wall. Ellis watched surreptitiously while the ladies fixed their coffee at the station.

" . . . so really, Grace, what else could I have done?" one woman was saying as she added two pink packets of sweetener to her coffee.

"I don't know that I would have done anything differently, dear." The oldest of the three—Grace, apparently—shook her head slightly. "Sometimes you just have to go with your gut."

"My gut would have told me to smack her over the

head with something," the third woman said drily. "She's lucky that you have more patience than I, because, really, Barbara . . . "

The voices trailed away as the women passed by. The woman called Grace, who had white hair tucked into a bun and a gentle face, turned to smile at Ellis.

"Hello, dear," she said softly without breaking her stride.

Ellis returned the smile and felt an unexplainable lump form in her throat. She turned her attention back to the cupcake and her coffee. So far, it seemed that St. Dennis was much like her mother had described: a small welcoming town populated by nice people. For about the one-thousandth time, Ellis wished she'd accompanied her mother on at least one of her trips here, but for Ellis, there'd always been somewhere else to go.

"Why waste your summer in some little nowhere place," her jet-setting father would say, "when you could be in London . . . ?"

If not London, then Rome or Madrid, or on the small island they owned off the coast of Greece. There'd been summer classes in Cairo when she'd been majoring in archaeology, and another in Paris the year she'd thought about majoring in French. Her father would take Ellis anywhere she wanted to go, as long as it wasn't St. Dennis, a place that *no one* who mattered had ever heard of. In retrospect, it seemed that her father had been manipulating both her and her mother for more years than anyone realized.

Well, those days were gone—not just the travel, but the manipulation—along with her mother, and any chance Ellis might have had to see St. Dennis through her mother's eyes.

She downed the last of the coffee and bused her table as she'd seen another customer do, before returning the plate and mug to the counter.

"Thanks," the young man told her. "Come back again."

"I'll do that." Ellis tossed her crumpled napkin into a nearby receptacle and started toward the door, stood back while other patrons entered, then stepped out into the sunshine. She was standing on the curb, waiting for the light to change, when she had the inexplicable feeling that she was being watched. She turned back to the shop, and saw the white-haired woman seated next to the front window. The woman raised her hand in a wave. Ellis waved back, then realizing that the light had changed, crossed and went directly to her car.

She slid behind the wheel and glanced back to the window. The woman had turned from the glass and appeared to be once again engaged in conversation with her companions, but there'd been something about the way she'd looked at Ellis, almost as if she knew her. Impossible, of course, Ellis reminded herself, since she'd never set foot in St. Dennis before today.

She pulled away from the curb and drove east, watching for the street where she'd make her turn.

The sign for Old St. Mary's Church Road was larger than the others because it also sported a plaque that marked the historic district. She made a right and drove three blocks, made another right, and parked along the street, as per the instructions she'd been given. She got out of the car, locked it, and stood on the sidewalk reading the sign over the door on the brick Federal-style building.

ENRIGHT & ENRIGHT, ATTORNEYS-AT-LAW.

This would be the place.

Ellis took a deep breath and walked along the brick path to the front door, pushed it open, and stepped into a quiet, nicely furnished reception area where an elderly woman sat behind a handsome dark cherry desk. The woman looked up when she heard the door, glanced at Ellis, then did a double take.

"I'm El . . . Ellie Ryder. I have an appointment with Mr. Enright." *Ellie Ryder*, she reminded herself. From now on, that was who she'd be, at least for as long as she stayed in St. Dennis, and possibly longer, depending on how much time it would take before the shit-storm subsided.

"I believe he's expecting you." The woman at the desk smiled warmly and got up from her chair. "I'll let him know you're here."

The receptionist disappeared into a room across the hall and stood behind the half-closed door. A moment later, a man who appeared to be in his midthirties emerged and came directly into the reception area, his hand outstretched to her.

"Ms. Ryder, I'm Jesse Enright. How was your trip? Can we get you some coffee? Have you had lunch?" His hand folded around hers with warmth and strength, and Ellis—*Ellie*—felt herself relax for the first time in days.

Reminding herself that he already knew the story, she smiled as she stood.

8

"The trip was fine. I arrived here in town with time enough to spare for a stop at the coffee shop in the center of town," she told him. "I had a great cup of coffee and a delicious cupcake."

"Vanilla with strawberry frosting?" he asked.

Ellis nodded. "You had one, too?"

"One last night and another at lunch. My fiancée is the baker." He patted his waist. "It's good news and bad news."

Jesse turned to the receptionist. "Violet, hold my calls, if you would . . . "

He led Ellis to his office and closed the door behind them.

"So how do you really feel?" He held out a chair for her, and she sat.

"Strange. It's strange to introduce myself as Ellie instead of Ellis. Ryder is my middle name, but I never use it, so that's strange, too."

"You don't have to do this, you know." Jesse sat behind his desk in a dark green leather chair. "I think you'll find people here to be much less judgmental than you assume."

"Over the past year, I've had more judgment passed on me than you could possibly imagine. Friends I thought for sure I could count on stopped returning my calls as soon as the news broke." Her best effort not to sound bitter was failing her. "My father had very little family, but what he has turned their backs on me, as if somehow this whole thing was my fault. My home was confiscated, my car, my jewelry, my bank accounts—I lost everything I worked for. If not for the one friend

9

who stuck by me, I wouldn't even have had a car to drive down here."

"The Mercedes you parked out front belongs to a friend?" Jesse raised an eyebrow.

When she nodded, he smiled. "Nice friend."

"The best," she agreed. "I don't know where I'd have been this past year without her."

"I understand that you've had a rough time these past ten months or so, but I'm asking you to keep an open mind as far as the people in St. Dennis are concerned. You'll find them welcoming and friendly, if you let them."

"I'm not here to make friends, and frankly, I hope I'm not here any longer than it will take to sell the house my mother left me." She looked at him across the desk and added, "You don't know what it's like to have people judge you because of something your father did."

"Oh, but I do." Jesse leaned back in his chair. "My father was the black sheep of the Enright clan. Still is, actually. Suffice it to say, I had to earn my grandfather's trust to join this firm, prove that I was good enough to call myself an Enright here in this town where Enrights have practiced law for close to two hundred years. So yes, I do know what it's like to be judged because of something your father did. I overcame it, and so will you."

"But you were still able to work as a lawyer somewhere, right?"

"In Ohio, before I came here, yes."

"I can't get anyone to even give me an interview or return my calls. I ran public relations for a major corporation for eight years, and I can't get anyone to hire me. Granted, the company was owned by my father—hence the confiscation of my worldly goods, since everything was considered 'fruit of the poison tree,' as the FBI told me repeatedly—but still, I was very good at what I did. One of the investigators even said that one of the reasons the entire scheme came as such a shock to everyone was that I'd done such a good job creating the company's image. So even though I had no hand in the fraud, I did have a hand in the public's perception of CC Investments." She blew out a breath. "When I think about all of the lives my father ruined, I get sick to my stomach. All the retired people who'd trusted him with their pensions, their mortgages, their futures . . . "

"What your father did was unconscionable, but you're not responsible for the decisions he made. As I recall, both the FBI and the SEC have totally exonerated you from any involvement in your father's scheme."

"Intellectually, I do know that I'm not responsible. I do. But then I think about all the suffering he's caused, and I just feel sick all over again."

"I understand," Jesse said. "But you're here to pick up the pieces and put your life back together again. I want you to know that you can call on this firm for anything, anytime."

"I appreciate that, Jesse. You've already done so much. My mother was wise to have entrusted the Enrights with her estate."

"Actually, it was your mother's great-aunt, Lilly Cavanaugh, who first came to us, as best I can determine from reading the file and from talking to Violet."

"Violet?" Ellis tried not to panic. Someone other than Jesse knew . . . ?

"My receptionist. You may have noticed she's a bit . . . advanced in her years."

"She knows who I am?"

"She knows that you are Lynley's daughter, and that you've inherited the house, yes." Jesse held up a hand. "There's no way she wouldn't have known. Violet's been here forever—she worked for my grandfather for many years. She typed up the original wills. But she also knows there's a confidentiality issue here, and she will not discuss it with anyone, I can assure you of that. That woman has kept more secrets than either of us will hear in a lifetime. Your identity is safe with her."

"I trust you, so I will have to trust her, I suppose. Though the way she looked at me when I came in . . . " She paused, remembering the woman in the coffee shop. "There was another woman, one in the coffee shop, who greeted me as if she knew me—"

"Don't let your imagination run away with you. I told you, it's a friendly little town."

"Still, I'd like to stick to the explanation we discussed on the phone."

"That you purchased the house from Lynley Sebastian's estate and you're fixing it up to sell it?"

"Yes."

"You're the client." Jesse pulled a thick folder to the center of the desk. "Now, I suppose you want to get on with the business at hand."

He pulled a sheaf of documents from the folder, explained each, and showed her where to sign. Twenty-

12

two minutes later, he handed her a small envelope with the address, 1 Bay View Road, written on the front in blue ink. She could feel the shape of keys inside, and her heart took an unexpected leap.

"The keys to your house," he said. "I drove over this morning and turned up the thermostat, so it should be nice and cozy for you. There's wood stacked outside if you feel like building a fire. The chimneys were all cleaned out four years ago, and to the best of my knowledge, none of the fireplaces have been used since. The bank accounts your mother set up years ago have paid the taxes and utilities and periodic repairs, and from time to time we've had the place checked inside to make sure that all was well, that the faucets weren't leaking, that sort of thing. It's been vacant for quite some time, you know. The house is fully furnished, everything just as it was the last time your mother saw it, I suppose. She had an alarm system installed but it kept shorting out, so I think it's been deactivated."

"I can't thank you enough for looking out for the place all this time. I'm sure my mother appreciated it."

"She was the one who made it possible. She set up the accounts a long time ago, with money she made during her modeling career. Once it was verified that she'd earned that money before she was married and that she'd set it aside before your father even started up his business, the feds weren't able to touch the account. Because your father's fingerprints weren't on any of it, you still have that money to work with. I never personally met your mother, but Violet spoke very highly of her."

"Violet knew my mother?" It had taken a second or

two for it to sink in that there were people in this town who had actually *known* Lynley. Ellis had been under the impression that the time her mother had spent in St. Dennis had been brief, and that she'd been very young.

"Sure. I imagine there are more than a few of the old-timers who knew her."

"But she left so long ago, I didn't think about people having known her."

"I didn't grow up here, so I can't attest to how much time she spent here, but I assure you, I remember Lynley Sebastian. After all, she was one of the first supermodels. Back in the day, every boy on the planet had one of her posters in his room." He smiled. "I know I did."

"Let me guess. The one where she's leaning on a fence and she's wearing a very thin pale pink dress."

"And the wind is whipping that long blond hair around her." Jesse grinned. "The very one."

"If I had a dime for every time someone brought that up to me . . . " She rolled her eyes.

"Speaking of money . . . " Jesse pulled another stack of papers front and center on the desk. "Here are the bank accounts I told you about. One savings, a separate account for checking. There's not a fortune left at this point, but if you're careful, I think you can easily manage until the house is sold, and barring disaster, should have something left over." He looked up at her. "You are still planning on selling the house?"

"Yes. The sooner the better. That's why I'm here."

"Well, keep in mind that it can't be any sooner than six months. I probably don't need to remind you that your mother's will specified that you had to live in the house

14

for a minimum of six months before you could sell it or any of the contents; otherwise, you forfeit everything and all the proceeds from the sale of the property will go to the charities she listed in her will."

"I've read the will"—Ellie nodded—"and the lawyers in New York made that very clear."

"I can put you in touch with a realtor when you're ready. Now, there might be some minor repairs that need to be done or perhaps some upgrades you might want to think about before you put it on the market. There's been no real updating in maybe thirty years, so I'm sure it all looks very dated. I can send Cameron O'Connor over to talk to you about all that. He's actually the one who's been taking care of the place."

"He's the handyman?"

"You could call him that." Jesse appeared to be suppressing a smile. "Now, here are the papers you need to take to the bank in order to have the accounts moved into your name."

"But if I put my real name on the accounts, then the people at the bank will know . . ." She frowned. So much for her desire for anonymity.

Jesse tapped a pen on the desktop and appeared to be considering other options.

"We can do this: we can maintain the accounts as they are now, in the name of your mother's estate. As executor, I've been signing the checks on behalf of the firm. I can continue to do so until the house is sold. You can submit any bills you have for repairs or whatever to me, and I'll pay them. If you need cash, we can arrange that as well. We can work under the pretext that the estate has

15

agreed to pay for any repairs to the property as part of your agreement of sale."

"Perfect." She sighed with relief.

Jesse gathered all of the papers, slid them into a brown legal envelope, and tied the strings to secure it.

"Here you go, Ms. Ryder." He handed it over to her.

"It's Ellie," she told him.

"Ellie, I wish you all the best." He paused, then added, "I hope you'll think about what I said, and that you'll give the folks around here a chance. Everyone isn't out to hurt you."

"I'll try to keep that in mind." She rose, the large envelope under her arm. "Hopefully, I won't be here long enough to find out. Well, no longer than six months, anyway."

Jesse opened the door for her and led her into the foyer.

"If you need anything, anything at all, let us know and we'll do whatever we can to help," he told her.

"Thank you, Jesse. I can't even put into words how much I appreciate everything you've done."

"You're welcome. Maybe we'll run into you at Cuppachino for coffee one of these days. It's the place where all the locals gather every morning."

"I don't know that I could handle one of those cupcakes every day."

"They are lethal, but I'll be sure to tell Brooke—she's my fiancée—that you enjoyed it."

"Please do." Ellis craned her neck to see if Violet was at her desk so she could say good-bye, but the room was empty.

16

Jesse held the front door open and stepped outside with her. "Glad to see the sun came out. It's been a little on the gloomy side the past couple of days."

"It's still chilly," Ellis noted.

"November moving headfirst into winter," he said. "Hope you brought some warm clothes."

"I did, thanks."

Jesse accompanied her to the end of the brick walk, his hands in his pocket. "Check in from time to time and let me know how things are going."

"Will do. Thanks again for everything, Jesse."

He nodded and waited at the sidewalk while she walked to her car, then waved before turning and going back into the building.

Nice guy, she told herself, and said a prayer of thanks that her mother's family had selected such a firm to represent them. She was well aware that another attorney might have been willing to sell her out. She could see the headlines now:

Daughter of Clifford Chapman Found Living Under Assumed Name in Small Maryland Town!

King of Fraud's daughter dumps his name, hides out on Eastern Shore!

Sad but true.

She slid behind the wheel and started the car. Following the directions Jesse had printed out for her, she drove around the square and made a left to head back to Charles Street. Once on Charles, she made another left and drove back through the center of town. Two blocks past the light, she took a right onto Bay View Road and drove all the way to its unpaved end. The number *1* was painted in dark green on a white mailbox that looked surprisingly new. She stopped in the middle of the street and stared at her inheritance.

The house seemed to have nothing in common with the others she'd passed on her travels through town, those imposing Colonial and Federal and Queen Anne styles that appeared on every block. This house was set at an odd angle to the road as if to gaze out upon the Bay and looked like an overgrown cottage, with misplaced gables here and there. The front porch didn't look original but it was impossible to tell when it had been added. It stretched across the entire front of the house and sagged a little on one side. The white clapboard siding could use a new coat of paint and the shutters were faded. Three brick chimneys—one of which listed slightly to the side—protruded from the roof. At the end of the driveway—which was covered in what appeared to be crushed shells—stood an outbuilding, a garage or a carriage house, the windows of which had been painted black. The shades in every window of the house had been pulled down, making it look as if it had something to hide. Two sides of the property were bordered by some of the tallest trees she'd ever seen. All in all, the impression was far from inviting, and yet something about the scene felt oddly familiar.

Like it or not, this was home.

She eased the sedan into the driveway and sat for several long moments before bursting into tears.

Chapter 2

EVENTUALLY, Ellie told herself, she was going to have to get out of the car.

"Why delay the pain any longer . . . ?"

She opened the car door and walked across the crushed shells to a path that wound its way leisurely from the driveway to the front steps. Her fingers traced the shape of the key inside the envelope Jesse had given her as she approached the porch. She ripped open the envelope, took out the key, and stuck the paper into her pocket.

"Here goes."

She fitted the key into the lock and turned it, pushed open the door, and stepped into a square foyer. The house was dark, as much because of the approaching dusk as because all the shades were pulled down to the windowsills. In spite of the chill outside, the house was warm—*Thank you, Jesse*—and very still, as if it had been holding its breath, waiting for her.

Ellie stood for a very long moment in the hushed foyer, her eyes adjusting to the dim light. The stairs to the second floor stood directly in front of her. Straight ahead to the left of the stairs was a long hall that led clear through to the back door, which also had a shade tightly pulled. There was a room to her right and another to her left. The furniture in both was covered with white sheets, giving what she could see of the downstairs the appearance of a ghostly landscape.

"Well." She spoke aloud to break the silence. What to do first, now that she was here?

After some deliberation, she walked into the room to her left and lifted the shades from the four windows—two facing front, one on either side of a fireplace. Paintings on the walls were draped with fabric and it took Ellie a moment to realize that the only things in the room that weren't covered were the carpets and the andirons on the hearth. She backed out of the room as if afraid of disturbing it, and went across the hall, where she found more of the same. There was no way to disguise that this was the dining room. A crystal chandelier, its ovoid drops covered with dust, hung over a long flat surface that lay beneath the expected white sheet. Against one wall, furniture lay hidden beneath more sheeting, and a peek under the draping on two smaller shapes revealed a sideboard and a tea cart. Peeling back the thin quilt from the side of the tallest piece of furniture, she found an empty china cupboard, the former contents having left round marks in the dust on the shelves. The placement of the windows and the fireplace exactly mirrored the room across the hall. The architect, she thought, clearly appreciated symmetry.

A feeling of déjà vu swept over her, and was promptly dismissed. Her mother must have described it all to her, she reasoned, and somehow she'd retained the images.

A door on the back wall swung open with a push and led to a butler's pantry that had glass-doored cabinets on

20

one wall, and an expanse of counter with a small soap-stone sink on the other. The cabinets were crammed with dishes, plates and bowls, and cups and saucers, all stacked haphazardly on top of one other.

The kitchen, a large square room, lay behind the pantry. Ellie pulled up the shades and looked for a switch for the clumsy overhead light fixture. Near the back door were the controls for a security system that obviously wasn't on, and the black push-button switch that served to turn on the light.

She wasn't sure the room hadn't looked better in the dark.

Chipped Formica in a truly terrible shade of yellow covered the counters. On the floor, there was dark linoleum of indeterminable age and a dreadful mustardy color. Wooden cabinets were built in along one long wall.

"I'll bet there isn't a thing in this room that isn't older than I am." She paused to consider the refrigerator, which looked much newer than everything else. "Well, maybe *that*. But not much else."

She walked to the stove. It, too, appeared newer than she'd expected. Not brand-new, but not 1950s, either. Curious, she thought.

A table with four chairs stood against the side wall under the windows. When she raised the shade, the last bit of afternoon sun spilled across the floor, highlighting the cracks in the old linoleum and the faded paper and paint on the walls.

Ellie stood in the center of the room, her hands on her hips, feeling more than a little bewildered, and stared at the wallpaper, blue-and-white-patterned teacups on a

21

background that was probably once white but was now yellowed with age. She'd seen that same paper—those same teacups—somewhere, but couldn't remember where.

She went to the back door and unlocked the dead bolt, which looked relatively new compared to just about everything else she'd seen so far, then stepped outside onto a small porch where she found nothing but a stack of wood. Like the shutters and the downstairs rooms, the porch needed a fresh coat of paint.

The yard was much deeper and wider than it looked from the house. Remnants of garden beds ran along the porch, the right side of the property, and the outbuilding—carriage house? garage?—that faced the driveway. A large shed with a door flanked by a window on each side stood in the back corner. She'd leave investigating that for another day. And there were those trees, huge things with long bare branches.

Bare branches where there'd been leaves not too long ago—but where were the leaves? She stepped off the porch and walked the length of the yard. She thought of the lawns she'd passed on her way into town, where the fallen leaves had carpeted the ground. Not here, though. She looked up at the trees and wondered if they were dead. She reached up to break a twig from the closest maple, and found it supple, not dry as one might expect from a dead tree. So where were the leaves?

A trip around the yard revealed a thick layer covering the flower beds.

Birdseed on the ground under the feeders that hung from the branches of several dogwoods meant that someone had filled them.

22

Raked leaves. Filled bird feeders. Wood stacked near the back door.

She glanced at the house nervously. Could someone be inside, hiding, perhaps, on the second floor? A squatter, maybe, someone who knew the house was empty, had been empty for years?

There was an outside entrance to the basement, double wooden doors that were God knows how old. Maybe . . .

Ellie took a deep breath and walked to the doors and gave one a good yank—but they didn't budge.

"Okay, locked is good."

She went back up the steps and stared at the pile of wood. Must have been Jesse, she decided. Of course. Hadn't he said they'd been looking out for the place? She hadn't thought that would mean raking the leaves into the flower beds and keeping the bird feeders filled, but those were nice touches. She exhaled and went back inside, making certain she relocked the door.

She walked softly on leather-soled flats back to the foyer. At the bottom of the steps she stood, as if listening, waiting to see if there was any sound from the second floor. Convinced there were no squatters—surely Jesse would have noticed—she climbed the steps slowly, almost on tiptoe. At the top of the stairs was a landing and a hall that, much like the one below, led to the back of the house. She counted the doors—there were five, all closed. Her hand paused at the one closest to her before grasping and turning it. She pushed it open and peered inside.

"More sheets. Where," she wondered, "did they find so many sheets?"

The wallpaper was peeling from one corner, the

23

flowers fading to the palest of yellows. She picked up a strip that had flaked off and fallen to the floor. The flowers, like the teacups on the paper in the kitchen, seemed to ring a very distant bell in her memory. She slipped the paper into her pocket and left the room.

One by one she opened the other doors, took a long studied look inside before closing them again. There were four good-size bedrooms and one large bath accessed from the hall. Two of the bedrooms had their own baths, all were fully furnished and had closets. Ellie resisted the temptation to open those doors, not sure of what she'd find hanging there.

She stood on the landing, looking at the doors she'd moments earlier opened then closed. She had to pick one to sleep in, and she needed to do that now so she could find sheets—*no problem there*—and hopefully, blankets. All of the bed linens would have to be washed, of course. Did this house have a washer and a dryer? She hadn't seen one on the first floor. Perhaps in the basement.

The basement where the squatters were hiding.

"You're being ridiculous. You've got the imagination of a ten-year-old," Ellie chastised herself as she returned to the first bedroom on the left, opened the door, and turned on the light switch. She pulled the sheet off the double bed and was happy to see there were pillows with pillowcases already on them. She removed the cases, punched the pillows a few times. A couple of feathers fluttered out, but no discernible dust.

"Real feather pillows," she noted.

She stripped the pale pink fitted sheet from the mattress and rolled it up with the top sheet and the pillowcases. On her way out of the room, she pulled up the shades and leaned on the sill to look out the window.

At the end of the street, a stone's throw from the house, was a dune, where tall grasses swayed in the light breeze, and beyond the dune, the Bay rolled onto a narrow stretch of beach in easy waves. Ellie dropped the bedding onto the mattress and forced open a window. When she raised the sash, the scent of the Bay flowed in as gently as the water nudged the shore. It was salt and pine and something she couldn't put her finger on, but the combination was pleasing and she smiled. Her mother had once mentioned how the Chesapeake smelled, and now here Ellie was, filling her lungs and experiencing the Bay much as Lynley had.

"You were right, Mom. It's delicious. At least, tonight it is." After a few minutes, the room grew cold, and she closed the window and locked it. "Not sure how it smells on a hot muggy day in August, but since I will be long gone by then, it won't be my problem."

She gathered up the bedding, turned off the light, and made her way back downstairs. She dropped her bundle on the floor, then went into the living room.

"Time for the big reveal," she announced. "Let's see what we've got hiding under all these covers."

She found a vintage dark green mohair sofa under one sheet, three club chairs—one green, two maroon—under others. She ran her hand over the upholstery and traced her fingers over the plush fabric. It was soft and velvety and comforting. She sat for a moment, her head resting back against the cushions, and closed her eyes, feeling strangely at home.

She got up with a start and turned on the lamps—

grateful to find they all still had bulbs—and removed all the protective coverings.

"Not bad, actually." She nodded when she was finished. "Not my taste, but I do know that there's a solid market for 1950s and sixties furnishings, so I should do all right here."

The paintings on the wall were an odd mix: a few landscapes and a dark painting of the Bay. The tops of the wooden tables were bare, but the bookshelves that ran along one wall were filled to overflowing. Ellie figured she'd have plenty of time to peruse the family library, since there was no TV. She could watch on her phone, but really, with everything that had to be done in the house, who would have time for television?

She added the sheets from the living room to the items she'd brought downstairs and carried the whole pile to the basement door. She found it locked; the sliding bolt opened easily. There was a switch at the top of the steps, but when she turned it on, the light-bulb downstairs popped.

"Crap. No way am I going down there in total darkness." She closed the door and relocked it. "Uh-uh."

She paused to think. It hadn't occurred to her to bring laundry soap, so she'd have to find a Laundromat anyway. Had she passed one in her travels today? She didn't recall seeing one.

Her grumbling stomach reminded her that she had to find dinner as well. She didn't know the lay of the land well enough to simply charge out the front door, so she consulted her phone. She discovered there was a Laundromat out on the highway and several restaurants and a food market nearby. Perfect. She could coordinate the washing/drying with grabbing some dinner and stocking up on some staples to take back to the house.

She followed the directions she got from her phone—so grateful for modern technology—and arrived at the Laundromat right before the sun set. She found the place empty except for an attendant who appeared to be in her late teens. Apparently Tuesday was not a big wash day in St. Dennis.

The young attendant extracted herself from the book she was reading long enough to make change so that Ellie could purchase a small packet of detergent. She loaded the nearest washer with the sheets and the required amount of cash and turned on the machine.

"Excuse me." She approached the attendant again. "How long do the wash loads usually run?"

The girl shrugged and took a sip from an almost empty bottle of Diet Pepsi. "I dunno."

"I need to do some food shopping at the market across the road. That's why I'm asking. I need to know how much time I have."

"Maybe thirty minutes?" The girl shrugged again. "I don't usually pay attention. But we're not busy. If you want to leave money for the dryer, I'll put the stuff in for you when the washer's done."

"That would be so nice of you." Ellie smiled gratefully. "Thanks so much. That would really be helpful."

The girl shrugged.

"I noticed there are several restaurants right along the strip here." Ellie paused near the door. "If I wanted to grab a quick dinner, which one would you recommend?"

The girl raised her head and appeared to think over the question.

"Real dinner or just like, you know, a sandwich or something?" she asked.

"I think real dinner."

"The Crab Claw at the end of the shopping center has pretty good stuff. Not as good as what you get in town, like at Captain Walt's or Lola's, but okay, I guess."

"Thanks. I'll give it a try."

Her itinerary set—market then pick up dinner then back to the Laundromat—Ellie drove across the road to the market. She hadn't made a list, and hadn't really thought too much about what she needed. Now that she was here and behind a cart, she felt overwhelmed.

Food staples first, she decided. Milk, eggs, bread, cereal, butter. Peanut butter. Maybe a can or two of tuna. Mayonnaise. She hadn't seen a coffeepot in the kitchen and doubted she'd find one, and she could not abide instant coffee. Which meant that she'd be driving into Cuppachino in the morning for a large take-out coffee until she could purchase a coffeemaker. In the meantime, she tossed a box of tea bags into her cart.

Purchasing food turned out to be much easier than selecting cleaning supplies, something she hadn't ever done before. There'd always been a housekeeper to dust and vacuum and clean the bathrooms and the kitchen— even when she was camped out at her friend's Boston town house this past year. Scanning the seemingly end-less rows of cleansers and plastic bottles threatened to give Ellie a headache until she decided to take the product that professed to be "all-purpose" at its word.

28

She hadn't cleaned bathrooms since that summer camp she'd gone to when she was thirteen. The counselor in charge of their cabin took her duties very seriously, and required all of the girls to clean not only the cabin but the communal bathrooms as well. At the time they'd lamented their bad luck in having drawn Judy Wilson's cabin, but in retrospect, at least Ellie had learned some lessons she'd never forgotten.

She picked up a second bottle. Who knew when the house had last been cleaned? She grabbed a jumbo pack of paper towels, cleanser, a large package of sponges, a sponge mop, and a plastic bucket.

That should pretty much cover everything.

She checked out, loaded up her car, drove back to the shopping center, and pulled in front of the Crab Claw, which seemed to be doing little more business than the Laundromat. She entered through a red door that had a giant crab painted on it. Inside the lighting was dim and the square wooden tables were set almost exclusively for four people. There were only a few parties scattered throughout the room and music played in the background. A plump waitress with short curly strawberry-blond hair and an overabundance of eyeliner approached with a menu.

"You gonna be meeting someone, hon?" the waitress asked.

"Ah, no. Actually, I was hoping for takeout," Ellie replied.

"Anything on the menu can be made for takeout." She handed Ellie the menu, a large slick number with a shiny picture of the same crab that graced the door.

"Thanks." Ellie opened the menu and began to scan it.

"The burgers are really good here," the waitress told her softly.

"I was hoping for more than a sandwich," Ellie said without looking up.

"A baked potato can be substituted for french fries, you could get a side salad." The waitress leaned a hand on a nearby chair and repeated pointedly, "Like I said, the *burgers* are real good."

Ellie got the message.

"Thank you. I'll have the burger, baked potato, side salad."

"Good choice. Dressing for the salad?"

"Vinaigrette?"

"I guess you could call it that." The waitress smiled and wrote down the order. "Can I get you a cup of coffee or tea, or something while you wait?"

"I would love a good cup of coffee," Ellie admitted.

"We're not Starbucks but I'll make a fresh pot."

"Thank you." Ellie took a seat at the closest table and checked out the decor. Crab traps hung from the ceiling and nets covered the walls.

A second waitress emerged from the kitchen with a tray that she served to a party of six—two tables pushed together, Ellie noted—and a few moments later, Ellie's waitress returned with the promised cup of coffee.

"Thank you," Ellie said.

"So, you just passing through?" The waitress leaned on the back of the chair opposite Ellie.

"How can you tell?"

"If you were local, I'd know you."

"Well, I guess I'm almost local. I inher—*bought* a place in St. Dennis and just arrived here today."

"Oh, which house did you buy? There weren't that many on the market, last I heard."

"It's on Bay View. An older place, needs a lot of work."

The waitress nodded. "A fixer-upper, estate sale? Best way to buy, if you're handy. St. Dennis is still a pretty hot ticket, draws a lot of visitors. 'Course, you probably already know that or you wouldn't have bought here, right? Prices aren't down here the way they are in other places. You should see this place in the summer." She shook her head. "You can barely get a table. Some weekends, there's a line out the door."

The door opened and three women entered.

"I hope you got a good deal on it," she told Ellie before she turned to greet the newcomers.

"I did."

"Good for you, hon." She patted Ellie on the shoulder as she walked past. "I wish you all the best luck with it."

"Thank you," Ellie whispered, suddenly a little choked up, though she couldn't have put into words why. Maybe it was the kind words from this stranger, or the nice offer from the girl at the Laundromat, but after almost a year of feeling as if she'd been batted around by just about everyone she'd ever known, the unexpected goodwill she'd met with today made her feel like crying. It had been quite awhile since she'd felt this emotional.

Not that she'd cry in a public place, but still.

The waitress brought out a bag with her takeout, and Ellie followed her to the cash register.

"Anything else, hon?"

"No, I think I'm good," Ellie told her. "Wait, yes. I'd like a Diet Pepsi."

"I only have fountain. That okay?"

"That's fine."

The waitress got the drink, added it to the bill, and Ellie handed over what she owed plus a tip.

"Oh, wait. You forgot to add the coffee," Ellie told her.

"It's on the house. Come back again when the rock-fish are running. The cook does a real nice job with the fresh fish. Off-season, the frozen ... not so much. But the burgers are always top-notch." She winked at Ellie and headed for the kitchen.

"Thanks ...," Ellie called after her, but the waitress had already disappeared through the door.

She carried the drink and the bag of food to the car, left the food, and took the drink into the Laundromat.

"Your stuff's done." The girl glanced up only long enough to see that it was Ellie.

"Thank you. I appreciate your help." Ellie placed the tall container of soda on the girl's small desk.

"What's this?" the girl asked.

"I noticed your drink was getting low." Ellie made her way to the block of dryers. "Which machine?"

"Oh. The third one from this end." Clearly surprised, the girl was still staring at the drink Ellie'd brought her.

Ellie opened the dryer, folded the sheets, and closed the dryer door again. She waved to the girl as she was going to the door.

"Wait, I didn't pay you for the soda," the girl called after her.

"No charge."

"Hey, thanks. This was ... nice. Really. You didn't have to," the girl told her.

"You didn't have to put my stuff in the dryer." Ellie opened the door. "See you."

"Hey, come back anytime."

Bet on that, Ellie thought as she loaded the clean laundry into the back of the car.

She drove back to the house and sat in the driveway for a few moments to watch the sun as it faded on the water.

Nice.

She remembered the burger that was getting colder by the minute, and took the food into the house. She sat at the kitchen table and ate with the plastic fork the waitress had tucked into the bag, used the plastic knife to put a touch of butter onto the potato, poured dressing from a small plastic cup on the salad, and used the bag as a place mat. Who knew when the table was last cleaned, and what might have crawled over it since?

The thought made her shudder.

The burger was, as promised, delicious, and the baked potato and salad just right. It was hardly the fare she'd been used to all her life, but she sensed that this was not a home where gourmet dinners had been prepared by master chefs. This was a place where comfort food had been prepared by loving hands, she felt certain.

Tonight she'd take the first steps to get the house cleaned up. She debated the merits of starting in the kitchen as opposed to starting in the bathroom. Before too long, she felt overwhelmed, so she finished eating and went back to the car to bring in her laundry and her purchases. At least she had clean sheets to sleep on, and she had enough food for the next few days.

She dug through the bags for one of the containers of cleaning product and a sponge. She was just about to head upstairs when her phone rang.

"Hey, you. How's it going? How's the new home?" Of course, Carly Summit, Ellie's best friend—her *only* friend, the friend who had opened her home to Ellie, loaned her a car and money, and stood by her when everyone else in her life vanished—would call to make sure everything was okay.

"It's . . . different. Different from what I expected, but in a good way. I mean, it isn't terrible." Ellie walked into the living room, turned on two of the lamps, and sat in one of the club chairs that faced the Bay. "Actually, it's quite charming in a shabby chic sort of way."

"You sound upbeat. That's good."

"I am upbeat. I think with some elbow grease and some paint, this place will clean up quite nicely." Ellie paused. "I'm talking a full crap load of elbow grease and buckets of paint, but still, the end result should be fine."

"Shades of Counselor Wilson at Camp Bedlam." Their shared name for Camp Bedlingham in the Berkshires where they'd spent several summers.

"That's exactly what I was thinking earlier. Though now I'm grateful for all those hours I spent scrubbing porcelain."

"So do you have a game plan?"

"Of course. Tonight I'm going to clean the bathroom I'm using on the second floor, then put sheets on the bed, after which I will fall face-first into it. That's all I've got so far. I'm exhausted."

"Long drive?"

"Not so bad."

"Look, Ellie, you know that if you need anything—I mean anything—all you have to do is call."

"I know that, and I appreciate it. But you've already done so much for me. I'll never be able to repay you for everything, Carly." Once again, that pesky lump tightened Ellie's throat.

"'Pshaw,' as my great-grandmother used to say. Have I done anything for you that you wouldn't do for me, if the tables were turned?"

"Of course not."

"Well, then, there you are. Who knows, someday, when things are super for you again, maybe I'll be down on my luck and you can give me a hand."

"Carly, you'll never be down on your luck."

"You never know. We'd have said the same about you two years ago."

"True enough but . . . " Ellie paused. "Carly, is everything okay there?"

"Perfect, as always. I was just trying to make the point that friends do what they can. Right now you're in a situation and I'm in a position to help out."

"But you'd tell me, right?"

"Of course. Who else would I tell?"

They chatted a little longer, Carly exclaiming, "Ohhhh! Waterfront! Fabulous!" when Ellie told her that the house faced the Bay. "I may have to buzz on down there soon."

35

"Anytime. Really. Please. I miss you," Ellie told her.

"I miss you, too, El. I'll fit in a trip when I get back to the East Coast. In the meantime, you can scrub up one of those bathrooms for me."

"Will do."

"Now, tell me all about your new house and that little town . . ."

After Ellie had told all and the call disconnected, she sat in the silent room, the phone still in her hand. Hearing Carly's voice reminded her that regardless of how it felt sometimes, she wasn't totally alone. Everyone else may have written her off, denied their friendship, and forgotten that she'd existed, but there was always Carly, and while Carly wasn't physically with her, talking to her had cheered Ellie. Such was the power of friendship.

Ellie locked the front door and carried what she needed upstairs, where she turned on the light in the room she'd claimed as her bedroom and went into the bathroom. She turned on the faucet, and jumped back when a stream of rusty water coughed out.

"Seriously?" She watched it run down the drain in rusty swirls. After a while the color began to lighten, and a few minutes later, the water ran clear.

"That's more like it." With cleanser and a sponge and the "all-purpose" cleaner, she managed to get the bathroom in respectable order in a little less than an hour.

"Not bad." She stood back to admire her work. "Not bad at all. Counselor Wilson, you'd be proud of me."

She changed the sheets on the bed, then realized she hadn't looked for blankets. She found a pile of old quilts in a chest in one of the other bedrooms and brought two of them into her room. One went onto the bed, the other she folded at the bottom. They smelled slightly of mothballs, but she decided it wasn't so bad that she'd risk freezing. She turned off the lights on the first floor and lowered the thermostat, took a quick shower, got ready for bed, and crawled under the covers.

Flat on her back and looking up toward a ceiling she couldn't see, Ellie relived the day, from leaving Carly's town house to driving straight through to St. Dennis, to meeting Jesse Enright. Stepping for the first time into the house she now owned, navigating her way to find the things she needed. She thought about the waitress at the Crab Claw who'd given her coffee and steered her away from the fish that might not have been so good, and the young girl at the Laundromat who'd offered to put Ellie's things in the dryer so that she could do her shopping and buy dinner.

"I told you, it's a friendly little town," Jesse had told her. And later, "I hope you'll think about what I said and that you'll give the folks around here a chance. Everyone isn't out to hurt you."

If everyone in St. Dennis were like the people she'd met that day, she'd concede that he was right. Of course, how kind everyone would be if they knew she was Clifford Chapman's daughter—well, that would be the test, wouldn't it?

Not a test anyone would be subjected to. When she'd told Jesse she wasn't there to make friends, she wasn't kidding. Friendship required honesty, trust, and Ellie knew she wasn't going to go there.

She'd trusted Jesse because she had to, but she wouldn't

be hanging around St. Dennis long enough to find out who else she could trust. After she'd been burned so badly by the two people who should have most loved her—her father and her fiancé—trust was hard to come by these days.

Ellie still couldn't wrap her head around the fact that her father—the same father who'd been her champion all her life and had always seemed to have put her, his only child, above everything else—was worse than a common thief because he didn't steal out of necessity but out of a greed so out of control there had been no end to it. If he hadn't been caught, she was certain he'd still be stealing the life savings and pensions of people who trusted him.

Ellie, too, had trusted him.

When the charges were first announced, she'd been blindsided. The moment when her father had looked her in the eyes and admitted that he—aided by Henry—was in fact guilty, that he had in fact done everything the FBI and the SEC said he'd done, Ellie had felt her entire world crack and shatter. That both her father and Henry—she'd planned on marrying that man!—had woven the tangled web in which thousands of people lost everything they had, devastated Ellie. Carly had been in Paris but had flown home the second she heard the news, had stood by Ellie while she was grilled six ways to Sunday by one investigator after another. When the interrogations were over and Ellie had been cleared of any involvement, Carly had taken her home, where Ellie fought off the pain and shame for the next three months.

The entire past year had been totally surreal, had turned Ellie's world inside out, and made her question everything she knew about herself, her life. What her father and Henry had done went beyond betrayal.

No, best to bury Ellis Chapman so that Ellie Ryder could get on with her life.

Chapter 3

CAMERON O'Connor parked his aging Ford pickup at the corner of Old St. Mary's Church Road and Cedar Lane, then walked the half block to the law offices of Enright & Enright. He didn't have an appointment, but given the foul mood he was in, he'd muscle his way past Jesse's elderly receptionist if he had to. He wasn't a man who was quick to lose his temper, but today he was *this* close.

He took a deep breath in an attempt to calm himself before he opened the firm's front door. As usual, Violet Finneran sat like a sentry at her desk to the left of the foyer. Cam was tempted to ignore her and just walk into Jesse's office, but better judgment prevailed.

"Miz Finneran?" he said from the foyer.

Apparently startled, the woman looked up from whatever it was she was reading, then a smile crossed her face.

"Cameron O'Connor, come in here and let me look at you," she commanded.

Anger was no excuse for poor manners. Cam went into the reception area.

"How have you been, son? It seems like months since I've seen you."

"Yes, ma'am. I'm fine, thank you. How are you feeling?"

"I'm doing just fine, too. And your sister? She's well?"

"Very well," he replied. "Thanks for asking about her."

"Of course. Please give her my best." Violet Finneran lowered her glasses and gazed at Cam. "Were you hoping to see Jesse?"

Cam nodded. "If he has a minute . . . "

"Let me check on that for you, dear. Why not have a seat?" She stood and walked across the hall, where she knocked softly on the first door. After a second, she went into the office, and a moment later was followed back out by Jesse.

"Hey, buddy. What's going on?" Jesse was his usual friendly self. "Missed you at the beer tasting the other night."

"Got tied up with a project." Cam could have added that he'd been working on a table he was making as a surprise gift for Jesse and his fiancée, but didn't feel like getting into that right now. "Got a minute?"

"Sure. Come on in." Jesse led the way back into the office, and Cam closed the door behind him.

"You finally getting around to writing that will, or are you—?" Jesse began as he seated himself behind his desk and pointed to one of the side chairs as an invitation for Cameron to sit.

"Is it true?" Cameron cut him off and ignored the offer of the chair. "Has Lilly Cavanaugh's house been sold?"

"Well, yeah." Jesse looked uncomfortable. "Where'd you hear that?"

"I stopped at Cuppachino this morning and Grace Sinclair mentioned it. She said some woman from up north bought it and she's—"

"Where did Grace hear about it?" Jesse asked.

"Someone saw lights on in the house and a car in the driveway a few nights ago and called the police. Beck stopped over to see what was what and was informed that the house had changed ownership."

Jesse nodded. "It did."

"Why didn't anyone in town know it was on the market?" Cam folded his arms across his chest. "More specifically, why didn't *I* know it was for sale?"

Jesse stared at Cameron for a long moment, then said, "The previous owner had given instructions to her lawyer in New York for the disposition of the house. Everything was handled there."

"By the previous owner, you mean Lynley Sebastian."

"That's right."

"She's been gone for how many years now? And the house is just now being sold? And sold so quickly that no one around here even knew it was on the market?"

"There may have been some entanglement with the investigation into her husband's affairs. I don't know the particulars because as I said, it was handled by the attorneys in New York who handled Lynley's estate on behalf of her heir."

"That would have been Lynley's daughter? I remember she had a little girl."

"I suppose." Jesse shrugged. "Want to tell me why you're so pissed off?"

"I would have liked to have had an opportunity to bid on the property."

"You'll still have that opportunity. The new owner is planning on doing some renovations before selling it."

"Seriously?"

"From what I understand, she has no interest in stay-ing in St. Dennis any longer than she has to. She just wants to clean the place up, make some necessary repairs, maybe spiff it up a little, then get what she can for it before moving on."

"She a professional?"

"A professional what?" Jesse frowned.

"House flipper. You know, people who buy houses that are run-down or outdated or that have serious prob-lems, fix them up, then sell them for a profit. Such as myself."

"I didn't get the impression that she's done this sort of thing before."

"So you've met her."

Jessed nodded. "The firm still represents some interests of the estate."

"What's her name? The owner."

"Ellie Ryder. She's from—"

"Ryder? *R-Y-D-E-R*?" Cam felt a tickle on the back of his neck.

"I think so. Why?"

"Lilly Cavanaugh's maiden name was Ryder, spelled just like that."

"I'm sure it's just a coincidence." Jesse brushed off any possible significance with the wave of his hand. "But just out of curiosity, how would you know that?"

"I knew the Cavanaughs pretty well when I was a kid. It's how I came to take care of the place," Cam said, his voice softened. "We lived on Bay View for a while. Miss Lilly was . . . well, she was a special lady."

"If you knew her, you must have known Lynley." Jesse sat back in his chair, a thoughtful expression on his face.

Cam hesitated. "When she was in town, we'd exchange a few words about cutting the lawn and raking leaves, looking after Miss Lilly, that sort of thing. I don't remember how old I was when I realized the connection between Miss Lilly's niece and that pretty face that was on all those magazines."

"Cam, if I'd known you had an interest in the property, that you had a history there, I'd have tried to help you out." Jesse appeared to be choosing his words carefully. "However, the house has now changed hands. I'm sorry. I had no idea that you'd want it, but I'll make certain that you know when the owner is getting ready to sell."

"I'd appreciate it."

Cameron felt his blood pressure lower. Of course, not having arrived in St. Dennis until last year, Jesse wouldn't have known Cam's family history. One of these days, Cam would have to tell him about the time he and his family lived on Bay View Road. But it wasn't going to be today. Maybe some night, when he and Jesse were testing beer flavors for Clay Madison and Wade MacGregor, whose local brewery, MadMac Brews, was still in the start-up phase, he'd tell the story.

Then again, maybe not.

Clay, who'd lived in St. Dennis his entire life, surely knew, but he was a friend and he'd never brought it up.

Wade was a little younger, and hadn't really spent much time here—except summers—until he was in his teens, so he might not have heard. Funny, Cam thought, the things that are so monumental to you, the ones that you carry around inside you and think are always on everyone else's mind, really aren't a regular topic of conversation among other people. He knew, though wasn't sure he totally believed, that if his family's circumstances ever came up at all, it was in passing, and was either precipitated or followed by the words " . . . and yet Cam and his sister have turned out so well . . . "

Cam let go a breath he didn't realize he was holding.

Of course, Jesse wouldn't have known. And of course, Lynley's New York lawyers would have been the front line, since surely efforts would have had to be made to keep the house out of the mess Lynley's husband had made. He hadn't followed the story all that closely—not much time these days to sit and read newspaper articles on issues that didn't directly affect him, given his busy contracting business. He had little interest in the Internet aside from searching for materials for a job now and then, and rarely watched television, preferring to spend his spare hours winding down by building furniture—tables, mostly—from old barn boards. The reports of the Chapman scandal had held only a passing interest to him. Had Lynley still been alive when it broke, he would have paid much closer attention. There had been references to Clifford Chapman's late wife, of course, but her connection to St. Dennis was rarely mentioned. So with her gone, Cam had merely shaken his head and turned to the sports page.

"But I was going to call you," Jesse was saying, "to ask

if you'd pay a visit to the new owner and maybe help her figure out what needs to be done. I know she doesn't have a lot of money to invest in the place and she's planning on doing as much of the work as she can herself, but there will be things that should be checked out or repaired or whatever that she might not be aware of."

Cam nodded. He'd been taking care of the property for years, long before Jesse arrived in St. Dennis. From the time he was eight or nine years old, the Cavanaughs paid him to help out around the yard, weeding the flower beds and assisting with the spring planting of the vegetable garden. Later, as a teenager, he'd cut the lawn with the old push mower that Mr. Cavanaugh had kept in a shed in the backyard. After her husband died and Miss Lilly was alone in the house, Cam stopped by every week to do whatever needed being done. As she aged, he found himself doing more and more for her, not that he ever minded one minute he'd spent helping her out. Then she passed away, and Lynley inherited the property, but he kept up with the yard and the flower beds that Miss Lilly had taken such pride in. Even after Lynley died, his stewardship continued, not because anyone had asked him to, but because he felt he owed it to Miss Lilly to keep an eye on things in return for all she'd done for him. But that, he reminded himself, was between him and Miss Lilly.

"Sure. I'll stop over this afternoon, see what's what."

"Maybe given your interest in the property, you can come to a deal about the eventual sale. You know, maybe give her a hand here and there, in exchange for a slightly lower sale price. Who knows?" Jesse stood. "The idea might appeal to her, especially since she isn't prepared to sink a fortune into the place. Of course, if she did, she'd be able to command a pretty steep price. St. Dennis real estate has more than held its own. And sitting right there on the Bay, we both know that place will be worth a nice chunk of change after it's fixed up."

"No argument there." Cam opened the door and stepped into the hall.

Jesse glanced at his watch. "You have time to grab some lunch? It's one o'clock already."

"Sure. How 'bout I meet you down at the Crab Claw for a burger?"

"They do have great burgers, but it's on the highway and I walked to work today." Jesse leaned against the doorjamb. "Unless I can hop a ride with you, but that means you'd have to drive me back."

"Sure. I have to come back into town to file for a permit for a kitchen remodel I'm doing over on Parson Middleton Road."

Jesse told Mrs. Finneran he'd be gone for about an hour and asked if he could bring her something from the Crab Claw.

"No, thank you, Jesse. I already had a sandwich." She waved from her desk. "Don't be such a stranger, Cameron."

"You take care, Miz Finneran." Cam waved back. The drive to the restaurant took five minutes, during which time the two men discussed next Sunday's football games and the statistics relevant to each team. Cam was still extolling the merits of one of his favorite running backs as he pulled into the busy parking lot at the Crab Claw.

A car was about to pull out at the end of the row, and Cam waited patiently while the driver strapped into his seat belt and prepared to back out.

"This guy made a first down damned near every time he touched the ball, so you'd think that someone would have figured out how to shut him down, and besides . . . "

Just then a woman walked out of the restaurant swinging what looked like a take-out bag. Of average height, she was lean in black leggings and a slouchy green sweatshirt and walked with an easy grace. A bright green scarf held back chestnut-brown hair, and her oversize glasses covered a good deal of her face. He wondered if the parts that were hidden looked as good as the parts he could see.

Cam momentarily lost his train of thought.

"Cam." Jesse tapped him on the arm.

Cam turned to Jesse, who wore an expression of amusement as he pointed at the now-empty parking space.

Cameron pulled into the space.

"What?" he asked Jesse. "What are you smirking about?"

"That woman, the woman you were just all but drooling over . . . ?"

"What about her? You know her?"

"That, my friend, was Ellie Ryder."

Cam swung around in his seat to take another look, but the woman had already disappeared into what looked like a fairly new Mercedes sedan.

He turned back to Jesse. "I was under the impression that she wasn't flush with cash. That's no cheapie compact she's driving. I'm guessing that sucker's worth eighty, ninety thousand if it's worth a penny."

Jesse merely shrugged and got out of the car. Cam got out, too, and watched the big sedan exit the lot and head for the light. Once it made the left toward St. Dennis, he turned and followed Jesse into the restaurant. Right now he needed a fat burger and a cold drink. He'd catch up with Miss Ellie Ryder later.

Chapter 4

FOR the fourth day in a row, Ellie headed toward the narrow beach when she needed a little bit of a break. She passed over the dune carefully so as to not disturb the sea grass that grew there and any little living thing that might be hidden beneath it.

The beach itself was an oddity to her, as beaches went. It was narrow and pebbly, unlike the beaches she'd sunned herself on in her old life, beaches that had miles of soft sugar-white sand with nary a stone in sight. Here, a large rock stood at the edge of the dune, and she'd taken to sitting on it with a mug of tea or coffee in the afternoons. The waves here were so gentle as they lapped at the shore, and the sunlight so soft, she almost wished she hadn't given up painting years ago. Of course, she wasn't sure she could replicate that pale light. It took on the most beautiful golden glow as it shimmered on the water.

Yesterday she walked along the shoreline until she came across the remains of what might have been a lighthouse. How tall had it been? When had it been built and what had happened to it?

The slamming of a car door shook her from her mental wanderings. Ellie stood and looked up Bay View

Road and was surprised to see a pickup truck parked at the end of her driveway. She jogged back to the house and arrived just as a tall blond man was about to ring her doorbell.

"May I help you?" she called from the foot of the drive.

He turned, his hands on his hips. "I'm Cameron O'Connor."

"And . . . ?"

"And Jesse Enright asked me to stop by." The man frowned. "I thought he'd told you."

"You're the handyman?" she asked.

His smile revealed a row of very white teeth. "Yeah, I'm the handyman."

"I'm Ellie Ryder, the new owner. Jesse said maybe you could give me a few pointers about things that need to be done to the house."

"Sure. How much work are you planning on doing here?"

"I haven't decided." She crossed her arms over her chest. "I guess I need to see what the place needs most and what I can afford."

"Well, how 'bout we take a look around the outside, then move inside to see what's what?"

"That sounds like a plan." Ellie met him halfway to the walk. "Things don't look too bad out here." She gestured to the front porch. "Well, except for the sag on the end there. Might need a little help with that. But the shutters look secure and in decent condition."

"You might want to think about paint out here for . . . well, for pretty much everything. The porch, the shutters,

51

the front door. Give it a little more curb appeal if you're planning on selling the place."

"I am going to sell it." She paused. "What exactly did Jesse tell you?"

"Just that you purchased the house from Lynley Sebastian's estate and you'd be looking to sell."

"I will be, but of course, I want to maximize what I can get. So I want to do whatever I can to increase the value of the house without bankrupting myself."

He turned and eyed her car in the driveway. She knew what he was thinking: why not sell that big old Benz and buy something a little smaller, less expensive, more economical? Which was exactly what she would do, if the car belonged to her; however, that was none of his or anyone else's business. Besides, if she sold the house tomorrow and left St. Dennis—which, thanks to her mother's will, she could not do—where would she go? She felt she'd relied on Carly's friendship long enough. If she stayed here and worked through the winter, she could put the house up for sale in the spring. Six months would take her to May, and by then she would have had more time to figure out her next move. Right now she was completely at odds with no clear goal, no destination.

And of course, the house would have greater value if put on the market in the spring, when people were more likely to be looking for a place on the Bay.

"You might need a new roof," Cam was saying as they looked up at the front of the house.

"It's not leaking," she hastened to tell him. "It's rained twice since I've been here and it hasn't leaked at all. I looked everywhere, even in the attic. The roof isn't leaking."

"Looks like it's at the end of its life span, though."

"There's nothing in the budget for a roof." She moved on around the side of the house with him. "That's not on the gotta-do-to-sell-the-place list."

"You will want to clean out those gutters, though, maybe have the downspout replaced." He pointed up toward the roof. "The gutter's filled with leaves and the water will just spill over instead of going down the downspout when it rains. Which it can't do anyway because the downspout's separated from the gutters. See here?" He pointed to the place where the two pieces disconnected and moved the downspout slightly. "I'm guessing all of the gutters are in the same condition."

He walked around to the back of the house and she followed.

Cameron grabbed the back-porch railing and wiggled it. "This is an accident waiting to happen. The top rail is loose and could give out if anyone leans too hard on it. Plus there are some rotting floorboards there on the deck, and a few steps are a little weak." He looked at her somewhat apologetically. "I meant to come back and replace that railing and it completely slipped my mind."

"You were the one who raked the leaves. You filled the bird feeders and stacked wood near the back door."

He nodded.

"Jesse said he was keeping an eye on the place. I thought he meant he was doing it himself. I guess he meant you were. Was the estate paying you?"

"No." Cameron appeared slightly insulted.

"Good Samaritan?"

"I knew Lilly Cavanaugh, a woman who used to live here. She was a very kind, sweet lady and she loved this house and her gardens. I figured the least I could do for her was keep up her place on the outside until someone decided to do something with it. She left the house to a niece who unfortunately never got to live here before she died." He paused. "You must know that the niece was Lynley Sebastian, since you bought the house from her estate."

Ellie nodded. "Did you ever meet her? Lynley Sebastian?"

"Sure. She spent some time here."

"Really? What was she like?" Ellie's heart skipped a beat.

"She was nice. Beautiful, even when she was sick."

"Wait." Ellie grabbed his arm. "She came here when she was sick?"

Cam nodded. "Not as much as she did before she got sick, but yeah. Why?"

"Just . . . curious, that's all." Ellie sought to recover. "I mean, you always saw her in magazines and on the society pages, but I don't remember seeing pictures of her when she was sick."

"Well, she came here, whether or not anyone was around to photograph her. I guess she didn't publicize her comings and goings."

Ellie tried to remember her mother leaving their home to go anywhere when she was being treated for the cancer that eventually took her life. Of course, Ellie was away at school much of the time, but still, would she have known if Lynley went away for a few days?

"Did she drive here on her own? How long did she stay?" The questions were out of her mouth before she could stop them.

Cam looked at her curiously. "She had a driver. He'd drop her off and she'd stay for . . . I don't really know how long. What's the difference?"

"She was a famous person and she owned the house I live in. It's just natural to be curious."

"I guess."

Cameron walked past her to the center of the yard. "The entire house needs a new paint job." He turned to his right. "Now, the carriage house needs more than just paint. It needs some hefty repairs."

She tucked thoughts of her mother aside and tried to focus on what he was saying. She stared at the old building and said, "Do you think maybe it should be taken down?"

"Are you crazy?" He turned and glared at her. "That's a historic structure. That carriage house was built by the first lighthouse keeper when the lighthouse was built. You can't just take it down."

His vehemence blasted her back a step or two.

"Sorry. I had no idea this was sacred ground," she said, no extra charge for the small amount of sarcasm.

"You can't destroy something just because it's inconvenient or shabby."

"Okay, I get it. Really. I do. I've apologized. The lighthouse you're referring to was out on that spit of land behind the trees?"

He nodded. "It was built in the early 1800s. Burned down twice and rebuilt each time. It came down for good in a hurricane in the 1940s."

"But the remnants are still there," she noted.

"Mostly just the old stone base, which no one's had the heart to haul away. Technically, I guess it belongs to you."

"The town doesn't own it?"

"I think if you check your deed, you'll see that that piece of ground is part of this tract. So yeah, it would belong to you now."

"Wow. That's . . . " She sought a word. When nothing better came, she said, "That's very cool."

"There used to be a dock there, too. It jutted out pretty far into the Bay, since the water is so shallow close to the beach."

"A lighthouse and a dock. How 'bout that?" She couldn't help but smile. It all sounded so . . . *romantic* somehow.

"So anyway, you're going to want to do something to shore up that carriage house, or make sure whoever you sell the place to understands its significance."

"Is there a historical register here? A historical society?" Hadn't she seen a sign somewhere for a historic district?

"Yes." He nodded. "Someone there can probably give you whatever information you're looking for."

"If it's all that historic, wouldn't it already *be* on the register?"

"Maybe. Probably." He started toward the house. "Let's take a look inside and see what she needs in there."

Ellie hustled to keep up with his much longer legs.

"I've been spending most of my time cleaning but I still have a long way to go." She reached the back steps a second or two after he did. He stepped aside to permit her to take the stairs first.

"There was some sort of security system installed at one time." She pointed to the control panel on the wall in the back hall. "It's not working, though. Jesse said it was disconnected a few years ago."

"Kept blowing fuses. The whole place needs to be rewired, brought up to code, given a little more juice."

"Great," she muttered.

"Beck keeps an eye on things, though, so you don't need to worry about break-ins."

"Beck's the police chief." She nodded, remembering his visit several nights ago when a neighbor had seen lights on, and suspecting a burglary in progress, called 911. "He said a patrol car passes by the house a couple of times throughout the night."

"Has been for years. Miss Lilly was a popular lady in St. Dennis. There's never been a problem here, as far as I know."

"So this is the kitchen." She stated the obvious as they entered the big square room.

"Where to start in here? New floor, new counter-tops, new cabinets, new—"

She held up a hand to stop him. "Unless something crazy happens—like I win the lottery—it's getting paint on the walls and the cabinets, and that's about all. Maybe a new floor if I can swing it, which frankly I'd love to do because that color is beyond heinous and I can barely stand to look at it."

57

Cam nodded and they moved into the butler's pantry.

"Likewise in here. Paint. A new light fixture would be great but it's not in the budget." She pointed to the floor. "More of the same from the kitchen. It's like it seeped under the door." She pretended to shiver.

Cam knelt down, opened one of the cabinet doors, and poked around on the floor for a moment with a penknife he'd taken from his pocket.

"What are you doing?" she asked.

"Just looking at the floor in here. Unless I'm mistaken, there's wood under the linoleum."

"Wood?" Her eyes widened hopefully at the thought. "Nice wood?"

Cam nodded. "Looks like heart pine to me. Very 'in' right now."

"Could I rip up the floor in here to find out?" She bit the inside of her cheek for a moment. "And if it's pine in here, might it be pine in the kitchen as well?"

"No guarantees, because I can't see through the linoleum, but that would be my guess."

"I'm definitely adding 'rip up kitchen and pantry floors' to my list of things to do."

"How 'bout you let me know before you start? There might be some old glue on the wood, and you're going to need to remove that very carefully."

"You know how to do that? You'd show me?"

"Sure." A smile played at the corners of his mouth.

"Great. Thanks." She made a mental note to call Jesse and thank him for sending Cameron over. He moved through the swinging door into the dining room and she went along with him.

"The wallpaper in here should come down." He turned to her. "Have you ever removed wallpaper before?"

"I was planning on just painting over it. Taking it down would be so messy."

Cam shook his head. "Painting over it is only going to make a bigger mess in the long run. The paper's loose in places and I see there's some old water damage up in that far right corner. See where it's stained?" He pointed to the wall. "It's all going to have to come down, Ellie."

"So I'll get a scraper and scrape away. It'll give me something to do over the winter."

"You're going to have to spray the paper with water to loosen the old glue before you scrape. And it's going to make a really big mess. You're going to need to put tarps down on the floor or all those little sticky scraps of paper will be a real pain to pick up."

"I have to do that in every room?"

"I'm afraid so."

Ellie's earlier enthusiasm was beginning to wane.

"I can loan you a ladder. And the sprayer, a tarp, and a scraper when the time comes."

"Thanks," she said more weakly than she'd intended.

He grinned and led the way across the hall to the living room.

"I always liked this room," he said admiringly.

"I'm growing quite fond of it myself. I sit in here and read at night." She gestured to the wall of bookshelves. "As you can see, there's plenty of reading material to be had."

He nodded, and for a moment, Ellie thought he was

going to speak. When he did not, she added, "No TV, of course."

"You probably have some sort of electronic device you can watch TV or movies on."

"I do, but it's not the same somehow as a nice big screen. Besides, there's nothing that I watch on a regular basis and *must* see." She shrugged. "Anyway, I'm finding myself so tired by ten o'clock it's an exercise just to get myself up the steps."

"Not used to all the physical work?"

"Not by a long shot."

"What did you do in New York, before you came here?" Cam asked.

Ellie paused before replying. "I worked in public relations."

"Let me guess. You lost your job due to a corporate downsizing."

"Something like that."

"Yeah, I heard there was a lot of that going around." She could feel his gaze on her face but couldn't look at him. Her job was the last thing she wanted to talk about. Well, almost the last thing.

"Did you like your job?" he asked. "Were you good at it?"

"Yes, to both."

"I figured. You don't strike me as the type of person who'd do something you didn't enjoy, at least not for too long. And I suspect you'd be very good at anything you decided to do."

She tilted her head to one side, and he recognized the question in the gesture.

"Just judging by the job you're taking on here." His hand waved around the room to take it in. "All the furniture's been uncovered and it looks like it's been vacuumed. Everything's been dusted and cleaned. It's been a long time since this place looked like someone lived here." He glanced at the fireplace, then did a double take. "And you found Ted Cavanaugh's decoys. Damn, it's been years since I've seen these things." He picked one up to admire it. "They weren't here last time I was in. Where'd you find these?"

"They were in a closet in the kitchen wrapped in newspaper." She paused. "Wait. Did you say the last time you were in here? Does that mean you have a key?"

"Actually, I do have a key." He glanced over his shoulder, the duck decoy still in his hand. "I have one, Jesse has one. But I'll be glad to drop mine off in the morning so you don't have to worry I'll come in during the night to rob you blind. Or something else more sinister."

She shook her head. "I don't think that of you."

"You don't know me." He replaced the duck on the mantel and picked up a different one. "Not that I'm inclined to do such things, but since I'm a stranger to you, you shouldn't be so trusting."

"Jesse sent you, though . . . "

"Do you know that for sure?" He turned to her. "Did you call him? Ask to see some sort of ID?"

She felt the blood drain from her head. She'd always been so cautious, and yet here she was, allowing a stranger into her house, one whose identity she'd not even questioned.

"I'm harmless, and I really am Cam O'Connor." He pointed out the window. "See? Name's right there on the truck. And now that I've spooked you—don't try to deny it, you're white as one of the sheets Miss Lilly used to cover her furniture with in the summer—I'm happy to show you my driver's license and you can call Jesse."

She peered out the window to the truck and saw that it did, indeed, have CAMERON O'CONNOR, GENERAL CONTRACTOR, painted on the passenger side door.

She exhaled. "I don't need to call Jesse."

He put the duck back. "I'd still ask to see the ID if I were you."

She put out her hand and waited while he took out his wallet and held up his driver's license.

"Thank you. I never thought to ask. I just figured . . . well, this is such a small sleepy town, and who else would know I was here and that Jesse said he'd be sending you over . . . " she rambled.

"By now, pretty much everyone knows you're here. And by the way, small sleepy towns have their share of crime, too. Even St. Dennis."

"What, stolen bikes, graffiti on the sidewalks, cars being egged on Mischief Night?"

"A couple of years back, a guy who lived in town was abducting, raping, and killing young women. His wife was one of the town's police officers. He killed her, too."

"Are you making that up just to scare me?"

He shook his head. "It really happened. The point's not to scare you as much as to remind you to be careful. When you're new in town, especially a town like St.

Dennis, it's easy to trust everyone because everyone is so friendly. All I'm saying is, be careful."

"Message received."

"Good." He went back to checking out the duck decoys. "These are just perfect."

"They are pretty, aren't they?" Ellie walked closer. "They look hand-carved."

"Oh, they are," he replied. "Miss Lilly's husband carved them. Ted Cavanaugh was a legend around here, won all sorts of awards for his decoys." He turned over the duck he was holding. "See? TJC. Ted—I forget his middle name—Cavanaugh; 1943. This one's a mallard. This one over here—" He picked up another and put the mallard down. "This is a ruddy duck. This one . . . " He pointed to a third. "This one's a pintail."

"How do you know all that?"

"I grew up on the Bay." He shrugged as if that was explanation enough, and perhaps it was. "If you decide you want to sell them, I'd appreciate first dibs. I know they're worth a lot of money. I'm not sure how much, but there's a museum down in Salisbury that might be able to help figure it out. And Nita Perry—she owns Past Times, one of the antiques shops in town—probably has a handle on what they're worth. She's been in St. Dennis forever." Cam smiled. "But if you contact the museum, don't let them talk you into handing the ducks over. I know they already have a few Ted Cavanaughs and I'm sure they'd be happy to have a few more."

"I promise I won't do anything with them without letting you know first." *And certainly not before six months have expired.*

63

"Say, have you thought about selling the house as is, before you put any work into it? Could be you'd save a lot of time and money."

"I hadn't thought about that, no." Actually, she had, but she needed to do some fixing up for her own sake, since she'd be living there for at least six months and she'd go crazy from the dust and depressing decor. Besides, what else would she do for the next hundred and eighty days?

"You might want to give it some thought. I'd be interested myself." To Ellie's eye, he appeared to be trying too hard to be nonchalant. "Would you think about it and let me know?"

"Sure." *As if she could sell it now anyway.*

"Thanks." He glanced at his watch. "I'm going to have to head out. I have an appointment with a customer at five." He reached into his pocket for his wallet. "Here's my card. If there's anything I can do to help you, call me, even if it's just a question you have about something. When you're ready to start on that wallpaper, or if you need a ladder, or you want to work on that linoleum— or you decide to chuck it all and sell it now—give me a call."

"I will. Thanks." She walked him to the door. "I'm sorry I can't afford to hire you to do what I can do myself, but I appreciate the tips you've given me."

"If you really want to do some of the work before you sell it, maybe we can work out some sort of arrangement for the tough stuff. Like a barter." He stood in the doorway, looking down at her with dark blue eyes, and for a brief moment, she was afraid to ask what kind of barter he had in mind.

64

Cam must have read her expression, because he laughed out loud. "Not that kind of barter." He pointed past her to the mantel, where the ducks were lined up at an angle. "That kind of barter."

"Oh, right. Sure. That could work. If you're sure."

"I'm positive. You think about what you need, and I'll figure out what it would cost—giving you the friends and family discount, of course—and then we'll see what the job is worth in decoys. Unless, of course, you want to sell it to me right now. As is."

"Ah, no. Not ready to do that."

"Then we're back to the 'friends and family discount' and the decoy barter."

"I like it. Thanks." She walked out front with him. The sun had almost set and the geese were settling in for the night at the wetlands around the bend from the remains of the old lighthouse. There was a strong scent of salt and something rotting over on the beach, but oddly enough, she found it appealing.

"Was that door unlocked the whole time you were outside?" Cam paused on his way to the truck.

She nodded.

"If someone walks in the front while you're out back and walks away with those decoys, I'm going to be really pissed." He went to the driver's-side door and opened it. "You get too careless, it's going to cost you. Like maybe a few days' worth of pulling up gunky flooring or stripping down some sticky wallpaper."

"Got it," she replied. "I'll be more diligent."

He backed the truck out, then waved as he started to drive on.

"Thanks again, Cameron."

He slowed the truck and looked back at her. "Anytime, Ellie ... "

She stood at the end of the driveway and watched the truck wind around the first bend in the road and disappear. She turned back to the house, went inside, and locked all the doors. Seconds later, the coming night closed in and she was alone again.

She sat in the living room, still as a stone, and thought about Lynley. Did her mother come here to keep Lilly company, or to find comfort during her illness? Through the worst of her battle, did she know she would, in the end, lose? Did she walk the beach where Ellie walked, watch the sun set across the Bay, listen to the scolding screeches of the gulls as they circled above her? Did she take solace in these walls, find some strength here that she could not find elsewhere? Had she, Ellie, failed to offer enough support and encouragement that her mother had fled to this house in this tiny town to find what she needed? Or had she simply wanted a change in scenery, a vista to look out at that differed from the view from their penthouse apartment?

"Mom, if I failed you back then, I'm sorry," Ellie whispered. "If there was something I should have done that I didn't do, I'm sorry ... "

She thought about all the years her mother had spent traveling for photo shoots, for filming TV shows and the occasional movie while Ellie had been away at boarding school or college or holidays. In retrospect, it seemed they were rarely in the same place at the same time, and yet she had adored Lynley, with the same adoration a child might bestow on a beautiful fairy princess, one who was above the mere mortals who surrounded her. There were times when she'd see her mother's face in a magazine and barely make the connection between herself and the woman on the page. Yet the times they were at home together, alone, there'd been a strong current of love that flowed between them, binding mother and daughter, and Ellie had clung to that in the last weeks of her mother's illness. Even then, Lynley had been beautiful. Even then, her smile could light the room.

Ellie sat alone on the sofa, wondering if Lynley had sat in that very room and worried about the daughter she would be leaving behind, if she'd brought her regrets and her sorrows here as well as her love for Lilly.

Ellie stared out the window at the Bay, and wondered if Lynley, in her day, had done the same.

Chapter 5

HAVING done the math and figured out that if she continued to buy a cup of coffee every morning for the rest of the month, she'd have spent the equivalent of the cost of a modest coffeemaker, Ellie decided that this morning's trip to Cuppachino would be her last. She'd become accustomed to the early morning trip into town and was pleased that the young man behind the counter now recognized her. Since she was alone almost all day every day, she found herself looking forward to that tiny bit of socializing in the morning. Of course, she told herself as she opened the now-familiar red door, there were other ways to socialize, if she were so inclined, that wouldn't cost her anything at all. Like joining the library. Volunteering at the nursing home or the local animal shelter.

Of course, socializing with the locals would expose her to a scrutiny she was trying to avoid, and therefore was pretty much out. There would always be questions she'd hesitate to answer, and seeing her hesitate, sooner or later, someone would start to wonder.

Better to keep to myself.

If she needed to talk to someone, she could call Carly. If she was really desperate for companionship, she could stop in to see Jesse, which she would have to do soon enough anyway because she would be needing cash. And then there was Cameron. She had to admit he'd come as a surprise to her; he wasn't at all the handyman she'd pictured in her mind. She'd expected a man somehow closer to fifty or sixty, with a little bit of a paunch, a receding hairline, and baggy pants.

Definitely not the tall, lanky blond guy—no bald spots as far as she'd seen, and no paunch, either—wearing well-fitting jeans and a really terrific smile who showed up on Bay View Road two days ago.

She walked to the counter and was greeted by the same young man—Josh, according to his name tag.

"Hey, good morning," he called to her from the latte machine. "Your regular?"

Ellie smiled and nodded. "Please."

Being recognized as a regular—albeit an anonymous one—made her feel just a tiny bit less alone, a little less like an outsider. Of course, she was an outsider—she knew that—but it felt nice to belong somewhere, even if only at the coffee shop, and only for a few minutes each day.

Josh delivered her coffee and she paid him, putting the change in the large white mug marked TIPS on the counter. She'd just fixed her coffee and snapped the lid on the take-out cup when she heard someone call her name.

"Ellie." Cameron stood near the front window table, where a small group—mostly women of varying ages—had turned to look at her.

Ellie flushed at the scrutiny. Her first thought was that someone would remember her face from all of the newspaper and TV coverage last year. She'd done what she could to change her look, darkening her blond hair and cutting it short. And certainly, her style wasn't that of a well-to-do Manhattan executive any longer. Gone were the designer suits and highticket shoes and accessories. She'd worn nothing but jeans and sweatshirts or sweaters since she arrived in St. Dennis. So chances were slim that anyone would connect her to the daughter of the King of Fraud.

Still, why take that chance?

She waved and smiled to Cameron, but headed toward the door all the same.

"Ellie, come here," he persisted. "Come meet some of your fellow St. Dennis residents."

Crap.

Slapping a smile on her face, she walked to the table, where four faces peered up at her.

"Ellie, meet Grace Sinclair. Her family owns the big inn that sits out on the Bay not far from your house. Grace also owns the town newspaper, the *St. Dennis Gazette.*"

The older woman who'd smiled at Ellie the first time Ellie stopped at Cuppachino smiled at her again now.

Swell. She owns the newspaper.

"Nice to meet you, Ms. Sinclair." Ellie may have been on edge, but she did remember her manners.

"Lovely to meet you, dear, and please, it's *Grace*. Cameron tells us you're fixing up Lilly Cavanaugh's old house. We can't wait to hear your plans for the place." Grace put out her hand and took Ellie's to give it a squeeze. "Welcome to St. Dennis."

70

"Thank you."

"And this"—Cameron touched the shoulder of the pretty curly-haired woman who sat directly in front of him—"is Brooke Bowers. She owns the cupcake shop across the street."

"The cupcake baker? You're Jesse Enright's fiancée?" Ellie asked.

"That would be me, yes." Brooke offered her hand. "Jesse mentioned you'd been in to the office to pick up the keys to your new house."

"Jesse's been really helpful." Ellie couldn't help but wonder if Jesse had shared with Brooke just how helpful he'd been.

"Nita Perry." Cameron indicated the woman in her late fifties who sat closest to the window. She had shiny black hair pulled back into a severe bun and wore large tortoiseshell glasses. "Nita has an antiques business here in town. I think I mentioned her to you."

"You did." To Nita, she said, "I'll be calling on you when I get around to inventorying the contents of the house. I'm going to want to sell some things."

"Oh, please do!" Nita's face lit up. "I know that house is filled with some wonderful pieces. Lilly never did get rid of a thing, you know."

"You'll be the first person I call when I get to that point," Ellie promised.

"I can't wait." Nita's shoulders shivered slightly with anticipation.

"And this is Clay Madison, Brooke's brother." Cameron pointed to the lone male seated at the table. "He has that big farm on the left side of the road when you turn off the highway. Clay grows organic produce and is just starting up an organic brewery with another guy in town."

"Organic beer?" Ellie raised an eyebrow.

Clay nodded. "Why not?"

"No reason, I guess." Ellie smiled. "Sounds good to me, anyway."

"We'll put you on the list for the tasting when we're ready for the big reveal," Clay told her.

"Clay's engaged to Miss Grace's daughter, Lucy," Cameron added.

"Congratulations." Ellie felt like her face was frozen in the smile she was still wearing. She needed to get out of here before it became permanent.

"Ellie, can you join us?" Grace asked.

"Oh, no, I have some errands to run." Ellie was grateful for an excuse to let the smile slide. "But thank you for offering."

"Another morning, perhaps," Grace replied.

"We're here almost every day by eight," Nita told her. "Please feel free to come in anytime and sit and chat with us for a while."

"That sounds great, thanks." Ellie turned to Cameron. "Good seeing you again, Cameron." She turned back to the table. "It was nice to meet all of you."

"We're happy to welcome you to town, Ellie." Nita turned in her chair.

"I'm happy to be here, thank you." Ellie glanced around the table one more time, committing faces and names to memory in the event she'd run into any of them again, which was likely, given the size of the town and the

72

length of her intended stay. "I'll see you all again, I'm sure."

"We'll look forward to it," Grace said.

Ellie forced her feet not to flee to the door. Once outside, she exhaled a long deep breath. She got into her car, which was parked three storefronts down from Cuppachino, and sighed. She put the key in the ignition and started the engine, her heart beating a little faster than normal.

"Fight or flight," she muttered.

She stopped at the light and watched a pretty dark-haired woman push a baby stroller across the street, where she stopped at the door of a shop and unlocked the door. The shop's windows were decorated for fall and held beautifully displayed clothing. The name of the shop— BLING—was painted across the front and side windows.

In another life, I shopped at places just like that, Ellie recalled.

These days, if Ellie shopped at all, it was for the things on her must-have list like cleaning products and sponges. She reminded herself that she needed to do exactly that. She made a left turn onto Cherry Street and drove around the block to reverse her direction on Charles. She headed toward the highway and the hardware store she'd passed on her way to St. Dennis, where she hoped to find that inexpensive coffeemaker.

Laden with a two-inch stack of paint-color brochures but no coffeemaker, Ellie returned to Bay View Road and parked all the way up in the driveway. When she got out of the car, she tried to peer through the carriage house windows to see what was behind the glass, but every pane had been painted black. She was just going to have to keep looking for the key, she supposed, so that she could satisfy her curiosity.

She went into the house through the back door and dropped her bag and the paint brochures on the kitchen table. Her planned project for the day was the cupboards. She'd started emptying them a few days ago, but got distracted by the cache of duck decoys and hadn't been able to resist taking them all out and placing them around the living room. Today she'd finish what she'd started.

The upper cupboards contained dishes that were stacked haphazardly, so she had a hard time knowing what was there. For two hours she emptied the shelves, then washed her findings. As she dried each piece, she sorted by pattern, and soon she realized that she had a complete set of Fiestaware, original, she was certain.

Nice.

She knew she'd need to paint the shelves at some point—*What do you think, Mom? A nice cream would show off the dishes quite nicely*—but for now, she merely wiped them, permitting them time to dry before replacing the turquoise, green, yellow, and pink dishes. There were several pieces of mismatched china, and these she wrapped in the newspaper she'd found the decoys in, and put them in a box she'd found in one of the bedroom closets. Perhaps Nita, the antiques dealer she'd met that morning, might have some thoughts on the age and quality of those pieces.

Next, to vary the view, Ellie tackled the cupboards below the counter. There were several old pots and pans, none of which matched the others, but she supposed that the concept of matching sets of pots might have come at a date later than the one on which Miss Lilly's house-keeping commenced. She set them all out on the counter to see what she had and what she might actually use. There was a large stockpot; maybe she'd make soup one of these days, so that was a keeper. She found several black cast-iron pans at the back of the top shelf, and while she wasn't sure what she'd use them for, she knew that reproductions were very popular right now and sold in some of the better housewares stores, so they—along with a griddle—made the cut. Besides, she thought as she washed the smaller of the two cast-iron frying pans, they just looked cool and old-timey, as if they belonged in the old house.

Had her mother cooked when she was here? Ellie had vague recollections of Lynley making breakfast or dinner but only when her father was away. He liked having a professional cook live in, and once he'd hired someone, Lynley practically never made so much as a cup of tea when he was around. But when Clifford was away—that was a different story. Even now, if she closed her eyes she could taste—smell—grilled cheese sandwiches and home-made tomato soup.

Where had that memory come from?

There'd been a time when she was home on a school holiday—Christmas, maybe?—when Lynley arrived from her latest photo shoot two full days before Clifford returned from a business trip. Lynley had given the sur-prised cook those two extra days off and had spent what to Ellie's mind had been forty-eight glorious hours at home, just the two of them. They'd baked Christmas cookies and drunk hot chocolate while watching a marathon of holiday movies together: *The Muppets Christmas* and *The Christmas Toy*, and *Miracle on 34th Street. A Claymation Christmas* and *A Christmas Story* and *It's a Wonderful Life.* Having two whole days with her mother had been the best present Ellie could have received, and she'd cherished the memory of Lynley singing along with Burl Ives while *Rudolph, the Red-Nosed Reindeer* played on the TV that was built into the kitchen wall so the cook could watch her soaps in the afternoon.

Dear God, that seemed so long ago. *Was* so long ago.

She wondered if her mother had baked cookies here, made hot chocolate and grilled cheese sandwiches to share with Lilly.

She pushed the past aside and forced herself to focus on the pots and pans that were in the cabinets.

There was a large pot that had a wire contraption that fit inside it and a lid. She had absolutely no idea what it could be used for. She added it to the closet where she'd stacked things to ask Nita about.

The doorbell rang, so she dried her hands and went tentatively to the front door. From the living room window she could see her visitor. Jesse Enright's fiancée—Brooke?—stood on the step with something in her hands.

Damn.

Ellie debated whether or not to answer the door. Finally, she opened it, feigning surprise to see Brooke.

"Hey, Brooke," she said as pleasantly as she could.

"Ellie, I'm embarrassed that it took meeting you this

76

morning to remind me that I hadn't stopped over to welcome you to St. Dennis." Brooke handed her a plate that was covered with aluminum foil.

"Oh, Brooke, you didn't have to . . ." Ellie protested even as she held the plate which could only contain cupcakes.

"I wanted to."

Convention and manners dictated that Ellie invite Brooke in. It also occurred to her that she'd have an opportunity to perhaps determine just what Jesse had told Brooke about her and how she'd obtained the property.

"Do you have a minute to come in?" Ellie heard herself asking. She lifted one corner of the foil and glanced at the cupcakes. "Wow, these are gorgeous. You're going to have to eat one of these. I don't dare eat them all myself."

She stood back so that Brooke could enter, then closed the door behind her.

"This was so nice of you," Ellie said.

Brooke glanced past her into the living room.

"Wow, not much has changed." She pointed into the room. "Except Mrs. Cavanaugh always had plants on that table near the window. She had tons of house-plants."

"She did? Wait, you knew her, too?"

Brooke nodded. "Sure. Everyone knew her. She was a real sweetheart. No kid ever missed Cavanaughs' on Halloween. She always had the best homemade caramel apples to give out. Sometimes she even dipped them in chocolate and rolled them in peanuts. I swear, she knew every kid in this town by name." Brooke walked into the living room uninvited and gazed around. "She didn't used to keep the decoys there, though. I think those were always on the bookcase." She pointed to the wall of shelves.

"And by now, I'm sure you heard that her . . . niece? second cousin?—whatever—was Lynley Sebastian."

Ellie nodded. "I did know that."

"Oh, of course you would, since you bought the house from her estate. Crazy about her husband, though, right?"

"Did you ever meet her? Lynley?"

"No. Wish I had, though." Brooke pointed to a chair that stood near the front window. "Supermodel, actress. I used to watch her in that TV show . . . I can't remember the name of it now but I'm sure you know the one I mean . . ."

Ellie did but she didn't volunteer the information.

" . . . and I'd daydream that she'd be in St. Dennis one day and we'd meet her and she'd be real friendly and she'd become friends with my mother." Brooke laughed self-consciously. "Silly, huh?"

"You're probably not the only person in town who wanted to meet her."

"That's for sure." Brooke pointed to a chair near the front wall. "Mr. Cavanaugh used to sit in this chair and look out the window, the year he fell ill. He'd wave to all us kids when we went past to go crabbing off the old dock that used to be out there. It fell into the Bay after a big winter storm one year." She smiled at the memory. "He was such a nice man. They never had kids of their own—I mean, I know they pretty much raised Lynley—but they were really nice to all the kids in town."

Ellie's ears perked up. "Wait, did you say they raised Lynley? Mr. and Mrs. Cavanaugh?"

Brooke nodded. "That's my understanding."

"Really." Ellie was stunned. She'd never heard such a thing. She'd never met her maternal grandparents, who'd died in a boating accident before she was born. Her father had told her they had lived in California but she assumed that Lynley had lived with them.

"So Lynley lived here ...? She went to school here?"

"At some point, but I don't know how old she was when she arrived and I don't know how old she was when she left. If you're interested, you could ask someone like Grace Sinclair—you met her at Cuppachino this morning. She's lived here forever, and her family's owned that newspaper for longer than that. It's the only newspaper St. Dennis ever had. If anyone knows the story, I'd expect it would be Grace."

The two women had gravitated back toward the entry, and Ellie's mind was racing a mile a minute.

"Can I offer you some tea?" she asked.

"Sure. That would be great. I have to watch my time, though. I left my mother in charge of the bakery and told her I'd be back in an hour." Brooke glanced at her watch. "Which gives me about twenty-five minutes, so sure. Tea would be nice."

Ellie led the way to the kitchen, and once there, apologized for the mess.

"I started cleaning out the cupboards this morning. I don't know what I was hoping to find. Except maybe a coffeemaker," she added drily.

She ran water from the faucet into the ancient stainless steel kettle and placed it on the stove.

"Why do you need a coffeemaker when you have the pot?" Brooke asked.

"What pot?"

"This one." Brooke picked up the old coffeepot and waved it.

"I thought that was a pitcher." Ellie frowned.

Brooke popped off the lid and removed the basket and stem from inside.

"Coffee goes into this little basket with the holes in the bottom, basket sits upon stem. Water goes into the pot. Put it on the stove, boil the water, and let the coffee percolate." Brooke demonstrated as she spoke. "When it stops perking—bubbling—it's done."

"I feel like an idiot. We always had those drip coffeemakers at home . . . " Ellie could feel her cheeks start to burn. She could have added that she'd rarely had to make her own coffee at home but she let that pass.

"Do you have any ground coffee?" Brooke asked.

Ellie shook her head.

"Pick some up next time you're out. These things make great coffee. My dad always made his in one just like this."

"Thanks. I'll be off to the market later this afternoon and I'll try it first thing in the morning."

"So if we never see you at Cuppachino again, I guess it will be my fault for telling you how to make your own morning joe."

"I doubt anyone would feel the loss."

"Are you kidding?" Brooke's eyebrows raised. "Everyone's intrigued by the city girl who moved to St. Dennis to renovate the home of one of the town's favorite

80

ladies. Lilly Cavanaugh was very well liked and had an army of friends, and of course, Lynley was a legend. Like a goddess."

"How do you know I'm a city girl?" Ellie turned the conversation from her mother and Lilly. "Is it that obvious?"

"No, but Jesse said you bought the house through a law firm in New York, so I just assumed . . ." Brooke confessed.

"I thought maybe my city roots were showing." Ellie glossed over it. "I did live and work in New York for years."

"How did you find out about the house being available?" Brooke pulled a chair out from under the table and sat.

"I'd worked with someone who knew someone at the law firm that represented Lynley Sebastian. My friend knew I'd lost my job in a corporate downsizing and had been thinking about investing in a property that might need some work that I could turn over for a profit, so she called me when the firm decided to sell the place." Ellie recited the story she'd known she'd need sooner or later.

"Oh, like a handyman's special. I am addicted to those TV shows where people buy a run-down place, work miracles, then sell and make a killing."

"I imagine the killings were a little bigger a few years ago." The teakettle shrieked and Ellie turned it off. "Though everyone says St. Dennis is still a good market."

Brooke nodded. "Without question. Plus, this house is so wonderful. Spacious and those high ceilings and all those windows and fireplaces." She sighed. "It's the house

I'd like someday, but I guess there are a lot of people in town who feel that way."

"I sure hope so, since I'll be selling it." Ellie was tempted to add that Cameron O'Connor had first dibs, but she didn't know Brooke well enough to engage in what could be considered gossip. And for all she knew, Cameron wasn't broadcasting his interest in the house.

Ellie prepared two cups of tea and placed one in front of Brooke, then took a seat across the table from her.

"So tell me what your plans are for the house." Brooke blew across the top of her cup to cool the hot tea.

Ellie went over what she had in mind for the down-stairs, and they pored over the paint-color brochures briefly, agreeing that a creamy wall color would be perfect in every room on the first floor.

"Except maybe the dining room," Ellie said. "I really like a little drama in there. Maybe red . . . "

"Red dining rooms are fabulous." Brooke turned her wrist to look at her watch. "Oops. My hour is up. Thanks so much for the tea and the conversation and for letting me sit and relax with you for a time. It's been so nice." She rose and Ellie did as well.

"Damn, I forgot about your cupcakes." Ellie made a face. "We should have had them with our tea. I am so not a gracious hostess."

"I'd have declined anyway, but thanks." Brooke laughed. "I have to taste a little from each batch to make sure all's well."

"Wow. A real hardship job." Ellie escorted Brooke to the front door.

"The hardship comes in keeping my work product off my hips."

"You could probably get someone to help you with that."

"Jesse and Clay are always happy to chow down. But when I'm experimenting with a new flavor, I need a more discerning palate, so I get together with the girls . . ." Brooke opened the door and turned. "You'll have to come to one of my cupcake-tasting nights which are really just an excuse to get together and kill a few bottles of wine. They're always a good time."

Before Ellie could respond, Brooke went on.

"Have you been to Scoop yet? One Scoop or Two, the ice-cream shop down near the marina?"

Ellie shook her head. "I saw the sign, but I haven't been. Is it good?"

"Best ice cream you will ever eat. Steffie MacGregor owns the place and she makes all her own flavors. She's been written up in magazines and she's had ice-cream companies try to lure her away and offers to franchise her stuff."

"But she's declined?" When Brooke nodded, Ellie asked, "Why?"

"Because she says all she ever wanted was to live in St. Dennis and make the best ice cream ever and marry the love of her life and raise a family here."

"How much of that has she done?"

"All of it, except raise the family. She just got married last year—to my brother's partner in beer—so she's working on that. Her best friend just had a baby a few months ago and I think it's inspired Steffie."

Brooke stepped outside and Ellie followed.

"Seriously, you need to come one night. Everyone's really friendly. It's a small group, but a dynamic one. Dallas MacGregor even comes sometimes."

"Dallas MacGregor? The movie star?"

Brooke nodded. "She used to summer here as a kid, then moved back last year and married her old sweetheart. Who happens to be the brother of the previously mentioned Steffie." Brooke continued to her car, which she'd parked on the street near the mailbox. "Steffie, to make things even more incestuous, is married to Dallas's brother, Wade."

Ellie nodded as if she'd followed, but in truth, she was thinking how drinking wine with a group of local women could be a disaster. Who knew what might slip out? Loose lips and all that.

"I'll give you a call next time we get together. I promise, you'll like everyone. They're just regular girls, like you and me." Brooke got into her car and turned it on.

"Thanks again for the cupcakes," Ellie said. "I really appreciate it."

"Enjoy them." Brooke made a U-turn in the road and waved as she passed by.

Ellie checked the mailbox and pulled out a handful of junk mail, underneath which sat a plain white envelope with her name neatly printed on the bottom. Through the paper she could feel the shape of a key. Cameron must have dropped it off, she realized, without letting her know he'd been there. She ignored a twinge of disappointment and tried to focus on Brooke's visit. She'd seemed very sincere and very nice, but Ellie couldn't help but wonder if she'd stopped by for something more than simply a welcoming gesture. Something like what, Ellie didn't know. She wasn't used to small-town life and she wasn't sure if the visit was exactly as it seemed, or an attempt by someone in the gossip chain to find out more about her purchase of the house. Ellie was pretty confident that Jesse's lips had remained sealed, as he'd promised. She'd expected as much from him.

Well, if Brooke had been on a mission, she'd learned precious little. And the irony was that Ellie actually learned more from Brooke than Brooke had learned from her.

She walked back to the house, mindful more than ever of its connection to her mother. Ellie'd known that Lynley had spent time here when she was younger, but she'd assumed it had been with her parents. Why, she wondered, had her grandparents sent her mother to live here with a relative? And how long had Lynley stayed?

Unfortunately, it appeared that everyone who would know for certain—everyone directly involved—was gone, and had been gone, for a long time.

It seemed the more she learned about her mother's life here in St. Dennis, the less she really knew.

Chapter 6

HAVING become increasingly tired of take-out burgers and fried chicken, Ellie resolved to start cooking for herself. Organizing the cupboards had helped galvanize her game plan. The few pots and pans she thought she might need were washed, dried, and back on their respective shelves, the remaining having been delegated to a box which she dragged into the closet by the back door. She doubted any of them would be of interest to Nita, but they could be donated to a thrift shop, if, in fact, St. Dennis had such a thing. She'd have to ask around.

She made a run to the grocery store late in the afternoon, and by seven was happily eating a piece of chicken she'd sautéed, a pile of green beans, and some organic sweet potato fries she found in the frozen food section. For dessert, she tackled one of Brooke's cupcakes. Deciding which one had been the toughest decision she'd had to make all day.

Nothing at all like my old life, she reflected as she covered the remaining cupcakes and put them into the refrigerator. *But satisfying in its own way.*

Her corporate world had been a constant round of meetings, and luncheons and dinners at some of the finest restaurants in Manhattan with Henry, her fiancé. She'd never been without her BlackBerry and spent hours each day sending or responding to e-mails. The view from her home and office windows had been defined by concrete, steel, glass, and a bit of Central Park. There'd been someone to clean her apartment, someone to drive her wherever she wanted to go. Someone to shop for her food, prepare, and serve it to her. A personal assistant to handle all those little details of life she hadn't time for: making her appointments, paying her bills, buying gifts for the significant people in her life, making her travel arrangements.

With her father's downfall, all of those people had vanished from her life like vapors, as if they'd never really existed, like her beautiful apartment on Mahattan's Upper East Side and the family's homes on Martha's Vineyard, in East Hampton and Vail, the town house in London, and the house she and Henry had bought two years ago on Martha's Vineyard. Her father's Greek island had been the first to go.

Sitting in the quiet of what had been Lilly Cavanaugh's cozy living room, with the wind picking up off the Bay to rattle the windows every now and then, Ellie wondered if she'd been better off then than she was now. The contrast between her former and present lives was about as stark as it could be, and yet, with almost a year between her and the worst days of her life, she reflected on how much of that other life she really missed.

She studied her fingernails. In the old days, she'd never gone more than five days between manicures. Now she was hard-pressed to remember when those nails had last been polished. Chipped and filed down with an emery board she'd picked up at the market, they were nails she barely recognized as her own.

Back then, she rarely gave much thought to money, because it was never an issue. From lunch to cars, jewelry, and homes, whatever she needed was always available. These days, she had to watch the price of everything she bought, and often found herself not buying at all.

And then there was Henry.

Henry, whom she'd loved, whom she'd planned on marrying and spending the rest of her life with. Ellis had thought that he'd loved her, too, until the house of cards he'd helped her father to build imploded. It hadn't taken Ellie long to realize that what Henry really loved was the media tag "the son Clifford Chapman never had." Even now, the truth still caused her cheeks to burn.

If she had to choose between then and there, here and now, would she go back to her old life? Well, maybe to the time when her mother was still alive, so that she could ask all those questions she wished she'd asked back then. And only if she could change things, like have her father develop a conscience and be something other than a criminal.

Other than those few things, given the choice, she just might choose to stay where she was.

While filled with ease and luxury, her entire life up until now had been built on fraud and lies. Since she arrived in St. Dennis, she'd done nothing but work. She'd had to learn to do things she'd never done because there'd always been someone else to do them for her. She had aches and pains in places she hadn't realized she had muscles or nerve endings, and yet she felt more alive here than she had in a long time.

At least what I'm doing now isn't hurting anyone. At least here life is more honest, and when someone offers you a hand in friendship, it isn't because they want something from you or are trying to figure out how to use you, she told herself. Not that everyone in New York was like that, but most of the people in Ellie's circle had proven to be disloyal and cowardly when it came to keeping up their friendship. Except, of course, Carly, who on general principles had promptly dropped anyone who'd dropped Ellie.

And at least here, no one pretended to be in love with her.

Her conscience made an attempt to remind her that, these days, she was the one doing the pretending, but she chose to ignore it.

When she laid her head upon her pillow, rather than lie awake worrying about the next day's meetings or the next press release or media campaign, she fell into a deep sleep within minutes. She'd awaken the next morning as she had every day since she'd been in St. Dennis, not to the shriek of an alarm, but to the sound of branches from an evergreen lightly scraping across the bedroom window, and geese calling as they landed or took off from the nearby marsh.

A loud and eerie *kronk* had awoken her early the previous morning, and she'd sat up in bed, eyes on the window, past which had flown a bird that looked positively Jurassic. When later that day she mentioned it to Linda, the waitress at the Crab Claw, Linda had laughed and said, "Oh, that's a blue heron. Some have already fled south, but others might stick around until it gets really cold. If we have a mild winter, a few might hang here straight through the season. As long as they're still catching fish and the temperatures are still mild, they'll stay."

This morning, Ellie took her second cup of coffee—brewed as per Brooke's instructions in the coffeepot she'd found—and wandered down to the beach before she started work for the day. The sun was bright and strong enough to have warmed the rock she often sat on, and she'd no sooner taken her seat than the heron passed overhead. She watched it land in the marsh and disappear among the reeds. She'd sighed with a contentment she hadn't expected to feel, sipped the rest of her coffee, and went back to the house to work. After years of having chased herself without even realizing she'd been doing so, she was finding the change of pace refreshing.

The room on today's list was the dining room. She'd started to dust the furniture two days ago, but organizing the kitchen had been more of a priority. She spent most of the morning polishing the mahogany table, sideboard, and china cupboard. She'd just stood back to admire her work when the doorbell rang.

Ellie held her breath for just a second. Unexpected company put her on edge lest she say something that might come back to haunt her. She peeked through the curtains and saw Grace Sinclair on the top step holding a basket in both hands.

Reluctantly, Ellie made her way to the front door. If

the people she'd met were determined to be hospitable and welcoming, she just didn't have the heart to leave them standing on the porch.

"Grace, nice to see you again." Ellie opened the door and greeted her visitor. "Please, come in."

"Thank you, dear." Once inside, Grace handed the basket to Ellie. "The chef at the inn made some delicious beef stew last night and I thought perhaps you'd enjoy some."

"You didn't have to . . . " Ellie checked herself. "But thank you so much. This is very thoughtful of you."

"There's also some bread that our new baker made earlier this morning, and some brownies they're serving for dessert at lunch today. I ran into Brooke this morning and she told me how hard you're working here and I thought you might like a home-cooked meal." She smiled. "Our chef makes everything we serve from scratch, so technically, it's home-cooked."

"Oh, my goodness, it all smells so wonderful." Ellie's rumbling stomach reminded her that she'd only had a light breakfast, and that was hours ago. "I might not wait until dinner."

"There's more than enough there for several meals, so you enjoy." Grace's eyes flickered from left to right, from the living room to the dining room. "I heard this old place was starting to look like a home again. You know, it's always been a happy place. Good people have lived here as far back as I can remember. I'm happy to see someone give it some love again."

"Well, I know that I have to show it in its best light if I want to sell it for the maximum amount," Ellie replied.

"Right now I'm just at the cleaning and let's-see-what-we-have-here stage."

"What you have here are years' worth of history." Grace smiled and walked to the dining room doorway.

"Cameron mentioned that a previous owner was the light keeper." Ellie pointed toward the place where she understood the lighthouse once stood. She'd been intrigued by the story Cameron had told and would have liked to hear more.

"Yes, but he was so much more. Benjamin Fray emigrated from Scotland as a boy of ten and was indentured to a local tobacco farmer who'd lost his only son to disease. The story goes that he took young Ben under his wing during the period of his indenture. So while Ben was working in the fields, he was learning everything there was to know about tobacco, from growing it to selling it. By the time his seven years were up, he'd amassed enough knowledge to start up his own business. His previous master sold him some acres on the outside of town, and he farmed until he was well into his forties, and was very successful. The farm, this house, and the lighthouse passed to his grandson, Eli, who in his later years was an active participant in the Underground Railroad." Grace smiled.

"And then, of course, there were the pirates . . . "

"Pirates."

"Oh yes, back in the day, more than one ship dropped anchor right out there in the cove. They'd come ashore for provisions—steal what they could and terrorize the locals a little while they were at it. But that's a story of its own."

"Who'd have guessed? The Underground Railroad and pirates, to boot. You certainly know your local history."

"I was on the committee that researched some properties to be proposed for inclusion on the National Register of Historic Places. I got to know a lot about many of the places in town."

"Is this property on the Register?"

"It's still in the proposal stage, I'm afraid. We've had to go house by house to establish a historic district in the area of Old St. Mary's Church Road, and that's been very time-consuming. Once that project is completed, we'll be starting on other properties in town. I'm sure that your house will qualify, though."

"It does sound like it has quite a history." Ellie thought for a moment. "So was the woman I bought the house from descended from Benjamin Fray?"

"No. The Ryders didn't come into the picture until after the Civil War. Sometime in the 1870s. They purchased the house from Eli Fray's widow. Eli died at Appomattox, fighting for the Confederacy, as some from around these parts did."

Grace glanced around the room, her gaze pausing on the sideboard.

"Lilly always kept a pair of silver candelabras there on the sideboard. They were a wedding gift from Ted's grandmother, and Lilly was very proud of them. She lit them every morning from Thanksgiving through New Year's Day, then didn't light them again until Easter Sunday."

"You knew Mrs. Cavanaugh well?"

"Oh, quite well. Perhaps not as well as my older brother, who was in her year at school. He had quite the crush on her back then, though he never would admit it. Now, if you want to know more about Lilly, you might talk to Violet Finneran."

"The woman who works for Jesse Enright?"

Grace nodded. "She and Lilly and Jesse's grandmother, Rose, were inseparable when they were younger. The three blossoms, people called them. Lilly, Rose, and Violet."

Ellie smiled. "I love that. I love the old-fashioned names."

"Violet could most likely answer any questions you might have about Lilly and her family." Grace paused, then added, "And you might want to speak with Berry Eberle as well. She lived next door to the Ryders at one time—that's Lilly's maiden name." Grace tilted her head for a moment. "Interesting that your last name is Ryder, dear."

"I'm sure it's just one of those cosmic coincidences." Ellie shrugged and changed the subject, all the while mentally kicking herself. For some reason, she'd always thought that Ryder had come down through her father's family. "Who's Berry . . . what did you say her last name was?"

"Eberle. She lives in that big Victorian place over on River Road. If you see it once, you won't forget it. You might have heard of her by her stage name. Beryl Townsend."

"The movie star from, what, the thirties? Forties? Fifties?"

Grace nodded. "Forties, fifties, sixties, and even later. She was born here, left town when she was, oh, seventeen or eighteen, thereabouts, to make her mark on the film industry. Her grandniece is Dallas MacGregor. I'm sure you've heard of her."

"I've seen many of her films. Brooke stopped over yesterday and she mentioned that Dallas lived here, married a local boy."

"She did. Grant Wyler is the local vet and has an animal rescue operation. If you're thinking about adding a dog or cat—"

"I'm not," Ellie said hastily. "No dogs, no cats. Maybe if I was staying longer, but I don't know where I'll be moving to, once the house is sold."

"Well, it's just a thought. Nice to have some furry companionship, especially on long winter nights. Always so nice to have a cat or a dog snuggled up next to you when you're reading in front of a nice fire. We always had pets growing up, but nowadays, it seems every other person has some allergy, so living at the inn, we just can't have animals anymore." Grace glanced at her watch. "Oh, dear, I need to hustle. Today's the day the ads come in for the newspaper and I'm running late. Do join us some morning for coffee. Everyone would love to get to know you better."

"That's very nice, but you know, I'm not going to be here very long." *And am so not interested in anyone knowing me better.*

"That makes no difference, dear. Friends are where you find them, and sometimes you find them when you least suspect, in the oddest places at the strangest times."

Grace patted Ellie on the arm. "Perhaps one of these days, we'll sit down together, you and I, and do an interview for my paper."

Not while I breathe, Ellie thought. Aloud, she said, "I'm really not a very interesting person, Grace."

"Everyone is interesting in their own way. Sometimes we just don't recognize it in ourselves." Grace opened the door, then stopped short. "Oh, for heaven's sake, I almost forgot. In St. Dennis, we celebrate First Families Day. It's always the third Sunday in November, and it's to honor those determined folks who first settled here and stayed long enough to start the town. I hope you'll join us for the little celebration."

"What exactly do you do?" Ellie asked, curious in spite of her determination to remain detached.

"Oh, we have the obligatory speeches on the square down on Old St. Mary's Church Road, there's always a reenactment of some sort—last year we chose the attempted shelling of the town by the British during the War of 1812—and then we have a dinner at the Grange Hall. Everyone in town attends, but over the past few years, we see more and more 'summer people' coming back for the weekend. Which of course is good news for the inn and the B and Bs. You should join us. I think you'd find it to be an interesting day."

"Thank you for mentioning it. I'll certainly think about it."

"Do. It would be especially fitting to have you with us this year."

When Ellie raised a questioning eyebrow, Grace added, "Because this house has a connection to our early history, and to some people we were so fond of. It's up to you, of course, if you're free. I'll have a ticket put aside for you, just in case you decide to join us."

Grace hurried down the steps and onto the path that led to her car, waving over her shoulder as she went. Ellie waited until Grace's car backed out of the driveway and passed by before closing the door. She'd been about to ask Grace about the Ryders' connection to the town history while at the same time trying to think of a way to politely decline the ticket, but the woman was gone before Ellie could get her mouth open.

I should have asked about my mother. I'll bet Grace knew her. She seems to know everyone in town. And I should have asked more about the pirates. Ellie shook her head. *Pirates indeed. Sounds like something Grace made up to sell newspapers.*

She put Grace's welcoming gifts in the kitchen then went back into the dining room and began to empty the sideboard, where she found some of what she assumed was Lilly Cavanaugh's silver, though not the candelabras Grace had spoken of. Not surprisingly, every piece she uncovered needed a good polishing. Silver polish was one thing she hadn't thought to pick up at the market, so she'd have to make a trip.

"Just as well," she muttered. "I am getting a little stir-crazy here."

She changed out of the sweatshirt she'd been cleaning in and slipped on a sweater that was a little more presentable and ran a brush through her hair. Her mother had always impressed upon her the importance of making a nice appearance.

"Even," Lynley had told her, "when you don't feel like it or you don't think it will matter."

Or, Ellie thought, *even when you don't know anyone who might possibly care what you look like.*

Of course, her mother had been a natural beauty and the chances of Lynley making anything but a great appearance were pretty slim. She thought about Cameron's remark, about how Lynley was beautiful even when she was ill, and the thought warmed her.

She stopped at the market and bought silver polish and a few other things she needed, then on her way back home, made an impulsive right turn onto Kelly's Point Road and parked behind One Scoop or Two, the local ice-cream shop she'd heard so much about. A little change in routine would be nice, she told herself as she got out of the car. She'd get a cone and walk along the water, maybe go as far as the marina and look at the boats that were still in the water. It was a beautiful day with lots of sunshine and no breeze off the Bay, and who knew how many more such days there would be?

The shop appeared empty when she entered, but the ringing bell over the door brought a tall woman from the back. She wore a Baltimore Ravens cap over honey-blond hair and an old sweatshirt very similar to the one Ellie had changed out of.

"Hi," the woman greeted Ellie. "What can I get for you?"

Ellie scanned the blackboard on which the day's flavors were written.

"Gosh, I don't know. There are so many choices." Ellie read the list a second time. "You make all these yourself?"

The blonde nodded. "I do. All in my little back room here. Today's new-flavor testing day." She pulled at the front of her sweatshirt where a smear of chocolate and something red could be seen.

"I feel so silly." Ellie laughed self-consciously. "I can't make up my mind."

"Want a taste of what I'm working on while you decide?" Without waiting for an answer, the woman disappeared into the back room, then came back holding a cardboard cup and a spoon. "Here. Try this."

She loaded up the spoon and passed it over the counter to Ellie, who obediently ate it.

"Oh, wow. That's amazing." Ellie's eyes widened. "What's in it?"

"It's a white chocolate ice-cream base, with cranberries and chocolate chunks."

"This is truly amazing. I'll buy a cone of this, if you have enough."

"Finish what you have there in the dish, but I don't really have enough to sell yet. Right now it's still in the testing stage."

"It's so good," Ellie told her, "I wouldn't change a thing."

"A good endorsement, thanks. I wanted something really special for the holidays."

"I think you've got it." Ellie finished off the small dish then went back to the board. "If that's a sample of your work, I have to say, I've never had better ice cream."

"Thanks." The shop owner blushed modestly. "It's really a labor of love."

"I'm going to try the apple cinnamon raisin, I think."

"Excellent choice. That's a big favorite. One of the first ice creams I ever made."

"What made you decide to make ice cream, if you don't mind me asking?" Ellie watched as the woman scooped the selected ice cream into a dish.

"I don't mind at all. When I was little, one of my grandmother's cousins used to make ice cream for us in one of those old crank things?" She smiled at the memory. "He used to let me turn the crank. Then, as I got older, he let me add things, and it just went from there to me making up the flavors. It's really all I ever wanted to do." She handed Ellie the dish. "Oh, I should have asked you if you wanted a cone."

"This is fine." Ellie met her at the cash register and was counting out change when the bell over the door rang again.

"Oh, look who's here!" The shopkeeper clapped her hands. "Aunt Steffie's favorite baby girl and her mama."

Ellie turned to see a pretty dark-haired woman struggling to get a stroller through the door. She left her dish and bag on the counter and went to help.

"Oh, thank you." The baby's mama flashed a smile. "The door doesn't stay open long enough to get the stroller in." She pulled the stroller over the threshold and parked it at the closest table, then turned it around.

Ellie looked down into the face of one of the prettiest babies she'd ever seen.

"With all that pink, I'm going out on a limb and guessing a girl," Ellie said.

"I know, right?" The mother laughed good-naturedly. "Pink blanket, pink hat, pink clothes . . ."

"You're such a girl, Vanessa." The shop owner came around the counter and crouched in front of the stroller. "How's Aunt Steffie's doll baby today?"

"She's teething." The mother—Vanessa, apparently—settled into a chair. "She's been a very unhappy girl for the past few days because of it."

"Well, she certainly looks happy now. Because she loves her aunt Steffie best, isn't that right, sweet pea?" Steffie unstrapped the baby's restraints and lifted her from the stroller.

"What's your baby's name?" Ellie heard herself asking. She was still at the counter, waiting to pay for her ice cream, a fact that the shop owner apparently forgot.

"Penelope Jane, but we call her Poppy." The baby's mother turned to address Ellie.

"That's adorable, and so is she."

"Thank you. We're pretty sure we're going to keep her."

"Aunt Steffie will keep her if you decide to the contrary." The shopkeeper held the baby up in the air, and the baby laughed. "Poppy can't wait until she's old enough for ice cream. And when she is, she'll have a flavor named just for her. We'll call it . . . Poppy Pink. Which reminds, me, Ness, I have a new flavor for you to try." She handed the baby to her mother, then gestured to Ellie and said, "We've had one big thumbs-up here so far."

"It's excellent," Ellie said.

"Of course it is. All of Steffie's ice creams are amazing. But sure," the dark-haired woman said. "I'm always up for a new flavor. What's this one called?"

"I don't have a name for it yet."

Before the shop owner could disappear into the back, Ellie said, "Excuse me, but I haven't paid for my ice cream."

"In one second." She continued on her way into the back room, then a moment later returned with a small dish and spoon like the ones she'd given Ellie, and handed it to her friend. "I'm sorry," she apologized to Ellie. "I totally lose my head when Vanessa brings Poppy to see me."

"Totally understandable," Ellie assured her.

The bell rang again, and a stack of white boxes appeared a second before Brooke did.

"Let me help you with those." Vanessa was out of her seat in a flash to grab the top box before it toppled off the pile.

"Thanks, Ness. I wanted to drop off what I have available now because for the rest of the week, I'll be baking nonstop for Sunday, and I'm not sure if I'll . . ." Brooke turned to close the door behind her and at the same time, saw Ellie. "Oh, hey! Ellie! Good to see you again."

The two other women turned to look questioningly at Ellie.

"Hi, Brooke. Nice to see you, too."

Brooke turned to the other two women. "Have you met Ellie?"

"Not officially." The shopkeeper stepped around from the back of the counter and extended a hand in Ellie's direction, which necessitated Ellie's putting down the spoon and meeting the tall blonde halfway. "I'm Steffie

MacGregor. The pretty mama of the world's most adorable girl is Vanessa Shields."

"Ellie, nice to meet you." Vanessa put down the boxes. "Any friend of Brooke's, and all that."

"Ellie just moved to St. Dennis," Brooke went on to explain, "She bought Lilly Cavanaugh's house and is fixing it up."

"I didn't know it was for sale. I love that house." Steffie's eyes lit up. "You're so lucky!"

"It is a great house," Ellie admitted.

"Which house is that?" Vanessa placed the white box on the counter.

"You know. The one I told you about. The one where the light keeper used to live out on Bay View Road."

"The house the pirates tried to burn?" Vanessa asked.

Ellie laughed. "That's the second time today someone mentioned pirates."

"Pirates were a real problem on the Chesapeake in the 1700s, definitely not a laughing matter back then," Brooke told her. "Even Blackbeard sailed the Bay."

"Are you going to tell me that Blackbeard tried to burn my house down?"

"No, it wasn't Blackbeard. It was that other one . . . " Steffie frowned. "Brooke, what was her name?"

"Her?" Ellie's eyebrows rose.

Brooke nodded. "A woman who dressed like a man. Anne—no one really knows what her real last name was, but she called herself André Bonfille. She'd drop anchor out there in the harbor and she and some of her men would row to shore in small boats, terrorize the town until they were run out. They rarely actually hurt anyone, but they'd round up a bunch of the townspeople and then ransom them back to their families. Every few years they'd be back. No one knew this pirate was a woman until she was hanged down in North Carolina. But you'll hear all about it on Sunday." Brooke placed the rest of the boxes on the counter next to the cash register. "First Families Day."

"Grace mentioned it," Ellie told her.

"Oh, if you're new in town, you have to come," Vanessa said. "It's so fun. The first year I was here, my brother made me go, even though I was thinking what a bore it would all be. But it was fun and I learned a lot. I wouldn't miss it for the world."

"Vanessa's brother is Gabriel Beck, the chief of police here in town," Steffie told Ellie.

"Oh, Chief Beck." Ellie recalled the polite officer who knocked on her door the second night she was there. "We've met."

"I've gone every year for as long as I can remember," Steffie was saying, "and I wouldn't miss it, either."

"Me, too," Brooke said. "Even after I moved away, I came back every year for First Families Day. It's a little hokey small-townish, but we love it anyway."

"I'll try to make it."

"You need a ticket for the dinner," Steffie told her. "I have extras. You're welcome to one. More, if you have someone you'd like to bring."

"Thanks, Steffie, but Grace mentioned she was saving one for me."

"Well, I guess we'll see you on Sunday. Great. Look for us when you get to the square, okay? We all hang out together, so you should join us, unless you have other friends to go with."

Ellie shook her head. "No other friends. And if I can make it, I'll definitely look for you."

"Great. We'll probably be toward the right side of the square, toward the corner where Jesse's law office is. You know where that is, right? Violet Finneran always has coffee on in the morning and sandwiches later in the day. Brooke is bringing cupcakes, so we can sneak in and grab a snack."

"Sounds like fun." Ellie nodded noncommittally and ate the last bit of ice cream. She stood and pitched the cardboard bowl and plastic spoon into the trash receptacle near the door. She wanted out before the questions became more personal. "I'll put it on the calendar."

"Oh, do. I know there's someone who'll be happy if you show up," Brooke teased.

Ellie tilted her head and asked, "What?"

"Jesse told me that Cam O'Connor thinks you're hot." Brooke grinned.

Ellie felt a flush creep up her neck to her hairline.

"Cam's hot," Steffie said. "Always has been."

"Stop it. You're married," Vanessa admonished.

"He is what he is. Marriage has not made me blind, nor has it erased my memory," Steffie replied.

Vanessa rolled her eyes and lifted her baby from the confines of the stroller. "Cam's hotness aside, join us on Sunday. We'll watch for you."

"Thanks for the invitation." Ellie turned to Brooke. "Great seeing you again."

"See you." Brooke went to the counter and Steffie met her there.

"Hey, Ellie, you should try one of Brooke's cupcakes before you go," Steffie called to her.

"I have a personal stash at home, thanks to Brooke. Best I ever tasted." Ellie smiled and opened the door to leave, the bell tinkling overhead.

"I dropped off a few yesterday," Ellie heard Brooke say as she closed the door behind her. "You know, a welcome to St. Dennis . . . "

Ellie walked to the edge of the wooden boardwalk that ran from Scoop to the marina. She mentally debated whether to take the time to walk its length or to go back to the house and polish silver. Because the sun was so warm and the afternoon so inviting, she continued past the boats, past the brown cedar-sided building that housed Captain Walt's, home of the best seafood on the Eastern Shore, according to its sign, and all the way to the marina. Gulls circled overhead, scolding one another for who knew what infraction, and the air smelled faintly of salt and gasoline. She stood at the end of the dock, looking across the Bay, thinking she hadn't realized how broad it was, how dark its waters. She watched the whitecaps, blown at a slight diagonal by the rising winds, and wondered what had brought those first settlers to this place, what they had found when they got here, and what hardships they'd faced in order to stay.

She thought of the pirates, and tried to imagine them coming up around the cove to drop anchor before they came ashore. How the people who lived in town must have shuddered when they saw the sails of those big ships billowing across the Bay.

For the first time that day, she began to consider the possibility of showing up on First Families Day after all, just for the hell of it.

Diary ~

Well, I was certainly right about something changing in our world but I couldn't have guessed what was coming! After all these years, Lynley Sebastian's little girl has come home.

Of course, she's not a little girl anymore, and she has no idea that I know who she is. Why she's calling herself Ellie Ryder, I can only guess that she fears that the sins of her father—and there have been many—have followed her and would cause folks to judge her in his light. She forgets that it's her mother whom St. Dennis remembers, not that scoundrel her mother married. I hope that in time she discovers that we all remember her dear mother with much affection.

I recognized her the minute I laid eyes on her.

She's fixing up Lilly's house—plans to sell it, she says. I don't know how Lilly or Lynley would feel about that. I think Lynley had hoped that one day her girl would find the same peace here that she herself found, the peace that kept bringing her back year after year. I do hope the girl gives us a chance. She's clearly a child who needs a place to belong.

I remember how Lynley would come back to relax—never with the husband, though, and only rarely would she bring the girl. She was Ellis then, not Ellie, but what's in a name? Lynley stopped bringing her when she was maybe three or four.

Back in those days, Lynley was still a celebrity. Sometimes she and Lilly would bring the girl to the inn for afternoon tea, and more often than not, Lucy and I would join them.

There are photographs somewhere—I should look.

Lynley Sebastian was a lovely woman—a very good

woman who never forgot where she came from. From what I can see, in spite of all the terrible things her father has put her through, Ellis—Ellie—has rolled up her sleeves and set to work to do what needs to be done. I believe Lynley would be proud of the woman her daughter has become.

~ Grace ~

Chapter 7

ELLIE turned on the faucet to fill the pot with water for her morning coffee when movement in the yard caught her eye. She leaned closer to the window and saw a man in a blue and brown flannel shirt ministering to one of the bird feeders. His shoulders were broad and the untucked shirttails hung over the back of his jeans in a nice curve. It was hard not to admire the view.

The thought occurred to her that she'd never seen her ex-fiancé, Henry, in a flannel shirt, doubted that he owned one. If he did, it surely wouldn't be faded and worn like the one that fit Cameron's frame so well. Henry's flannel—should he ever have owned one—would have come from some high-end store and would have been pressed within an inch of its life so that not a wrinkle or fold showed. The colors would not have been faded because he'd wear it once—if he wore it at all—and it would have been tucked into neatly pressed khakis.

Of course, these days, Henry's wardrobe consisted of orange jumpsuits, so the point of her mental meandering was pretty much moot.

Cameron turned to pick up the large bag of birdseed that he'd placed on the ground and hoisted it in one hand.

Real men, she decided then and there, wore well-worn flannel, and they never tucked it into their jeans.

Real men like Cameron, who, word had it, thought Ellie was pretty hot.

Likewise, my friend. Likewise . . .

Ellie hastily filled the coffeepot's basket with fresh grounds and turned on the stove. Grabbing a sweater from a wall hook near the back door, she tossed it over her shoulders before stepping outside and leaning on the porch railing, which swayed in response.

"Hi," she called. The morning was rich with scents from the Bay, brilliant sunshine, birdsong, and promise.

"Good morning." He finished filling the feeder and walked toward the house, carrying the bag of birdseed, which he placed on the bottom step. His eyes were hidden behind dark glasses as he strode toward the porch. "I wouldn't lean on that railing if I were you. I haven't gotten around to fixing it yet."

"It does have a bit of a sway to it." She straightened up. "You're up and out early."

"Got a lot to do this morning."

"Like driving around St. Dennis filling bird feeders?"

"Just these. Everyone else can fill their own." He pushed his glasses on top of his head and fixed those blue eyes on her. "I put these feeders up a few years ago, and it's become a habit to check on them, especially during the migration season and into the winter. I noticed they were getting low on seed when I was here the other day." He stared up at her. "Does it bother you . . . ?"

"Oh, no. No. I think it's really nice of you. I just don't want you to feel obligated . . . "

111

"I don't. Well, maybe to the birds. They become accustomed to finding food at certain places, so I want to make sure there's seed here for them. I'd suggest you continue filling the feeders yourself, except that I've hung them for my height. You'd need a step-ladder to do the job. Of course, I suppose I could lower the feeders."

"Would that confuse the birds?" she wondered.

"They'll adapt, though the lower the feeder the easier it is for the squirrels to raid them." Cam smiled. "So we can leave them where they are and I can stop over once or twice a week and refill them."

"That's up to you. In the meantime, I'll pick up some birdseed. I saw some in the market the other day."

"You want the kind that has a high percentage of thistle and sunflower seeds. Anderson's out on the highway usually has the best prices for the good stuff."

"Oh. Okay." *The good stuff?* She hadn't known there were different kinds.

"The cheaper varieties usually are heavy on the smaller seeds and really light on the stuff the birds need," Cam went on to explain. Perhaps he sensed her ignorance on the matter.

"Like thistle and sunflower seeds."

"Exactly." He stood with his hands on his hips, his sleeves rolled almost to the elbow. "You want to buy the right food for the birds you have."

"What kind of birds do I have?" She frowned. She'd seen several flitting around the backyard, but none close enough that she could tell robin from blue jay.

"This time of the year, you have chickadees, nuthatches, wrens, tufted titmice, cardinals. The usual suspects."

"Oh, right." She nodded as if she knew. Through the door wafted the smell of percolating coffee. On impulse, she invited him in.

"I've got a minute, thanks. I was going to grab some takeout from Cuppachino on my way to the job." He followed her into the kitchen and looked around. "Someone's been busy."

"I've cleaned out all the cupboards and washed up just about everything in this room and the dining room."

"It's looking like someone really lives here now."

"I know, right?" She poured two mugs of coffee and placed them on the table. She added two spoons, the sugar bowl, and a container of milk. "Help yourself," she told him.

"Thanks." Cam added a teaspoon of sugar and just enough milk to turn his coffee a few shades lighter. "So you think you might be almost ready to paint the first-floor rooms?"

"Not quite yet, but I'm close. I thought I'd wait until I got the upstairs in better shape and then paint everything at once."

Cam raised an eyebrow. "You're going to get awfully tired of painting if you try to go from one room to the next until they're all done. The only way I'd ever recommend that would be if you had a crew come in and paint for you."

"What would you suggest?" She fixed her own coffee and leaned back against the counter.

"I'd do one room at a time." He looked around the kitchen. "I'd start here, maybe. Paint the cabinets, the walls and woodwork."

"After I do the floor," she added.

"That's a whole 'nother thing," he reminded her, "since that old linoleum has to be pulled up and the floor sanded."

"Maybe I should start that project before I get into anything else. Or maybe I'll paint the dining room first. I think it will be easier." She sighed. "After I strip off the wallpaper, of course."

"Whichever room you decide, remember to wet the walls first and the paper should scrape right off, depending on the type of glue the paper hanger used. I was serious about loaning you a pressurized sprayer. It'll make the job much easier."

"With my luck, it will be the antique version of Super Glue."

"Like I said, I'd complete one room at a time. If you want to start in the kitchen, start with the floor. Then when you have it stripped down, you can start taking down the wallpaper. Either way, call me first and I'll come over and give you a hand."

"I'd appreciate that, thanks." Ellie turned to the counter and picked up a silver bowl that she'd polished the night before. "I found silver in the sideboard. I still can't believe that this house has been vacant for all these years, and it hasn't been broken into."

"Like I said, a lot of people have been keeping an eye on the place."

"Including you."

"Especially me."

Before she asked if there was a reason for that, he'd finished his coffee in one long drink and placed the mug on the counter next to where she stood. "Thanks for the coffee."

"Thanks for feeding the birds and the lesson on bird-seed."

"Anytime."

She walked him out to his truck, which was parked across the end of her driveway.

"So I guess you've heard about First Families Day." Cam opened the cab door but made no move to get in.

"From just about everyone I've run into over the past few days."

"Are you going to go?"

"I'm thinking about it."

"You should. It's a fun event, involves the whole town."

"I have to admit I'm curious. Mostly about the pirates."

"Oh?" His mouth slid into a slow smile. "Curious about the pirates, are you?"

"How could I not be? I mean, I heard they burned down the house that originally stood here."

"Not exactly where your house is standing now, but you can see part of the foundation for that first structure inside the carriage house."

"Really?" She turned and looked down the driveway at the old building she'd yet to investigate. "Maybe I'll get lucky and find the key. I'd hate to break a window to get in there."

"Yeah, you don't want to expose the interior to the elements," he told her. "Especially with winter coming on. But who knows? Maybe the key will turn up." He swung himself into the driver's seat.

He started up the engine and rolled down the window. "I hear it's going to go down to the thirties tonight," he said right before he closed the door. "You might want to bring in some of that firewood from the back porch."

He slammed the cab door and she waved before turning to go back to the house as he drove away.

I hear it's going to go down to the thirties tonight. You might want to bring in some of that firewood from the back porch.

Jeez, way to dazzle with your wit, O'Connor. Could you have been any smoother than that?

What a dumb-ass.

He watched in the rearview mirror as Ellie leaned down to pick up something from the ground. There was no denying that she intrigued him on more than one level. He liked the way she looked, liked that she didn't appear to fuss with herself too much. And that he was attracted to her . . . well, what guy wouldn't be? Besides her good looks, there was a grace about her, in the way she moved and the way she gestured and spoke. She gave every indication of having been well educated, but poorly prepared for the task that she'd set for herself here in St. Dennis.

And that, to Cam's mind, was just the start of where the problems came in.

Something just wasn't quite right about Ellie Ryder.

There was something about her that just didn't ring true. He'd tried—given it some thought after his visit the other day—but just couldn't seem to put his finger on what it was about her that was off. Oh, there were the little things—like how she claimed to have little money for renovations but was driving that big Mercedes sedan. And, who, having no money to hire a contractor and admittedly no skills to do the work yourself, would buy a house that needed as much work as Lilly Cavanaugh's house needed?

Of course, there was the possibility that she'd spent everything she had to buy the house and didn't realize just how much work the place needed until she moved into it.

He'd give her that much, but the house itself was only half of what weighed on him where Ellie was concerned. Her hands were definitely not hands that had done much hard work in the past. They were soft and refined, not hardened by the type of tasks she was taking on, and who in their right mind would take on such a huge project without having some experience?

Then there was that feeling that they'd met before. There was something about her eyes, something familiar, and yet not. It really bugged him. He couldn't imagine where they might have met in the past—certainly she didn't give any sign of having met him before—and yet there it was. Every time he looked at her, he got that same feeling.

He slowed the truck in front of the vacant lot on the opposite side of the street and three houses down from the old Cavanaugh place. He just couldn't seem to drive past without stopping, however briefly, to reflect and remember the house that once stood there, the family that had once lived there.

Of course, the house, like the family, was long gone.

He gunned the engine and continued on his way.

Cam turned into the drive that ran between Grant Wyler's house and his veterinary clinic and parked behind a white pickup that was parked near the garage. He hopped out and waved to the plumber he'd called in to get an estimate on the work Grant and his wife, Dallas, wanted done on the house. New expanded kitchen, new bathrooms, new sunroom. Offices in the attic and a new four-car garage. It had all the makings of one very sweet job.

He'd have to put his curiosity about Ellie aside and focus on the task at hand. There'd be time enough to discover just what was what. In the meantime, the possibility that she'd be at the square on Sunday gave him a little something else to think about, his reservations about her having done little to diminish his attraction. The errant little thought he'd had earlier began to take on a life of its own.

If Ellie was intrigued by the pirate tales, he'd just have to make sure she'd have a ringside seat—or better—come Sunday afternoon.

Chapter 8

EVEN the chilliest morning of the week couldn't keep Ellie from heading toward the beach with her coffee, and this morning, a breakfast sandwich she'd made for herself. Modeled after something offered by a fast-food drive-through, it had a sausage patty topped with a scrambled egg topped with a slice of cheese on a toasted English muffin. She'd tried it out the day before and was so pleased with the results she couldn't resist making another one. She sat on her rock, mug in one hand, sandwich wrapped in foil in the other, and took a deep breath. Despite the damp and the chill in the air—Ellie was thinking that life was pretty sweet in the here and now. Having decided that looking back at what used to be was pointless, she'd made a promise to herself to look at each new day as an opportunity to learn and to grow and to just enjoy and be grateful to be in this place.

She unwrapped her sandwich, balanced it on her knee, and watched a very large bird swoop low over the white-caps out on the Bay, then rise up swiftly, and just as swiftly, dive headfirst into the water. Seconds later, the bird emerged, a struggling fish in its mouth. She'd seen the bird—or one like it—every day when she came to the beach, but she didn't know what it was.

I should know what that bird is, she told herself. *I will know. I will learn what that one is. I'll find an app for my phone that has seabirds on it, and I'll bring it with me when I—*

Motion in the dune grass to her right caused her to freeze, the sandwich in her left hand almost to her mouth. She held her breath, wondering if the fox she'd seen a few days earlier had returned. It had poked out of the grass, and she was pretty sure that both she and the fox had been equally surprised to see the other. They'd both stopped in their tracks to stare, the moment suspended in time, before the fox flicked its tale and disappeared back into the grasses. It had been bigger than she'd supposed foxes to be, more like a medium-size dog.

Ellie sat still as a stone, wondering if she and the fox were about to have another face-to-face, but when she shifted her eyes to the right, she saw not the fox, but a small gray dog standing at the edge of the dune. It watched Ellie as she watched it before taking small, very tentative steps in her direction. Its little nose sniffed the air, and she realized it had been drawn by the scent of her sandwich.

"Hey, pup."

At the sound of her voice, the dog cocked its head to one side. It paused for a moment, then took another few steps in Ellie's direction. It was close enough for Ellie to see it had no collar.

"Are you a runaway? Got out the back door when the kids left for school? Chased the mailman? What's your story?"

The dog came closer, and without thinking, Ellie broke off a piece of her sandwich and extended her hand in the dog's direction.

"Are you hungry, pup?"

Its eyes downcast, the dog crept nearer until it was almost to the food. Then it raised its head and looked at her as if waiting for assurance that the morsel was truly meant for it.

"It's okay. Take it. Don't worry, I won't hurt you." She leaned forward, her arm outstretched, and the dog took the food so gingerly that Ellie wasn't sure it was actually gone. The dog sat at her feet, chewed and swallowed, then looked up at her hopefully.

"Another piece?" She broke off another bit of sandwich. The dog wagged its stub of a tale and waited patiently for her to offer it. "You have lovely manners, you know that? Someone has trained you very well."

The dog's tale wagged more, and Ellie couldn't resist giving it another bite, and then another, until the sandwich was all gone.

"It's okay," she told the dog. "I can make myself another one." She reached out her hand to touch the dog, and the dog met her halfway, nudging its head under her palm. What could she do but pet it? "You're a cutie, but I'll bet someone is out looking for you right at this very moment, so you should probably be on your way now."

Ellie looked skyward as a breeze blew across the beach, almost flattening the grasses.

"It's going to rain soon and it's getting cooler. You should scoot along home now. You don't want to get caught in the storm."

Ellie rose and took her last sip of coffee. "Where's your collar?" she asked. "If you had a collar with some tags on

121

it, I could call your owner and let them know where you are."

She walked over the dune and onto the road, the little dog at her heels.

"No, you can't come with me. Go on home, now. And stay off the dunes, hear? You don't want to run into that fox. He might think you look a little too much like lunch."

Ellie kept walking, the dog trailing her at a distance. When she reached her driveway, she turned and told the dog, "Seriously. You need to go home. Someone is worried about you. I know I would be, if you were my little dog."

She leaned down and patted the dog on the head one last time, then walked to her front door and went through it, leaving the dog at the foot of the driveway.

"It'll go home now," she told herself. "It was just waiting to see if there would be more food to mooch."

Ellie was torn between starting on the kitchen or the dining room walls. They would all have to be scraped, she trusted Cameron on that, but which would be the best place to start?

Probably the kitchen, she decided. Getting the walls stripped down as well as the floor would be time-consuming and messy, maybe the messiest task.

Start with the floor, she reasoned. Cameron said there was nice wood under the old linoleum, so maybe we rip up a piece of the crappy floor and see what we can find.

Sounded like a plan.

She began in the butler's pantry, working on the area where Cam had lifted the linoleum to reveal the pine floor. It took her all of the morning and part of the afternoon, but as it turned out, the old floor wasn't so hard to remove after all. Surprisingly, the tiny black iron nails that held down the flooring popped mostly without resistance. By noon, the pantry floor was back to its original pine, in need of a good cleaning, but she could see the beauty of the wood. When she talked to Cameron again, she'd ask him the best way to clean that floor and she'd tell him that there'd been no glue used when the floor in the pantry had been put down. She hoped that proved true in the kitchen as well.

A clap of thunder caused her to jump nearly out of her skin, and she realized she'd been working in total silence. She found her iPod at the bottom of her bag and scrolled through her playlist until she found some tunes she could work to. She bundled the ripped-up flooring and put it out on the back porch. She'd call the town hall to find out how best to dispose of it, but for now, it could stay where she left it.

The rain was falling harder and slanted toward one side of the house. She was happy to close the door behind her and shivered as she returned to the warmth of the kitchen. She put on a pot of coffee, determined to take a little break, and went upstairs to grab a sweatshirt to pull over her turtleneck. On the way back downstairs, she paused and looked out through the front windows and was relieved to find the little dog gone from the lawn. She hoped it had made it home before the storm hit. It really had been a very cute little thing.

The mail truck came down the street and she walked to the door to see if it would pause at her mailbox. She stood watching for a moment, listening to the sounds of the storm outside, the howling of the wind and the pine branches scratching at the glass. She started to turn from the window when she looked down, and saw a gray mass huddled near the door.

"Oh, dear Lord," she said aloud.

She reached for the doorknob, then hesitated for a second before she ran upstairs, taking the steps two at a time, and returned in a moment with a pile of towels. She opened the door and scooped up the shivering animal and brought it inside wrapped in a towel.

"I thought I told you to go home. I know that your people are worried about you. What were you thinking, taking off like that from wherever it was you came from?"

She rubbed the dog dry with the first towel, but the shivering didn't stop.

"You're cold right through, aren't you." She carried the dog into the kitchen and sat it on the floor next to the sink while she ran warm water. She lifted the little dog into the sink and ran warm water over its back. The water ran brown with dirt.

"No doggie shampoo here, so we're going to have to go with the stuff I use for the dishes. Sorry, pal, but that's all I've got." She lathered up the dog's fur, then rinsed off the suds. Dark specks that did not look like dirt floated in the water. Ellie peered closer. Some of the specks appeared to be swimming.

"Fleas? Seriously? I bring you in from the cold and you bring me fleas?" Ellie grimaced. "Okay, we're going to have to run through this routine again. Maybe there are more . . ."

There were. She washed and rinsed several times more until no new culprits appeared in the water and all had been sent down the drain.

"Your owner is going to thank me for ridding her—or him—of those pesky little bloodsuckers. And you're going to thank me, too, because you won't be scratching."

She picked up the dog, set it on a towel she'd placed on the floor, and dried it off with a second towel.

"Ah, you're a little girl, I see. And your coat's not so dark now that it's clean. You're really quite a lovely silvery color." Ellie continued to dry the dog's fur. "You're a good little dog and very cute, but you have a home somewhere and we're going to have to find it." She bit her lip. "Not sure the best way to go about doing that."

The dog leaned up and licked Ellie's chin.

"Oh, you're welcome. I'm glad you feel better. We'll keep you warm and dry this afternoon, but then we'll have to find your home."

The dog licked her chin again.

Ellie piled the dry towels on the floor and placed the dog on top. She poured herself a cup of coffee and sat at the table.

"You can curl up right there while I drink my coffee and call the police department and see if anyone reported a missing dog."

She pulled up the town's website on her iPhone, then punched in the numbers for the town hall. She was transferred twice before talking to someone who took her name and number and promised to call if anyone reported a missing dog, but so far, no one had.

"Maybe you sneaked out when your owner left for

work and no one realized you'd gone." Ellie turned to the dog, who sat up on the pile of towels. "In the meantime, I have a job to do, so you can just sit right there while I work on this floor."

The dog whined.

"Sorry, I don't have any more cooked sausage and I'm not giving it to you raw." She watched the dog that was watching her and seemed to be waiting for something. "Are you thirsty? Would you like some water?"

The dog wagged its tale as if it understood.

"Water it is." Ellie took a small bowl from the cupboard and filled it with cool water, then placed it on the floor. The dog drank until the bowl was empty.

"Wow. You *were* thirsty."

The dog wagged its tail and returned to its nest atop the towels.

"How long were you out there, anyway?" Ellie knelt down next to the dog and smoothed the fur on the top of its head. "More than just today, I'm thinking."

The dog curled up, closed its eyes, and went to sleep. Ellie finished her coffee, and encouraged by her success that morning, went to work peeling up pieces of the kitchen floor.

By four in the afternoon, the rain had stopped, the wind died down, the sun came out, and the dog woke up.

"Good timing on your part," Ellie told the dog. "You probably need to go out right about now."

The dog followed Ellie to the back door and went down the steps into the grass.

"I wish I knew what to call you, friend," Ellie murmured, and watched the dog run around the yard for

126

several minutes. Her phone began to ring and she answered without looking at the ID. Maybe, she thought, someone called the police department about the dog.

"What's cooking?" Carly asked when she heard Ellie's voice. "How's everything going?"

"Pretty good. Just spent the past two weeks working my little fingers to the bone trying to clean and organize this house. Lucky for me I'm not allergic to dust." Ellie put her hand over the phone and whistled. The dog stopped sniffing the tall grass at the rear of the property, turned, looked toward the house, then ran full tilt to the porch. "What are you up to?"

"Just got back from a quick trip to London to look over some paintings the gallery was interested in. They were lovely, but upon close inspection, my expert eye recognized them to be fakes."

"Good girl! What a good girl you are!" Ellie praised the little dog after she ran up the steps and sat at Ellie's feet, wagging her tail happily.

"Why, yes. Yes, I am." There was a pause on the line. "You know, you have an odd way of phrasing things sometimes."

Ellie laughed. "Sorry, Carly. I was talking to the dog."

"Dog? What dog?"

"The dog I found on the beach this morning that followed me home and waited on my front porch until I capitulated and took her in."

"What kind of dog? What's her name?"

"She's ... I don't know, some sort of terrier maybe. Small and light gray, a little white on her chest. Little stubby tail and floppy ears. Cutest thing. No collar, no tags, so I have no idea what her name is."

"Well, what are you calling her?"

"'Girl' is the closest I've come to calling her anything."

"Well, that won't do. She needs a name."

"She's got one, and somewhere, someone knows it. I'm not keeping her. She's just staying here until I can find her owner."

"Still, she needs to be called something. Where did you find her? On the beach?"

"She kinda appeared on the dune."

"Dune, then. Call her Dune."

"I think she knows 'Girl.' She wags her tail when I called her that."

"She needs something better than that. Call her Dune."

"Sure. Okay." Ellie shrugged her shoulders and rolled her eyes. As if the dog would be there long enough to recognize Dune as her name. "Dune it is."

"I can't wait to see her. She sounds adorable."

"Well, unless you expect to be here within the next twenty-four hours, you're probably going to miss out. I called the police and left my number so that the owner can contact me. I'm sure whoever owns her is frantic to find her."

"How long ago did you find her?"

"Around eight this morning."

"And no one's gotten frantic yet?"

"I'm thinking maybe she got out when her owner left for work this morning and hasn't been missed yet."

"I suppose that's a possibility. But . . . "

"But . . . ?"

"Maybe she doesn't belong to anyone. Maybe she's a stray."

"No chance. This dog has been well trained. She has excellent manners. No, she belongs to someone who cared enough about her to teach her how to behave. Someone is missing her. This is a small town. Sooner or later, her owner will be looking for her."

"In that case, don't get too attached," Carly warned. "You never had a dog before, so you don't know how quickly they become part of your life, or how much you can love them."

"I don't expect to have her long enough to become attached." Ellie paused and heard Carly yawn. "You sound really tired."

"Beat to a pulp," Carly admitted. "Too much travel, not enough days in between trips."

"Maybe you should plan on taking some time off."

"I'm taking off tomorrow, as a matter of fact."

"Any special plans?"

"I'm visiting my BFF in her new home. That is, if she doesn't have any plans of her own . . ."

"Really? You're coming here? To St. Dennis?"

"I am. You know how my curiosity always gets the best of me. I can't stand not seeing your new house or that idyllic little bayside town you're calling home these days."

"Yay! When will you get here? How long can you stay?"

"I think it'll probably be sometime tomorrow afternoon by the time I get my act together and get on the road."

"Oh, cool. You'll be here for Sunday."

"What's happening on Sunday?"

"St. Dennis's First Families Day. Sort of like founders' day, from what I understand. I don't know exactly what they do, but everyone I've met down here keeps telling me I have to go."

"Cool. We'll do it."

"Want me to give you directions?"

"GPS, El."

"Right. So how long do you think you can stay?"

"Maybe till Monday. I have something tentatively scheduled for Tuesday in Philadelphia, but we'll see. I'm hoping we can move that up so I can take a few extra days. Assuming it's all right with you."

"Of course. Stay as long as you can. I can't wait to see you."

"I can't wait, either. I'm dying to see that fabulous little town—and of course, Miss Dune. You, too."

"I doubt the dog will still be here. I totally expect someone to call tonight when they get home and find her missing and call the police department."

"Well, I'm hoping they're out of town for the weekend so I can meet her. I can't tell you how much I've missed having a dog since Bowser crossed over the Rainbow Bridge."

"Is that a euphemism for . . . ?"

"See, if you'd had a dog even once, you'd know. You'd know and you'd understand."

"My father wouldn't let us have a dog. He didn't think animals belonged in the house."

"Just goes to show what he knows." Carly yawned. "Sorry."

"Hang up and go right to bed, get lots of sleep so you can make the drive tomorrow without falling asleep at the wheel."

"Good point. I'll give you a call if I think I'll be later than three tomorrow afternoon."

"Great. Have a safe trip, Car."

"Will do."

Ellie disconnected the call and left the phone on the coffee table.

"What should I do first?" she wondered aloud, then realized that she was talking to the dog.

"I'm talking to a dog."

The newly christened Dune tilted her head to one side.

"I'll bet that's nothing new to you. I'll bet your people talk to you all the time because you're such a good listener."

Ellie got up from the sofa and looked around the room. "Things look pretty good in here and in the dining room. The kitchen can wait until the morning. Of course, the floor in there is partially ripped up, but that can't be helped. So I'm thinking that now is a good time to get a room ready for Carly." She started toward the stairs and the dog followed her. "Which room do you think? The one next to mine, or the one across the hall?"

Dune's nails tapped on the hardwood as she kept up with Ellie.

"Right. The one across the hall. That's what I was thinking, too. So she'll have her own bathroom. Good choice."

Ellie stripped the bed of its sheets and the faded green chenille bedspread and took the whole pile to the first floor, where she stuffed it all into a laundry basket that had spent the past who-knew-how-many years in a closet on the second floor, and left it near the front door. First thing in the morning, she'd make a run to the Laundromat. Maybe she'd even make a stop at the supermarket to pick up a small bouquet of flowers. She'd put them in one of the art pottery vases she found in the pantry and place them on the table next to the bed in the room she—and Dune—had selected for Carly.

Maybe, she thought as she checked the locks on the front, back, and basement doors, she'd look through that box of recipe cards she'd uncovered in a kitchen closet and actually attempt to bake something to share with her friend over tea tomorrow afternoon.

The important thing was that Carly was coming to visit. The one person—the only person—who'd stood by Ellie, who knew all of her secrets and all of her warts and loved her anyway, would be here tomorrow, and for just a few days, Ellie could drop the pretense and the outright lies about who she was, where she came from, and where she was going.

She wondered how it would feel to be Ellis Chapman again.

It might be nice.

Chapter 9

EARLY the next morning, a thumping sound from the back of the house sent Dune barking and Ellie to investigate.

"I hope I didn't wake you." Cameron O'Connor stood at the top of the tall metal ladder that stretched all the way to the roof. He glanced over his shoulder at Ellie as he tossed a glob of leaves to the ground. "Don't worry. I'll clean that up before I leave."

"What are you doing?" she asked from the porch.

"Cleaning your gutters. We're in for one heck of a rain come Monday, if the meteorologists know what they're talking about. Not that they always do, but why take a chance?" He held up another glob of wet leaves. "Your gutters are worse than I thought. I should have kept a closer eye on them."

"What's the problem?"

"The problem"—he started back down the ladder—"is that the gutters get clogged with leaves, then the water can't get to the downspout, where it could just flow nicely to the ground. Instead, it overflows the sides of the gutters and can rot your siding eventually."

He picked up the leaves he'd dropped and pitched them into a bucket near the base of the ladder.

"This is really very nice of you, but you know, you don't have to . . . "

"Actually, I do." He smiled at her, then turned to move the ladder a few feet toward the end of the house.

Ellie leaned against the porch rail but straightened up when she felt it give a little. She watched Cameron climb the ladder, watched the way his sweatshirt stretched across his shoulders. There were worse ways a girl could spend a few minutes early on a Saturday morning.

"So when did you get the dog?" he asked without looking down.

"I didn't get a dog. She followed me back from the dune yesterday and I couldn't leave her outside in that storm. I called the police station and told them I had her in case her owner reported her missing but I haven't heard back from them."

"Cute little thing."

"She is. And she's very sweet. I know someone is missing her."

"Maybe she's one of Grant's dogs."

"Grant?"

"Grant Wyler. The local vet. Good chance he'd recognize the dog if it's local. He also runs a rescue shelter over at his clinic, gets dogs from kill shelters down south and tries to find homes for them."

"Someone else mentioned him. I can't imagine she's a shelter dog, though. She's very well trained."

"Lots of rescue dogs are well trained. There are all sorts of reasons why dogs end up in shelters. Their owners die or lose their jobs and can't afford to take care of them, or

134

they have to move and can't have pets in their new place, or their kids are allergic, or they—"

"Stop." Ellie put her hands over her ears. "It's too sad. I can't imagine how hard it would be to give up a pet that you loved."

"When did you say you found this dog?" He turned and looked down at her.

"Yesterday."

"And you're already this attached?"

"I'm not attached. It's just sad, that's all."

"Right." Cam went back to scooping handfuls of gook from the gutter. He dropped another handful of leaves. "Good luck."

"Yes, well." She watched him climb down the ladder. "Thanks again, Cameron. For . . . " She gestured toward the roof and the gutter.

"You're welcome, but I should have done this back in September."

"I appreciate that you're doing it at all. I wouldn't have known that it had to be done."

"So I take it this is your first house."

"First one I've been responsible for."

"Always lived in apartments?" he asked.

"Yes." *Well, except for the several mansions I used to call home, but for the purpose of this conversation, they don't count, because there was always a staff to handle whatever had to be done.*

Ellie couldn't remember her father ever asking about having the gutters cleaned in any of their former homes. Someone was always there to just do it. She wondered if her father even knew that such things had to be done.

135

Cameron was back on the ground and moving the ladder to the corner of the house.

"Can I offer you some coffee or something?" she asked.

"No, thanks. I need to get this done and get to a meeting." He flashed a smile again. "I'll take a rain check, though."

He really has a pretty terrific smile, she thought as she watched him ascend the ladder once more.

"Sure." She stuck her hands in the pockets of her jeans and thought about all the things she had to do between now and Carly's arrival. "Well, I guess I'll let you finish up so you can make your meeting."

She called to the dog, who'd been sniffing at the clots of wet leaves that dotted the ground near the ladder, then opened the back door.

"Hey, Ellie."

She turned back and looked up toward the roof, shielding her eyes from the early morning sun.

"There's live music at Captain Walt's tonight, down near the marina. Want to join me for some great Maryland seafood and some mediocre jazz?"

Surprised by the invitation, Ellie hesitated for a moment. "Thanks, Cameron, but I'm having company this weekend. Maybe another time?"

"Sure," he replied from the top of the ladder. "See you tomorrow?"

"Tomorrow?" She frowned. "Oh, you mean the First Families thing. I guess so."

"Maybe we'll bump into each other."

She went back inside and Dune scooted after her. She

washed the breakfast dishes and tried to decide how she felt about Cameron asking her out.

She searched for the to-do list she'd had in her hand when she came downstairs earlier. She found it and sat at the table to go over it. If she concentrated really hard, she could ignore the fact that a really great-looking guy was at that moment climbing around her house and cleaning her gutters, and that he'd just asked her out on a date. It had come so unexpectedly that she hadn't had time to think much about a response. Of course, she'd been unable to accept, but if not for Carly's visit, would she have?

Tough call, she thought.

On the one hand, seeing anyone socially could lead to complications. What if one date led to another, and that one to another still? Dating implied a relationship, and what kind of a relationship could you possibly have with someone you're lying to about the most fundamental things? Like who you are and where you came from and how you really acquired the house you're living in.

On the other hand, Cameron O'Connor seemed like a special kind of guy, a guy who was thoughtful and interesting and nice to be around, not to mention that he was pretty hot. If she were to date anyone in St. Dennis, he'd be the first guy she'd want to spend time with.

And then there was the fact that it might be nice to connect with someone here in St. Dennis who remembered—who *knew*—her mother, even if he wasn't aware of the relationship.

Interesting—curious, even—that he still felt such a strong sense of responsibility to this house and to Lilly

Cavanaugh. He'd said that he'd known her and that she was very kind and sweet, but surely there had to be more to it than just remembering a sweet, kindly old woman who'd been dead for many years.

All of her senses told her there was a story there that he wasn't sharing. She thought back to a conversation she'd had with him a week or so ago. She'd shown him silver she'd found in the sideboard and had polished the night before.

"I still can't believe that this house has been vacant for all these years and it hasn't been broken into," she'd said.

"Like I said, a lot of people have been keeping an eye on the place," he'd told her.

"Including you."

"Especially me."

She'd wanted to ask him at the time if there was any particular reason for his vigilance, but he'd polished off his coffee and headed out before she could inquire. Maybe if he asked her out again, she should go, if for no other reason than to find out why his attachment to this house was so strong.

Of course, the fact that the guy was very easy on the eyes would be merely a bonus.

A glance at the clock told her she was running behind her self-imposed schedule. She'd found a recipe for scones that looked pretty simple, and thought she'd mix up a batch of them so she'd have a snack to offer Carly when she arrived later this afternoon. She grabbed her bag, closed Dune in the kitchen, and went out through the front door. Cameron was still working on the gutters on the side of the house when she drove past. If he was still there when she returned from running her errands, she'd take him coffee or a bottle of water, but she suspected he'd be long gone by the time she got back.

Sure enough, the pickup was no longer parked near her mailbox when she arrived home. The laundry had taken longer than she'd planned, and she'd been held up in the grocery store by Grace Sinclair, who insisted on introducing her to several other ladies, all of whom appeared to be of Grace's era. But she did manage to pick up a copy of the *St. Dennis Gazette*, Grace's newspaper. Ellie tucked the paper into her shoulder bag, thinking that at some future date, she'd follow up with Grace to see what the older woman recalled about Lynley's time in St. Dennis.

Once inside, Ellie cut the stems of the mixed bouquet she'd picked up at the market and arranged the flowers in a dark blue vase. She carried them up the stairs in one hand and the sheets for Carly's room in the other. She made the bed, rearranged the flowers, and opened one of the windows to bring in some fresh air.

She got out the ingredients for the scones on the counter and turned on the oven to preheat it, then mixed the scones, which she baked on a cookie sheet she found in one of the cupboards. By the time she heard a car's engine out front, the scones were cooling on a plate.

"Yay, Carly's here." Ellie grabbed a sweater from the back of a kitchen chair and dashed out the door, Dune at her heels. She slowed as she crossed the lawn, staring as her friend got out of the sleek sports car parked in the driveway. "Whoa, Carly! Those are some fancy wheels."

"She's something, isn't she?" Carly tossed an oversize

bag over her shoulder and slammed the door of the shiny silver Porsche 911. "I just picked her up yesterday. Thought I'd take her on a test run."

"How'd she do?" Ellie met Carly with a hug near the front fender.

"She's perfect." Carly embraced Ellie in a bear hug, then stood at arm's length to take a long look at her old friend. "You look fabulous. Working your fingers to the bone apparently agrees with you."

Ellie laughed and held up her hands, which Carly grabbed and pretended to scrutinize.

"Girl, you weren't kidding. When was your last manicure?"

"Too long ago to remember." She gave Carly an extra squeeze before letting her go. "But strangely, I don't miss my once-lovely nails."

"Well, if I had to choose between this place and that old apartment of yours on Madison, I'd definitely choose to be here." Carly stood back, her hands on her hips. "It's a wonderful house, El. I can't wait to see the inside. Come on." She grabbed Ellie's hand. "Show me everything."

"Want to get your bags?" Ellie paused.

"Later. I'll come back out and . . . oh, is that Dune?" Carly knelt down next to the little dog. "Oh, she's so cute! Maybe you'll get lucky and her owner won't look for her."

"I'm sure someone's looking. How could they not? Maybe they just haven't called the police station. I was thinking this morning that maybe they're still looking around the neighborhood, or putting up posters or

140

something. Or maybe they're away." It occurred to Ellie then that she'd forgotten to call the vet. "Cameron suggested I call the vet in town. Apparently he's involved in some rescue dog group and—"

"Cameron?" Carly stood and fell in step with Ellie. "Who's Cameron?"

"Oh, he's . . . well, at first I thought he was sort of like a handyman because he was doing little things around here, but he's really a contractor. At least that's what it says on the side of his pickup." Ellie opened the door and held it for Carly, who stepped inside, then paused, looking around.

"There's just something about a guy with a pickup that—oh, Ellie! This is so cool. Look at your dining room. Was all this furniture here?" Carly pointed to the sideboard. "Oh, that's so pretty. My grandmother had furniture something like that. And check out your living room. I love that sofa!"

Carly dropped her bag on the floor and went directly to one of the club chairs and sat. "Real mohair circa 1940. This stuff is in prime condition, El. And totally back in style. Dealers in Manhattan would kill for this stuff."

"I know. I've been checking online."

Carly ran her hand along the wooden insert in the chair's arm. "You're so lucky, you know that? Once you start selling off things, you should make out quite nicely."

"I think so. I'm planning on having a dealer come in to look things over for me."

"Excellent idea." Carly stood and walked to the fireplace and ran her hand along the wood. "Your mantel is beautiful. And look at these ducks." She lifted one and turned to Ellie. "Decoys?"

Ellie nodded. "Lilly Cavenaugh's husband, Ted, was a well-known carver. Cameron thinks they're worth a lot of money."

"There's that name again." Carly grinned. "Who is this person?"

"He's been sort of looking after the house. You know, keeping the grass cut and just making sure that nothing was amiss. He knew Lilly, and for some reason that I'm not sure I understand, he's felt obligated to keep up with things around here."

"Maybe he had a crush on Lilly."

"Lilly would be, oh, I suppose maybe around one hundred if she were still alive."

"And how old is Cameron?"

"About our age. Midthirties."

"May-December romance." Carly shrugged.

"I think she probably died when he was in his teens."

"You mean she's been gone for twenty years?"

"I'm not really sure when she died. Easy enough to find out, I suppose. Everyone around here seems to have loved her." Ellie sat on the arm of the sofa. "And there are people here who remember my mother."

"Well, you've said she used to come here when she was little, right?"

"Even later than that. Cameron remembers her. He knew her, Carly. He said he remembered when she came here when she was sick." Ellie felt her throat constrict. "I'm not sure that I even knew that she came here when she was sick. If I knew, I don't remember."

"Well, how old were we when your mother was first diagnosed? We were still in high school, weren't we?"

"We were sixteen."

"Sixteen and living at boarding school. It's very possible that you don't know a lot of what went on back then."

"And from what I'm hearing, she even lived here for a while."

"Here? In this house?"

Ellie nodded. "I was always under the impression that she just visited here sometimes, but now I'm hearing differently."

"You said that people remember her. You can probably ask around and find out."

"And if I were Ellis Chapman, I'd have reason to do that. As Ellie Ryder, though ... " Ellie shrugged.

"Good point." Carly bit her lip. "There must be someone you can trust."

"I trust my attorney, but he didn't grow up here, either, so he wouldn't know. His secretary, who has to be in her eighties if she's a day, knew Lilly and knew my mom. I've thought about asking her. I think she knows who I really am."

"Well, then, ask her what she remembers."

"And there's Grace Sinclair. She owns the little newspaper in town." Ellie got up, opened her bag, and pulled out the issue of the *St. Dennis Gazette* that she'd picked up earlier. "I can always call her, I guess. Her number's in here."

"I'd ask." Carly nodded vigorously. "I'd definitely ask. El, you can't be living in this house where your mother once lived and *not know*."

143

"I know. I keep thinking about it."

"Too bad you can't ask your father."

"As if he would know." Ellie made a face. The last thing she wanted was contact with her father. "He always acted as if this place didn't exist. To hear him tell it, St. Dennis was just someplace that my mom passed through before she became famous and only stopped in now and then on her way to someplace else. I had no idea that she'd spent anything other than an occasional vacation here."

Her voice dropped, remembering. "My father only wanted to go to places that he thought were important, places where the beautiful people went. St. Dennis wasn't important, in his book, and the beautiful people never came here, so we never did, either."

"You never came here with her?"

Ellie shook her head. "My dad always planned our vacations. My mom never had anything to say about it. Besides, she was always off someplace working. She almost never went with us. Usually she met up with us wherever we were going."

"But she continued to come back here?"

"That's the thing, I'm not really sure when. She talked about St. Dennis and about her aunt Lilly—her mother's aunt, actually—and from what Cameron told me, she did come to visit when Lilly was still alive. But you're right about me not knowing what my parents did while we were away at school. It never occurred to me to ask what they did while I was gone."

"So she still had strong ties here, at least as long as her great-aunt was still alive."

"I think she must have."

"She was famous, people would have noticed." Carly leaned forward, her elbows on her knees, her chin resting on her fists. "Maybe while you're here, you can find the answers to all those questions I know you have."

"I'm going to try."

"Nothing like a good mystery," Carly said. "I bet with a few well-directed questions to the right people, you can find out everything you need to know."

"I haven't had much time to think about it, to tell you the truth. I wasn't kidding when I said I've been working my butt off here. I can't even begin to tell you how tired I am at night. I hit that pillow, and I'm gone."

"Totally worth it." Carly looked around the room from the fireplace to the built-in bookcase that lined one entire wall. "I'll bet your mom came here every chance she had. It's a very comfortable house. I can see you snuggled up here with a glass of wine or a cup of something hot, a soft cozy throw, reading a good book, a fire blazing in the fireplace. Dune next to you on the sofa." She smiled. "Don't you have the feeling that others have done exactly that? Lilly, maybe even your mother. It seems like a happy house, for all it's been vacant all these years. It feels like a house that's been loved."

"From everything I've been hearing, everyone loved Lilly and her husband. Even the neighborhood kids liked them."

"As evidenced by the fact that people who knew them were watching over the house for many years after they were gone."

Ellie nodded. "You know, it's hard to explain, but I've

felt at home since the first night. Maybe the fact that my mother lived here and spent time here over the years and came back when she was sick has something to do with it, I don't know. But I think my mother must have loved this house. Otherwise, she would have sold it after Lilly died and she wouldn't have arranged for its care and maintenance all these years. She wouldn't have wanted to save it for me."

"I think you're right. And I think that sooner or later, you'll find the answers to all the questions you have about her time here." Carly stood. "Now, think of someplace you'd like to go to have dinner while you take me for a stroll around your property. I want to get some pictures while it's still light . . . "

Chapter 10

"LOLA'S really is a lovely restaurant. The decor is charming and the food was delicious." Ellie folded her napkin and placed it next to her now-empty coffee cup. "I've only been to one other restaurant in town since I arrived but I stopped going when I realized I was eating far too many take-out burgers."

"You're living on the Chesapeake Bay and you're eating burgers every day?" Carly made a *tsk-tsk* sound. "With all the seafood they have on the menu here?"

"What can I say?" Ellie shrugged. "I was going for cheap."

"Well, cheap was not on the menu tonight, since we're celebrating your new home and dinner's on my dad and mom," Carly said. "They send their love and wanted you to know how much they miss you."

"I love and miss them, too. I'll never forget how kind they've been to me."

Carly dismissed the comment with a wave of her hand. "You know they think of you as a second daughter. After all, we've been friends for a million years."

"I'll never stop being grateful for that, too, Car. You've been the best friend that anyone has ever had."

"You'd do the same, and there's not going to be any

more discussion on that subject." Carly finished the last of her wine.

"So let's talk about you, then. How's everything in your world? How're things with Todd?"

Carly gave the thumbs-down sign. "Kaput."

"What happened?"

"It's hard to explain." She paused. "Oh, the obvious is easy to explain. I'm pretty sure he has a girlfriend in Toronto. He's spending more time there than anywhere else."

"Seems pretty straightforward. So where's the hard-to-explain part?"

"Oh, that's the part where for some reason, I don't think I really care. My first reaction was more akin to relief than shock."

"Then maybe the universe did you a favor by removing him from your life. That way, you don't have to go through any sort of hassle to break up with him."

"Exactly what I thought." Carly nodded. "You'd think that after having been together for two years, it would have been shocking, devastating even. But no. I only felt relieved. It made me realize that I hadn't been paying much attention to the relationship lately, if the breakup was that painless. In retrospect, I can't blame him for finding someone else. If I were in his place, I might do the same thing."

Ellie shook her head. "You'd do the breakup thing first. You wouldn't cheat."

"True enough. Anyway, that's done." Carly signaled the waiter for their check and handed him a credit card. "What? You want to say something. I know you do."

"I never liked him," Ellie whispered sheepishly.

"I know." Carly sighed. "Neither did my parents, but they never mentioned it, either, until we broke up."

"Sorry."

"Don't be. Water over the dam and all that." Carly smiled. "Just promise me that next time you don't like someone I'm dating—if there ever is a next time—you tell me straight out."

"I promise." Ellie crossed her heart with her index finger. "But you need to do the same."

"I've always pretty much liked everyone you dated. Though there was that guy freshman year who was such a colossal jerk."

"The sax player?"

Carly shook her head. "The football player."

Ellie made a face. "After a while, I didn't like him much, either."

"Explains why it didn't last very long." Carly sighed. "You know, it's been years since we were both single at the same time. It could be fun."

"True enough. At least it could be if we were in the same place all the time." Ellie nodded. "However, if I were to guess, I'd say I'll be single for a lot longer than you will be."

"How do you figure?"

"You're going to be globe hopping and meeting all sorts of fabulous guys who will sweep you off your feet. I'll be here in St. Dennis, scraping wallpaper and dripping Corsica White on my head as I attempt to paint the ceilings."

"You'll probably have more fun. Besides, must be some

single men around. Watermen. Oyster fishermen. Boat-builders. Manly types."

Ellie thought about that flannel stretched across Cameron's shoulders. "Contractor."

Carly raised an eyebrow. "You mentioned a contractor earlier."

"Cameron. He's pretty hot."

"And single?"

"He asked me out, so I guess he is."

"When?" Carly signed the slip the waiter brought. "Ready?" she asked Ellie.

"I'm ready."

The two women stopped at the coatroom to pick up their wraps, then headed out into the evening air and to the parking lot.

Carly unlocked the doors, and once they were both inside the Porsche, turned to Ellie and said, "So finish. When did this guy ask you out?"

"This morning." Ellie settled back into her seat and fought the urge to hold on as Carly peeled away from the curb.

"And I'm just hearing about this now because . . . ?"

"It didn't come up before now." Ellie shrugged. "We've been talking about other things."

"So when are you going out with the hottie with the hammer?"

"I'm not. First of all, the date was for tonight, which was out of the question for obvious reasons. And secondly, I don't think I should go out with anyone while I'm here."

"Why not?"

"Because when you go out with someone, you talk. And the talk always turns to 'So, where are you from? Where'd you go to school?' and those questions beget other questions. Sooner or later, it comes down to lying or telling the truth, and I don't want to do either to someone I like."

"So you like this guy."

"I mean, in a general sense, sure. What's not to like? He's good-looking and responsible—did I mention he's been taking care of my house and property for years just because he liked Lynley's great-aunt Lilly? Carly, turn at the next street."

"But . . . " Carly put on her turn signal.

"But when you like people, you want to be honest with them and I can't be. I don't want to make friends that I have to lie to all the time. Especially since he knew my mother. I can't even tell him that."

"I understand. But you know, you're going to get pretty darned lonely if you stay here long enough."

"So I guess the solution is to not stay any longer than I have to. Which, as you know, is six months."

"Six months can seem like an eternity when you're alone."

"I don't have a choice about that."

"Have you given any thought to where you'll go from here?" Carly pulled into Ellie's driveway and cut the engine.

"Not really." Ellie released her seat belt. "Carly, this car is just amazing. I wish you tons of luck with it." She opened the car door and got out.

"Thanks. She is a sleek little beast, isn't she?" Carly

emerged from the driver's side, locked the car, and patted the hood. "You can always stay with me, you know. I'd love the company when I'm home, and when I'm off on a trip, you'll have the place to yourself."

"Thanks, but sooner or later, I have to get a job."

"Any idea what you might want to do?"

Ellie shook her head. "I have no options. I spent years doing a great job in PR, but that ship has sailed. The only company I ever worked for belonged to my father, so I have no references."

"You have me. I could be your reference."

"I never worked for you."

"I could say you did. I know the quality of your work, I watched you for years. Besides, you were the one who gave me the ideas for several of our most productive marketing plans."

"Still, I didn't have a hand in implementing them and I wouldn't ask you to lie."

"You're not asking me. I'm volunteering. If your future is on the line, I'd have no problem saying that you worked for Summit Galleries International. And please, no protests. You'd do the same for me." Carly paused in the driveway. "Actually, I could hire you to do PR for the galleries."

Ellie shook her head. "That would bring me right back into the world I left."

"True. But think about it. We could set you up in a different city. Boston, maybe. You've always liked Boston."

"Thanks, Carly, but I don't know if I want to get back into that game again."

"It's up to you. Now let's take a walk on your beach. There's still some light left."

"Give me a minute to get Dune. She should be ready for her walk right about now."

Ellie disappeared into the house and emerged moments later, Dune on the end of a shiny red leather leash.

"I was afraid to walk her off the property without a leash and collar, so I picked these up at the grocery this morning. Honestly, the pet food options are just staggering. It took me twenty minutes to figure out what to buy, but she seems to like the organic chicken and rice."

"I like organic chicken and rice, too," Carly noted.

"Probably not the same stuff she eats."

They walked the short distance to the dune and stopped to take off their shoes.

"Watch out for the grasses," Ellie told her. "They're trying to preserve the native plants along the Bay. I read about it on the town's website."

"I like your little beach." Carly stood with her hands on her hips and gazed out across the Bay to the western shore, where the sun had all but disappeared.

"It's not exactly the Riviera."

"True. But it's nice. Different, but nice."

"The sand is really coarse along here, but you're right. It's a nice little beach." Ellie sat on her rock. "I come here most mornings and drink my coffee and think about things."

"What things?" Carly made Ellie scootch over so that they could share the rock.

"Well, lately, I've been thinking mostly about ripping up the kitchen floor." Ellie smiled. "And pirates."

"Pirates?" When Ellie nodded, Carly grinned. "I've always had a thing for pirates, ever since *Peter Pan*."

Ellie pointed out toward the Bay. "Back in the 1800s, pirates used to come up the Bay, drop anchor out there in the middle, then row ashore in small boats and terrorize the residents. They burned down a house that once stood on my property."

"Any chance they buried some of their loot in your backyard?"

"Sadly, no. Apparently they just came into town to bully the populace until they were run back out to their ship by the locals."

"Too bad. Pirate booty would come in handy right about now."

"True."

They sat and watched the small waves unfurl quietly onto the sand.

Finally, Carly said, "You know, all things considered, you ended up in a really good place, a place that feels right. You have a great house that's loaded with character. I know you feel connected to your mother's spirit here, and that's a good thing. I think you've needed that for a long time."

"I have. I always adored my mother, but over the past few years I've come to realize how little I really knew her. Partly because she was always off someplace else, partly because when I was younger and so full of myself, it never occurred to me that I didn't know her the way I should have. Being here does make me feel closer to her."

"That's a good thing, El." Carly went on, "And when you're ready to put the house on the market, I think you're going to be surprised by how much you'll get for it. The location couldn't be more perfect."

"I'll do really well when the time comes," Ellie agreed. "Assuming I can do the work that it needs to pass inspection."

"You will. And you know, it's good that you're having time away from everything and everyone from the past, time to cleanse your palate, so to speak."

"There's no question that I need to put all of that behind me. This last year has been hellacious."

"Do you hear from Henry?" Carly asked.

Ellie shook her head. "I hope I never do."

"I think he cared about you, El. I really do."

"He cared about me to the extent that he could gain access to my father. He cared about being 'the son Clifford Chapman never had,' as the newspapers called him. He didn't so much care about me." Ellie drew a circle in the sand with the toe of her shoe. "He never even apologized. He never said he was sorry for his part in the whole scam. It didn't seem to register with him that he'd played a huge part in ruining a lot of lives. Mine was only one of them."

Carly rubbed Ellie's shoulder. "Well, he's behind you now. Your life is far from ruined. And hey, there's your contractor . . ."

"He's not my contractor," Ellie protested.

"We'll see." Carly stood and pulled on Ellie's hand. "Let's go back to your house and make coffee and look through some of the books on those shelves in the living room. I'm dying to see what's there."

"Ice cream first." Ellie tugged on Dune's lead, and the

dog trotted obediently, a piece of driftwood in her mouth. "I stopped at One Scoop or Two this afternoon. That's the local ice-cream place where everything is handmade in small batches right there in the shop."

"What flavor did you get?"

"Maple walnut surprise."

"What's the surprise?" Carly caught up with her.

"I guess we'll find out."

Ellie came into the living room with a tray that held two bowls of ice cream, two spoons, a pile of napkins, and a bowl of pretzels, Dune dancing behind her with joyful anticipation.

"I found out what the surprise is," Ellie was saying. "It's cranberries. I cheated and took a taste. It's amazing."

Carly stood with her back to the door, staring at one of the paintings on the wall. "Ellie, this painting . . . " she said without turning around.

"What about it?" Ellie placed the tray on the coffee table. Dune patiently stared down the bowl of pretzels.

"It's signed Carolina Ellis."

"I know. There's a bunch of her stuff hanging throughout the house."

Carly turned slowly. "There are *more*?"

"A half dozen or so."

"Ellie, do you know who Carolina Ellis is? Was?"

Ellie shrugged. "No. But it sounds as if you do."

"You could say that. Carolina Ellis's work was 'discovered' by the art world about twenty years ago, but she's since been recognized as one of the more important

156

women artists of the very early twentieth century. Her *Life Along the Chesapeake* hangs in the Met."

Ellie tilted her head. "So, her work's valuable?"

"The last painting to come up to auction sold for a bundle."

Ellie frowned. "I wonder how Lilly came to own them."

"Them?"

Ellie pointed to the opposite wall. "There's another right there."

"Holy crap." Carly all but sprinted across the room and studied the painting for several minutes before asking, "Ellie, notice anything different between the two paintings?"

Ellie walked to the other side of the room and stood in front of the painting. "This one is darker than the other. In that one," she pointed back to the first painting, "the colors are much lighter, the feel of the painting is lighter."

"I've only seen one Carolina Ellis painting where the colors and the subject matter are this dark," Carly told her. "The few that have come to auction over the past few years have all been painted during her lighter period."

"The ones in the dining room and the ones upstairs are even darker."

Carly put a hand over her heart as she crossed the foyer to the dining room. "I cannot believe this. I doubt anyone in the art world has any idea that these exist."

Ellie joined her across the hall.

"Pinch me," Carly said. "This is by far the largest example of her works that I've ever seen."

"It is larger than the others," Ellie conceded. "I take it that's good."

"Very good, as in very rare. This storm scene . . . " Carly shook her head. "The way the waves are swirling just like the sky . . . it's beautiful. Just beautiful." She turned to Ellie.

"You realize that one of these beauties could pay for the repairs and the renovations on this house."

"Yes and no." Ellie leaned on the back of one of the dining room chairs.

"What do you mean?" Carly frowned. "You inherited the house and the contents, right?"

"Well, first I'd need to see Lilly's will to see if she bequeathed them to my mother. And there's that pesky clause in Mom's will that stipulates that nothing can be sold until I've lived here for six months. It hasn't even been a month yet."

"Maybe you can use them for collateral."

"Assuming they belong to me. Can you appraise them?"

Carly nodded. "Of course. But I'll want to have them cleaned and removed from their frames and run some tests on them first."

"Don't let me stand in your way."

"I don't have anything with me to work with. I'd have to take them back to my gallery."

"So bring your tools and work here."

"I might have to do that." Carly stared at the painting on the wall, a smile on her face. "On second thought, I should take them to my house. I wouldn't want word of this find to get out. I think I want to keep them under

wraps, then, when they've all been cleaned and cata-
logued, we'll do a fabulous exhibit."

"Why the smile?"

"Oh, was I smiling?" Carly laughed. "I'm just imag-
ining the stir these paintings will create when I announce
that Summit Galleries has located a cache of hitherto
unknown Carolina Ellis paintings." She turned to Ellie.
"You will let me display them all, right?"

"Of course. If they're mine."

The two women stared at the storm that was rising
chaotically on the canvas in swirls of oils, shadows that
went from dark to darker still.

"Ellie, it couldn't be a coincidence that your first name
and her last name is the same."

"I was just thinking that same thing. It would be really
cool to find out that I was named for a famous artist."

"She wasn't famous when you were named. She hadn't
been 'discovered' yet. And there's still so little known
about her." Carly sighed. "This is blowing me away. I
come to visit my best friend and look what I find."

"You drove hours to visit an exiled friend," Ellie
draped an arm over Carly's shoulder, "so it's only right
that you are rewarded in some way."

"I want to see the others."

"They can wait five minutes. Right now, our ice
cream is melting, and trust me, you're going to love every
delicious bite."

Carly looked torn.

"The ice cream is melting now. On the other hand,
the paintings have been here for a very long time and
most likely will still be here in ten more minutes."

"You said the surprise was dried cranberries?" Carly raised an eyebrow.

Ellie nodded and pointed toward the door. "Just in time for the holidays."

They each grabbed a bowl of softening ice cream and a spoon, and sat on either end of the sofa.

"Dune, give it up," Ellie told the dog. "Those pretzels are salty and I don't think salt is very good for dogs."

Dune, who'd been eye-level with the bowl of pretzels, sunk to the floor with a soft groan.

"You know, if Carolina Ellis was an ancestor of yours, it explains why your mom's great-aunt had so many of her paintings. They were probably kept in the family. Carolina's work has become well known—what there is of it that's hit the market—though as I said, not much is known about her."

"I'm afraid I can't help you there," Ellie told her. "I don't know anything about her either."

"Oh, my. This is decadent. Oh, and there are shards of dark chocolate in there, too. Yum."

"How did I miss chocolate?" Ellie frowned and dug for a dark shaving in her bowl.

"So how do you suppose Lilly would have been related to Carolina?"

Ellie thought for a moment. "Lilly was my great-grandfather's sister. My grandmother's aunt. So she would have been Carolina's daughter." She frowned. "Lilly's maiden name was Ryder, so her mother's last name would have been Ryder, too. Why wouldn't she have signed her paintings, *Carolina Ellis Ryder*?"

"Good question."

"I'll bet Grace Sinclair would know. She knows everything about everyone in St. Dennis."

"Can you call her?"

"I don't have her number but I'm pretty sure she lives at the inn that her family owns. It should be easy enough to get a number for it."

It was. A quick search on her phone brought up an app for the Inn at Sinclair's Point. She called the number and in minutes had been connected to Grace's line. After a few preliminary niceties, Ellie cut to the chase.

"Grace, I've found some paintings in my house that were all done by the same artist, Carolina Ellis, and I'm curious about her. Would you happen to know . . . ?"

"Of course, dear." Grace cut her off. "Carolina Ellis was Lilly's mother."

Ellie gave a thumbs-up to Carly. "But I wonder why she didn't sign them 'Carolina Ellis Ryder.'"

"Oh, her husband wouldn't have stood for that. He wasn't at all pleased to learn belatedly that he'd married a serious artist," Grace said. "For a time, he'd actually forbidden her to paint. Said she spent too much time locked away with her paints, that it was unhealthy. But it's more likely that he was jealous of the time she devoted to her work. Less time devoted to him, you see. The story I heard was that she became so depressed that he finally relented and allowed her to work again, but only if she never signed his family name to any of her paintings, and she wasn't permitted to sell them."

"So if she wanted to sign her paintings, she had to sign only her maiden name?"

"That's the way I heard it from my grandmother."

"Sounds as if he ... her husband ... had some real control issues."

"Not particularly uncommon in the early part of the twentieth century. A woman's place was in the home, you know. That meant taking care of the house and the children and the husband. Any other pursuits were not encouraged." Grace laughed. "Thank God that's all changed."

"Interesting. Thank you, Grace. I appreciate the information."

"I'm glad I could help," Grace said before she hung up.

Ellie put her phone back into her pocket. "Carolina's husband didn't like the amount of time she spent on her work and forbade her to paint. She became depressed, he gave in, let her work again but she couldn't sign her paintings with her married name and she wasn't allowed to sell any of them." Ellie paused. "That last part seems strange ... "

"Not when you consider the time. No husband of means wanted his wife's hands to be sullied by currency, for heaven's sake. That was *his* place."

"I guess, but it still seems silly."

"It's outrageous to us, but that was the way it was. If your wife worked, it meant that you couldn't afford to support your family."

"I feel very badly for Carolina—I mean, all this creative talent and to not be able to find an outlet for it must have been hell. No wonder she became depressed."

"On the other hand, if she'd been able to sell her paintings," Carly pointed at the paintings on the walls, "these wouldn't be hanging here now for you to sell."

162

"An excellent point," Ellie agreed.

"So barring any other bequests on Lilly's part, the paintings could all belong to you outright through your mother." Carly appeared thoughtful. "Any idea how you could get a copy of Lilly's will?"

"The same law firm drew up Lilly's and Mom's wills, so I should be able to get a copy on Monday."

"Great. Maybe you could give them a call first thing and ask."

"I will."

Carly sighed again.

"What?" Ellie asked.

"Every gallery owner dreams of finding some great work that no one's seen before. Some work that, up until that time, had been unknown. And here there's a whole collection of work that I doubt anyone even knows exists. It's such a thrill for me . . . I don't have words."

"Don't get too excited. Maybe no one will care."

Carly laughed. "The art world will care. What a coup for Summit Galleries, to be able to display such treasures." A dark cloud crossed her face. "Is there a security system in place here?"

"My mom had one installed but it hasn't been updated in terms of the technology. It was pretty basic to begin with and hasn't been on because it kept blowing fuses. But the locals keep an eye on the place, so the house has been surprisingly secure given how long it's been vacant."

"Now might be a good time to beef up the amps in this place and have the security system updated. If someone breaks in and steals them . . . "

"Seriously, I doubt anyone knows they're even here,

Carly." Ellie brushed her off. "People around here just think of this place as Lilly Cavanaugh's old house, and the people in town who knew her have taken great pains to protect it."

"You lucked out there."

"I know. It was a bit of a shock to find some silver pieces in the sideboard and a few others here and there. And the duck decoys are worth something as well, from what I understand. No break-ins, no thefts."

"Like I said, you've been very lucky, but I'm still not comfortable with all this incredible artwork at risk." Carly finished the last of the ice cream in her bowl and plunked the spoon down inside it with a *clunk*. "Finish those last few bites or I'm taking off for the second floor without you."

Ellie laughed. "You go on ahead. I'll take these things back into the kitchen so that Dune doesn't help herself to something she shouldn't have, then I'll join you."

"How will I know where to look?" Carly paused in the doorway.

"Think of it as a scavenger hunt."

Carly had already hit the top of the stairs. "Oh, my God. One, two, three ... right here on the landing. I didn't even notice them before. Oh, my God, Ellie ... "

"Guess she found something she liked," Ellie said to Dune. "Come on, girl. I'll give you one of those little liver treats you like for being such a good girl. Then we have to find some smelling salts and take them up to Aunt Carly, because when she sees what's hanging over the bed in that back bedroom, she's going to—"

"Oh. My. God. Ellie ... !"

Chapter 11

"YOU make the best pancakes ever." Ellie leaned an elbow on the kitchen table and watched Carly at the stove.

"It's true." Carly flashed a grin over her shoulder. "I love to cook. I've missed it these past few weeks while I've been traveling. I was so happy to see the blueberries in your refrigerator this morning."

"No accident there. I have to admit I had high hopes for those berries this morning."

"They're not bad for out of season." Carly popped one into her mouth before pouring a measured amount of batter into the hot frying pan. "And I love using this old cast-iron pan to make them in." She paused for a moment. "Remember when your parents' cook taught us how to make these in sixth grade?"

"I remember she taught you how to make them. It all went right over my head. I wasn't much interested in cooking back then."

"And now?"

"Now I wish I'd paid more attention because a cook did not come with this house. Though a lot of what my parents' cook taught me is slowly coming back."

"Cooking is easy," Carly told her. "All you have to do is read and follow the directions."

"I'm learning. I can now honestly say I know how to make something other than reservations."

"You can make dinner tonight."

"I'd planned on it. I found a recipe for chicken that uses red Thai curry paste and chickpeas that looks interesting."

"Have you made it before?"

Ellie shook her head.

"You know you're not supposed to try out a new dish on company, right?"

"Where's your sense of adventure?"

"Left it in London."

"And since when have you been company?"

"Good point."

Carly lifted out the first of the pancakes and stacked them on a plate. "What time do we have to get to this . . . what is it?"

"First Families Day." Ellie twisted around so she could see the clock on the stove, which she'd found to be forty-three minutes slow. "Everyone said we need to be there by eleven if we want to hear the speeches and see the reenactment of whatever it is they're doing this year."

"No one said what they're doing?"

Ellie shrugged. "I guess we'll see when we get there."

"And who's 'everyone' who said to be early?"

"Just some people I met from town." The coffeepot finished percolating and Ellie rose to fill their mugs.

"Cameron the contractor?"

"Among others."

"So maybe I'll get to see this guy?" Carly wiggled her eyebrows.

166

"Maybe." Ellie shrugged as if the prospect of running into him hadn't occurred to her. "He mentioned that he'd be there."

"Well, then. I suppose I should speed up this production." Carly flipped a pancake onto the waiting plate. "I'd hate to miss an opportunity to meet him."

"We're going to take Dune with us." Ellie changed the subject. "Maybe her owner will be there."

"And if he or she isn't?"

"Then we'll bring her back and wait to hear from the police. I keep meaning to call the vet here in town to see if he recognizes the description of the dog, or if he's gotten a call from anyone reporting her missing, but I keep forgetting." Ellie watched the dog, which at that moment was standing on her hind legs and sniffing the air. "She's thinking I should have bought bacon to go with those pancakes."

"She's right. But who needs the calories and the fat? I'd rather save up for more ice cream from that shop where you got last night's entry for best ice cream ever." Carly sighed and put several more pancakes on the plate. "It was certainly the best I ever had."

"I've had the apple cinnamon raisin and it was phenomenal."

"Perhaps we'll have to stop there after the festivities."

"An excellent idea. The weather forecast has promised us an unseasonably warm day."

"Great." Carly put the last pancake on the plate and brought it to the table along with the maple syrup that Ellie had heated.

167

Ellie poured more coffee and the two women sat and ate for a moment in silence.

"Delicious," Ellie finally said.

"If I do say so myself," Carly agreed. "You know, I'm almost tempted to stay here and spend the day going from painting to painting and just staring. I'm black and blue from pinching myself."

"Maybe when we get back, we should look in the attic and see if there's—"

Carly stood up and looked as if she were ready to bolt from the kitchen.

"Down, girl. I don't know that there are any more in the house."

"Can we go look now?"

Ellie glanced at the clock. "We need to leave here before eleven. How 'bout if we save the attic for later?"

Carly groaned.

"It's always good to have something to look forward to, don't you think?" Ellie grinned and helped herself to another pancake.

"The suspense may kill me."

"Doubt it."

"Do you think there are any paintings up there?"

"I saw some landscapes and a couple of portraits when I was up there last week, but I didn't check the signatures."

"Carolina Ellis didn't paint portraits," Carly said, "and she isn't known for landscapes, just seascapes and beachy paintings."

"The ones that are up there are probably nothing, then."

"We should still check," Carly told her.

"And we will. Later. Right now we're going to get dressed and go to the First Families Day whoop-de-do." Ellie drained her coffee mug. "I doubt it'll last more than an hour. It's a small town. How long could it take for a couple of speeches, and I doubt there's much to reenact."

Cam rechecked the contents of his gym bag before closing it. The last thing he wanted to do today was to get into town and find he was missing some vital part of his costume for today's reenactment. He tucked his hat under his arm and headed into the kitchen, where he washed down half a bowl of soggy cold cereal with the remaining mouthful of coffee in his mug. He'd been looking forward to this day since the idea for this year's reenactment was first proposed by Clay Madison, and he didn't want to be late.

He left his breakfast dishes in the sink and headed out to his pickup, his gym bag in one hand and his hat in the other. It had been a long time since he'd had a chance to play dress-up games with his friends. Last year he'd been laid up with a broken foot—dropped a table saw and didn't get out of the way quickly enough—and he'd missed out on the reenactment of the War of 1812. The other guys got to shell the harbor with a fake cannon that was mounted on the bow of Hal Garrity's cruiser. He'd had to watch from the dock while his buddies got to send those blasts of smoke out over the Bay. This year, he planned on being right in the middle of the action. They'd gotten the okay to use the cannon again, so that was cool. Any day a guy got to blow things up—even for pretend—was bound to be a good day.

He drove into town with a smile on his face, thinking about the role he'd be playing. Heh. Good times for sure.

Even the weather was cooperating. It was another sunny and warm November day, a day when a sweater was more appropriate than a jacket.

He drove along Charles Street, Clapton's latest blues CD blaring and the windows down to coax in the sea air. He was tapping his fingers to the beat on the steering wheel when the two cars up ahead stopped while a very sexy silver Porsche attempted to parallel-park in what appeared to be the last spot on the street.

Sweet wheels. Very sweet. He watched as the driver struggled to fit the car into the minuscule spot. The passenger finally got out and tried to direct the driver. It took Cam only a second to recognize the woman on the sidewalk giving directions. Traffic being backed up, he sat back and just enjoyed the view.

Ellie Ryder was one good-looking woman. She was wearing dark jeans and a gray pullover, the same big round dark glasses she wore the first time he saw her, and her hair was in a ponytail that had been pulled through the back of a red baseball cap.

Traffic started moving once the sports car was tucked into the parking spot. Cam tried but couldn't see inside the Porsche as he drove past. Must be the "friend" she had visiting for the weekend. He wondered who the lucky guy was who had not only the car Cam lusted after but the girl who'd caught his eye. Probably someone she knew before she moved here. Maybe someone from the city who wore a suit all day and rode a desk. He felt his mouth melt into a frown.

Damn.

Jealousy wasn't an emotion he recognized, and even if it was, he'd never admit to envying a guy over a car. The girl, on the other hand   that was something else.

He kept driving, and allowed himself one glance in the rearview mirror but was too far away at that point to see Ellie or her friend.

He had a moment or two to decide whether this friend of Ellie's was going to result in a change of his plans.

Nah. He'd go with the script, and her friend was just going to have to live with it.

The entrance to Old St. Mary's Church Road was blocked off with orange caution cones, so Cam slowed and rolled down his window.

"I'm one of the reenactors," he called to Susan Alcott, the police officer who was directing traffic away from the street.

"So I heard," she called back, and motioned for one of the men on the side of the street to remove the cones so that Cam could pass by. "Have fun."

"I'm planning on it." Cam waved a salute to her and to the officer who'd moved the cones and proceeded to the parking lot behind the library, where he left the pickup. The bells in the tower at the Episcopal church down the street chimed eleven. He had plenty of time to stroll through the crowd and see who was where. It would make everything easier later on.

There was a microphone in a stand on the front steps

of the library, and to the left, a patch of lawn set off by rope tied from one sawhorse to another to form a square.

At one of the front corners, Clay Madison stood talking with Grace, his future mother-in-law, and Wade MacGregor.

"Are you the masterminds who constructed this?" Cam pointed to the square. "It looks like something you'd herd cattle into."

"Hey, if you think you can do better, you can be our guest." Wade crossed his arms over his chest.

"Yeah, I didn't see you here early this morning trying to figure out how to make this thing work," Clay said. "It's as historically correct as we could make it."

"It just looks dumb." Cam shrugged his shoulders.

"Not much to argue about there," Clay agreed. "But it's for charity, so let's just ignore how crappy the thing looks."

The three men walked through the gathering crowd and made their way across the square to the far corner where Jesse Enright's law office stood.

"You got your stuff?" Wade asked.

Cam held up his duffel bag. "Where's yours?"

"Dropped it off early." Wade pointed to Jesse's office. "You might as well hang on to yours now since we'll be going in to change soon enough."

"We've got time." Cam scanned the group gathered on Enright's lawn.

"Looking for anyone in particular?" Clay asked.

"Maybe," Cam replied.

"They're all over there by the oak. Stef, Brooke, Lucy . . . " Wade pointed to a large tree that had yet to shed all its leaves. "Steffie wanted to be in the shade during the speeches in case they lasted too long so she wouldn't get too hot standing in the sun."

"Steffie just didn't want to be so close to the speakers that she couldn't gossip with her friends. I'm betting she couldn't care less about hearing the First Families Day speeches again." Clay added, "Let's face it, we've all heard the same thing a hundred times."

"Which is why the reenactments are important," Cam told them as they joined the women under the tree. "It's the only good part of the day."

"You guys are all just grown-up little boys." Brooke turned at their approach.

"You're right." Her brother nodded. "And boys just want to have fun."

Steffie rolled her eyes. "Just don't make such a fuss that you scare Poppy. Vanessa just took her inside to change her but she'll be back before the festivities start." Her eyes narrowed. "You make that baby cry and you will all answer to me."

"I'm shaking," Clay deadpanned. He turned to Cam. "You?"

"Absolutely. Wade?"

"Leave me out of this. I'm married to her." He gestured with his head in Steffie's direction. "We'll have to be quiet when we ... well, you guys know what I mean, right?"

"Right." Clay nodded.

Cam continued to scan the crowd, searching for the red baseball cap. Finally, he saw her moving along the sidewalk, the dog at the end of its leash. There were others walking his way and it was difficult to know for certain who she was with but she seemed to be talking to a short woman whose long blond hair was twisted up on top of her head in a tight knot.

Ellie looked up as they came closer to the tree, a smile of recognition lighting her face.

"Hey, Cam. Hi, Steffie. Brooke. Everyone." She walked toward them, stopping once while Dune sniffed at a spot on the ground.

"Hi."

"Glad you made it, Ellie."

"Oh, cute dog."

Cameron looked around for the suit.

"This is Carly, my friend," Ellie was saying. "She's visiting for a few days."

Cam's first thought was, *Great. No guy.* His second was, *That's a lot of car for a small woman.*

He knew better than to voice either.

"That's the dog you found?" Steffie asked Ellie, who nodded in reply. "Did you call my brother? The vet?"

"It kept slipping my mind," Ellie said. "But I thought I'd walk her around today and see if anyone recognized her."

"We'll show her to Grant and see if he knows who she belongs to," Steffie told her. "She looks adorable and very well behaved."

There was a lot of chatter as Vanessa and Grady Shields, her husband, joined the group with the stroller and the appropriate fuss was made over the baby at the same time others were welcoming Carly to St. Dennis and Ellie to her first First Families Day. Cam had no real

174

opportunity for conversation with Ellie, but it was okay. He'd have a little one-on-one time with her later.

Grace Sinclair was testing the microphone, and moments later, introduced the mayor, Christina Pratt, who gave the welcoming address and began her annual First Families Day speech.

"This is the same speech she gave last year," Vanessa said out of the corner of her mouth. "I remember the line about 'and right where we stand now, the townspeople gathered to protest . . .'"

"It was the same the year before, too," Steffie added.

"Hey, there's only so many ways you can describe how the settlers made their way up the Bay, fighting off mosquitoes and the elements and the natives," Lucy noted.

"I think she just said what you said, about the settlers making their way up the Bay . . ." Vanessa whispered.

Wade tapped Cam on the shoulder, and the two men, along with Clay, slipped quietly from the group and made their way into Jesse's building, where they, along with several other reenactors, changed into their costumes.

"So how is this going to work, exactly?" Jesse joined them in the conference room, already dressed for his part. "How are we going to know when to go out onto the square?"

Cam pulled his sweatshirt over his head and reached for his duffel bag.

"When the mayor gets to the part in her speech where she says, 'And the town was terrorized for three days while the pirates held the women of St. Dennis hostage,' Grant is going to call out to Hal Garrity on his boat, and he's going to shoot off three rounds on the cannon. That's our signal to invade the town."

"Got it." Jesse grinned. "I guess we can figure out who your hostage is going to be."

"Anything for charity," Cam replied.

Wade put his hat over his wig and straightened his beard. "I think I heard the cannon."

Jesse opened the front door. "Yep. That was the second blast. You guys ready?"

"Yo-ho-ho." Cam headed for the door and the motley band of pirates spilled out onto the lawn.

Those in the crowd who knew what to expect faked frightened cries and there was even a feigned faint or two.

"Good one, Barbara," Cam complimented the bookshop owner on her graceful collapse to the ground.

"Thanks." She opened one eye as he passed. "I've been practicing all week."

Cam headed toward the oak. There his unsuspecting target stood, dog's leash in hand, looking around the crowd and laughing as first one woman then another was swept up and carried across the lawn to the library.

She never saw him coming.

Ellie's shriek was real when Cam scooped her up.

"Hand off the dog to your friend," he told her as he tossed her over his shoulder.

"What? What are you—"

"Here, Ellie, I'll take Dune." Laughing, Carly reached out and grabbed the leash.

"What are you doing?" Ellie was struggling.

"Getting ready to ransom you off." Cam hoisted her a little higher. "And could you work with me here and quit

176

wiggling around so much? You're making this harder than it needs to be. I'd hate to drop you on your head."

"Cameron?" She went still and looked back over her shoulder.

"You were expecting Blackbeard?" He carried her to the library, lifted her over the ropes, and set her down with the other women who'd been carted off across the square and left inside the makeshift enclosure. If his hands rested on her arms a few seconds longer than necessary, it was only because they'd never been that close before, and he was reluctant to let her go.

"Now what happens?"

"First of all, you're supposed to be terrified. You've just been carried off by a bloodthirsty pirate. Could you please have enough respect for us swashbucklers to try to look a little afraid?" *God, but she smelled good.*

"It's tough to take you seriously when your beard is crooked like that." Her eyes were smiling and she held his gaze. He could neither look away nor step away.

"It is?" He reached up to feel where it had shifted.

Ellie laughed and reached over the rope, straightened the beard so that it covered his face equally on both sides. "There. Now you look quite fearsome."

"Thank you," he said with as much dignity as he could muster under the circumstances. The spell broken, he let her go.

The last woman was deposited unceremoniously over the rope, and the pirates faded into the crowd.

Mayor Pratt returned to the microphone and took the stand again.

"Today, we recall those souls who came before us,

those staunch men and women who braved not only the elements and the natives, but the pirates who invaded yearly to steal their women and ransom them back to their families. Those hardy folks who first made St. Dennis their homes in the wilderness ... "

Her voice droned on for several more minutes before she ended with the announcement that the bidding would begin in ten minutes.

"Bidding?" Cam heard Ellie say as he turned to sprint back across the street to change back into his "civilian" clothes. "Bidding?"

Hal had already auctioned off two of the hostages by the time Cam and the others returned to the square. Fortunately, neither of them had been Ellie. Steffie was the first of their group to be led to the steps, and the bidding was lively between her father; her husband, Wade; and her brother, Grant. When Wade finally emerged successful, he thanked his in-laws for driving up the price.

"I'm worth every damn cent and you know it," Steffie called back from the steps, and the crowd burst into laughter.

Brooke went next. Since no one bid against her fiancé, Jesse, Hal banged the gavel at what Brooke declared was an insultingly low amount and she refused to leave the steps until Jesse bid against himself until she was satisfied.

Ransom was paid for several other of the hostages before Ellie was led to the steps. Hal was just about to start the bidding when he heard a woman's voice from behind call out, "I'll bid a thousand dollars."

Cam turned and saw Carly approaching, Ellie's dog trotting by her side.

"We have one thousand dollars." Hal looked across the crowd. "A very respectable opening bid. Anyone else?"

"I'll go eleven hundred." Cam raised his hand.

"Fifteen hundred." Carly immediately countered his bid.

"Cam? Back to you?" Hal asked.

"It's for charity, right?" Carly asked as she stepped closer to Cam.

"Well, yeah, but, you see . . . " Cam sighed. How to explain . . .

"Oh, wait. You wanted to be the one to spring her." Carly looked slightly abashed. "I'm sorry, it didn't occur to me . . . "

"It's okay." Cam turned back to Hal and raised the bid.

"Miss? You still in?" Hal asked.

Carly shook her head.

"The ransom will be paid by Cameron O'Connor," Hal announced. He turned to Ellie. "You're free to go."

"Thanks." Ellie smiled and made her way to where Cameron and Carly stood. "That was fun."

"Probably more fun for you than Cameron"—Carly spoke before Cam could—"who is now out a considerable chunk of change, thanks to me driving up the price."

"It's okay," he told them both. "It's for a good cause."

"What's the charity?" Ellie asked.

"The women and children's shelter out on the highway gets one half of the money and the library gets the other," he told them.

"Looks like they raised quite a bit today," Ellie noted.

Cam nodded. "Yeah, we did pretty well."

"So what happens next?" Carly asked.

"Well, right about now we usually go into Jesse's office, where there are snacks—sandwiches and drinks and some of Brooke's cupcakes," he replied.

"Yum." Ellie turned to Carly. "I've had Brooke's cupcakes. Fabulous."

"Great. Let's go." Carly took a few steps then stopped. "Which way?"

Cam pointed to the red brick building on the corner.

"And are you sure it's all right to bring extra people?"

"Positive," Cam said. "I think everyone's expecting you to stop in since we were all together earlier."

"Actually, Brooke did mention it. But what about the dog?" Ellie looked pensive.

"She'll be fine. And I know that Grant's going to be there, so you can ask him if she looks familiar to him." He added, "And you'll get to meet Dallas MacGregor. Grant's wife."

"I'd love to meet Dallas MacGregor. She's my favorite actress ever." Carly's eyes widened and she turned to Ellie. "Ellie. *Dallas MacGregor.*"

"Lead the way." Ellie tugged on the dog's leash and followed Cam across the lawn.

The conference room and kitchen at Enright & Enright, Attorneys-at-Law, were both packed, and Cam did his best not only to keep track of Ellie and Carly, but to make sure they were both introduced to as many people as possible. After Dune was stepped on twice, Ellie picked her up and carried her, which made it easy for her to show the dog to Grant Wyler.

"I figure she got away from someone here in town," Ellie explained. "Someone's taken good care of her, and she's been well trained. I thought perhaps you'd recognize her as one of your patients."

"I recognize the scamp all right," he replied, "but not as a patient. She was on a transport from a shelter in South Carolina last week, and when they stopped here to exercise the dogs, this little monkey broke free and ran off. We looked for her for almost an hour before the van had to leave again."

"What does that mean, exactly?" Ellie asked cautiously. "A transport from a shelter . . . "

"There are a lot of dogs and cats that are surrendered to shelters for whatever reason. There are some shelters—like the one I run here in St. Dennis—that will keep the animals until homes can be found for them, no matter how long that might take. There are others that are known as 'high-kill' shelters, which are just what they sound like. Seems to be a lot more of them in the southern states than there are up here. There are rescue groups, like Middle Mutts, for example, that transport animals from down south to the shelters up north, like mine, where, as I said, we make every effort to find good homes for them. That's what was happening when this little gal slipped away." Grant stroked Dune's back and the dog wagged her tail appreciatively. "Looks like you found a nice home after all, girl."

"Oh. Well, no, I hadn't planned on keeping her." Ellie frowned. "I just thought I'd take care of her until we found her owner."

"I think she did find her owner," Carly said.

"I wasn't planning on having a dog." Ellie looked unsure.

"But you don't really want to give her up, do you?" Cam had listened to the exchange.

"Not really. Still . . . "

"Why don't you keep her until you decide what you want to do? If you find you really don't want her, you can bring her into my shelter and we'll keep her there until the next transport arrives. In the meantime, call my clinic tomorrow and make an appointment to bring her in this week so that we can check her out, make sure she's healthy."

"I'll do that. Thanks."

"Have you met my wife?" Grant asked as a beautiful woman with pale blond hair made her way through the crowded room. "Dallas, this is Ellie. She's just bought a home in St. Dennis. And this is her friend . . . I didn't catch your name . . . "

"Carly Summit."

To Cam's eye, both Ellie and Carly looked starstruck. Well, who could blame them? Dallas was an A-list movie star, someone you don't meet every day.

"Nice to meet you both." Dallas turned to Ellie. "I saw your ransom was paid earlier, and quite handsomely, too." She poked Cam in the side.

He nodded and repeated what was beginning to sound like his mantra. "Anything for charity."

The crowd began to thin and it was clear that Ellie was getting tired of holding Dune, so Cam walked outside with her and Carly.

"Where are all those people going?" Ellie indicated a steady stream of pedestrians ambling across the square.

"The Historical Society is open, and there's a walking tour of St. Dennis," he told them.

"Want to?" Ellie asked Carly.

"Sure." Her friend nodded.

"I guess you've seen it all before." Ellie turned to Cam.

"About a hundred times. But I wouldn't mind another stroll through town."

"Great." Ellie looped her arm through Cam's on one side and Carly did the same on the other. "Let's do it . . ."

It turned out to be a long day. Cam hadn't thought about doing all the First Families Day events, but he couldn't bring himself to give up a chance to spend the afternoon with Ellie, even if they were accompanied by her friend and her dog. They watched footraces at the park and toured the side streets, stopped at Scoop for ice cream, and sat at a small table outside and watched gulls circle over the Bay in large graceful swirls of wings. Cam had extra tickets for the dinner that night, and talked the two women into joining him. Ellie had to take the dog back home and Carly wanted to get her car, which she'd left parked on Charles Street all afternoon, but they agreed to meet him at six at the Grange Hall.

Cam had time for a quick shower and change of clothing before hopping into his pickup and heading for the Grange. Dinner was the same every year—baked ham, sweet potatoes, green beans, salad, and pumpkin pie—but everyone in town went and it was always noisy fun. The local ladies cooked and served and the guys cleaned up. It was the type of community dinner that could be found in just about any small town in any state in the country. But the routine never grew old, and Cam wouldn't have missed it.

First Families Day was one of those annual events—

like Christmas or Thanksgiving—that he looked forward to. It was part of his past, something that had remained the same for as long as he could remember, even when other things in his life changed so totally and so quickly—and so violently. Some years had been better than others—the years he'd gone with his family were a blur, though he had memories of his mother making a scene once. He'd been too young to understand what she was fussing at his father about, but he remembered how people at their table had looked away with embarrassment when she'd removed the flask from her bag and offered to pass it around. Then there were other years—better years—when he and his sister went with his aunt after she came to live with them. Most of those years, they'd sat at the table with Lilly and Ted Cavanaugh, and everyone in town knew that the O'Connor kids were going to be okay.

Tonight would be different because Ellie was there. He wanted to get to know her better, wanted to assure himself that those things about her that hadn't been sitting right with him were all in his mind.

It had taken less than ten minutes for his suspicions to be reinforced.

He'd sat between Ellie and Carly at dinner, and at one point, when Ellie had been engaged in conversation with Clay on her left, Cam turned to Carly and asked, "So how long have you and Ellie been friends?"

"Forever." Carly smiled. "We went all through school together."

"Where did you go?" he'd asked, and her face had frozen.

"What?" she'd asked.

"You said you and Ellie went to school together. I asked where."

She hesitated for a moment, and he'd said, "Was that a tough question?"

"Oh. No. Of course not." She forced the smile back onto her face. "We went to Rushton-Graves in Massachusetts."

"You grew up together, then?"

"You could say that." Carly turned her attention back to her dinner, the smile still tightly fixed to her face.

"What do you do, by the way?" he'd asked.

"I manage an art gallery." Carly had become visibly uncomfortable.

"Sounds interesting."

"It is." She took a sip of her ice water.

And that was that, as far as Miss Carly Summit was concerned. She barely said two words for the rest of the night, and her "So nice to have met you" as she and Ellie left was more than a little on the cool side.

Cam wasn't sure what was going on, but he was more convinced than ever that something about Ellie wasn't adding up. It might take awhile, but one way or another, he was going to figure it out.

Chapter 12

"THAT was fun," Ellie said as she unlocked her front door. "I didn't expect it to be so much fun. A little on the hokey side, but fun."

"Of course you had fun. You got carried off by a hot pirate," Carly reminded her. "Shiver me timbers."

"You know, that whole thing was so silly, it's hard to believe that an adult thought it up." Ellie unfastened Dune's leash and followed the dog to the kitchen. "Grown men dressing up like pirates, women being carted off like sacks of rice . . ."

"Good times."

Ellie nodded. "Best time I've had in a couple of years."

"Silliness—laughter—can have that effect on the best of us." Carly stood in the kitchen doorway while Ellie filled Dune's water dish from the faucet. "Not to mention the effect of the aforementioned cute pirate."

"He *is* pretty cute," Ellie agreed.

"El, I might have said something to him that could backfire." Carly looked uncomfortable.

"What are you talking about?"

"Cameron. He asked me how long we'd known each other and I said forever, that we went to school together."

"So? All true."

186

"The bad part came when he asked me where we went to school, and I didn't know what you'd told him."

"And . . . ?"

"And I probably waited a little too long to answer him. I think he might have wondered why I couldn't just answer such a simple question without having to think about it." Carly looked uncharacteristically sheepish. "Actually, I know he did."

"You told him Rushton-Graves?" Ellie leaned back against the counter.

Carly nodded. "Of course. But if he looks it up, he'll know there's money in your background, El."

Ellie shrugged. "There are always ways to get around that. I can say a grandparent or a wealthy uncle paid my tuition."

"I didn't mean to complicate things for you. I'm really sorry."

"You didn't complicate anything."

"You sure?"

"Positive," Ellie assured her even while the thought niggled that Cameron was probably too smart to have overlooked Carly's hesitation.

"Good." Carly straightened her back. "Let's go up to the attic and look at paintings."

"You have a one-track mind when it comes to that stuff."

"Damn right. That's why I am so good at what I do." Carly started toward the steps. "That's why in the world of art, Summit is a very highly respected name. Soon to be the talk of that very same art world when I announce the discovery of all of those lovely Carolina Ellis paintings."

187

Ellie caught up with her friend at the top of the steps, and opened the door to the attic. Carly needed no invitation to climb the stairs.

The attic was dimly lit, the contents covered with a thick layer of dust.

"I haven't spent much time up here, as you can see," Ellie said. "There's been so much to do on the first two floors. I thought I'd save this to go through with one of the antique dealers in town. There's a lot of furniture and trunks filled with who knows what."

Carly had already pulled the drape off a group of paintings that were stacked against one wall. Ellie knelt down and began to study them, one by one. Every once in a while, she heard a quiet gasp, as if Carly's breath had caught in her throat. Ellie busied herself looking through a trunk that she found to be loaded with hats. She took them out, one by one, and tried them on.

"Carly, tear yourself away for a moment and check out this hat." Ellie plopped a wide-brimmed dove-gray felt number adorned with a trio of peacock feathers onto her head. She turned to show it off and realized that Carly was crying.

"Car? What's wrong, honey?"

"This . . . " Carly pointed toward a painting she'd separated from the others and placed against the window wall.

"What's wrong with it?" Ellie leaned closer to get a better look at the portrait of a very young woman.

"Remember I said Carolina Ellis never painted portraits?" Carly sniffed.

"I guess."

"I was wrong." Carly turned to Ellie, her face wet with tears. "She painted this one. It's her daughter."

"Lilly?" Ellie's eyes widened. "Why do you think that's Lilly?"

Carly turned the painting around. A piece of vellum glued to the back of the canvas read, *Lilly at sixteen*.

"Oh, but she was pretty, wasn't she." Ellie knelt down in front of the painting. "Look how pretty she was."

She looked back at Carly. "But I don't understand why it's making you cry."

"Carolina Ellis is a woman whose works are just getting the recognition they deserve. Her landscapes are exquisite, but nothing she's done comes close to this. It's beautiful in every way." Carly smiled. "You can tell she loved her daughter very much. And it's something totally unexpected. I have never felt so overwhelmed in my life. It's what Howard Carter must have felt when he looked into Tutankhamun's tomb that first time."

"So this is a real find, is what you're saying."

"My head is spinning." Carly leaned against a nearby trunk. "And, Ellie, that's not all. Lilly apparently inherited her mother's talent. There are some lovely paintings here with her signature."

"I want to see." Ellie stood up and started toward the stack.

"There's something else you should see." Carly walked to the paintings and went through them one by one, searching for something. Her hand stopped on a large painted frame. "You might want to sit down for this one."

"Why?"

"Did you know your mother painted?"

189

"I know she dabbled in watercolors sometimes." Ellie nodded. "But I don't remember that she was ever very serious about it."

"If she wasn't, she should have been." Carly lifted the painting and turned it around for Ellie to see.

A very young golden-haired child sat in the midst of a garden, tall white daisies and some low-growing pink flowers surrounding her.

"That looks like . . . " Ellie came closer, her eyes narrowed.

"You."

"It *is* me." Ellie momentarily struggled for words. "I've seen that dress before. I found it in a box with some other baby clothes that my mother must have saved. But how do you know for certain that she was the artist?"

"She signed it here, in the corner." Carly pointed out the name in black print.

"Lynley Rose," Ellie murmured. "Not Lynley Sebastian or Lynley Chapman. Just her first and middle names." She smiled. "Years ago, a cosmetic company marketed a nail polish and lipstick called Lynley Rose. There was a big marketing campaign, magazine ads, billboards. I was only about five or six then, but I remember."

She stared at the painting a moment longer. "I must have been two or three when she painted this." She looked up at Carly. "I wonder why she didn't sign her full name."

"Maybe she was hoping to exhibit it someday and wanted to be judged by her talent alone, not her celebrity name," Carly suggested.

"Maybe."

"Ellie, didn't you say that you'd never been here before?" Carly asked after studying the painting for another moment.

"As far as I know, I hadn't been." Ellie lifted the painting and brought it into better light. "But that's the carriage house here in the background. And right over here is the corner of the back porch." Ellie looked up. "She could have painted it from memory."

"Maybe she brought you here and you just don't remember."

Ellie shook her head. "I don't think my dad would have let her."

"Maybe she did it when he was away on business. He used to travel a lot, as I remember," Carly reminded her.

"That would explain a few things," Ellie conceded. "Like why some of the wallpapers look vaguely familiar. Funny how she must have loved it here so much, and yet he could never understand the attraction it held for her."

"Do you?"

"Oh, yes. I do now, anyway. Back then, when I was younger, it was all glitz and glamour with my dad." Ellie dusted the glass over the child's face with her fingers. "Everywhere we went with him, it was like New Year's Eve and the Fourth of July and Christmas all at the same time. He always made St. Dennis sound like the last place in the world anyone would want to come to."

"Your father was wrong about a lot of things."

"So true." Ellie held the painting. "Let's take these downstairs and wash off the glass so we can see them better."

191

"We'll take them down but we'll just dust with a dry cloth. I'd hate for any moisture to find its way under the glass and spoil a masterpiece."

"I don't think my mom's dabbling would qualify as a masterpiece."

"We'll see what we see once we're downstairs in better light." Carly grabbed the portrait of Lilly and headed for the steps.

It took several trips, but soon all of the paintings from the attic had been brought into the living room. After they'd been propped up against the bookcases and dusted, Carly sat on the sofa and just stared at their findings.

Carly looked up when Ellie came into the room, carrying two mugs of tea.

"I made chamomile," Ellie told her. "It's supposed to soothe and relax."

"It's going to take more than tea to relax me tonight." Carly wrapped her hands around the mug Ellie offered her. "This has been the most incredible weekend of my life."

Ellie laughed. "I really doubt that."

"It's hard to explain what a find like this means to someone like me." Carly took a sip of tea. "I've worked very hard to make Summit Galleries a respected name in the art world, and yet there are so many people who still consider me a lightweight because my parents funded the start-up. I always feel like the Rodney Dangerfield of the art world."

"Your parents haven't supported you or the gallery for years."

"Absolutely true. But no one knows that. I can't very

well shout from the rooftops that yes, family money started me off but yay! Now I'm self-supporting." Carly made a face. "It sounds like the lady protesteth too much." She took another sip of tea. "But these paintings ... this find ... " She shook her head from side to side. "Maybe now people will take me a little more seriously."

"You certainly deserve it," Ellie agreed. "I'm so happy to have a small part in that."

"A small part?" Carly laughed. "You own these paintings. At least, we're assuming you do. For you to entrust them to me is huge."

"There's no one else I'd consider entrusting them to."

"Thank you, sweetie. I promise to get as much for each of them as I can. When this is over, you'll have enough money to start up a new business or go and do whatever you want."

"That would be nice. I still don't know where I'll go or what I'll do, but it's nice to know I'll have some options I hadn't planned on."

Carly returned her attention to the paintings while Ellie sat on the sofa, Dune curled up next to her, the dog's head on her lap. For a few moments, the only sounds were the clock ticking on the mantel and the dog's breathing.

"You used to paint, too," Carly said. "I remember at school, you did some watercolors that were really pretty. I seem to recall the head of the art department entered a couple of them in state and regional competitions."

"I won a few of those." Ellie smiled grimly. "The feds permitted me to keep the awards since I'd earned them before my father started robbing unsuspecting folks of their life savings."

Several other minutes passed in silence before Carly said, "I have an idea."

"Should I be frightened?"

Carly smiled. "I think you should write a book about these women. Your great-great-grandmother. Your great-aunt. Your mother. We'll self-publish it if we have to, but it could be incredible. We could have pages of photographs of the paintings and release the book right before we put the paintings on display." She turned shining eyes to Ellie. "The publicity will be phenomenal. Three generations of artists in the same family, written by their one common descendant. You have to do it, El." Carly paused. "We could include a few of your works, too."

"Forget that. I don't have any 'works.' Just a few old amateur paintings and I don't even know where they are. Besides, I was never serious about it and I really wasn't that good."

"That can be debated." Carly looked pensive. "Well, what about your grandmother? Lynley's mother? Did she paint as well?"

"I have no idea." Ellie shook her head. "She and my grandfather moved to California before I was born. They died out there in a boating accident. I don't know anything about them, really. Since I came to St. Dennis, I did learn that they more or less handed my mother over to Lilly when Mom was just a child, but I don't even know much about that."

"Maybe someone in town can shed some light on all that, too. But it doesn't matter. If we market this all the right way, when we finally send the paintings to auction, you're going make a fortune."

"The book is a fabulous idea, Car, except for one thing." Ellie momentarily stopped petting the dog and Dune pawed at her to resume. "I know nothing about Carolina, very little about Lilly, and apparently I didn't know my mother as well as I thought I did."

"There are still people here in St. Dennis who remember Lilly. You could interview them." Carly's enthusiasm for the idea was growing. "And I'll bet you could learn a lot about your mother's life here at the same time."

"I don't know what I'd say to people. How can I interview people here as Ellie Ryder and then have this book written by Ellis Chapman, surrounded by all the publicity you're talking about. Everyone will know what a liar I am." Ellie got up and began to pace. "Everyone will know what a fraud I am."

"Well, I guess that's a choice you're going to have to make," Carly said slowly. "On the one hand, you can maximize what you'll make on the paintings through the book and the publicity, which will reveal who you really are, or you can skip the book and continue to protect your identity, and make half—a third—of what you could have gotten for the paintings."

Ellie felt her stomach churn with anxiety.

"I guess the real question is, do the people here mean so much to you that you'd forfeit making a potential killing? I mean, all along you've been planning on leaving and not looking back anyway, right? So what's the difference what they think of you?"

Ellie thought about the look in Cam's eyes when he set

her on her feet after he'd carried her across the library's lawn, about the feel of his hands on her arms and the way her heart had skipped a beat or two when she realized he was drawn to her as much as she was drawn to him.

"I don't know," she told Carly. "I think a book with my name on it might bring back the scandal all over again."

"Maybe. But you have time to think it over. In the meantime, let's get some cloths and start cleaning up these beauties. And then let's go back upstairs and see if we missed any the first time around . . . "

Cameron turned on his back-porch lights, stepped outside, and inhaled deeply. In the warm months, the nearby marsh was sometimes unpleasantly odoriferous. Now, in November, he caught whiffs of the very last of the sweet autumn clematis and the scent of drying cattails, but no decaying fish or rotting vegetation, for which he was grateful.

All in all, Cam had liked living here. In the daylight hours, he could watch the osprey and the hawks hunt and the red-winged blackbirds flit across the wetland area. Now, at night, the marsh wrapped in deep shadow, there was sound but no sight. Some small creature, a rabbit, most likely, shrieked in the darkness as the deadly talons of an owl sank in and carried it off. The owls were nesting now. He'd heard their calls back and forth from tree to tree over the past week, mate seeking mate. One night he'd even seen a pair sitting on the branch of a tree outside his bedroom window, their bodies silhouetted against the moonlit sky.

The bungalow that sat a long stone's throw from the edge of the marsh was the latest in Cam's home improvement projects. He'd watched the market closely and picked up the place for a song when the children of the former owners decided the house would require more work than they wanted to take on. So far, Cam had replaced the roof, the front and back porches, and two bathrooms. He'd stripped and repainted all the rooms and was partly through the kitchen renovation. Once he finished replacing the cabinets, floor, and installed new appliances, he'd be ready to sell and move on to his next project.

He already had a place in mind. But that house wouldn't be flipped. That house—the Cavanaughs' house—was meant to be his, pure and simple.

Why Ellie wouldn't just sell it to him right now and spare herself the time and the money she'd have to put into it—well, that just didn't make any sense at all.

Cam wouldn't mind helping her out, of course. Whatever he did in the house now would be less he'd have to do later, and he'd be paid in Ted Cavanaugh's duck decoys to boot. How sweet a deal was that? Cam meant to earn every one of them. They should stay in St. Dennis—preferably in that house.

Besides, he figured if he had a hand in the renovations, things would be done to his satisfaction and done right. Nothing worse than having to rip out someone else's shoddy work. He'd been down that road more times than he could count, and he wasn't about to let some hack muck up his house. If Ellie were left to her own devices, God only knew who she would end up hiring to do all those jobs she couldn't do herself.

Which brought him right back to the question of why would she bother when she had a buyer right under her nose, willing to negotiate a fair sale price today.

He would miss the big garage here, though. The Cavanaugh house did have the carriage house, but it, too, needed a lot of work. The garage here not only housed the tools he needed for his contracting work, but provided space for his sideline, making furniture—mostly tables—from reclaimed barn boards. The entire second floor of the oversize garage was filled with boards he got from Clay when one of the old barns on the Madison farm was razed. Clay had offered Cameron all of the salvage wood in exchange for Cam helping to dismantle the building and for aiding in the construction of a hop barn where Clay and Wade could cure the hops they were growing to make their beer. Of course, Cameron had jumped at the chance; prime aged barn board was becoming increasingly scarce. His latest project was almost finished: a trestle table for Brooke and Jesse that was intended as a wedding gift. It was especially apropos, he'd decided, the wood being from a barn on Brooke's family farm, and he'd been working on it for several months whenever he had a few minutes to spare.

He turned his wrist to look at his watch. It was later than he realized and he had an early day tomorrow. He went back into the house and locked the door, the thought heavy on his mind that if things had worked out the way he'd wanted them to, he wouldn't be home alone at this hour. He'd hoped to spend some time with Ellie this evening, but she and Carly had opted to leave the

Grange right after dessert was served. But even if they'd stayed, well, three's a crowd.

There was no way to deny that he was becoming more and more attracted to Ellie. He liked everything about her—the way she looked, the way she smiled, the way she laughed, the way she'd felt when he'd carried her in his arms. But he still couldn't put his finger on what exactly it was about her that bothered him. Something about her just didn't add up.

So which was stronger, he wondered: his attraction or his curiosity?

His laptop was on the kitchen table, and he pulled up Magellan Express, his search engine of choice, and typed in *Ellie Ryder*. When nothing relevant came up, he entered first *Ellen* then *Eleanor Ryder*—assuming that Ellie was short for something else—and hit search, but the links to the women that appeared were clearly not Ellie.

Curious.

He deleted Ellie's name and typed in *Carly Summit*.

He studied the screen that appeared for a moment, then whistled. Carly Summit, age thirty-two, was the only child of Patrick Summit of Summit Industries, and was the sole owner and CEO of the very upscale Summit Galleries International.

Cam snorted. "That's some little art gallery you *manage*." According to the magazine article he skimmed, Carly owned the New York gallery outright, along with smaller galleries in Boston, London, and Istanbul.

So how did Ellie—who is so broke she has to do all the painting in her house herself because she can't afford to hire someone to do the work—become best friends with someone who was obviously among the super-wealthy? It occurred to him that perhaps Ellie wasn't as bad off financially as she pretended. For one thing, there was the matter of that Benz . . .

But why pretend? Why insist on doing all the work on the house herself—the type of work she's obviously never done before? Grunt work. Nothing fun about pulling up floors and scraping layers of wallpaper.

Yeah. Something's wrong with this picture.

He cleared the screen and typed in *Rushton-Graves*.

The link for the school's website pulled up immediately. Cam clicked on it and waited for the site to load.

"Wow," he muttered when the home page pulled up.

The campus of the Rushton-Graves School in Massachusetts's Berkshire Mountains took up most of the town of Endicott, a small village that appeared to exist solely to support the school. Rushton-Graves's buildings were of brick construction in the Federal style, the lawns spacious and meticulously clipped, the student body neat and shiny and ridiculously preppy in their appearance, and the tuition, room, and board astronomically high.

How could Ellie Ryder afford to attend such a place?

He scanned idly through the website, only half paying attention to the photos, until he came to a page that posted pictures from an alumni field hockey game from ten years ago. There in living color, smiling, her arms around her teammates on either side, stood Carly Summit. On her left was a dark-haired girl identified as

Megan Granville. On her right, a platinum blonde: Ellis Chapman.

The hair was different—blond instead of chestnut brown, long past her shoulders instead of the shorter style she now wore, but the smile was unmistakable. *Ellis Ryder Chapman*, the caption read.

It was Ellie, all right.

Cam stared at the picture for a long moment, then returned to the search engine and typed in *Ellis Chapman*. This time, the results went on for pages.

"Oh, jeez," he said aloud. "*That* Ellis Chapman."

The Ellis Chapman whose father had been named Villain of the Year last year.

The Ellis Chapman whose mother was Lynley Sebastian.

THAT Ellis Chapman.

It was all starting to make sense.

He read one article after another, most of which described her father's crimes in excruciating detail. There were photos of Ellie—the blond Ellie—walking into the courthouse during her father's trial accompanied by a dapper older man in a well-tailored suit who was identified as her personal attorney. Photos of her during the press conference in which the district attorney announced that Clifford Chapman had changed his plea to guilty in order to avoid a trial. Photos of her ducking into a limo, her eyes behind the dark glasses he now recognized. Photos of her and Carly in the hallway outside the courtroom where her father was sentenced. Photos of her dodging questions about her former fiancé.

Photos of the former fiancé himself. God but he looked like a tool. Cam wondered how a man—any man—could trade a chance for a lifetime with a woman like Ellie for something as fleeting as wealth.

All in all, Cam learned more about Ellie—*Ellis*—in that one hour than he had since the day he met her. The bottom line was that her father was the worst kind of crook and her ex-fiancé was the world's biggest fool—and Ellie as much their victim as the thousands of people they'd defrauded.

He scrolled back to a photo that was taken of her seated in the courtroom at her father's arraignment. Her face was a study in confusion and pain. It was clear even to Cameron that she'd been totally blindsided by his arrest. He pulled up pages of articles and the accompanying photographs to form a time line of the past year of her life, and found it telling that the only people in the photos with her were either her attorney, or Carly. No other family. No other friends.

It wasn't hard to figure out why she was hiding her identity.

Cameron completely understood the fear of being judged against the actions of a parent. He knew too well how the sins of the father—or in his case, the mother—could burn into your soul and haunt every day of your life.

It occurred to Cam that Ellie needed to remember that she was Lynley's daughter as well as that weasel Chapman's. That she isn't responsible for what her father did any more than he, Cam, was responsible for his mother's actions. Of course, it had taken him years to come to that conclusion. Maybe for Ellie, it was all still too raw for her to view the situation with a more rational eye.

Cam turned off his computer and sat back against the chair. Now that he knew the truth about her, what was he going to do about it?

It took him a moment to realize he wouldn't be doing anything. It wasn't his place to confront her, to try to force her into talking about something she wasn't interested in discussing. If she wanted to continue living a lie, that was her choice, her business, and he didn't have the right to try to make her confess a secret she wanted to keep. She obviously had her reasons, and he of all people knew how the sins of a parent could mess with your head and make you question who you were and how you felt about yourself.

Cameron had been there and done all that.

No, there'd be no confrontation. What would that prove, beyond the fact that he was clever enough to ferret out her secret, and that wasn't who he was. He'd be respectful of her privacy as long as she felt it necessary to keep up the facade.

He did wish she'd come to trust him enough to tell him the truth herself, though, but he knew that he'd have to earn that trust, and it would take time.

Cam sat at his desk for a while longer, still trying to process everything he'd just read. If anything, he was left with more questions than answers.

Finally he turned off the lights and locked the doors and was halfway up the steps when his phone rang.

"What's up, Jesse?" he asked after a glance at the caller ID screen.

"Just wasn't done busting your stones about having to put out such a hefty sum to ransom Ellie this morning. You're a good sport to pay that much for a woman you've never even taken to dinner."

"I believe the record shows you paid more for Brooke," Cam reminded him.

"Yeah." Jesse's chuckle had a smug ring to it. "But I get to see Brooke naked . . ."

Chapter 13

"I WISH you could stay longer." Ellie stood in the doorway watching Carly pack.

"So do I. And next time, I will." Carly glanced up from packing and smiled. "Assuming I'll be invited back."

"Of course. Anytime. No special invite needed." Ellie walked to the bed, sat, and scooched back to lean against the headboard. "Besides, I'm holding the Porsche hostage."

"Just one more reason why I'm glad I loaned you the sedan. There's no way I could fit the paintings in the little 911." She grinned. "Room for all in the Mercedes, though."

"I'll take good care of the beast for you."

"I know you will." Carly squeezed her toiletries into the suitcase and zipped up the sides. "I just wish I could have rescheduled tomorrow's meeting. I really thought I'd be able to do that so I could stay a few days longer."

"Who are you kidding?" Ellie laughed. "You can't wait to get those paintings back to your house."

"Well, there is that." Carly feigned nonchalance but the gleam in her eyes at the mention of the artwork she'd be taking with her gave her away. "I will buzz through that meeting tomorrow at the speed of light and I've canceled everything else I had on my calendar for the next week. This is such an amazing find."

She hoisted her suitcase and reached for a jacket she'd left on a chair.

"I'll get it." Ellie stood and grabbed the jacket. "Got everything from the bathroom?"

Carly nodded. "No harm if I forget something, though. I really will be back as soon as I've finished with the paintings. I'll clean the oils myself and see about having the watercolors backed with acid-free paper." She paused on the way out the door. "Of course, your mother may have taken care of that herself. It's hard to tell how old her paintings are."

Ellie led the way down the steps. "I keep getting little flashbacks of her standing at an easel in a big room on the third floor of our house in Connecticut. There were big windows that looked out over the sound and there was always a lot of light there."

"I wouldn't be surprised if she did a lot of her painting here as well. Next time I'm here, we'll search for clues."

They reached the first floor and Carly set her bag on the floor near the door.

"What kind of clues would there be?" Ellie asked.

"The most obvious would be drips of paint on the floor. And you'd want a room that had a lot of light, just like you described. Then again, maybe you'll find some supplies in a closet or notes, sketches that she later turned into paintings."

"It seems there's no end to the surprises this house holds."

"I know. Isn't it great?" Carly reached for her jacket and Ellie handed it over. "You know, I feel so much better about you being here. I admit I was worried at first, but after seeing your wonderful house and meeting your new friends—"

"I don't know anyone here in St. Dennis well enough to consider them friends," Ellie interjected. "And frankly, that works for me."

"I think I may have already reminded you that it's not fair to judge everyone you meet by the people who dumped you in the past," Carly cautioned.

"It wasn't just that I was dumped. It was as if I'd been collectively erased from the memories of everyone I've ever known. Like I just don't exist anymore."

"But you have a chance to start over here. The people I've met all seem to accept you at face value."

"That's because they don't know."

"And when they find out?"

Ellie shrugged. "I'll be out of here before next summer, so it isn't going to matter."

"Is this the same woman who was worried last night about people finding out that she lied?"

"That was in a different context. That was when we were talking about me mining their memories for a book about people they knew." Ellie shoved her hands into the pockets of her jeans. "That seems actively dishonest."

"As opposed to passively dishonest?"

"Something like that."

"So it's all right to pretend to be someone else as long as things don't get personal."

"What's your point?" Ellie sighed.

"My point is that you have to live somewhere, El." Carly picked up her bag from the floor. "You have to have a *life* somewhere."

"It's not that easy."

"Not saying it would be. But you can't spend the rest of your life moving from place to place because you're afraid everyone you meet is going to turn on you." Before Ellie could respond, Carly added, "Anyway, you're in a good place here. Whether or not you want to stay, that's up to you."

Ellie grabbed a sweater she'd left on the newel post, wrapped it around her shoulders, and opened the front door. Dune came running at the sound of the door opening.

"There's my little friend." Carly knelt down to give the dog a scratch behind the ears. "You behave yourself until I come back, hear?"

Ellie stepped outside and held the door for Carly, and Dune followed.

"You know, I'd been envisioning you in a house that was falling down around your head, no heat, no electricity, no running water . . . "

Ellie laughed.

"Well, you said the house had been vacant at least since your mom died, and that's been twelve years. I figured it would be a ruin by now. You do have lots to do here, but it's a house that gives you roots, you know?" Carly stood halfway along the path and looked over her shoulder at the house. "It's a place your mom loved, and that should give you some comfort."

"It does, actually."

"Well, if you have to start over, this is the place to be. Lick your wounds until they're clean, babe. Rechart your course. Move ahead."

"You sound like one of those motivational speakers you see on TV."

Carly laughed as she opened the trunk. "Some nights when I'm traveling and I can't sleep, there's nothing else on cable." She tucked her suitcase next to a pile of paintings that were carefully wrapped in sheets. "I still can't believe what we found in your house, and that you're actually letting me take these precious paintings with me."

"If Jesse hadn't confirmed this morning that they're really mine, I wouldn't have been able to. Fortunately for you, Lilly's will spelled out that they all passed down to my mother." Ellie opened the driver's-side door for Carly. "Jesse said Mom's will specified that all the contents of this house were to go to me, so there we are."

"I'll be pinching myself all the way home." Carly turned and looked back at the house. "Who'd ever have dreamed that this house held such treasures . . . "

"Certainly I did not." Ellie looked back as well. "I have to admit this place has grown on me."

"Find lots of other cool stuff while I'm gone." Carly hugged Ellie before getting into the car. "Who knows what other treasures are tucked away in there?"

"That's a fun thought that will get me through the winter." Ellie closed the car door, then stepped back onto the grass.

Carly rolled down the window. "Where's the dog? I don't want her to chase the car."

"She's over on the lawn," Ellie said. "I've never seen her chase a car, so I think you're good."

The big sedan backed slowly toward the road, then rolled past Ellie, Carly waving as she passed. Ellie waved back and watched the departing car for a few seconds before checking the mailbox and pulling out a few pieces of mail. She called for Dune, and wrapping her sweater around her midsection against the cool Bay breeze, went inside.

The house was as quiet as it had been the day Ellie arrived, as if it, too, missed Carly's presence.

"She'll come back, Dune," Ellie found herself saying as she went into the kitchen.

It was too early for lunch but Carly had been in such a hurry to get on the road that there'd been no time for much more than toast and coffee for breakfast. Ellie put the dishes in the sink and reheated the coffee while she looked through the mail. There was some correspondence from her father's lawyers and a letter with the return address of the prison where her father was serving time. She held both envelopes in her hand for a long moment before tossing them unopened into the trash. There really wasn't anything he—or his lawyers—could say that she would want to hear. Maybe someday she'd be willing to speak with him, but right now it was all still a little raw. She just wasn't able to get past what he'd done to destroy so many lives. If he hadn't been caught, he'd probably still be robbing people blind. It still devastated her to think that her father was not the wonderful man she'd always believed him to be. As painful as Henry's betrayal had been, discovering the truth about what her father had been doing had been mind-blowing. She hadn't grown up worshipping Henry.

She sat at the table staring out the window. Her enthusiasm for the day had departed with Carly. *I could start ripping up the kitchen floor,* she told herself.

Then again, she could start painting the kitchen walls. She had to paint the woodwork, too, but couldn't remember whether the walls or the woodwork came first.

"Chicken or egg?" she asked Dune, who sighed and rolled over.

"Walls first, I'd think," she reasoned. "If you do the woodwork first, wouldn't paint get on it when you painted the walls?"

She looked down at the dog, who'd apparently decided it was time for a morning nap. "Of course you would, because you'd be using a roller."

She headed for the living room, where she'd left the paint and brushes in the closet, but once in the room, she paused. The space looked so odd with the paintings gone, the walls now naked. The pale rectangles on the wall where they'd hung for so many years reminded her of a photograph she'd seen once, where someone had hung empty picture frames on the wall.

"Ghost paintings," Ellie murmured.

She paused at the bookcase, one of the glass doors of which stood ajar. Carly had started poking around for something read before she'd found the paintings. As Ellie moved to close the glass doors, her eyes were drawn to the shelf below, where a series of faded red leather volumes were lined up. There were no titles on the spines, so Ellie grabbed the closest one to her and pulled it from the shelf. She opened the book and tilted it toward the window and the light that was spilling through.

Lilly Angelina Ryder. This is her journal.

Ellie sat on the arm of the sofa and turned to the first page. Lilly's handwriting was tiny and precise and in places difficult to read, and even with her reading glasses, Ellie had a hard time deciphering every word.

Today is my fifteenth birthday, and Rose and I are going to watch the sailboats race. Mother said I could go if Rose's mother was going, too. I believe she will. At least, I hope she does! Rose's brother told Rose that T.C. will be sailing with Curtis Enright and she said she just has to be there. It's no secret that Rose is sweet on Curtis and that Curtis is sweet on her as well. As for me, if I get to see T.C. it will be a happy birthday indeed!

Ellie smiled. T.C. must be Ted Cavanaugh. Even at fifteen, Lilly knew what she wanted, and from what Ellie'd heard, Lilly and Ted had lived a long and happy life together.

Her phone rang in her pocket and she placed the journal on the coffee table while she answered the call.

"Ellie Ryder."

"Ellie, it's Cameron. I was wondering if you'd be working on that kitchen floor of yours anytime soon."

"Actually, I was thinking I'd start on the walls first."

"Don't know that you'd want to do that," he said. "You're going to kick up a lot of dust when you do the floor. You'd hate to have to clean those newly painted walls."

"So you're saying I should do the floor first?"

"I would."

"Then I guess I would, too."

"I had a crew working on another house in town and they just finished up. I thought I'd drop off a scraper for you."

"I didn't really need one for the pantry floor," she reminded him.

"The kitchen floor is a much larger expanse than the pantry floor. I'm willing to bet it was put down with some sort of adhesive and they would most likely have used a greater quantity of it. You're going to need a tool to scrape it off the floor. I'll show you how to use it so that you don't gouge the wood underneath."

"That would be great, thanks. I'd appreciate the use of the tool and I appreciate the advice."

"How 'bout I drop it off on my way home later? Around four-thirty?"

"I'll be here."

"Great. See you then."

"Nice of him to call and offer help," she told Dune after she'd hung up, "but that sort of blows my plans for the rest of the morning and the early part of the afternoon since I was going to spend that time working in the kitchen.

"Oh, well," she said as she picked up the journal, "guess I have no choice but to read a little more. After all, why start something now that I'll only have to put aside later?"

She toed off her shoes, propped her feet on the coffee table, put a pillow behind her back, and opened the book where she'd left off, at Lilly's high school graduation. When Dune began to bark at some gulls that had landed on the lawn, Ellie shushed her.

"Hush, Dune. I'm just at the part where she's trying to decide whether to go to college or marry Ted that summer." She peered over the top of the journal and told the dog, "That's a big decision for an eighteen-year-old to make."

When Dune barked to announce that someone was at the front door, Ellie stood, looked out the window, then checked her watch for the time.

"I had no idea it was so late," she told Cameron after letting him in.

"Is this a bad time? Are you in the middle of something?" He stepped inside, then leaned over to pet Dune.

"Yes, one of Lilly's journals." Ellie held up the leather-bound book. "I found a bunch of them in the bookcase."

She closed the door behind them and led the way into the living room.

"I just got to the part where she's talking about her wedding. She had decided to finish college before she and Ted were married, but then he signed up to fight in World War Two, so they had the wedding before he left. She continued to live at home and she'd finished college by the time he came back." Ellie reached for Cam's jacket when he finished unbuttoning it.

"Miss Lilly taught fourth grade in St. Dennis for years," Cam told her. "She taught my dad and just about everyone else in his age group."

"Really." Ellie put the book back on the table. "That explains why everyone remembers her."

Cam shook his head. "Everyone remembers her because she was such a good person. If anyone in town had a problem, Lilly Cavanaugh was the first person there to lend a hand. Mr. C., too. He was just as nice. People may have known her because of her teaching, but they remember her for the good things she did through the years."

"That's nice to hear. Nice to know that my ... my *predecessor* here in the house was such a good person." Ellie turned her back to hang up Cam's jacket. She'd need to watch herself. She'd almost said her *relative*.

"She was the best. I never met anyone who ... "

Ellie turned around to find Cam staring at the wall next to her.

"What happened to the painting?" He looked from one wall to the next, frowning. "What happened to all the paintings?"

"Carly had to leave and I let her take some of the paintings back with her. That's why the Porsche is in the driveway but the sedan is gone. She needed to take the bigger car because the paintings wouldn't fit in the sports car. It's hers, anyway. The sedan, that is," Ellie heard herself confess. "She loaned it to me because I don't have one."

"You don't have a Mercedes?" Was he teasing her?

"I don't have a car. Any car. I had the Mercedes because that's what Carly had to loan me."

"That was really nice of her. You know what that baby was worth?"

"Less than the 911," she replied.

Cam nodded. "But maybe not by much."

Ellie waited for him to say something, like "Why don't you have a car of your own?" The answer to which was

Because the feds took it when they took my house and my jewelry, my investments, and everything else I owned.

Instead, Cam said, "Carly did mention that she ran an art gallery. I guess she's going to try to sell them for you."

"Eventually, I suppose. I mean, when she has space in the gallery, I guess she'll exhibit them." It was a good time to change the subject. "So what's that thing?"

Ellie pointed to the long-handled tool Cam had brought in with him.

"It's a scraper. We'll use it to get the residue of adhesive off the floor after the linoleum is removed." He tossed her the bag he'd held under his arm. "Here's a little present."

"Thanks. You didn't have ... " She peered into the bag, then laughed. "Rubber gloves?"

"You're going to need them if you plan on pulling up that floor and scraping the walls." He took one of her hands in his and held it up. "Unless you don't care if this gets beaten up in the process."

"Thanks. I should have bought a pair. My hands already look as if they've been beaten." She pulled the gloves out of the box and tried them on. "Just fit." She held up both gloved hands to show them off.

"Good." Cam gestured toward the kitchen. "Want to get started?"

"I do, and I certainly don't want to take all of the rest of your day." She pushed the swinging door that stood between the living room and the kitchen and held it open for Cameron. "I know you're probably tired from working all day today and playing pirate yesterday."

Cameron grinned. "It was fun. Not something you get to do every day, and let's face it, at some time in his life, every little boy dreams of being a pirate when he grows up."

"It's nice when our childhood fantasies come true, isn't it?" Ellie laughed again and reached for the scraper.

"Uh-uh." Cameron shook his head. "I think I'll do this part until we see what we're dealing with here."

"I don't expect you to pull up my floor for me," she told him. "I thought you were just going to show me what to do."

"It's easy to damage the wood if you don't know what you're doing. And you'll still be pulling up the floor. I'll be removing the old glue."

He scanned the floor, then selected his starting point at the entrance to the back hall. After leaning down to see where the linoleum appeared to be most loose, he donned a pair of gloves and peeled back the flooring to reveal the wood. "Beautiful pine, but a little soft." He pulled back more of the flooring. "Got something to put the old flooring in?"

"I have a couple of paper bags," she replied.

"We need something stronger and bigger."

Ellie made a face. What else was there in the house that she could use?

"I have a couple of buckets in the back of my truck." Cam stood the long-handled scraper up against the wall. "I'll be right back . . . "

She heard the front door open and close, then reached for the scraper. It was heavier than it looked,

217

and the blade didn't appear all that sharp, a fact she noted when Cameron returned with a white bucket in each hand.

"It doesn't have to be sharp," he told her. "If it were too sharp, it would do a real number on the wood. Most of the time, old adhesive is dry and brittle. It only takes a little pressure to pop it off the floor. Much of the time, it's stuck to the back of the linoleum anyway when the floor is pulled up."

He broke off a piece of linoleum and showed her where the glue coated the back.

"This stuff is really old," he observed. "I'm betting this floor has been down for at least fifty years."

"Well, someone got their money's worth." She looked around at the entire floor. "It all stayed down until I started pulling it up."

Cam tossed the piece into one of the buckets.

"How 'bout we pull up some more of the flooring, then you can break it up and put it in the buckets while I work on getting up the adhesive?"

"I didn't mean for you to do all this." Ellie stood in the middle of the floor, a piece of linoleum in her hands. "I really can't afford to pay you."

"You're paying me in duck decoys, remember? I figure this job is worth . . . " He seemed to calculate how long it would take him to finish the entire floor. "Maybe half a duck."

"Half a duck," she repeated.

"Right." He looked up at the ceiling, which clearly needed painting. "Maybe the ceiling in here and one other room might be the other half."

"Or I could sell you the duck and you could have a little downtime. Don't you do this all day long?"

"I have a crew," he said simply. "Besides, the more I do now, the less I'll have to do later."

He looked up from the scraper, which had loosened a clump of black glue, and he smiled. "I still intend on being the highest bidder for the house when you're ready to sell it."

"You know, when it comes to buying a house, the last thing the buyer should do is let the seller know how much he wants the property."

Cam shrugged. "That cat was already out of the bag. I told you that the first time I met you. I figure at this point it's only a matter of when and how much."

Ellie knelt on the floor and peeled back a long strip of linoleum that she broke into smaller pieces.

"I'm not sure why you won't sell it to me right now, but I guess you have your reasons." He moved the scraper along the floor, then leaned over to pick up another glob of glue. He tossed it into the bucket. "It just seems to me the it would save you a lot of time and wear and tear on your nails."

Ellie's eyebrows arched. "I'm not afraid to get my nails chipped."

"Well, that was clearly the wrong thing to say," he muttered. "What I meant was, it's a lot of work, renovating a house this size, one that hasn't been touched in ... " He stood and tilted his head to one side. "I'm guessing since even before Lynley inherited it from Lilly. She got sick right about then, and about all she had time to do was buy some new appliances."

"How would you know that?" She stopped what she was doing and turned to stare at him.

"I remember when they were delivered." He shrugged. "They were top-of-the-line when they were new, but not so much anymore. I imagine they still function well enough, though. You probably wouldn't want to replace them."

"I never thought about replacing them. I couldn't afford to do that."

"You could sell that sweet little automobile out there in the driveway."

"You know that's not mine"—she laughed—"but I bet it would bring a pretty penny."

"Maybe Carly wouldn't notice."

"Yeah, good idea. When she comes back and asks, 'Where's my Porsche?' I'll say, 'What Porsche?'"

"Yeah, that'll work." He leaned the scraper against the wall and helped her with a wide piece of flooring that was lifting but not releasing. They struggled with it for a moment before it broke free. "So tell me what you learned from Lilly Cavanaugh's journals that you didn't know."

"Well, I learned that Lilly's mother suffered from depression." Ellie straightened up and tried to work the kinks out of her back. "I guess it's that artistic temperament you hear people talk about."

"Those paintings that Carly took . . ." Cam sat back on his heels. "Those were all painted by Lilly's mother. You knew that, right?"

Ellie nodded. "Carolina Ellis. How do you know about her?"

"St. Dennis born and bred," Cam reminded her. "Had Carly heard of her?"

"She had. She said that Carolina was just being recognized as an important woman artist of the early twentieth century."

"So I guess she was surprised to find the paintings here."

"Was she ever. I have to admit, I was surprised, too. I didn't know that . . . " She was about to say, *That my great-great-grandmother was an accomplished artist.* "That there was that connection to the house when I bought it."

"I guess the lawyers knew, though, right?"

"What?" She frowned.

"Wouldn't you think that the lawyers for Lynley Sebastian would have known who Lynley's grandmother was, and that there were valuable paintings in the house?"

Caught off guard by the question, Ellie took a few seconds to recover. When she did, she said, "Maybe Lynley didn't tell them. Maybe at the time she arranged for them to handle her estate, Carolina's work hadn't been 'discovered' yet, so it wasn't considered particularly valuable. Maybe it wasn't an issue." She took a breath. "Don't you think the paintings would have been removed by the lawyers if they'd known they were valuable and in a house that was relatively unsecured?"

"Good point." Cam nodded and returned his attention to the floor, but Ellie wasn't sure that there wasn't just a hint of a smile on his lips. "So what other tidbits of information did you find in Lilly's journals?"

"Lilly talked a lot about a friend named Rose who married a man named Curtis Enright." She started

221

breaking up the piece of flooring. "I'm thinking maybe someone related to Jesse?"

"His grandparents. Rose died years ago but old Mr. Enright is still living. He practiced law forever here in town, and just turned the practice over to Jesse last year. He has that mansion over on the other side of town. It takes up the whole last block of Old St. Mary's Church Road. It isn't the oldest house in town, but I think it might be the biggest." Cam handed Ellie another piece of broken flooring. "I think I need to dump those buckets in the back of the truck. You've filled them both."

Cam grabbed a bucket with each hand and headed for the front door, Ellie watching his smooth stride eat up the hallway.

He was back in minutes with the empty buckets. He set them on the floor and said, "Help me move the table and chairs into the hallway so we can do the other half of the room."

"Cam, it's almost seven o'clock." She pointed to the wall clock.

"Your point?" He paused, a chair in each hand.

"Aren't you getting hungry?"

"I'm always hungry." He looked as if he was still waiting for her to make her point.

"We could stop. I could go back to this tomorrow."

"You really want to come downstairs and look at this first thing in the morning?" He pointed to the floor, half of which had exposed wood and the other linoleum that appeared to have been chewed on. "I wouldn't."

"It'll be okay."

"It won't take that long," he assured her as he carried the chairs into the hall.

"If you say so." Ellie picked up the other two chairs and followed him, squeezing past him in the doorway when he returned for the table.

"I feel really badly about keeping you here all this time," she said when she'd resumed pulling up the flooring.

"My choice, so don't." He scraped at a few leftover clumps of glue on the newly uncovered wood floor. "I can't wait to see this all refinished. It's going to be real pretty."

"I guess there's someone around who can do the refinishing." Looks like she'd be making another call to Jesse this week. She was going to need some money from that account her mother left to fund renovations on the house. Refinished floors would definitely qualify.

"Dave Freeman does floors," Cam told her. "But I doubt he works for decoys." He tossed a wad of glue into the bucket. "I can sand and refinish the floor but I suggest you do that before you start painting. Sanding makes a mess of dust."

"Swell," she grunted.

"As does scraping off the old paper. Which you have to do before you can paint anyway," he reminded her.

"I forgot about the scraping part." Ellie frowned and eyed the old wallpaper.

"You were hoping to forget that part. The prep work is always the worst part of painting." He reached over and put one hand on her biceps. "Scraping paper is going to wake up muscles you never knew you had."

"I'm in good shape."

"Yeah, well, we'll see just what kind of shape you're in once you've spent a few hours scraping at those walls."

She made a face and cracked a large piece of linoleum over her knee.

It took another hour, but the last bucket of linoleum was finally dumped into the back of the pickup. When Cam came back into the house, Ellie expected him to ask for his jacket.

"It's after eight," he said. "I imagine you're as hungry as I am. How 'bout splitting a pizza with me?"

She started to decline, but heard herself say, "I love pizza. But I couldn't possibly go anywhere looking like this." Bits of dried linoleum clung to her knees and the front of her sweatshirt. She looked him over. "Why don't you look as grubby as I do?"

"You're a novice. I'm a professional." Cam leaned against the counter. "I can run out and pick something up."

Before she could respond, he'd taken out his phone. "Pepperoni okay?"

"It's great, but . . . "

He had already speed-dialed a number and was starting to place an order.

"Done. Fifteen minutes."

"Cam, I don't know how to thank you for everything. You're doing so much here . . . "

"Protecting my investment." He corrected himself. "My potential investment."

"I hope you feel it's worth it."

"There's no doubt in my mind that it will be." His voice trailed down the hall. "I'll be back in a few."

224

And that quickly, he was out the front door.

Well, he was certainly a guy who knew what he wanted, and he clearly wanted this house.

Ellie got out the vacuum and cleaned up as much of the dust and dirt from the floor as she could. She fed Dune, then wet a paper towel and rubbed it lightly on her face. When she saw how much dust she'd been wearing, she was appalled. It was a miracle Cam didn't take the opportunity to leave and not come back. She'd just tossed the paper towel into the trash when she heard him at the front door.

"Can we eat in here?" He nodded in the direction of the living room. "There's a lot of dust in the kitchen."

"Sure."

He placed the pizza box and a bag on the coffee table.

"I got a couple of bottles of water," he told her as he emptied the bag. "I wasn't sure what you liked to drink."

"Water is fine." She disappeared into the kitchen for plates, flatware, and napkins.

"I hope that knife is for the brownies and not the pizza," he said when she handed him a plate with the flatware on top. "Around here we eat pizza with our hands."

"I'll remember that." She peeked into the bag. "You got brownies?"

"The mother of the guy who owns the pizza place in town makes wicked desserts." Cam sat on the edge of the sofa cushion and opened the pizza box. "I wasn't sure what to get."

The smell of the sauce and cheese all but made Ellie swoon. She hadn't realized just how hungry she was.

Cam turned the box in her direction so she could select first. She put a slice on her plate and sat next to him.

"You can never go wrong with brownies," she assured him.

She took a bite of pizza and rolled her eyes. "Oh, my God, this is good."

"Yeah, Dominic makes the best pizza around. Most of St. Dennis is seriously addicted." He opened one of the water bottles and handed it to Ellie. "Wade and Clay are talking about making a beer flavor specifically to complement Dominic's pizza."

"You're making that up."

"Nope. They were talking about it at poker the other night." He opened the second bottle of water and took a long drink, staring at the bookcase on the opposite wall. "Mr. C. had a great collection of mysteries from the 1930s and forties. I can still see him sitting in that chair over there near the window, his glasses perched at the end of his nose, the book practically in his face. He really needed to have his glasses changed but he wouldn't admit that his eyesight was failing."

"How long ago was that?"

"Twenty-five years or so."

"You must have been, what, eight? Nine back then?"

"Something like that."

"How did you know the Cavanaughs so well?"

"We were neighbors."

"I didn't realize that. Which house did you live in?"

"The one that isn't there anymore." He looked as if he was about to say more, but thought better of it.

Before she could ask, he changed the subject. "Do you have plans for Thanksgiving?"

"Thanksgiving?" The pizza in her hand stopped halfway to her mouth. When was Thanksgiving?

"Strictly American holiday. Fourth Thursday in November every year. People get together with family and friends and eat more than they should. It's a tradition we observe here in St. Dennis. I'm surprised you haven't heard of it."

She laughed. "It's this week already?"

Cam nodded.

"If you tell me that you cook, too, I'll be totally intimidated," she said.

"I do cook, but not this holiday. A lot of us have dinner at the inn on Thanksgiving every year. Why don't you join us?"

"I'd love to. Thanks for the invitation."

"Good. I'll let Grace know there will be one more. It's a good holiday. A lot of us around here have much to be thankful for." He eyed the last piece of pizza.

"It's all yours," she told him. While he ate, she said, "You know, if you want to borrow any of Mr. Cavanaugh's books, you're welcome to."

"I've read most of them, but I wouldn't mind reading a few of them again."

"Take whatever you want."

"Thanks." He tossed her a brownie, and she shook her head. "I couldn't eat another bite."

"Save it for breakfast." He stood and started folding up the empty box.

"Don't bother with that," she told him. "I'll take care

227

of it. Why don't you grab a book or two before you leave?"

"Thanks. I think I will."

He scanned the shelves while she cleaned up the debris from their impromptu dinner.

"Mickey Spillane," Cam announced. "*I, The Jury*. His first Mike Hammer novel. Published in 1947." He turned to Ellie with a smile. "Only one of the best detective novels ever written."

"Take it. Please, take whichever books you want. With my thanks for all your help."

"I thought we agreed I'd be paid in decoys."

"This isn't payment." She watched his face as his eyes scanned the titles. In that moment, he looked like a happy little boy on his birthday, one who'd just been told he'd be getting that new bike he wanted. She wouldn't have suspected that the books would mean so much to him. "This is a thank-you, one friend to another."

"In that case ... " He reached into the cabinet and took two books from the shelf. "Thank you. These two were Mr. C.'s favorites. Miss Lilly scolded him like you wouldn't believe when she found out he'd let me read them."

"When you were eight or nine?"

"No, no, older than that. Fifteen, sixteen, maybe."

"So you were always sort of friends with them."

"You could say that." Cam tucked the books under his arm. "Thanks again, Ellie. These mean a lot to me."

He turned, and for a moment, she thought he was about to kiss her. All it would have taken would have been for him to lean forward just a bit to close that tiny space between them. But he didn't.

After she'd closed the door behind him, she wondered why he hadn't.

Then again, why hadn't *she*?

Chapter 14

DUNE sat upright on the chair she'd been sleeping on in the corner of Ellie's bedroom and tilted her head as if listening to something outside right before turning into a barking machine.

"Who needs a burglar alarm when you're around?" Ellie stumbled out of bed and pulled back the curtain. It was barely dawn. Cam's pickup was in the driveway, the driver's-side door open, but Cam was nowhere to be seen. "Looks like we have company."

She tossed on an old sweatshirt, traded her pajama bottoms for sweatpants, grabbed her slippers, and danced into them on her way to the stairwell.

"Hush, Dune." She attempted to quiet the dog, which now stood howling at the top of the steps.

Ellie ran down the steps just as the pickup drove past the house. She unlocked the front door and found a ladder propped up against the wall, a bucket, a pile of plastic sheets, and an odd contraption that looked like something an exterminator would use to spray an infestation of ants. Two short-handled scrapers were in the bucket and a plain white envelope was taped to the top step of the ladder three feet above her head.

She stared up at the white rectangle that fluttered in the breeze. "Cute, Cam."

She dragged the ladder inside and rested it against the foyer wall, then brought in the bucket and the plastic while Dune danced impatiently around her feet.

"You need to go out, of course you do. Sorry. I got distracted."

Ellie managed to get the ladder into the kitchen on her way to the back door. She stood on the back porch shivering while Dune went about her early morning business. The breeze out back wasn't quite as stiff as the breeze that blew directly off the Bay out front. Still, there was no question that November had moved in, and as Jesse had said, was moving headfirst into winter. The dog paused in her patrol of the yard to scamper after some birds that had landed on the ground and were pecking at seed fallen from the bird feeder. Moments later, she was chasing a squirrel up a nearby tree and barking gleefully. When it became obvious that there was more pleasure than business being conducted, Ellie called her back to the house.

"It's too cold to play outside," Ellie told the dog as it followed her inside. "Maybe later it will warm up."

Ellie put a pot of coffee on the stove, then opened the ladder. It was metal and had some age on it, so it seemed a bit cranky until she'd opened it all the way. She yanked the envelope free when she got to the top step and read Cam's note.

Ellie,

Just trying to keep you honest—here are the items you'll need to scrape the wallpaper. Fill the tank with

231

*water and spray down the wall in small sections. Spray,
wait a few minutes to give the water time to soften the
glue, then scrape the paper pretty much the way I scraped
the floor yesterday. Just be careful not to put holes in the
plaster. Get some big plastic trash bags for the stuff that
falls on the floor. It's going to make a big mess.*

*Tape the plastic over the doorway leading into the hall
or you'll have paper dust everywhere. Put one of the sheets
on the floor to catch the stuff that falls.*

I think you know what to do with the ladder.

Call me if you have any questions.

Under the last line, he'd written his phone number,
which Ellie programmed into her cell. She turned off the
flame under the boiling coffeepot, then dialed the
number he'd written down.

"Keep me honest, eh?" she said when he answered.

"I was afraid that without proper guidance you'd be
painting right over the paper. I just thought I'd remove all
possible excuses."

"I admit to momentarily considering it."

"Sorry I had to drop it all off so early. I had a meeting
at seven with a potential customer in Ballard. I hope I
didn't wake you."

"I was awake," she fibbed. "So am I going to be graded
on the work I do on the kitchen walls?"

"No pressure but I can spot shoddy workmanship a
mile away." She could hear the smile in his voice as he
teased. "And since I intend on buying that house someday, I'd think you'd want to get the best price out of me
that you can."

"I get the point. I'll follow your instructions to the letter."

"I'll be by later to check it out," he said before he disconnected the call.

Ellie filled the tank with water and sprayed a mist of water onto a small section of wall. She waited a moment, then scraped at the paper until she got a tiny rip that she could exploit. It took a few minutes, but she got down through three layers of paper and several layers of paint to the plaster wall.

"This isn't so bad," she told Dune. She pulled the ladder across the floor and climbed halfway up. "We'll just start in one corner and move right across to the next. We'll be finished in no time."

She sprayed more water, waited, then scraped. Spray. Wait. Scrape.

Spray. Wait. Scrape.

She found the rubber gloves Cameron had brought her, picked up all the pasty strips of paper that had fallen onto the floor, and stuffed them into a plastic trash bag that wasn't nearly big enough for all the debris. She made a mental note to make a run to the market after lunch to purchase larger bags as she stuffed two more. She'd tossed them into the hall before she remembered about the plastic sheets that Cam had given her to tape up over the doorways and cover the floor. She hastily rectified the error and went back to work on the next section of paper.

Spray. Wait. Scrape.

By three in the afternoon, Ellie could barely raise her hands over her head.

"This looks so easy when they do it on TV," she told

233

Dune, fighting an urge to wail. "All those DIY decorating and remodeling shows make it look like a snap."

Dune wagged her tail and hopped over the clouds of pasty paper on the floor to get to the back door, where she barked.

"Thank you for giving me an excuse to stop." Leaving the scraper on the top ladder step, Ellie climbed down and pulled on the jacket she'd left in the back hall closet.

Walking around the backyard with Dune was both pleasure and pain. Pleasure because she was no longer reaching over her head and scraping away those little strips of paper that dispersed dust into the air and stuck to her arms. Pain because she had been reaching over her head for hours and she was pretty sure she would be useless for very possibly the rest of her life.

Cameron did try to warn me, she reminded herself. But who knew it would be so hard?

A cold rain began to fall in fat drops from a dark gray sky, so she headed back toward the porch, Dune at her heels. The dog apparently disliked the cold and wet as much as Ellie did. Once back inside, she made herself something hot to drink and decided a break was in order. She wrapped herself in a throw, curled up on the sofa, and fell asleep.

The next thing she knew, her cell phone was ringing.

"How'd it go?" Cameron asked.

"Pretty good." She stifled a yawn and tried to figure out what time it was, day or night. How long had she slept?

"How do you feel?"

"Tired," she admitted. "Actually, my arms are killing

me. I doubt I'll ever be able to wash my hair again. Volleyball and tennis are definitely out, probably forever. But I did a damned good job."

"Did you finish?"

"Almost."

"Well, open the door and let me check it out."

She got up and looked through the blinds. Cam's truck was parked in front of the house and he was standing on the front porch, a hand raised in a wave.

Ellie had already unlocked the door and opened it when she caught a glimpse of herself in the hall mirror. She cringed at her reflection. Bits of gooey paper stuck to her hair and her clothing. There were streaks of dirt on her face from the wet dusty paper.

"Looks like you really were busy today." Cam pulled a clump of paper from the back of her head and handed it to her.

"Thanks." She took the wad of paper but avoided his eyes. Could she look any worse than she did right at that moment? She wanted to kick herself for answering the door.

"So let's see the progress." Cam headed for the kitchen, Ellie trailing behind, picking sticky little flakes from the sleeves of her sweatshirt.

"Hey, you're doing a great job." He walked closer to the wall, silently inspecting, smoothing away tiny bits of wallpaper that clung tenaciously to the plaster. "No gouges in the wall, very little glue left behind. Very nice." He turned to her. "Best novice work I've ever seen. Some of my guys have left more residue than you have. Want a job?"

"A job?"

Cam nodded. "We're in the midst of a big renovation and we've got an entire house with a lot of walls that need to be stripped. I could use you."

Ellie couldn't tell if he was kidding or not, but it didn't matter. She would be totally useless. She shook her head. "Everything hurts. My hands hurt. My neck is all crinked up. It's probably going to be days before I can raise my arms above my shoulders." She lifted her arms chest-high and winced. "Noodles. My arms are noodles and my neck is so stiff I can barely turn my head."

"That'll all pass in a day or so. Here. Maybe this will help." He turned her around and put those big hands to work gently massaging her neck. "Put your head down."

"I can't."

"Little by little."

She inched her chin toward her chest. His thumbs worked at the knot of muscles in the back of her neck.

"Ow."

"Sorry." He switched to her shoulders and she groaned. "Wasn't this bothering you while you were working?"

"A little."

"Why didn't you stop?"

"Because it didn't bother me that much at the time." An *ohhh* escaped her lips when he hit a particularly sore spot.

"Sit." Cameron led her to a chair and she sat. He massaged the neck and her shoulders. "Better?" he asked after a few moments.

"A little. Thanks."

236

"Do you have anything you can take for pain?"

"I don't think so. I haven't had headaches or anything since I got here." She stood slowly.

"I have some Advil in my truck. Let me get it."

He walked from the room before she could respond. She went into the hall and took the opportunity to pull more gunk from her hair. She balled it up in her hand and stuck it in her pocket when she heard Cam on the front steps.

"Here you go. Two now, two before you go to bed." He handed her the container.

"And call you in the morning?"

Cam smiled. "If you like."

Ellie tried to get the childproof lid off the container. Her fingers were stiff and sore and uncooperative.

"Where's a four-year-old when you need one?" she grumbled.

He took the container from her hands, struggled with it for a moment before it opened, then handed it back.

"Thanks." She dumped half a dozen tablets into her hand. "This should do it. If my muscles are still this sore tomorrow, I can run to the store in the morning and—"

She'd been focused on getting the lid back onto the container and hadn't realized how close he'd moved, how near his face was to hers. When she looked up, she was looking into his eyes.

Ellie tilted her head to one side, her eyes locked on Cam's. When he leaned down, she stretched up. His lips brushed against hers so softly that at first, she barely felt them. She wanted to put her arms around his neck, but her leaden limbs wouldn't move above chest level, so she sank one hand into the front of his flannel shirt, the tablets clutched in the other, and pulled him closer. The kiss that started out as little more than a feather's touch deepened in the blink of an eye.

One thing she learned in that split second was that Cameron O'Connor kissed as if he meant it.

His lips were soft and warm and lingered just long enough for Ellie to want more of him, but his mouth moved to the corner of hers, teased her with his tongue before he rested back against the wall. His hands moved from her shoulders to the tops of her arms.

"So we're good for Thanksgiving, right?" His words were soft against the side of her face, and somehow felt as intimate as the kiss.

"We're good." Ellie forced herself to breathe normally again. "What time?"

"I'll check with Miss Grace but they usually serve their 'family-and-friends' dinner around two in the afternoon. They open the dining room to the public at five." His hands began to caress her aching biceps.

"What's the dress code?" She tried to ignore the warmth that was spreading through her, as if there was a direct line from the soft skin on her arms to the rest of her body.

"Just, nice. You know."

"Nice casual or nice dressy casual?"

Cam looked at her blankly. "What's the difference? Nice is nice."

"I think I'll ask someone else."

"Maybe Brooke, or Steffie down at Scoop."

"I'll stop down there tomorrow," she told him. "It'll give me an excuse to get ice cream."

"Maybe you should take tomorrow off." His hands continued to gently knead her arms. "Give your muscles a chance to recover."

"I was hoping to finish that last little bit of kitchen wall."

"Leave it and we'll work on it after dinner on Thursday, work off some of that big meal we're going to have at the inn." Unexpectedly, he kissed her mouth, a short sweet dip to her lips, then released her arms. "In the meantime, rest up. Take a hot bath, then some of the Advil. Pretend you're a nine-to-fiver again and that tomorrow is a day off. Pretend it's Saturday."

"I didn't used to take days off," she confessed. "I almost always went into the office on Saturday."

"You know what they say about all work, right?" His fingers hooked with hers.

Ellie shrugged. "It was sort of a habit."

"I read somewhere that it takes three weeks to break old habits and form new ones." With his free hand, he pulled a few more pieces of paper from her hair. "Downtime is important. Which is why weekends matter. They should be observed in the spirit in which God and the five-day workweek intended."

He started for the door, his hand holding hers.

"Most people who work a regular workweek don't rest up on Saturday anyway," she noted. "That's the day most people use to run errands and shop. Sunday's the day for relaxing."

"Then tomorrow will be your Saturday and Thursday will be your Sunday. By Friday, you should be ready to work again. And I'm sure you can find something to do that

239

won't require you to torture yourself until your muscles stop screaming."

"Well, there are all those journals of Lilly's . . . " Hadn't she been itching to find and read the next one?

"Bring in some firewood and make yourself a cozy fire. I'll bet those journals are real interesting." He leaned down, kissed the side of her face, and added, "No telling what you might learn from them."

She stood aside in the doorway while Cam passed her on his way out, Dune at her feet, then watched him follow the path to the drive. When he reached the truck, he turned and waved before getting into the cab. He'd barely disappeared down the street when she raised her fingers to her lips and traced the path his mouth had made across the side of her face.

"Wow." She sighed. "Just . . . wow . . . "

He'd only been half kidding about the job but dead serious when it came to kissing Ellie.

He forced himself to focus on the former and try to ignore the latter. The work she'd done had been good: he hadn't been patronizing her when he'd said it was the best amateur work he'd seen. She was neat as a pin and had taken obvious pains—no pun intended—to get every speck of glue off the wall, and she'd missed damned little. He liked that meticulous attention to the small details because he was like that himself.

But the kissing part—he hadn't planned that. It had just sort of happened. Not that he was sorry. Kissing Ellie had been the highlight of his recent life. There was something about her that drew him closer every time he saw her.

Oh, who am I trying to kid? I've been wanting to kiss her—to touch her—since I saw her walking out of the Crab Claw.

Well, yeah. Pretty much.

It was a little strange, though, her being Lynley's daughter. There were things about Ellie that reminded him of Lynley. Like her eyes being the same shade of green, and the way she tilted her head to one side when she was thinking. And the way she avoided looking at you when she didn't want to talk about something. Things he'd pretty much forgotten about the mother until he realized that he was looking at the daughter.

Cam had looked up Clifford Chapman on Magellan Express, and after studying his face for a few moments, decided that Ellie favored her father in the looks department. Where Lynley was tall and willowy, Ellie was shorter and more compact. He'd never met Chapman, but he'd known Lynley better than he'd let on. Not that he'd known her well, but they were more than passing acquaintances. Once he'd gotten past the initial infatuation, he'd found her to be sensitive and thoughtful and caring. Their common bond was their love for Lilly. Lynley trusted Cam to look out for Lilly when she was away, and Cam had never let her down.

He parked his truck in his driveway, and before he went into the house, walked to the end of the blacktop to where the brown stalks of cattails bent with age and the season. The marsh grew right up to the back of his property, and sometimes on nights like this, he stood at the edge and listened for the first of the night sounds. The hush of the wings of an owl on the hunt, the screech of its prey. The soft wind through the cordgrass. As much as he was looking forward to buying Lilly's house when Ellie was ready to sell, he knew he'd miss this place.

Funny she seemed in no great hurry to sell it, but he supposed she had her reasons. Maybe she needed the time to connect with her roots. He wasn't sure how much she knew about Lilly, or for that matter, Lynley. She seemed surprised to learn that her mother had spent so much time in St. Dennis.

He couldn't help but wonder what Ellie would learn about her mother from reading the journals—and what she might learn about herself in the process.

Chapter 15

"I'VE been so excited about the paintings, I forgot that Thanksgiving is tomorrow," Carly said when she called Ellie on Wednesday afternoon. "Throw some clothes into a suitcase and toss Dune into the car and drive up to my parents' and have dinner with us. They just got home this morning and decided to do a big Thanksgiving and want you to come."

"Thanks, Carly, but, actually, I have plans for tomorrow."

"Don't tell me you're cooking a turkey."

"Nope. Cameron invited me to dinner. Apparently a lot of St. Dennis folks go to one of the local inns for dinner on Thanksgiving."

"Sounds like fun."

"We'll see. But please thank your parents for me." Ellie paused. "You know, Car, I've been thinking. It's not going to work for me."

"What's not going to work?"

"The book about Carolina and Lilly and Lynley."

"Why not?"

"I've been reading the journals, Lilly's and Carolina's, and they're fascinating. I've learned so much about my family. But I'm not a writer, and I just don't have the time or the ability to do their stories justice."

"El, I spent two hours on Monday when I got home scanning the Internet for information about Carolina and found practically nothing. There were a number of articles about her work, but nothing about her personally. I think this book really needs to be written. People should know who Carolina was and her contribution to early twentieth-century art."

"And you're just the person to tell them."

Carly began to protest, but Ellie cut her off. "Look, I'm not an art historian like you are. I think you should take the journals and read them and write the book yourself. You can do it in such a way that it enhances what you're going to do with the paintings. And besides, as much as I'd like to help you, as much as I understand the importance of what you're doing, the bottom line is that I have an awful lot of work to do in five months. I've totally underestimated how much there is to do to get the house ready to go on the market by May. I'm going to need every penny I can get out of this house."

After a moment passed, Carly said, "All right. I'll do it if there's no other way the book can be written. I feel so strongly that this is the perfect opportunity for Carolina's work to get the recognition it deserves. So yes, as long as you don't mind me taking the journals for a while."

"You're welcome to them for as long as you need them. I think you'll find there's a lot of information to work with." Ellie opened the door to let Dune out. "Besides, this way, when I start asking questions around town about Lilly, I can say I'm helping you research a book you're writing about Carolina's recently discovered paintings. People here met you and they know you work for a gallery and they won't think it's strange for me to be helping you out."

"All true. Relieved that you won't have to lie?"

"I am."

"Then it's settled. I do think that as Lynley's daughter, Ellis Chapman should at least write a foreword but we can talk about that later." Carly paused. "Oh, and before I forget, and speaking of Ellis Chapman, I got an e-mail from Jenny Wilson today. She wanted to know if I was still in touch with you, and if I knew how you were holding up and if you were okay."

"What did you tell her?"

"Nothing yet. I thought maybe I'd forward the e-mail to you and you could respond directly."

"I don't know. I haven't heard from her—or anyone else from school—in a long time." Ellie bit the cuticle around her index finger.

"She doesn't know how to approach you directly, El. She just doesn't know what to say. I think there are a lot of people who feel that way, like they want to reach out but don't know how."

"Maybe. Would you mind just telling her that I'm fine and thank her for asking?" She thought for a moment before adding, "And yeah, forward the e-mail to me. Maybe I'll get around to writing to her one of these days."

"Will do."

"So how are you doing with the paintings?"

Carly sighed. "The more I study them, the more

stunning they are. It's time-consuming, as I expected, but they're cleaning up beautifully. I'm having one of the best times of my life."

"I'd like to think your life has been a little more exciting than that."

"I've had my moments, but this sort of thing transcends the everyday good time."

"I'm glad you're enjoying them. Do you want me to send the journals to you?"

"If that wouldn't be a problem for you, I'd love to be able to read through Carolina's thoughts while I'm working on her paintings."

"I'll pack them up and mail them off. I've already gotten through all of Carolina's and maybe half of Lilly's."

"Keep the ones you haven't read yet," Carly said. "You can send those along when you've finished."

"Will do. Thanks again for inviting me for tomorrow."

"I think you've had a better offer. You'll have to let me know how it goes."

"I will," Ellie promised. "Give your mom and dad my love . . . "

Ellie stood and stretched, her attention drawn outside, where the mailman was placing something in her mailbox.

"More junk," she grumbled. "There has to be a way to opt out of all that trash mail."

She grabbed a jacket from the front hall closet and slipped into it on her way out the front door, Dune racing ahead, chasing the shadows of the gulls that swept overhead. Ellie opened the mailbox and removed a handful of paper circulars and two envelopes. One was from the electric company. The other was from prisoner number 524782.

"Thanks, but no thanks, Dad. It's all still too raw. I'm not ready to deal with you yet." She tucked the unopened letter into her jacket pocket and called to Dune, who, anticipating a walk on the beach, had raced to the edge of the sand and stood wagging her tail, waiting.

Ellie followed the dog along the waterline, where pale foam marked the level of the last waves to stretch onto the sand and Dune made a game out of chasing the receding water. The envelope seemed to vibrate against her hip but she ignored it. The last thing she wanted to think about right now was her father. Henry ran a close second.

She wanted to think about her house. She wanted to think about Cameron and how kissing him had been such a delicious surprise. She wanted to think about tomorrow's Thanksgiving dinner at the inn and discovering family she hadn't even known she had but who were becoming a part of her life through their words and through living beneath the same roof they'd lived under. She wanted to think about how it felt to spend hours doing hard but surprisingly satisfying work that wore her out physically but stimulated her mentally. She wanted to think about the time she spent walking the beach with Dune and Carly writing a book about the women artists in her family.

She wanted to think about a future that might outshine her past.

But no, thank you, she did not want to think about her father.

She pulled the envelope from her pocket and tossed it

into the Chesapeake, where an incoming wave snatched it up. She watched the white paper roll toward the shore then retreat as wave after wave tossed it about. What could he have to say now that could be relevant to the life she was making for herself, the life that would take the place of the one he'd destroyed? She turned her back on the Bay and called for Dune, who'd taken off into the grass. She started back to the house, Dune catching up with her before she reached the driveway.

Tomorrow was Thanksgiving, a day to count blessings, to give thanks for all the good things in life. The past year had held precious little for Ellie to be grateful for, but since she arrived in St. Dennis, the tide of her life had seemed to turn and she was determined to ride it. The last thing she needed right now was a reminder of all the dark days that she was trying so hard to leave behind.

Thanksgiving morning was bright and clear but colder than it had been since Ellie arrived in St. Dennis. She stood in front of her closet and surveyed her meager wardrobe. She hadn't planned on having much of a social life, so she'd left most of her clothes at Carly's house, where she'd moved them once the feds gave her the green light to retrieve her belongings from the house she'd shared with Henry. Her pricey designer clothes and jewelry had been confiscated by the feds—not that she'd wear such fancy things here in St. Dennis, but still, she wished she had something a little dressier than black pants. Maybe she'd ask Carly to bring some of her things the next time she visited.

Ellie tried on a number of tops with the black pants,

but in the end settled for a dark gold turtleneck, an animal-print scarf, and black ballet flats. She wore her hair down and a pair of large gold hoop earrings she'd found in the corner of one of the dresser drawers in the back bedroom that she liked to think had belonged to her mother, though she had no way of knowing for certain. She spent more time on her makeup than she had in the last three months. She'd once been the master of the smoky eye, and she hoped she hadn't lost her touch. The look on Cam's face when he came to pick her up was her first hint that she hadn't.

"You look great," he said. "Really . . . great."

"Thanks." She smiled at his awkwardness and let him help her on with the black tweed blazer that probably wasn't going to be warm enough but looked really good with the outfit and therefore trumped the warmer one. "So do you."

And he did. Cameron did for khakis what he did for worn jeans. He, too, wore a sweater—his a dark blue crew that fit nicely over his shoulders and matched his eyes—under a soft tan suede jacket. He looked surprised by her compliment but tried to act as if he wasn't.

"Thanks. Ready?"

"I am." Ellie turned to Dune, who seemed to think she was included in the outing. "I'll be back. I'll see if I can sneak out a tidbit of turkey for you."

"Turkey's not really good for dogs," Cameron told her as he held the door for her, then closed it behind them.

"I didn't know," she said. "I've never had a dog before. I guess I should get a book."

"Sounds like you're keeping her." Cam opened the passenger door of the truck and Ellie climbed in.

"I guess I am. Grant seemed pretty sure that she was one of his rescue dogs. I took her over to his clinic yesterday and he checked her out," she told him after he'd slid behind the wheel and started the engine. "He said she's healthy and that she's only a year or so old. There was some paper on her that the rescue group had brought up with them from the shelter where she'd been dumped but it didn't have much information on it. Just what shots she'd had before she'd been loaded onto the transport that brought her here." Ellie sat back against the seat. "I hadn't thought about getting a dog, but she's really grown on me. Grant said I could bring her in and he'd try to find a home for her if I didn't want to keep her, but really, what kind of person would I be if I did that? I mean, she's used to me. She's already lost one home. How would she feel if she lost this one?"

"So what you're really saying is you can't part with her now because you really like her."

"I really do." Ellie laughed. "All of my rationalizing is just so much smoke. I'm really starting to love that dog."

"Good. Everyone should love a pet at least once in their life. More than once, if possible."

"Do you have one? Dog? Cat?"

"Not right now, though Grant keeps threatening to drop off one of his rescue dogs." He reached over and took her hand as he spoke. That the gesture felt so natural took her by surprise. "I work crazy hours most weeks. There are days when I leave the house at six in the morning and don't get back until well after seven. It's not fair to an animal to keep it locked up all that time by itself."

"But you've had a dog before?"

"Yeah, but that was a long time ago."

He slowed as they passed the vacant lot toward the end of the street, his eyes flickering slightly to the right as if he were caught between wanting to look and not wanting to look. He sped up till they reached the stop sign at Charles Street, and they rode in silence to their destination.

The Inn at Sinclair's Point was built by ancestors of Grace Sinclair's late husband. Now run by her oldest son, Daniel, the inn had become one of the go-to places on the Eastern Shore. The parking lot was almost filled to capacity when Cameron and Ellie arrived. They found a spot near the cabins behind the inn and walked hand in hand along the flagstone path to the back entrance. Ellie stopped to take a long look at the building, then turned to look over her shoulder at the Bay behind them.

"Something wrong?" Cam asked.

She shook her head. "No. For a moment I thought the building looked familiar." She stared at the white clapboard siding and the long windows with their dark shutters. "Maybe I drove past it when I first came into town." She paused. "But of course you can't see the back of the building from the road and I know I didn't drive up here, so maybe it just reminds me of some other place I've been." She tried to remember what other place that might have been, but couldn't. Still, it seemed the most logical explanation.

They climbed the steps and went into the lobby, where Grace greeted them.

"Ellie, I'm so happy that Cam was able to talk you into joining us for dinner." Grace took both of Ellie's hands in hers and held them for a moment.

"So am I," Ellie replied. "Your inn is beautiful."

"She's holding up pretty well." Grace gave Ellie's hands a squeeze before releasing them. "Now, go on into the dining room and have a glass of wine and some hors d'oeuvres and mingle. Cam, I'm trusting you'll introduce Ellie to anyone she doesn't already know."

"Will do, Miss Grace." Cam took Ellie by the arm and steered her into the dining room.

Ellie took three steps inside the door and stopped. There was that feeling of déjà vu again. Even the tables with their white cloths set for parties of six or eight or ten with their milk-glass bowl centerpieces of small gourds and pumpkins all seemed familiar somehow. The bank of windows on two sides opened to the Bay, just as she knew they would.

"But I've never been here before," she heard herself whisper.

"What did you say?" Cam leaned closer.

"I was just thinking aloud. Never mind." She gestured to a table on her right. "There's Mrs. Finneran, Jesse Enright's assistant. Is that her husband?"

Cam turned to look. "You mean the white-haired gentleman? That's Curtis Enright, Jesse's grandfather. He and Mrs. Finneran have been friends for ages. She and Curtis's wife, Rose, were good friends."

"I think Grace may have mentioned that." Ellie

paused, remembering what else Grace had said about Violet's childhood friendships and her connection to Lilly. "Let's stop at their table and say hello."

Violet Finneran seemed pleased that Ellie had remembered her, introduced her to Curtis, and invited Ellie and Cameron to join them.

"Don't be silly, Violet," Curtis said. "They don't want to sit with a couple of old fogies like us. They want to be with the young folks."

"No, no, I'd love to join you." Ellie glanced at Cameron. "Unless you've already arranged—"

"No arrangements." Cam pulled out the chair next to Violet for Ellie and she sat. "Will Jesse be joining you, Mr. Enright?"

The white-haired gentleman nodded. "He's picking up Brooke and her mother. I think Clay and Lucy have already arrived, but they're off somewhere."

"Can I bring you something from the bar, Miz Finneran?" Cam asked. "Another glass of wine?"

"No thank you, dear. I'm approaching my limit and want to save a little to have with my dinner."

"Ellie? Mr. Enright?" Cam took their orders and disappeared into a room off to the left.

"So how are you liking St. Dennis, Ellie?" Violet asked.

"I'm liking it very much, thank you," Ellie replied.

"And your new house? You're settling in?"

"Temporarily, yes. You know that I'm planning on selling the property after I finish some improvements. But it needs a lot of work."

"Which house is that?" Curtis asked.

"Lilly Cavanaugh's place," Violet told him.

"Oh, right. I heard that it changed hands." He nodded slowly and seemed to be looking at Ellie with new interest. "You know, my late wife, Rose, and Lilly were good friends back in the day. Along with Violet here."

"I believe I did hear that, yes." Ellie smiled, recalling Lilly's recounting of Rose's crush on the man who now sat across the table, aged and wrinkled, but still handsome in his way.

"Oh, yes, I spent a lot of time in that house of yours when we were growing up." Violet sighed. "And of course, Lilly and Ted lived there after they married. It's a wonderful house. I'm so happy to hear that you're enjoying it." She leaned closer and lowered her voice so that only Ellie could hear. "If there's anything you want to know ... about the house or the people who lived there ... please don't think twice about asking me. I'm sure you must have questions."

"I do." Ellie nodded, very much aware that Violet was one of the few people in St. Dennis who knew who she really was, and as such, could be an important source of information in the coming months. "I've been reading Lilly's journals and the more I read the more I realize how little I know."

"I'll be happy to help fill in any of those blanks that I can for you, dear." Violet patted Ellie's hand, and Ellie felt tears well up behind her eyes.

"Thank you," she whispered. "I have so many questions ... "

"I'm sure you do." Violet started to say something else, but was interrupted when a large group of elderly men and women stopped by the table. She introduced Ellie to each of them.

Everyone seemed to know her house and Lilly and Ted, and Ellie was impressed once again by how many people had fond memories of the couple. When the introductions were made, Ellie recognized several names from Lilly's journals: Douglas Montrose, who'd been their class daredevil, the one who'd given Lilly her first kiss. Marjorie Trimble, the girl who'd tried to break up Lilly and Ted by spreading rumors about Lilly. Matthew Divine, whom Lilly liked to tease that, with a name like his, he'd have no choice but to enter the seminary (he did). Millie Passel, who'd been voted class clown and who still seemed to have a healthy sense of humor.

The familiarity of it all settled around Ellie and made her feel a part of something she hadn't belonged to even six weeks ago. When Cam returned to the table with their bar order, he glanced at Ellie and looked as if he was about to say something before having second thoughts.

"What?" Ellie asked.

"Nothing. You just looked ... happy, I guess, is the best word." Cameron sat next to her, his arm across the back of her chair.

"I guess I am." The thought hadn't occurred to her, not in so many words, but it was true. She did feel happy. "There's such a nice group of people here."

Ellie looked around the room and was struck by the number of faces she recognized. "Doesn't anyone in St. Dennis eat Thanksgiving dinner at home?"

"Sure, but it's been a long-standing tradition for a lot

of families to come to the inn. I don't know how it got started. Grace would know."

"Did you used to eat here when you were growing up?"

He seemed to give more thought to the answer than a simple question would merit.

Finally, he said, "After a time, we did."

There was a touch of something she couldn't name— sorrow? melancholy?—in his voice, but she sensed there was a story there that was part of a larger one, one he wasn't ready to tell. She could appreciate that. There were things she wished she could say, but couldn't.

Jesse and Brooke arrived with her mother, and Clay came by to claim a seat at the table.

"Where's Lucy?" Cam asked him.

"Orchestrating," Clay replied. "Big events are her thing."

"I hear your big event will be after the holidays," Violet said. "Grace told me that you and Lucy have set a date."

"She's been so busy making sure that everyone else has the perfect wedding that she hasn't been able to plan ours," Clay told her. "When the wedding she had booked for New Year's Eve canceled, she jumped on it. She's done so many weddings she can plan them in her sleep. She knows exactly what she wants and how to get it done, so we're good."

"Not in on the planning, eh?" Cam leaned forward to make eye contact with Clay.

"I just want to marry Lucy." Clay shrugged. "How, where, day, night, what we eat, what the cake looks like, what kind of flowers ... whatever she wants is fine with me."

"But there will be exceptional beer, right?" Cam asked. "You're going to be making a special wedding brew."

"Oh, hell yeah." Clay nodded vigorously. "Wade and I are already working on that."

Waitstaff began to bring trays and bowls and platters laden with traditional dishes to each table for family-style service. Soon the room was dense with chatter and requests to pass the potatoes or the green-bean casserole or the oyster stuffing. It was unlike any holiday dinner Ellie— an only child—had ever taken part in, filled as it was with so much laughter and conversation. But it was also the most memorable meal she'd ever shared. By the time dessert was served, she barely had room for the pumpkin pie that everyone insisted she try. Ellie left the inn with ribs aching from laughing and her jaws sore from talking so much. When you live alone for any length of time, you just don't have much occasion to talk, she reminded herself, and fewer occasions to laugh out loud. Even when she'd lived with Henry, in retrospect, she couldn't recall that they'd talked—or laughed—all that much.

Ellie and Cam said their good-byes and strolled into the lobby, where once again, Ellie was overcome by a sense of having been in this place before. When Cam stopped to talk to an old friend, she took the opportunity to walk around the lobby and study its appointments. She paused before the massive fireplace and tried to remember where she might have seen its like before.

"Is something wrong, dear?" Grace startled Ellie when she came up behind her and placed a hand on her back.

"Oh, no. I just thought I'd look around a little. It's crazy, but I keep having the feeling that I've been here before."

"Ah, but you have," Grace said softly.

"That's impossible." Ellie shook her head. "I've never been in St. Dennis before."

Grace took one of Ellie's hands. "Ellie, your mother brought you here several times."

Ellie's heart began to beat so loudly she was certain everyone in the inn could hear it, that any minute someone would call 911.

"You know?" Ellie whispered. "How did you know? Did Violet . . . ?"

"No one had to tell me. I knew you the minute I saw you in Cuppachino," Grace replied gently. "Lynley and Lilly used to bring you here for afternoon tea when you were just a toddler. Very often Lucy and I would join you. There are photographs somewhere. I'll try to find them for you."

Ellie covered her face with her hands, trying to remember, but she couldn't bring up a memory.

"But you couldn't possibly have recognized me."

"I knew you all the same, Ellis. Ellie." Grace smiled. "Lilly just loved to dress you up and show you off around town. We had some lovely times here together. Lilly never had children of her own, you know, and she doted on you."

"I don't remember being in St. Dennis." Ellie tried, but there was nothing concrete. "Sometimes I think I

258

might recognize some little thing, but I can't say I have any real memories." She hesitated, then said, "Miss Grace, I've just learned that my mother lived with Lilly in my house when she was young."

"Oh, yes." Grace nodded.

"Do you know why?" It might not have been the best time, or the best place, to have this conversation, but Ellie couldn't keep the words from tumbling from her mouth. "I'm just beginning to realize how little I know about my mother, particularly her childhood."

Grace took Ellie's arm and steered her from the main throng in the lobby. They stopped next to a window that looked out over a vast expanse of lawn where a gazebo stood. In the background, the Bay looked dark blue as a light mist began to fall. "Were you aware that Lynley had younger twin sisters?"

"No." Ellie frowned. "I was under the impression that she was an only child. I never heard her mention having sisters."

"I'm not surprised that it wasn't something she'd talk about. They were not quite two when they died. One caught a lung infection that she shared with the other. They passed on within a few days of each other."

"Oh, my God. That's horrible. I never knew." Ellie felt blindsided, as if she'd just taken a fist to her stomach.

"After they died, your grandmother—Evelyn—went into a terrible depression. Her husband moved the family to California thinking the change of scenery would help her to cope, but she seemed to sink deeper into her depression. Peter—that is, your grandfather—called Lilly and asked if he could send Lynley to live with her and

259

Ted until Evelyn was well again." Grace sighed. "Of course, Evelyn never did get better."

"My mother told me that her parents drowned in a boating accident, but other than that, she almost never spoke of them."

"Well, there's not much question that they drowned, and it doesn't surprise me to hear that Lynley didn't have too much to say about them. Imagine how you might feel as a young child, being shipped off by your parents and never seeing them again. That must have had a terrible effect on Lynley. But whether or not there was an accident . . . no one will ever know for sure."

"What do you mean?"

"All we really do know is that Peter took Evelyn out on their boat, and they were never seen again. Weeks later, the boat was found miles down the coastline—no damage to the boat, but no one was on board. People around here figured that Evelyn had become suicidal and that Peter couldn't stand to see her suffer so much, but he couldn't let her go alone. I'm of the mind that he probably just ran the boat until it could run no more. He and Evelyn most likely eased themselves overboard and drowned together."

"Oh, my God." Ellie felt sick. "Why would you think that?"

"Because two weeks before the 'accident,' he mailed an envelope to Lilly which contained his will and other information one would need to probate an estate. Of course, it could have been a coincidence, but I believe he wanted to make certain that Lynley was well provided for."

"This is all so tragic."

"Oh, dear. I've upset you. I'm sorry, Ellie. I probably shouldn't have been so blunt." Grace took her arm and led her to a settee that stood near a doorway and urged her to sit.

"No, no, please don't apologize. I had no idea that my grandparents ... or that my mother ..." Ellie paused. "How old was my mother when all this happened?"

"Well, let's see ..." Grace appeared to be calculating. "I think she was around four or five when the twins were born, so she'd have been six or seven when they passed on. I think she stayed out west with her parents for another year or two, so I'm thinking she was around eight or nine when she came here to stay."

"My poor mother." Ellie tried to imagine what Lynley must have been feeling. Rejected? Frightened? Unloved? Lonely? Surely all of that and more. "I had no idea. I've been reading Lilly's journals in chronological order but I haven't gotten past her young married life. Lynley wouldn't have been born yet. All of this explains so much about my mother."

"Lynley had a difficult time when she first arrived in town, as I recall, but Lilly and Ted loved her as they'd have loved their own child, and in the end, it was most certainly for the best. They were much more stable than Lynley's parents were. Evelyn was always very high-strung and, well, frankly, a bit of a drama queen. She was always quite self-absorbed."

"That explains my mother's attachment to Lilly and the house and St. Dennis," Ellie said thoughtfully. "I wonder if my father knew ..." For a second or so, she almost wished she hadn't tossed Clifford's letter into the Bay.

Before Grace could respond, Cameron joined them.

"You about ready to leave?" He placed a hand lightly on Ellie's back.

"Yes." Ellie turned to Grace. "Thank you again for . . . for everything. Dinner was absolutely delicious."

"As always," Cam added.

"Thank you. I'm glad you enjoyed your meal." Grace patted Ellie's hands. "Now I should tend to our other guests and help Lucy get ready for the next seating. But promise you'll come and have tea with me one afternoon. Just call. Anytime. We'll have Lucy join us."

"I'd love that, thank you." On impulse, Ellie hugged the older woman briefly.

"Make it soon, dear."

"I will," Ellie promised.

She slipped into her jacket and made her way with Cameron through the crowd of similarly departing diners, trying not to think about everything Grace had told her. Once outside, she took a deep breath, filling her lungs with cold air that hinted at pine and the Bay beyond the trees.

"Is everything all right?" Cameron asked.

"Sure." She nodded but didn't trust herself to look at him.

When they reached the pickup, she paused at the passenger-side door and said, "Thank you. This was one of the nicest days I've had in a long time."

"The day isn't over," he told her as she climbed into her seat. "As the poet said, there are miles to go. I think

262

he was referring to miles of wallpaper that needed to be scraped. Miles of brushstrokes to be painted on miles of walls."

"Look, about that." She snapped on her seat belt. "We don't have to do any of that today. I'm sure you have better things to do on a holiday than scrape someone else's walls. You could use the rest, I'm sure."

"Nope. Nothing I'd rather do." He closed the door and walked around the front of the truck.

"I thought holidays were supposed to be days off."

"You took off yesterday, didn't you?"

"Well, yeah, but I was referring to you. Couldn't you use a little downtime?"

"I don't do downtime."

Cam started the engine and backed out of his parking spot.

"That was the most amazing dinner ever. I can't remember the last time I ate that much." Ellie leaned back against the seat and closed her eyes. "I may not be able to get out of the truck."

"You and me both. We might have to spend the rest of the day here in the truck."

Cam turned on the radio and searched for something other than static. Ellie kept her head back and her eyes closed as her mind zipped back and forth through her conversation with Grace, trying to grasp it all. Her grandparents had lost not one, but two children, and Evelyn—her grandmother—had gone into a deep depression, so deep that her grandfather thought that Lynley would be better off on the other side of the country, being raised by a couple she barely knew. Had he felt that he had to make a choice between his wife and his daughter? Had he been trying to protect Lynley from what may have been a nightmare situation with an unstable mother? For years Ellie had wondered why her mother had been all right with sending her daughter off to boarding school at such a young age. Having been sent off herself as a child must have made such a separation seem normal.

For the first time since the day her father had been led away in handcuffs, Ellie wished she could speak with him, if only to ask him what her mother might have told him about her childhood. Then again, there were still so many journals on the shelves. Surely Lilly, who wrote about everything, had written about the day her grandniece came to live with them.

The truck came to a stop and the engine was cut. Ellie opened her eyes and began to unfasten her seat belt when she looked out the window onto an unfamiliar scene.

"Where are we?"

"At my place. I thought I'd stop and change my clothes if we're going to try to paint out those kitchen walls." Cam pulled the keys from the ignition.

"Are you sure you don't want to change your mind? I really didn't expect you to spend your Thanksgiving working in my house," she told him.

"I spent the last two days taking down plaster walls. I'm looking forward to something sweet and easy." He hopped out of the cab. "Want to come in while I change?"

"Sure, but really . . . "

He ignored her and went straight to the front door,

which he unlocked and swung open. Ellie followed, her bag slung over her shoulder.

"This is so nice." She stopped about ten feet from the front porch and took a good look at the bungalow that was sided in brown cedar shakes and trimmed with crisp white paint.

"Thanks. I'm almost done here," he said as he held the door for her. "I only have the one big room on the second floor to finish painting and I'll be ready to put it on the market." He snapped on the hall light. "I just can't decide whether I should put this one up for sale before your house or if I should wait until the sign goes on your front lawn."

He grinned and led her into the living room. "I don't want to be caught without a place to live if this place should sell before you're ready."

"I'm thinking I'll be ready by May," she told him.

"If you put your mind to it, you could be finished well before then."

"No, May's my target." No reason for him to know she couldn't sell it before then.

He tossed his jacket over the newel post.

"Can I get you anything? Something to drink, maybe . . . ?"

"No, no. I'm fine, but thanks."

"It won't take me long to change. Make yourself at home," Cameron said as he disappeared down a short hall.

Ellie heard a door close softly. She stood for a moment before walking to the bank of windows that stood along the far wall. She drew aside a curtain and looked out onto a pond where dried cattails bent at odd angles to one another. Between the pond and the house was the driveway, at the end of which was a garage that was sided in the same cedar as the house. She walked to the back door, opened it, and stepped onto a porch where two rocking chairs faced the backyard and a marsh beyond. She wondered who sat in the second chair to watch the sunset with Cameron, who shared quiet mornings over coffee watching the red-winged blackbirds land on the reeds.

"Here you are." Cameron stood in the doorway in that well-worn plaid flannel shirt and the jeans with the hole in the back pocket. "For a moment I thought maybe you started home on foot."

"I was just enjoying the scenery." She leaned against the railing, which she noted was much more secure than the one on her back porch. "It's pretty here."

Cam nodded. "It's a nice street and a quiet neighborhood. I think I'll make out really well when I sell it."

"Have you done a lot of work here?"

"A ton. All the mechanical systems replaced. New windows. New kitchen, new baths. Everything's been painted except for that one last room. So yeah, I've done a lot of work."

"I'm surprised you want to sell it right away instead of staying and enjoying it. I'd think you'd be more attached to it after doing all that."

"I bought it with the intention of fixing it up and selling it." He crossed his arms over his chest. "Just like you're doing."

Ellie tried to think of a quick retort but couldn't.

"Besides," he went on, "this is what I do for a living. Buy, fix, sell."

"But you have a contracting business, too, right?"

"I do. A couple of years ago, when business started to slow down, I had the opportunity to buy a run-down place out on River Road. I spent three months fixing it up while I lived there, then sold it for more than twice what I paid. I've been in the renovating business ever since."

"That's why you want my house? To buy, fix, sell?"

"I'd never sell that house." He came out onto the porch. "That one's for me."

He put an arm around her. "Having second thoughts about selling?"

Ellie shook her head. "Not at all. And for the record, I'll still give you the first shot at making an offer."

"I appreciate it." He turned slightly toward her and reached down to tuck a strand of hair behind her ear. Tiny jolts of what felt like electricity trailed in the wake of his fingers. "Maybe you'll come back and visit me there."

"Maybe I will."

He leaned down and kissed her, but this time she'd been waiting—hoping—for him to kiss her again. His lips were softly demanding, his arms pulling her closer until she was fully in his embrace.

A strong breeze blew through the marsh and she shivered in spite of the warmth that had started to spread through her.

"It's getting chilly out here," he said as he eased his lips from hers. "You're not dressed for winter."

He took her hand and led her inside.

"I think we need to get back to my place." Ellie

watched him lock the back door. "I think Dune will need some tending to."

"Good point." He lit the lamp that stood on a table inside the front door and picked up the tools he'd left near the door. On their way to the driveway, Cam pulled up short and pointed to the sky, where a long ragged string of Canada geese was passing. "You know winter is coming when the geese start moving in flocks that large."

"Don't they stay all year round?" she asked as she got into the truck.

"Some do. A lot still migrate from the northernmost states. The diaries of the early settlers talk about huge flocks of geese arriving right about this time every year."

A light rain started to fall as they drove through several side streets to Bay View Road. Cam parked in Ellie's driveway, close to the path leading to the front door.

"Someone's having a lot of company." Ellie gestured to the row of cars that lined the road.

"The Walshes have a big family thing over Thanksgiving weekend," Cam told her as she unlocked her front door. "They have six kids and they're all married and have kids and everyone comes back to St. Dennis for the long weekend."

"You know the family?"

Cam nodded. "Jackie Walsh and I went to school together."

"And you lived on this street at one time, you said?"

She slipped out of her jacket and hung it in the hall closet, then reached for his and hung it next to hers.

"Right." He walked into the kitchen, carrying the tools he'd brought from his house.

Dune greeted them madly, running from one to the other in a happy dance of *Welcome home now feed me walk me pet me*. Cam offered to walk the dog while Ellie changed into work clothes. Ten minutes later, when Ellie came downstairs in her old sweats, she found Cam and the dog in the living room, seated together on the floor, in front of the bookcase, a stack of books by his side.

"Thanks, Cam, for taking her out. I appreciate . . ." She'd taken four steps into the room. "What are you doing?" she asked.

"Oh." Cam seemed flustered. "I just remembered that this was here . . . I didn't think you'd mind."

She knelt next to him on the floor and leaned into the now-empty shelf. Along the back wall, a hole opened in the wall. "Is that, like, a secret panel?"

He nodded.

"How did you know it was there?" she asked.

"I spent some time here when I was young," he said simply, as if that were explanation enough.

"You mean, visiting Lilly?"

Cam's face was a study in uncertainty, of hesitation, of pain. Finally, he sighed, then stood and reached down to help her up.

"Come on." He looked sadly resigned "Get our jackets. There's something I need to show you . . ."

Chapter 16

CAM set a brisk pace down the driveway and across the street, leading Ellie by the hand, her steps hurried as she tried to keep up with him. What earlier had been rain was now mist that settled on the ground, and they pushed through it, all the way to the vacant lot in the middle of Bay View Road.

"My dad bought this lot and built a house for my mother. He didn't want to marry her until he had a house for her." Cam slowed partway up the driveway. "It was a pretty great house. Three bedrooms and two baths, a big kitchen and family room with a big brick fireplace. As soon as it was finished, he proposed. His family did everything they could to keep that wedding from happening."

"They didn't like her? Approve of her . . . ?"

"They thought that something wasn't quite right about her."

"Any particular reason?"

"Yeah, she was an alcoholic. Before they were married, she did her best to hide it, but my grandparents saw through her from the first. My dad didn't. He loved her very much. In spite of everything that happened, he loved her until the day he died."

"Cam, what happened to the house?" Ellie glanced at the trees and shrubs that grew in no particular pattern.

"It burned down years ago."

He led her deeper onto the lot. In the wet ground up ahead she could see the outline of what had been the foundation of the house that no longer stood.

"Things were always very volatile in our house. When my mother was sober, everything was fine. Normal. We were like any other family. My sister and I would come home from school and there'd be a snack waiting for us. We'd do our homework and Mom would help us if we needed it. The house would be clean and warm and there'd be dinner on the stove and stories at bedtime. My mother and my father would be happy and everything was like one of those families you'd see on TV.

"But when my mother was drinking . . . " He took a deep breath before continuing. "We'd know right away, as soon as we opened the front door. There'd be no Mom waiting for us and the house would be a mess. There'd be no snacks on the table and no dinner cooking on the stove. If my mother hadn't already passed out, she'd be incoherent, often abusive and threatening, always angry and argumentative. She scared me but she terrified Wendy, my little sister. So we'd have to hide from her until our dad got home and could calm her down. Sometimes that took hours. Then he'd make dinner for us and we'd go to bed and pretend we weren't afraid to go to sleep."

His face was filled with so much pain that Ellie didn't think she could bear it. She turned her body to his as if to block the memories from hurting him all over again.

"After a while, the uncertainty of it all, one day to the next, became the new normal. But my dad never stopped loving her, never stopped believing that one day she'd get herself straight and she'd be the girl he'd fallen in love with and we'd all live happily ever after."

"Cam, you don't have to . . . "

Ignoring her protest as if he hadn't heard, he drew closer to the foundation. "One day it all just seemed to boil over. She was always angry when she drank, but this one day, she was beyond anger and beyond reason. And she had a handgun. I never did find out where she got it."

Ellie wanted to slap her hands over her ears, didn't want to hear the rest, hoped he'd stop there, that that would be the end of the story.

"She was sitting in the kitchen when we got home from school, a half-empty bottle and the gun on the table in front of her. She waved the gun at me and I knew something bad was going to happen. I panicked and grabbed Wendy and took her into my room and we hid in the back of my closet. When my father came through the back door about twenty minutes later, we thought we were saved. Wendy and I got up and I opened the closet door, and then we heard the bang. My mother shot him in the chest, point-blank range. And then she came looking for us."

"Oh, my God, Cameron." Ellie gasped at the horror of it, could almost picture the scene in her mind.

Cam's voice was surprisingly calm, but there was immense sadness in his eyes.

"Wendy and I huddled in the back of the closet and I had my hand over my sister's mouth to keep her from

272

screaming. She'd gone stone still and quiet when we heard the gunshot but I was afraid that any second she'd understand what had happened, and she'd start screaming. I knew right away what my mother had done, and I knew that sooner or later, she was going to find us, and she was going to kill us, too."

He paused for a moment, as if reliving that terrible night.

"And then, there was a miracle. The doorbell rang. Lilly Cavanaugh had heard the shots and she called the police, then she ran across the street and rang the doorbell. My mother didn't answer it, but Lilly started talking to her through the door. As soon as I heard her voice, I knew we were going to be okay. A few seconds later, I heard the police sirens coming closer and closer. And then we heard one last gunshot."

"Your mother . . ."

Cameron nodded. "When she realized she wasn't going to get to Wendy and me, she shot herself." Through the growing mist, Ellie could see Cam's eyes starting to well. "Miss Lilly rang that doorbell knowing that my mother could just as easily turn that gun on her, but she didn't care. She knew we were in there and that we were in danger, and she did what she had to do to create a distraction before the cops arrived. She said later she'd have found a way to knock the door down, if she'd had to."

"She saved your lives." Ellie stated the obvious. No wonder he took such care of her house—Lilly's house. No wonder he spoke of the woman with such love.

"Miss Lilly saved us in more ways than one. She took

Wendy and me home with her and went through all the red tape so that we were allowed to stay with her and Mr. C. until my aunt—my dad's sister—could find a place for us to live. She found a house here in St. Dennis, and the Cavanaughs helped her to get a mortgage, helped her to find a job. They were our lifeline. We wouldn't have survived without them."

"Cameron, how old were you when this happened?"

"Eight. Wendy was five. She had just started kindergarten."

"I can't imagine what a nightmare that must have been for you. I'm so sorry for what you went through. But thank God there was someone there for you. I'm glad it was Lilly," Ellie said softly. "I'm glad that my house was a sanctuary for you and your sister. I'm glad that you'll be buying the house when it's time. It should be your house."

They stood close together while a cold rain fell around them, soaking them to the skin. Finally, she tugged at his hand until he turned and they headed back to the last house on the street.

"You didn't have to tell me," Ellie said when they were back inside, "but I'm glad that you did. I'm so sorry that you and your sister had to witness such terrible things."

"I didn't tell you so you'd feel sorry for me." He looked horrified at the thought. "I felt like I wasn't being honest about myself and my relationship with Lilly and this house. I felt like I was deceiving you, and I thought you deserved better than that. I wasn't lying to you but I wasn't being up front with you, either."

Ellie took their wet jackets into the kitchen and left

them on the backs of two chairs. To her surprise, Cam followed her and knelt next to the tool bag he'd brought in earlier.

"I guess I left the sander in the truck. We need it to go over that wall before we paint," he said. "I'll be right back."

Before she could react, he was almost to the front door. Ellie went into the hall and watched in disbelief as he disappeared through the doorway, stunned that he could go from discussing the fact that his mother had murdered his father—and apparently had intended to kill him and his sister—to sanding her kitchen wall.

"Seriously, Cameron?" she muttered. How could he make such a leap?

Maybe he's thinking he said too much. Maybe he wishes he hadn't said anything at all. Ellie could understand that. She knew what it was like to feel every day that she had to live down what her father had done.

And let's face it, what had happened to Cameron and his sister was so much worse than what had happened to me.

So okay, she got it. If he wants to talk about plaster, they'd talk about plaster.

He returned a moment later, the sander in his hand.

"The sandpaper's pretty thin, but I don't have another piece with me, so it will have to do. I think it will be okay, though, because you did a damned fine job on this wall, Ellie."

He ran his fingers over the plaster. "A damned fine job." He looked over his shoulder at her. "Are you sure you've never done this before?"

"Positive."

"I have guys on my crew who aren't this meticulous. I could sure use you next week. I can think of three jobs I could put you on. Anytime you want to make some extra money, you let me know. I'd hire you in a minute."

"I don't have any experience." Nor did she have any money. The offer definitely turned her head.

"You can get experience, but not everyone has as good an eye as you. There's barely a scratch on the wall." He stood back and took a long look, then nodded. "Yeah. Anytime, you let me know and I'll put you to work."

He slipped on a mask, handed one to Ellie, then turned on the sander before she could respond.

The idea of working, of getting paid for what she was doing here for free, did have a certain amount of appeal, she thought as she watched him smooth first his hand, then the sander, over the plaster. She could use the money, and besides, it could be fun. She hadn't really minded the scraping—had actually liked the physical work—except of course for the fact that she hadn't been able to raise her arms for forty-eight hours. But if she did it more frequently, wouldn't her muscles get used to it? And as an added bonus, she'd get to look at Cameron all day.

It was something to think about.

He turned off the sander. "Where's your vacuum cleaner? I'll need to clean up the plaster dust."

"I'll do it."

She pulled the old vacuum out of the hall closet, trying to think of a way to get back on the topic of his childhood and the time he spent living in this house and his relationships with its occupants. His story was so tragic it was surreal. That he had survived—in no small part thanks to a member of her own family—that he had lived here, in this house where her mother had lived, where she now lived, seemed meaningful to her in ways she had yet to explore. She had so many unanswered questions, but how to broach the topic again if he'd turned his back on it? Obviously the memories were still very painful for him, and yet he'd gone out of his way to share this part of himself with her. All of which left Ellie feeling very confused.

She brought the vacuum cleaner into the kitchen and plugged it in, then ran it as far up the wall as she could reach. Cameron took it from her hands to finish up the area nearest the ceiling, then turned it off and dragged it back into the hall.

"Ready for paint?" he asked.

"Sure. Walls first, right?"

"Right."

They found the can of Brackenridge Cream and divided the paint into two smaller containers. Ellie started on the cutwork at the bottom along the baseboard, Cameron on the door surround. She set up her iPod on the counter and selected what she thought would be good music to paint by.

She'd just dipped her brush into the paint when Cam said, "You know, there are several little hidden compartments around the house. The one in the living room is only one of them."

"You know where they all are?"

"Well, I know where some of them are. I don't know that we ever found them all."

"Lilly showed you?"

Cam nodded. "She was in her sixties when Wendy and I stayed here, but she still had the best sense of fun of anyone I ever met. She loved surprises and she loved all the little quirks in this house."

"I really wish I'd met her." More and more every day, Ellie realized.

He looked about to say something but hestitated.

"What?" she asked.

"Nothing. I'm sure she would have liked you a lot, that's all." He dipped his brush into the paint. "Anyway, about those little compartments. Sometimes Lilly'd leave little treats in there for Wendy and me. She used to buy these chocolate oranges that had slices wrapped in orange foil. Every once in a while she'd put two in there, one for each of us."

"She sounds like a very thoughtful person," Ellie said. "I like what I've learned about her from her journals and from what I hear from the people in town."

"I've never met anyone else like her. You've heard the expression that someone was 'the soul of kindness'? That was Lilly. After everything that had happened, coming here to stay was like walking out from a long dark tunnel into a sunny day. There was never any drama with Lilly. No threats, no violence, no ramblings. There was structure and there was consistency. There was kindness and there was love. Not that my mother was always unkind, or that she didn't love us," he hastened to add. "I think she did, when she could. But she was caught in the grip of something that was relentless, and that something always trumped everything else in her life. I think she'd planned all along to kill herself, but maybe she just lost track of time. Then we came home and my dad came home and things just spun out of control from there." He painted a long strip of color on the wall. "Hal Garrity was chief of police back then, and he told me once that he believed that she'd planned on just taking herself out, that when Dad came home and saw her with the gun, he might have tried to take it from her and he was shot accidentally. When she realized what she'd done, maybe she decided she didn't want to leave Wendy and me alone, so she was going to take us out, too. We'll never know for sure, but given the alternative, I like his version better." He smiled wryly. "It's probably pure fiction, but I like it better."

"I do, too." Either way, Ellie didn't like thinking about a mother who would deliberately hunt down her children to coldly murder them.

"It's hard enough to know that your mother was an alcoholic murderer, without remembering that you were one of the people she wanted to kill for no apparent reason."

"But she didn't," Ellie reminded him, "and she probably could have."

"She heard Lilly at the door and she heard the police cars coming—"

"And she probably would have still had enough time to . . . to do what she'd set out to do, but in the end, she chose not to. Not much consolation, I imagine, but still."

"Still." The brush in his hand made several more long smooth strokes along the wall. "Anyway, I just thought you should know. I didn't feel right not telling you. I

279

wasn't sure how you'd react, but I felt it was important. Some situations call for full disclosure, and this is one of them."

"Because?"

"Because of the way I feel about you."

"About me or about my house." She sat back on her heels and looked up at him.

"I thought we already agreed that when you're ready to sell the house, I'd be the buyer."

"We did."

"So that's a nonissue. That's going to happen when you're ready."

"I'll be ready by spring," she told him. "I'm thinking May at the earliest, June at the latest."

"And then what?"

"What?" She looked up at him.

"What will you do after you sell the house? Where will you go?"

"I have no idea." Ellie turned her attention back to the job at hand. "I haven't thought that far ahead."

"I find that hard to believe."

"Why?"

"You're just so organized and methodical about everything else, it seems odd that you don't have a plan."

She could have said that the burden of living a lie, of not being herself, was proving to be greater than she'd anticipated. Or, she could have said that she didn't know where she could go where she'd be accepted for who she was. Or that she felt more like her true self after living here as someone else, and how confusing was that? How to explain that she'd never felt so relaxed, so free, as she did over the past month, that inside, she felt more like Ellie and less and less like Ellis, and she was all right with that?

More than all right, actually.

She could have told him the truth right then and there. The words were starting to swirl and form in her mind but she wasn't sure of the right thing to say, how best to begin. Should she start out with something like "Cam, you should know that I'm Lynley's daughter"? Or maybe "Remember that big financial scandal last year? The one involving Clifford Chapman? He's my father. I just thought you should know. Of course, that makes me Lynley's daughter. Small world, eh?"

All she had to do was think of the right way to say it. It occurred to her that this was especially hard, after having pretended to be someone else. "The tangled web we weave" never felt more true, or more tangled.

"You know, I never thought I'd say this after the meal we had this afternoon, but I'm actually getting hungry," he was saying.

"I think I am, too. How could that possibly be?"

Cam rested his brush sideways across the paint can. "Nothing's open today. We can't do takeout. Maybe I have something home in the refrigerator."

"Let's see what I have." Ellie opened the fridge door and looked inside. "Bread. Cheese. We could have grilled cheese sandwiches."

"Sounds good to me."

"I should feed Dune first and take her out." Ellie set the bread and cheese on the table.

"I'll do it. Where's her food?"

Dune came scampering when she heard the can opener. Cam fed her, and when she was finished, took her out the front door. Ellie searched for the cheese slicer and had just started to butter the bread when she heard the front door open and close a few minutes later. She prepared the sandwiches for the frying pan, but Cam hadn't appeared back in the kitchen. She went into the living room to see what was what.

"Are you ready for me to start cooking the . . . " She paused in the doorway.

Cam was seated on the floor near the bookcase, returning the stacks of books to the shelves.

"You know, you always hear people talk about being instantly attracted to someone, but you don't understand until it happens to you," Cam said without looking up. "The first time I saw you, I got a jolt."

His lips formed a half smile. "A first for me, by the way. And that was before I knew you'd bought this house."

"What? Where was that?" She tried to remember if she'd seen him before he showed up in her backyard. She'd have remembered, if she had.

"You were coming out of the Crab Claw with a take-out bag when Jesse and I were waiting for a parking spot. You just sort of floated along that sidewalk. I liked the way you looked. I liked the way you moved."

She sat behind him and wrapped her arms around him. "Tell me more."

Her hair fell over her shoulders and he reached back to toy with a strand of it.

"I'd gone to Jesse's office in a huff because I'd found

out this house had been sold and I was pissed off because I'd waited so long to buy it and here it had been snatched out from under my nose. He told me how you'd bought the place from Lynley's estate and that it had all been arranged through her lawyers in New York. After I calmed down, we went to lunch. Jesse saw me eyeing you while you walked by and told me who you were."

Her hands played with the top button on his shirt because she needed to touch him. The flannel was soft and faded, a total turn-on.

"Well, I have a confession to make, too." She moved closer and pressed her body against his. "I admit that the first time I saw you here, that first time you stopped over, I got a bit of a jolt myself."

She smiled. "Actually, I think you were wearing this shirt."

"You remember what I was wearing?"

Ellie nodded.

"That's nice." He turned her around and drew her into his arms.

"You weren't happy I was here. I could tell that right away." Her heart began to beat a little faster.

"I *was* happy you were here. I just wasn't happy that you were in my house." He ran his fingers through her hair. "But I was happy you were here. And you were even prettier close up."

She edged closer, wanting nothing more at that moment than to feel his mouth on her, his hands on her skin. She wrapped her arms around his neck, her lips drawn to his and demanding that he kiss her with the same fervor. She unbuttoned his shirt and ran her palms on his chest, and his breath caught in his throat.

"Ellie . . ."

"Shut up, Cam."

"Okay."

He leaned back against the bookcase, knocking over the stack of books that had yet to be put away, and pulled her onto his lap. His thighs were rock hard beneath hers and his chest solid under her hands, and when she kissed him, she felt as if her lips were on fire. His tongue teased the inside of her mouth and she felt her body move against his as if it had a mind of its own, tension building inside her like the springs of an overwound clock. When his hands slid under her shirt, she eased back to give him access to her breasts, aching for his touch. Mouths and tongues still entwined, she reached back to unhook her bra, a moan from deep inside escaping when his hands found her skin. She sat back farther as his hands skimmed over her from her throat to her waist. His mouth moved to her neck, long slow kisses that fanned the fire that was growing out of control within her. Her clothes were suddenly too tight, too hot, too much in the way, and when he moved her onto her back, she pulled her sweatpants over her hips.

"Let me . . ." he whispered, and she felt the smooth fabric glide over her hips and her thighs.

She pushed his shirt off over his shoulders and tugged on the waist of his jeans. She pulled her sweatshirt off over her head and tossed it . . . somewhere. Then he was covering her with his body, and when she opened to him, she felt him in every cell. He slid into her and she arched her back and barely heard the "ohhhh" that escaped her lips. Cam moved inside her slowly at first, his hips in concert with hers, the rhythm fogging her mind. He buried his face in her throat for a long moment, then moved his mouth to her breast, and she shattered into a thousand pieces.

"Want to move to the sofa?" Cam asked, his breath still ragged.

"No. I want to move upstairs to my room. Third door on the left . . . "

The house was quiet—too quiet—when Ellie opened her eyes. The sun was already up and peeking through the curtains, the open shade spilling light across the floor and onto the bed. She rolled over and put out a hand to touch Cameron . . . and found only empty space. She sat up and looked around the room. His clothes were gone, and so apparently was he.

He must have gotten up and left at some point, though she had a vague sense of him having been there earlier. Had he found that sleeping with her after having emptied his soul to her had overwhelmed him? Had he regretted the telling or the long night of sex or both? Still, she wouldn't have picked him for the kind of guy who crept out in the middle of the night, and was disappointed to find that he had.

Reluctantly, Ellie got out of bed and went into the bathroom, where she showered, then towel-dried her hair. She started to get dressed, then stopped, tilting her head to one side, and sniffed the air much like Dune might have done.

She stepped into the hall and sniffed again. She smelled . . . bacon?

She finished dressing and went downstairs to the kitchen, where Cam stood in front of the stove, Dune at his feet, her tail wagging like crazy.

"Coffee's ready," he said without turning around. "I love these old percolating coffeepots, don't you? Was this one here when you moved in?"

"I found it in the cabinet."

"I remember Lilly making coffee for Mr. C. every morning and every evening after dinner. Lilly never drank it, she was strictly orange pekoe. Never had any use for herb teas, though. Said they tasted like boiled grass."

Ellie stood for a moment, watching him, the flannel shirt unbuttoned, the mussed hair, and felt a wave of something inside her surge. She wrapped her arms around his waist and kissed the back of his neck.

He half turned and she could see the smile on his face. "Plant one here," he said, and she did.

"Now make yourself useful and crack a few eggs," he told her.

"Where'd the bacon come from?" She took a bowl from the cupboard and a fork from the drawer.

"I woke up early and hungry, remembered we never did get dinner last night. So I took Dune out for a walk, and then the two of us drove to the market and picked up a few things." He turned the bacon over, then reached for his coffee.

"How do you like your eggs?" she asked.

"Scrambled, if you do."

"I do." She scrambled the eggs and looked through the

cupboard for the small cast-iron frying pan. When she set it on the stove, Cam said, "I remember that pan, too."

"You have a lot of memories here," she observed.

"Good ones," he assured her.

Now was the time to tell him, she decided. All she had to do was open her mouth and let it come out naturally. He'd trusted her with his secrets. She could trust him with hers.

She just hoped it wouldn't sound as if she thought it was tit for tat. *He showed me his, I should show him mine.*

It doesn't matter, she told herself. Cameron wouldn't go running out the front door, horrified at her lineage.

But would he have told her everything he had about himself if he'd known that she was Lynley's daughter, that she was no lucky buyer of this house, but that it had been her inheritance? Would he be embarrassed at having poured his heart out to her only to find that she was related to the woman who'd saved his life?

Ellie watched butter sizzle in the bottom of the black pan, wondering how Cameron would take the news.

"Hey, unless you're trying to brown the butter, you might want to turn the flame down."

"Oh, crap." She lowered the heat and poured the eggs in.

Over breakfast, she'd tell him. She'd say, *Cam, I haven't been completely honest with you . . .*

"Ellie."

"What?"

"Your phone's ringing."

"Oh." She found the phone where she'd left it the night before, on the kitchen table. "Hello?"

287

"Ellie, it's Jesse Enright. Sorry to call so early . . . "

She glanced at the clock. It was almost eight.

"What's up, Jesse?"

"You need to come down to my office. There's something we need to talk about."

"This morning?"

"The sooner the better." Jesse's voice was tense and hurried.

"Is something wrong?" Was the account out of money? Had the feds found a way to take what had belonged to Lynley in their zeal to punish her father?

Had her father found a way to get out of prison?

"I think it's best if we discussed this in person." Jesse cleared his throat. "I'm on my way into my office right now. I can meet you there."

"All right."

Ellie held the phone in her hand, her heart pounding like thunder.

"Something wrong?" Cameron asked.

"I don't know. Jesse wants me to come into his office as soon as I can get there but he wouldn't tell me why."

"No clue?"

She shook her head. "None."

She started out of the room and Cam grabbed her by the hand.

"No point in running out." He steered her in the direction of the table. "Whatever it is, it can wait. Sit down and eat."

While she was on the phone, he'd finished scrambling the eggs and divided them between two plates. He brought both coffee mugs to the table along with the bacon and a few slices of toast. He took the seat next to hers and handed her the plate of bacon.

"Thanks." Her nerves were on edge and anxiety seeped through her. Jesse had sounded very somber, very disturbed. What the hell could it be?

" . . . and it's a good thing she texted me early, because I forgot all about it. Can't imagine what had distracted me, can you?"

"What were you saying about texting?" She frowned. "I'm sorry. My train of thought . . . "

"It's going to be fine, whatever it is." Cameron covered her hand with his.

She nodded and tried to smile. "What about a text?"

"Wendy. Wanted to know what time I'd get to her apartment. She's moving today and I told her I'd help her." He glanced at his watch.

"What time was she expecting you?"

"About a half hour ago."

"Where is she?"

"Baltimore. She's been living in a studio for the past four years but has finally decided to go for a little more space. Frankly, I don't see how anyone could live in one of those tiny one-room places, but different strokes, I guess."

Dune begged for bacon and Cam broke off a small piece for her. Ellie wanted to tell him she didn't like feeding the dog from the table but the thought was lost inside her head and got mixed up with the resolve she'd made to tell him who she was and the fear that had risen inside her.

"What's the worst thing it could be, Ellie?" Cameron pushed his plate aside and put an arm around her.

"I don't know. I really don't know." She put down her fork, her appetite having been banished by the dread that had settled inside her.

"Look, whatever it is ... " He seemed to search for words. "Understand that I'm here for you, whatever. Just ... whatever."

"Thank you." Her hands shook slightly when she picked up her mug but she forced a smile. "Do you need to get going to Baltimore?"

"I do, but I—"

"I'm fine. Really. I'm just overreacting. I'm sure it's nothing as bad as what I think." She pushed back her chair and studied his face, and realized he was studying hers.

"Want me to stick around in case ... I don't know, in case—"

"No, no. Go help your sister." Ellie leaned over and kissed him. "Thank you, though."

"I'll call you later."

Ellie nodded.

"And you'll tell me it was something ridiculously silly like the town's building inspector forgot to file a U and O or forgot to get a termite inspection." He held her face in his hands for a long moment, then kissed her.

"Could that happen?" she asked.

"All kinds of things can happen when a house is sold," he assured her.

Ellie clung to that thought all the way to Old St. Mary's Church Road.

Diary ~

Well, another Thanksgiving Day has come and gone and we've all survived it. Seems that every year we're serving more and more folks at the inn, and that's a good thing, of course, though so exhausting at my age to greet everyone and act the hostess. Yes, I know, it's hard to believe but I'm no spring chicken anymore! Ha!

I joke, but the truth is that my advancing age is no laughing matter. By the time we were just getting into our evening seating for dinner, I was done. Fried, as my granddaughter would say —and she did. Thank God for Lucy. She sent me up to my room—I want to go on the record as having protested, but I admit it was merely to save face— and she took over for me. I had a lovely nap that lasted until six this morning. What can I say? I'm old and I was tired!

Before I pooped out, I had a chat with Ellie Chapman— that is, Ellie Ryder, as she prefers these days—and I'm afraid I may have said too much. But for heaven's sake, no one ever told that girl what had gone on in her mother's life and she was entitled to know. Why Lynley had never told her about Evelyn's depression and the eventual suicide of both Evelyn and Peter, well, I can only speculate on that. All right, speculation combined with what I glean from Lilly from time to time. I must say that Lilly isn't always forthcoming when it comes to sharing but she does occasionally permit me some insight through the portal, so to speak. It's difficult for me to present as fact what I learn from Lilly via my Ouija board and the things that come to me in my dreams. So for me to tell Ellie that I know that Lynley hid the full story of her

291

parents' tragedy because she'd had so much conflict over the whole thing, well, surely she'd wonder how I knew. But here's the truth of it: Lynley had been devastated by the loss of her sisters, but no one seemed to acknowledge her loss. Evelyn, that silly, self-absorbed woman, was only mindful of her pain, and none of the pain of others. She wallowed in her grief to the exclusion of everything else, including her living daughter. While Peter sending Lynley to live with Lilly and Ted may have broken Lynley's heart at first, in the end, it was the best thing that could have happened, because they allowed her to grieve. They made her the center of their lives, and in doing so, helped her to heal from the trauma of losing her siblings. I speak from firsthand knowledge of that sort of pain, having lost a brother when I was nine. Steven's death had shattered all of us, but none of us children ever were lost in the shuffle of our family's sorrow. Anyway, it's Ellie's right to know the truth about her family. If I can help her to discover that truth, I'll do so.

At least, until Lilly tells me to shut up.

~ *Grace* ~

Chapter 17

JESSE met Ellie at the door, his face grim.

"What's happened?" Dread washed over her again, and she knew this had nothing to do with code violations.

"You need to sit down." Jesse led her into his office and closed the door, even though Violet Finneran had the day off and no other clients were in sight. "I've been trying to figure out how to tell you . . ."

"Tell me what?" Her legs shaking, Ellie sank into the first chair inside the door. "Just say it."

"I got a phone call last night around nine thirty from your father's personal attorney."

"Max Forester?" Ellie frowned. "What was so important that he had to call you on Thanksgiving night? What did he want that couldn't have waited until this morning?"

"He wanted to talk about your sister."

"What sister? I don't have a sister."

"Apparently you do."

"You're not making any sense." She shook her head as if to clear it. "I'm an only child."

"Ellie . . . there's just no other way to say this."

Jesse sat in the chair next to her and turned it to face hers. "Your father began an affair with a woman in New

Jersey about sixteen years ago. They had a child together."

"That's preposterous. The feds went over every second of his life for the past thirty years. If there'd been another woman there, they'd have found her and everyone would have known about it a year ago."

"Does the name Marilyn Hansen ring any bells?"

"No. I've never heard it before. She's the one?"

Jesse nodded.

"That's crazy talk," Ellie scoffed. "Oh, wait. Let me guess. She's looking to get some sort of payoff from him by claiming that a child of hers is his. Ms. Hansen's obviously way behind in her reading. Every newspaper and magazine in the country ran the stories of how everything he owned—everything *I* owned—was turned over to the FBI and the SEC to sell to repay his victims. Surely Max told her that."

"I don't know what Max told her but it hardly matters now, since she was killed in a car accident two weeks ago."

"This woman's dead?"

"She's dead, but her daughter is alive."

"Wait a minute, this supposed daughter—"

"Not supposed. There was a paternity test years ago. She's definitely Clifford Chapman's daughter. He acknowledged her a long time ago. That's not in dispute, Ellie. I had Max fax over all the papers this morning. Her birth certificate, the results of the DNA testing, copies of the mother's bank account."

"He was supporting her?"

"Evidently quite well."

"How did he manage to hide that during the investigation?"

"Cash payments every month to her mother." Jesse leaned back in his chair. "Which I'm assuming stopped once the investigation began."

"They had to have shown up somewhere," Ellie insisted.

"Your father's business brought in a ridiculous amount of money. You of all people must know that."

"Yes, but I made a lot of money working for him and I had to account for all of it."

"I know, but you're honest, and he wasn't. It appears that he managed to hide a lot over the years."

"So what does this girl have to do with me?"

"Put bluntly, your father is asking that you take her in."

"Take her in? What does that mean, take her in?"

"Her mother has no family and her father is in prison. Clifford has asked that you agree to become her legal guardian."

"You mean, have her live with me?" She choked back a laugh. "Is he delusional?"

"She's been staying with the Foresters but that was supposed to be temporary, and quite frankly, they don't want her. They're turning her over to the state to put her into foster care on Monday if she has nowhere else to go. And other than you, there is no one, no place, for her to go."

"Well, she's not coming here, either." Ellie got up and began to pace. "My father has colossal nerve to even think of asking me to raise his . . . his child."

She slammed a hand on the back of the chair she'd been sitting in.

"What is wrong with that man, anyway?"

Jesse sat back, apparently willing to let Ellie blow off as much of her anger as she needed to.

"And who is this girl? How old is she?"

"She's thirteen." He got up and reached for a file on his desk. "Her name is—"

"Don't tell me her name. Don't tell me anything about her. I don't want to know. He's crazy if he thinks for one minute that I'd . . ."

Jesse closed the file and Ellie walked into the hall, paced some more, then came back into the office.

"Did you speak with my father directly?"

"No, only Max. He said that both he and your father had tried to contact you by mail but you hadn't responded."

Ellie thought about the letters she'd received—two from her father and one from Max's law firm—and tossed away. She groaned and sat for a few seconds, got up, paced once more, then sat again.

"Where is this girl now?" she asked.

"She's with Max and his family, but they're not willing to keep her. Actually, they're supposed to be leaving on a cruise tomorrow and want her gone today. Max sounded extremely put out that you hadn't contacted him to make arrangements for her, so that he and his family had to share their Thanksgiving Day with her." Jesse paused, then asked, "Is Max as big a jerk as I make him sound?"

"Bigger," she told him. "You have no idea."

"Oh, I have some idea. He said having her at dinner yesterday put a damper on their family's holiday. That she was sullen and antisocial."

296

"Oh, gee. She was sullen? Really?" Ellie snorted, her sense of fair play tweaked. "Ya think it might have had something to do with the fact that her mother's dead, her father's in prison, and her choice is between foster care or a half sister she's never met? Can't imagine why she wasn't in more of a party mood."

"That was pretty much my reaction, too. It can't be easy for this kid."

"Don't make me feel sorry for her." Ellie put both hands over her face and groaned. "Jesse, I don't want to do this. I really don't want to do this."

"I understand. I don't know how I'd feel in your shoes. I don't know what I'd do."

Ellie paced a little more and wished she could turn the clock back to early this morning when she had nothing on her mind except Cameron and memories of their night together. She hadn't had time to process it— needed time to process it—but here she was, being asked to decide the fate of a hitherto unknown girl. Her sister.

Her little sister who just lost her mother and probably didn't have much of a relationship with her father and was probably scared shitless about what was going to happen to her.

"All right." She sighed. "What's her name?"

"Gabrielle. She's in ninth grade and she—"

"I need to think."

"Want some coffee while you do?"

"Yes, please."

"I'll be right back."

Ellie sat back in her chair and closed her eyes. She did

not want to be responsible for her father's love child. She didn't know anything about teenage girls other than that she'd been one once. She had no idea where she'd go or what she'd be doing once her time in St. Dennis was over. How could she take on the responsibility of someone else? A stranger? A kid, for God's sake. Keeping Dune had been a big step for her.

No, she did not want this girl—this half sister—to come to St. Dennis. No. No, no, no.

She picked up the file that Jesse had left on his desk and opened it. Inside were the faxed letters from Max on the letterhead of Forester, Fox and Oxenhauer, the DNA report, and the birth certificate of Gabrielle Amelia Hanson naming Marilyn Jean Hanson as her mother and Clifford Andrew Chapman as her father.

Amelia was Ellie's paternal grandmother's name. *Nice move on Marilyn's part.*

The last item in the file was a photocopy of a photograph of a young girl with dark bangs that fell like fringe over her forehead almost to her eyes. She wore a floppy hat and sunglasses and a big smile. Her cheeks hadn't yet lost their childhood roundness and her face still held a semblance of innocence. Ellie sat and held the picture in front of her.

She didn't know this girl, didn't want to. She didn't want to share her house with Gabrielle Hansen—or did she go by Chapman? She didn't want this girl's problems to become her own. Ellie was just starting to come to terms with her past and still had no idea what the future held. Did she really need a teenager at this stage of her life? What did she know about raising a child?

But what she did know about the foster care system in this country could fill volumes.

Three years ago she'd done some free PR for a private organization that was promoting adoption of kids who were caught in the system through no fault of their own. She'd wept when she watched the film they produced, showing how kids got sucked into foster care and how so few ever got out. How, as they grew older and older, they became less and less adoptable. How they were kicked out of the system at eighteen and how many of them disappeared into the vortex of street life.

Could she really sentence a young girl—her own sister, for crying out loud—to such a future?

On the other hand, what about *her* life, the life she was trying to build for herself?

Crap.

Jesse returned to the office, a mug of coffee on a tray along with sweetener and a container of skim milk.

"We're out of half-and-half," he apologized, and held up the small carton of milk. "This is the best I could do in a pinch."

"It's fine, thanks, Jesse." Preoccupied, Ellie fixed her coffee and sipped without tasting.

"Why don't you go home, take a few hours to think things over?" Jesse suggested.

"That won't be necessary," she said. "I've already made up my mind. I really don't want to do this, Jesse."

"I totally understand. I'll contact Max this morning and tell him to make the arrangements with child services."

"No. To bring her to St. Dennis."

"I thought you just said you didn't want to take her."

"I don't. I don't know her, and for all we know, she really is a sullen, antisocial little brat and I'll be at my wits' end before the weekend is over and I'll wish I'd told my father to go screw himself. But I know that foster care can be really, really rough. I've never heard a good thing about it. I can't in good conscience send this kid into that without at least giving her a chance. What's happened to her to turn her life inside out isn't her fault and it isn't fair," she told him, "and I know all about that."

She stood. "So go ahead, call Max and tell him I said yes. Get whatever paperwork we'll need. But tell him I want her driven down here in a hired car with all her things at his expense. He can afford it. After all the money my father paid him over the years, he can at least have the decency to do better than a bus ticket."

"Do you want to talk to him yourself? Make the arrangements . . . ?"

"No. I don't want to talk to him. God forbid I should sound sullen or distracted. I might ruin his cruise."

It was almost four in the afternoon when Jesse's SUV pulled up in front of Ellie's house. Max had the girl and everything she owned dropped off at Jesse's law office, either because he wanted to annoy Jesse or because he felt it lent some greater legality to the situation.

To ease her nerves, Ellie had taken Dune on a long walk, then she'd called Carly.

"Hey, I was just thinking about calling you to see how Thanksgiving dinner—" Carly began when she answered Ellie's call.

"You're not going to believe this. My father had an affair. He had a mistress in New Jersey and they had a child. A girl. She's thirteen. Gabrielle. Marilyn—that's the mother—my father's mistress—she died, and my father wanted me to—"

"Whoa! Back up! You're babbling. Slow down and start over from 'My father had an affair.'"

"He did. It started sixteen years ago. You realize that was even before my mother was sick, right? Bastard. I never thought he'd cheat on her. I thought he loved her and that they were happy together. I thought that—"

"Excuse me, but at the risk of sounding rude, that part isn't relevant at the moment. Go back to the part about him having a child with this woman. How did you find out?"

"My dad's attorney called Jesse Enright when he couldn't get in touch with me. He'd sent me a letter—and my dad wrote to me as well—but I didn't read any of the letters, I just felt so over that entire mess, I didn't want to hear from my father or anyone else connected with all that. So I threw the envelopes away, thinking they were just some blah-blah-I'm-so-sorry stuff."

"Jesse is your lawyer there, right? Engaged to the cupcake queen?"

"Right. Anyway, Max—my dad's personal lawyer, not to be confused with his criminal lawyer—called Jesse because the girl—Gabrielle—had been staying with his family since the funeral and they wanted her out."

Ellie related her conversation with Jesse.

"Wow. That's gotta hurt," Carly said when Ellie finished filling her in on the details. "So what happens now?"

301

"Now I wait for her to show up here this afternoon. Car, tell me the truth. Am I nuts? What if we hate each other? What if she hates me? What if she's obnoxious and takes drugs and—"

"Stop it. Stop it now. You're giving me a headache," Carly protested. "Look, you've made the decision to give her a chance; now do it."

Ellie paused. "You're right. I need to be rational."

"Just take a deep breath and don't imagine the situation will be worse than it will be. She could be a perfectly nice kid." Carly paused. "Or she could be demon spawn. Either way, you won't know until she gets there."

Ellie heard the car doors slam and looked out the window to see Jesse and a slim girl almost as tall as she standing behind it, the hatch open. Jesse placed several items in the girl's arms before sliding a suitcase onto the ground.

"Which is now. I'll call you back . . . " Ellie disconnected the call and put the phone in her pocket.

"Here we go, Dune," Ellie said to the dog, who was standing on her hind legs to look, too. "Wish all of us luck . . . "

Ellie opened the front door and went outside, meeting the girl halfway up the drive.

"Gabrielle, I'm—"

"I know who you are. You're Ellis." The girl studied Ellie with sea-green eyes through round wire-framed glasses. She had dark brown hair—ironically, the same color that Ellie'd dyed hers—that came to her shoulders and she wore a College of New Jersey sweatshirt and jeans. "I've seen your pictures. Where should I go with this stuff?"

Ellie took one of the two boxes from Gabrielle's hands and said, "This way."

"You have a dog." Gabrielle stopped on the walkway to stare down at Dune. "I didn't know you had a dog."

"Her name is Dune." Ellie was on the porch and was pushing the door open with her foot.

"What kind of dog is she?"

"Not sure. Some terrier mix, I think. She's a rescue dog."

"So you've done this before." Her eyes huge behind her glasses, Gabrielle looked up at Ellie from the bottom of the steps. "The rescue thing. Good to know you've had experience with the homeless."

She came up the stairs and walked into the foyer, past Ellie, whose mouth was hanging slightly open. Jesse followed with the suitcase, and whispered to Ellie on his way into the house, "I see you've met Gabrielle."

"Sullen? Antisocial?" Ellie raised an eyebrow.

"Not that I could tell."

"Maybe she didn't like the Foresters."

"Smart girl." Jesse put the suitcase down.

"This is a really old house, isn't it?" Gabrielle stood in the middle of the living room floor, taking it all in. "Our house was new. Everything was new. This place looks a little shabby."

"I've only been here for a month," Ellie told her. "I'm working on it."

Gabrielle nodded and looked toward the stairwell. "Do I have a room?"

"You do. Third door on the right."

"Great. Thanks." The girl picked up the box and trotted up the steps, Dune racing her to the top, where Gabrielle paused and looked down at Jesse. "Do you think you could bring that up for me, please, Mr. Enright? It's a little heavy and I'm just a kid . . . "

An amused look on his face, Jesse carried the suitcase upstairs muttering, "Yeah. Thirteen going on forty-five."

Ellie sighed and followed him with the box in her arms.

"It's nice that the room looks out at the woods." Gabrielle had put the box she'd carried onto the bed and was looking out the back window. "And over there I can see the water. Is that the Chesapeake Bay? Mr. Forester said St. Dennis was on the Chesapeake Bay."

"That's the Bay, all right." Jesse set the suitcase next to the box on the bedspread. "I'll get the rest of your stuff."

After Jesse left the room and his footsteps pounded on the stairs, Gabrielle turned to Ellie. "I know you didn't want me to come here. It's okay. I'll try not to be any trouble."

"Gabrielle . . . do you like Gabrielle or maybe Gabi?" Ellie asked.

Gabrielle shrugged. "Whichever you like."

"No, it's whatever you like."

Again, a shrug. *Not sullen*, Ellie realized. *Resigned.*

"I prefer Ellie to Ellis."

"Okay," Gabrielle said. "It must feel weird to find out you have a sister you never knew about. I'm sorry."

"No reason for you to apologize," Ellie told her. "It isn't your fault. And it has to be equally hard for you."

304

"No, I knew about you. I know all about you. I looked at your pictures online all the time." She looked up at Ellie with eyes as light as Ellie's own. "You were the one he owned up to."

"Lucky me." Ellie grimaced, and regretted the words the second they were out of her mouth. Too late to take them back.

"Were you?" Gabrielle sat on the edge of the mattress and asked somewhat wistfully, "Was he a good father to you? It looked like he was, in all the pictures online."

"He was a great father," Ellie answered honestly. "Until he wasn't. I don't know why he did the things he did, but they were pretty terrible."

"I read about that, too. My mom said people get addicted to all kinds of things, and that he just got addicted to making money instead of drugs."

"That's about as good an explanation as any that I've heard." It was an apt comparison. Her father had exhibited all the signs of addiction, had she been paying attention. "How 'bout you? What kind of a father was he for you?"

"Okay until I was about eight or nine, then he sort of lost interest," she said matter-of-factly. "I guess I was cuter when I was little, or maybe he and my mom got along better then. And he was never, like, 'Oh, you're Daddy's little girl' or anything like that. He always supported us, though. He wanted me to go to private school but my mom didn't want me to go away. He was going to pay for that because he said education was important."

"But no warm fuzzies?"

"Not so much." Gabrielle tried to force an I-don't-really-care attitude that didn't match the look in her eyes. "But it's okay. My expectations weren't all that high."

"I'm sorry," Ellie heard herself say.

"It's okay. I had a really good mom." Ellie expected Gabrielle to burst into tears, but instead, she held her chin up and met Ellie's gaze with an acceptance that Ellie would not have expected.

"Are you hungry?" Ellie asked when she couldn't think of anything else to say.

"A little. I didn't get lunch."

"I don't know what you like to eat."

"I like pretty much everything. My mom wasn't a real good cook," Gabrielle said.

"I don't know that I'm much better, but I'll see what I have that we can whip together." Ellie leaned against the doorjamb. "You know, you can choose another room, if you like. Why not look into all of them while I make us a something to eat?"

"Okay, thanks."

Ellie was on the landing when Gabrielle called to her.

"You're nicer than I thought you'd be, Ellie."

Ellie went back to the room and poked her head in. "Did you think I wouldn't be nice?"

"I thought you'd be mad. I didn't think you'd want me to come."

"Why did you think that?"

"Because Mr. Forester said you were a being a bitch about it because you didn't answer his letter."

"I didn't answer his letter because I didn't read it. I thought it was about ... well, I don't know what I thought it would be about, but I didn't expect ... "

"You didn't expect me."

"No, I didn't." Ellie decided to be completely honest.

"I'm sorry," Gabrielle said once again.

"Don't be sorry, kiddo. I'm not," Ellie said, surprised to realize that she meant it.

"You're not?"

"I'm sorry that so much has happened to you in so short a time. I'm sorry that you lost your mother and you got jerked around by Max for the last couple of weeks." She wouldn't be surprised if, sooner or later, Max billed her father for those hours. "I'm sorry that your father—our father," she corrected herself, "wasn't a better dad to you. He should have been."

Ellie went downstairs, where Jesse was just delivering a pile of boxes.

"That's the end of it, I think," he told her.

"Jesse, I can't thank you enough for getting her here."

"Is she going to be all right?" he asked. "Are you going to be all right?"

"I think we'll be okay after we get to know each other a little. I can't help but feel sorry for her. She seems like a really nice kid who deserves better than to be just one more person who got screwed over by Clifford Chapman."

"Agreed." Jesse let himself out the front door. "Call me if you need anything."

"Will do," she told him.

Ellie went into the kitchen and tried to make sense of the entire day, which had gone from fabulous to crazy in practically no time at all. She'd planned on spending much of this day just basking in what remained of the glow of her night with Cameron. Instead, she was pushed once again into the harsh light that seemed to accompany everything connected with her father these days.

She heard Gabrielle moving upstairs, the floorboards squeaking as she moved from one room to the next, trying to decide which one she wanted. Ellie hadn't had time to figure out how she felt about this hitherto unknown half sister of hers. She seemed like a genuinely sweet girl, one who'd been handed a particularly nasty hand. How things were going to play out, Ellie couldn't even begin to guess.

One thing she did know was that what her father had done to her didn't hold a candle to what he'd done to Gabrielle.

Ellie made open-faced tuna sandwiches since she and Cam had used most of what little bread she had for toast earlier. She and Gabi—as Gabrielle announced she really did prefer—ate in the kitchen, trying to talk past the strangeness.

"Did you decide on a room?" Ellie asked.

"I think I like the back room on the left side of the hall best. Would it be okay if I moved my stuff into there?"

"Of course."

"Thanks." Gabi looked down. "Why does the floor look like that?"

"The old linoleum was hideous, so I tore it up. The wood hasn't been sanded yet."

Gabi pointed to the wall Cam and Ellie had worked on the night before.

"Nice cutwork around the doorway," she told Ellie. "Did you do that?"

"No, my friend did. And what do you know about cutwork?"

"I know that you paint with a brush around the molding and then you finish the rest of the wall with a roller. My mom always did all our paint and stuff." Gabi took a bite of her sandwich. "Who's your friend? A boyfriend?"

Ellie thought about how to categorize her relationship with Cameron. "Sort of."

"What's his name?"

"Cameron."

"That's a cool name. There was a boy in my old school named Cameron. He was a jerk but at least he had a cool name." She took a drink of water to wash down the tuna and bread. "Where am I going to go to school?"

"I don't know where the school is. I'll have to ask someone."

"Are there any kids on this street, you know, my age?" Gabi asked.

"I don't think so. Most of the houses along here belong to summer people, so they're empty this time of the year. There's an older couple who live across the street, and a few young families closer to Charles Street, but I haven't seen anyone your age. I'm sure there are lots of kids in town, though. That's something else I can ask around about."

"Never mind. I guess I'll meet kids when I go to school." She took another bite and chewed it slowly. "Will that be on Monday?"

"Do you want to go on Monday?"

Gabi nodded. "I love school. I'm very smart and I get very good grades. I'm a pretty good athlete, too."

"What sports do you play?"

"I play field hockey and lacrosse at school and I run track with the girls' club."

"The same sports I played," Ellie noted, and Gabi beamed at this bit of news.

"So, we'll do our best to get you to where you need to go on Monday." Ellie thought for a moment. "I think we'll need to get your records from your last school, though."

"I think Mr. Enright had all that stuff. Mr. Forester had a big folder that he gave to Mr. Enright. I think it's in that box you took upstairs."

"We'll look for it." Ellie grew thoughtful. "And I probably need something to show that I'm your guardian."

"Is that going to be okay with you?" Gabi's face was suddenly very serious.

"I think it's going to be fine."

"'Cause, you know, I heard foster care wasn't all that bad if you got a nice family." Gabi straightened her back. Her attempt to look brave was obvious.

"We're taking the whole foster thing off the table," Ellie told her.

"Good. I'd rather stay here." Gabi drained her glass of water to hide her relieved sigh. "Thanks for making lunch, Ellie. Could I take Dune out for a walk?"

"Sure. She'll like that. Her leash is in the back hall, near the door."

Ellie moved their dishes to the counter and rinsed them off, then went to the front door. She was about to open it and call to Gabi to suggest that she might like to walk along the beach, when she saw Cam's pickup in the driveway.

"Hi," she heard Gabi's voice. "Are you the sort-of boyfriend?"

Cam stopped on the path to stare at the girl before smiling. "Yeah. Sort of. Who are you?"

"I'm Ellie's sister, Gabi."

"Since when does Ellie have a sister?"

Gabi pointed to Ellie, who stood in the doorway.

"I think you'd better ask her . . . "

Chapter 18

UNTIL he looked up and saw the stricken look on Ellie's face, Cameron thought the girl was just kidding around. He was pretty sure that Ellie was Lynley's only child, which left Clifford Chapman suspect. Would Cam be surprised that Chapman had fooled around on Lynley? Would a man who would cheat so many people out of their life savings have qualms about cheating on his wife? Not likely.

Cam walked up the front steps to where Ellie stood, leaned against the side of the house, and asked, "So, what's new?"

"I tried to call you a couple of times." Ellie seemed to be looking everywhere except at Cameron.

"I forgot to charge my phone." He watched her face. She looked like she was about to jump out of her skin. "My sister ended up having a few of her friends help her move. She really didn't need me, so I decided to come back and spend the day with my sort-of girl-friend."

Ellie held the door open for him, a grim look in her eyes. She looked past him to where the girl and the dog stood in the middle of the lawn.

"It's okay, Gabi," Ellie called to her. "You can go on

down to the beach. Just keep an eye on the sky. It looks like it might rain."

Gabi nodded and jogged off toward the beach with Dune. Ellie closed the door behind her.

"I could use a cup of coffee," Cam told her, sensing that Ellie was at loose ends.

"Okay." She followed him down the hall to the kitchen.

She busied herself at the sink—emptying out the remains of that morning's coffee, rinsing out the pot and the basket, measuring water, measuring coffee. Cam could tell by her expression that she was conflicted and trying to decide what to say.

"Take your time, Ellie," he said softly.

She nodded without looking at him. When the coffee was finished percolating, she poured a cup for him and brought it to the table, where he sat, waiting for her to join him.

"What I have to say, I should have said before." She swallowed hard. "Early this morning, I rehearsed what I was going to say but then Jesse called and I went to his office . . . and . . . " Her hands fluttered in the direction of the beach.

"She really is your sister?"

"Half sister. I learned this morning that my father had had an affair that resulted in . . . Gabi."

"You didn't know about the affair?" Cam had read a lot about Clifford Chapman, but he didn't recall reading that he had an illegitimate child somewhere. He was pretty sure he'd remember that, if for no other reason than that he'd find it hard to believe that anyone in their right mind would cheat on Lynley Sebastian.

"I had no clue," Ellie said.

"So why is she here all of a sudden?"

"Her mother was killed in a car accident two weeks ago. It was here or foster care."

"Tough all the way around. Tough situation for her, tough decision for you."

Ellie stared at him for several seconds, one eyebrow raised. Finally, she said, "You didn't ask about her father. Our father. You didn't ask why she didn't go to live with him."

For a brief moment, Cam considered saying something like "I was just about to ask," but he figured the farce had played itself out. But before he could say, "Because I know he's in prison," Ellie surprised him.

"Our mutual father is Clifford Chapman, the King of Fraud."

"I know," Cam said simply.

"You know?" Ellie frowned. "How could you know?"

Admitting that he'd read everything he could find on the Internet about her was not going to be easy. It might sound as if he'd been stalking her, and that wasn't behind his quest for information.

"You guessed because of my middle name, right?" She went on. "I thought I was being so clever, going by my middle name. Who'd have thought that Ryder was so well known here?" She paused. "Then you know who my mother is."

"Yes. Lynley." Time to fess up. "But it wasn't because of your name."

"Then what . . . ?"

"I did an Internet search."

314

"You . . . you looked me up on the Internet?" She looked as if she wasn't sure she'd heard correctly. "You did a search on me?"

Cam nodded. "Magellan Express. When I couldn't find Ellie Ryder, I looked up Carly Summit and I looked up the school she said you attended. There was a picture of the two of you at some reunion a few years ago. Carly Summit and Ellis Chapman. I looked up Ellis Chapman, and *bam* . . . everything anyone would want to know."

"But why did you search in the first place?"

"Because something just didn't add up, Ellie. I can't explain it, but there was just something about you that . . . " He struggled for the right words. "I knew the minute I met you that you would be important to me. That you were going to mean something in my life. I needed to know who you were, and my gut was pretty sure you weren't going to tell me, so I had to find out on my own."

"How long have you known?"

Cam shrugged. "Awhile."

"The conversations we had about my mother . . . "

"I didn't know, at first."

"Why didn't you say something? Why didn't you tell me you'd figured it out?"

"I figured if you wanted to talk about it, if you wanted me to know, you'd tell me. The bottom line is that it really wasn't any of my business. I didn't feel it was my place to try to force your hand. That's how I felt at first, anyway. Lately, I've just been wishing that you'd trust me enough to tell me."

"I was going to tell you. I was afraid of how you'd

react. I came here as Ellie Ryder because I was afraid of how everyone would react when they found out that Clifford Chapman was my father."

"You need to understand that your father doesn't matter."

"Tell that to the thousands of people he defrauded."

"That has nothing to do with you."

"It has everything to do with me. My father is one of the biggest crooks in the country."

"Did you help him?"

"Of course not. My fiancé did, though."

"Yeah, I read about that. If you don't mind me saying, he looked like a dick."

Ellie smiled. "You're extremely perceptive."

"No one's going to judge you by your father's crimes, Ellie."

"A lot of people have judged me over the past year. I can't tell you how many friends turned their backs on me."

"And you call them friends?" He scowled. "Friends don't turn their backs. Friends ride the storm with you. Like Carly did."

"She was the only one."

"With a friend as good as she is, maybe you only needed one. But you don't have to pretend to be someone you're not to have people here like you."

"I was tired of explaining." She threw her hands up.

"I can understand that. For years I went out of my way to avoid meeting new people so that I didn't have to explain where my parents were or how they died. I felt responsible for so long. Like somehow it must have been my fault. My fault that my mother was an alcoholic, my fault that she wanted to hurt us. My fault that she killed my father . . . "

Ellie reached across the table and took his hands.

"You know that none of that is true."

"I do. As a rational adult, I do. As a child, though, I wondered. It took me a long time to understand that we're not responsible for the actions of others."

She sat quietly, playing with his fingers.

"As a rational adult, you know that you are not responsible for what your father did. You know that, right?" He grabbed her fingers and held them still.

"I do know. I don't feel guilty because of what he's done. What I do feel is anger that he and Henry could act so normal while all the time they were finding ways to steal money from people who trusted them. Whole pension funds were wiped out, people lost everything they owned because of them, and all the time, they thought they were so damned clever." She swallowed hard. "And I admit that I am angry, too, over the fact that I was judged so harshly, especially by people who'd known me for years."

"I think you'd find that people here would be different."

"People are people." She shrugged. "Why would I expect people in St. Dennis to be any different from New York or anywhere else?"

"Because no one around here cares about Clifford Chapman. No one ever did. The story was all over the news last year, as you very well know, but hardly anyone around here talked about it except for the occasional 'You hear about how Lynley's husband bilked all those people out of their money?' Now, if Lynley'd still been alive last year when all this broke, it would have been different, because it would have involved her, she'd have been at the center of it, and it would have hurt her. But your father's a nonentity here. Lynley, on the other hand, was very much admired. She was ours, and you're her daughter."

Ellie nodded. "I get it. I do. But it isn't easy to tell someone that you are not who they think you are."

"Oh, but you're exactly who I thought you were." Her eyes had welled with tears and he reached over to wipe them away with his thumb. "Changing your last name isn't going to change who you are. I don't like you any more because you're Lynley's daughter, and I don't like you any less because you're Chapman's."

"I didn't know how to tell you. I didn't want it to come out wrong. I didn't want you to get up and leave."

"That will never happen."

"I'm sorry I didn't tell you the truth before we ... " She stopped. "Well, actually, at one point last night, I did come into the living room to tell you but I got distracted."

"I'm hoping to get you distracted again very soon."

The front door slammed.

"Ellie, can we come in now?" Gabi called. "We're getting cold."

"Of course. We're in the kitchen." Ellie smiled at Cameron. "To be continued."

Cam shook his head. "Nothing more to say on the subject, unless you do."

"I don't know if I do."

"Feel free to revisit whenever you need to."

Ellie squeezed his hands and got up to meet Gabi in the doorway.

"We're just having coffee," Ellie told her. "Would you like some?"

"No, thank you." Gabi unhooked Dune's leash and took it to the back hall to hang up. When she returned to the kitchen, she said excitedly, "We saw an eagle. At least, I think it was an eagle."

"Very large bird, huge wingspan, white head?" Cam asked.

Gabi nodded. "I didn't know they were that big. I never saw one before. It took my breath away."

"You'll see them from time to time around the Bay," he assured her.

"I was afraid it would come after Dune, so we came back." Gabi addressed Ellie. "Is it okay if I unpack some of my clothes and put them in the dresser and the closet?"

"Of course," Ellie assured her.

"Thanks." She turned back to Cameron. "It was nice meeting you."

"Nice meeting you, too, Gabi."

Gabi's footsteps padded down the hall and up the steps.

"She seems to be adjusting awfully quickly," Cam noted. "Is that normal?"

"I think she's trying really hard to make me think she is, but she has to be hurting. She's tried to act as if this is all very normal when it decidedly is anything but. No one adjusts that quickly when their life is turned upside down. But I have to give her a lot of credit for the effort she's making. I don't know that I was as strong at her age."

"Well, I should probably go and give you some time to be with her. You have a lot to talk about, I'm sure."

"I don't know where to start."

"You've been doing okay so far. The two of you will figure it out."

"What about us?" she asked solemnly. "Are we good?"

"We haven't *not* been good. We were good yesterday and last night and this morning. We're good now, and we'll be good tomorrow and the day after that."

He took a strand of her hair, wrapped it around his finger, and used it to gently pull her closer to him. He brushed his lips across hers, then kissed the side of her mouth. "We're good, Ellie."

The rain began as misty drops that showed up silently on Cam's windshield as he made his way home. By the time he pulled into his own driveway, it was a steady beat against the hood of the pickup. He jumped out of the truck and ran to the side porch. Once under the overhanging roof, he fitted the key into the door and pushed it open. The house was quiet, as if too well mannered to greet him with anything other than the hush from the hot-air vents. Usually he appreciated it. Today he could use a little more than white noise to drown out the cacophony in his head.

All he'd been able to think about all day was Ellie. He'd never experienced that kick to the gut he'd heard other guys talk about, but the first time he saw her, he felt sucker punched. Still did. She was everything he'd ever looked for and never thought he'd find. Funny that the two things he wanted most in life were so deeply entwined. The woman and the house.

How ironic that, to have the one, he'd have to say good-bye to the other.

Not for the first time, Cam wondered why life couldn't be less complicated and more simple.

The Cavanaughs' house had been a sanctuary to Cam, the calm in the midst of the storm. It had been a refuge for him and Wendy that terrible day when the whole world had shifted and they were suddenly cast out from their family—such as it had been—and became "the O'Connor orphans." It had been their first taste of what a normal home life might be like, their first up-close-and-personal with consistently rational adults. Meals were at the same times every day and everyone was expected to be at the table at six o'clock every night. Homework was expected to be completed, and if there was a problem understanding something, Lilly or Ted would be there to offer help. People spoke kindly and listened when others spoke and engaged in real conversations, no shouting, no screaming, no slamming doors or loud cursing. The Cavanaughs' house was definitely a no-drama zone. Even as an adult, when things bothered him or he felt confused or conflicted about something, he'd stop by the house at the end of Bay View Road. When Lilly was still alive, they'd sit and talk, and Cam would always feel better—calmer—just for having spent some time with her. After she passed, sometimes he'd let himself in and he'd sit for a while, sometimes in the living room, sometimes in the kitchen, and he'd let the memory of her spirit and loving heart soothe him.

Cam believed that if he'd grown up to be a good man, he had Ted Cavanaugh to thank for being the role model he'd needed, when he needed it, and Lilly to thank for loving him and Wendy when they'd most felt unlovable. The Cavanaughs' house represented all that was good in St. Dennis to Cameron, and knowing that it would be his by summer—when Ellie said she'd be ready to sell—should have gladdened his heart.

But that was before he'd acknowledged his feelings for Ellie, before he realized just how deeply those feelings went. Before he understood that he'd gladly give up the house if only the woman would stay.

Chapter 19

ELLIE took her time washing the coffee cup that Cam had used, drawing out the process by rinsing it first in hot water, then in cold. She wanted to curl up in the corner all by herself and sort out the events of the past twenty-four hours but there simply wasn't time. Any sorting or thinking she was going to do would have to wait until she crawled into bed that night and could go over it all: the night spent with Cam and the new direction their relationship was taking; the fact that he'd known who she was and didn't tell her that he knew; the revision of what she'd believed to be her parents' love story from that of total mutual devotion to a husband who'd cheated. Gabi . . .

Ellie wondered if her mother had known that her father had strayed. Had she known about Gabi? Was Clifford's infidelity the reason Lynley began spending less time at home and more time working, accepting modeling jobs that would find her on any given day in some exotic place far from home?

Ellie had to accept the fact that those were questions that most likely would never be answered. The questions about Cameron and their relationship—those were very different. Her feelings for him left her totally confused.

She'd thought she was in love with Henry, but Henry had never ignited her whole being the way Cam did. When she was with Cameron, she felt totally alive, totally engaged in whatever they were doing or talking about. Her mind didn't wander onto mundane things like a pair of shoes she'd seen in the window of a shop earlier that day or which trendy restaurant they'd go to for dinner. Cameron was always in the present, and he brought her with him and kept her there.

It was so strange to think that what had begun as the most difficult time of her life was turning out to be the most rewarding in so many ways.

And then there was Gabi.

Ellie'd agreed to take her in because she couldn't bear to send any kid into the hell of foster care and the possibility that she'd be bounced from one foster home to another. It wasn't Gabi's fault that Clifford had cheated on his wife with her mother. It wasn't her fault that her mother was dead and she had no one else to turn to. It wasn't her fault that there was no one living who loved her enough to give her a home. Ellie hadn't really wanted her, but she wasn't heartless enough to turn her back on a kid who needed her. Even if the last thing Ellie needed right now was a kid to complicate her life.

Right now that kid was upstairs trying to make herself at home in a place where she had to know she hadn't been wanted.

Ellie turned off the voices in her head. Too much had happened today for her to think rationally about any of it. It was time to shut down the inner chatter and deal with things in order of priority.

She went upstairs and stood in the doorway and watched Gabi sorting through her clothes. She was struck by Gabi's obvious attempts to make even this task seem, well, normal.

"I have more clothes than dresser space." Gabi looked up when she heard Ellie in the hall. "I hung stuff in the closet, but I have a bunch of other stuff that doesn't fit anywhere."

"You can use a dresser from one of the other rooms if you like. There's one that matches this one across the hall." Ellie looked around the room. "We could move out that chair and put the dresser there."

"I was thinking that would be a good place to read," Gabi told her. "I like to read at night before I go to bed."

"An excellent habit. Did you bring any books with you?"

"A few. Just my favorites. I didn't have time to pack up everything. I don't know what's going to happen to all our stuff. All my mom's stuff." A dark cloud crossed Gabi's face. "What happens to people's stuff when they die?"

"Depends. If your mother had a will, then things will be divided up in accordance with the instructions she left." Even to Ellie, that explanation sounded stiff. "Do you know if she had a will, or if she had a lawyer?"

"She had a lawyer." Gabi's eyes lit, remembering. "That's how I got to go to the Foresters. Because her will said that if anything happened to her, I was to go to my father." Gabi made a face. "I guess she wrote that part before he went to jail."

"Do you know the name of the firm?"

"Mr. Forester would know."

"Maybe it's in that envelope that you brought with you. Do you know where it is?"

Gabi nodded and leaned into one of the big boxes Jesse had carried up for her. "It's here." She handed it over to Ellie, who immediately opened it and started leafing through the papers.

"Let's see if we can find ... oh, here it is. Donald Ansel. Germaine, Ansel and Gallagher." She glanced at her watch. "It's probably too late to call now but we can call on Monday." Ellie paused. "Actually, maybe we should have Jesse call ... "

"He can find out where my mom's stuff is? Where the rest of my stuff is?" Gabi looked hopeful.

"I don't know why not." *And I don't know why Max Forester hadn't dealt with this, but whatever. It will be dealt with now,* Ellie resolved.

"I didn't have much time to pack." Gabi sat on the edge of her bed and Dune jumped up next to her. "It was hard to know what to take."

"Didn't anyone help you?"

"Mrs. Carroll, next door, helped. She said I should just take my winter stuff because the cold weather was coming." Gabi stared at the space between her feet on the carpet. "She said I could only take a few books because there wouldn't be room in the car."

"Mr. Forester's car?"

Gabi nodded.

"We'll work this out next week, and we'll see if we can get your books and your other things."

"My summer clothes, too?"

326

Ellie knew Gabi wasn't thinking about what she'd wear next year as much as where she'd be. She was asking if she'd still be here.

"Whichever of your things you want, we'll bring. Maybe you could make a list," Ellie suggested. "In the meantime, let's see where we could fit another dresser in here, maybe rearrange the furniture if we have to . . . "

The furniture was rearranged, the second dresser brought in and filled, and dinner made and eaten by eight thirty. They'd barely finished eating when Gabi began yawning, her eyes at half-mast.

"Why don't you turn in early?" Ellie suggested. "You've had one heck of a long day."

"A life-changing day," Gabi replied. "A day after which my life will never be the same, ever."

Ellie suppressed a smile. Had she been this dramatic at thirteen?

"We'll need to put clean sheets on your bed," Ellie told her.

"I did that already. I switched the sheets that were on the bed in the first room. They smelled clean."

"They were. Good thinking." Ellie mentally added *independent* and *self-sufficient* to *intelligent, adaptable*, and *good-natured*.

"Can I take Dune up with me?"

"If she wants to go, sure. But I don't let her sleep on the bed."

"Come on, Dune." Gabi snapped her fingers and Dune got up and trotted after her, leaving Ellie to wonder if she'd just lost her dog to this child.

"I'll be up in a while to say good night."

"I'll be awake for a while. I like to read before I turn off the light. I like to have nice things in my head before I go to sleep."

"What are you reading now?"

"*Anne of Green Gables.*" Gabi hastened to add, "I know it's a kid's book, but I really like it. I've read it, like, a million times."

"That was my favorite when I was a girl," Ellie told her.

"I like that Anne was always so hopeful. I mean, she was an orphan and still believed that good things would happen when she went to live with Matthew and Marilla." She paused, then added, "And I like the way she looked at things, like everything was special. Like the Violet Vale and the Lake of Shining Waters. I was thinking about that when I was looking at the Bay today, but Bay of Shining Waters doesn't sound quite the same."

Ellie couldn't help but smile.

"And at first, after my mom died and no one knew what to do with me, I was thinking I was like Anne. You know, an orphan coming to live with strangers who don't understand her. But I told myself that I'm not quite an orphan, that I do have someone." She looked across the room to Ellie with her huge round eyes and said, "I have you. And while you don't understand about my mother, you understand about my father."

"All too well." Ellie nodded. "But I can relate to how it feels to lose your mother. My mother died, too, though I wasn't a kid when that happened."

"I remember about your mother. My mom had a

People magazine that had her picture in it. She was beautiful, like a fairy princess."

"I always thought so, too. But how could you remember that?" Ellie asked. "You were only a year old or so when she died."

"I found the magazine in my mom's room. I guess she kept it for some reason." Gabi's fingers twisted in her hair. "You probably don't like my mom very much, do you?"

"I didn't know her," Ellie answered honestly. "I don't know what went on between my dad and my mom, or Dad and your mother. I doubt we'll ever know."

"She was a really good mom, Ellie." Gabi's voice was thin and tight.

"I'm sure she was. Judging by the fact that you seem like a really good kid, she'd have had to have been a really good mom."

The tension that had been building in Gabi's face began to vanish.

"Gabi, you know that you can talk about your mom anytime you want," Ellie assured her. "Your mom, or anything else you want to talk about."

Gabi nodded several times, then ran up the steps, Dune close at her heels.

It wasn't hard for Ellie to recall how lost she'd felt when Lynley died, and she'd been twenty at the time, halfway through college. But she was an adult, and had handled Lynley's death with a certain amount of maturity with the help of her father. At thirteen, Gabi not only lacked the maturity, but she hadn't had the support of her father, and from the little she'd said, there didn't seem to be another adult in her life who could help her to navigate such deep waters.

Whatever the relationship between Marilyn Hansen and Clifford Chapman might have been, their daughter did seem like a good kid—despite the lack of attention from her father—a kid who deserved a better hand than the one she'd been dealt. Ellie covered her face with her hands. The last thing she'd expected when she arose that morning was to find herself with a very young teenager to raise, but there it was. And if Gabi could make such a brave effort to adjust, so could she.

Ellie cleaned up the kitchen from dinner and closed up the house for the night, turning off lights as she went through the downstairs to the stairwell in the foyer. She started to grab a book from the stack of journals she'd yet to read, then put it back. What if she discovered something else that she didn't really want to know about? She had enough to keep her mind racing through the night, so why look for trouble?

She stopped in Gabi's room to say good night, and found her already asleep, book in one hand, the other resting on Dune's back. The dog's tail began to softly thump when Ellie walked into the room to turn off the light, her little dog face looking chagrined at having been caught on the forbidden bed.

"It's okay," Ellie whispered, her hand briefly touching Dune's head as she reached for the book. "Keep her company, Dune. Good girl."

Ellie left the book on the bedside table and turned off the lamp. In her own room, she stripped down for the shower and grabbed a long nightshirt from a drawer. She took a long, hot shower, dried her hair, and dressed for bed. The last time she'd felt so drained, mentally and physically exhausted, had been last year when the charges were made against her father and Henry. Ellie had been so shocked, so devastated, so disbelieving. She'd had to be shown the evidence in order to believe it, and the agents who'd investigated the case undercover for months had been happy to lay it all out for her, hoping for her testimony. But since Ellie had never been involved in the investment side of the business, and because both her father and her fiancé had gone to extraordinary lengths to make sure she was kept in the dark, the government had had little use for her. She'd been deprived of the comfort of both men in her life, and had been left with Carly and Carly's family to hold her together.

She couldn't imagine going through something like that without Carly to help her through. Yet here was Gabi, going through so much more, with no one. Well, no one except Ellie.

The wind picked up outside and the branches of the trees smacked against the glass. Ellie turned off the light, pulled the blankets up to her chin, and tried to get comfortable. The last time she'd crawled into this bed, she'd been with Cameron. If not for Gabi, he'd probably be here now.

Not a good idea to have a sleepover with a guy the first night Gabi was here, she'd realized. Not a good message to send the kid. She pulled over the pillow Cam had used and held it against her body. It was a poor substitute, but she could smell the faintest bit of his aftershave lingering on the pillowcase.

She'd been shocked when Cam admitted that he knew who she was, surprised that he hadn't made more of an issue out of it and that he'd never let on. She tried to focus on this one thing, her eyes closed in the dark, an attempt to calm her brain because there was way too much swirling around in there tonight.

On the one hand, she felt that he'd deceived her by not letting her know that he knew, for letting her keep up the pretense. On the other, she'd be the world's biggest hypocrite for accusing him of being deceitful when she—liar, liar, pants on fire—had so deliberately kept her identity a secret.

He knew, but he hadn't told anyone, not even her. He'd respected her right to privacy, he'd said. How could she be angry with a man who hadn't grilled her or confronted her, but who'd left it up to her when to reveal her secrets?

She fell asleep, thinking he was a one-of-a-kind guy. A guy it would be really hard to say good-bye to when the time came. But they had from now until summer, and that was going to have to be enough.

The first snow of the season was falling on Saturday morning, the fat flakes drifting down like feathers onto the grass and the trees. It wasn't a snow destined to last, nor would it stick to the ground, but it was a pretty snow, and Gabi had been excited to see what it looked like on the beach, so she and Ellie put on their heavy jackets and took Dune down to the water's edge to watch the snow fall onto the sand and dissolve into the Bay.

Gabi had pointed across the Bay. "You can hardly see

the other side, the snowfall is so thick. It's like everything out there is white."

Dune leaped to catch the snowflakes even as Gabi caught them with her tongue. The grasses held a thin covering of white that the occasional breeze blew onto the sand. They walked down the beach as far as the remains of the lighthouse, then turned back, the wind having shifted to send cold gusts along the shore.

"Brr. It's really cold today," Gabi was saying as they returned to the house. "How can it be so cold today when it was only chilly yesterday?"

"I guess this time of the year, you can expect almost anything," Ellie replied.

"Is that your car?" Gabi stood in the driveway near the path to the front door. "That is so cool!"

"It belongs to my friend Carly. She let me borrow it because I don't have a car."

"Why don't you have a car?" Gabi asked.

Ellie hesitated for a moment. *Honesty*, she reminded herself. *Total honesty.*

"I bought my car with money that I made from doing public relations work for my father's company. The government said that the money he paid me had been gotten through defrauding his clients, so they took the car to sell it and put the money into a fund to pay back the people he'd stolen from."

Gabi stared at Ellie, the color draining from her face.

"Can the government take anything that was bought with money he made?" she asked, and Ellie nodded.

"They could take the town house and my mother's car and our clothes and—"

"Whoa, there. Let's not look for trouble, all right? I don't know if the FBI even knows about you. And if they do, or if they find out, we'll deal with it if we have to." She put her arm around Gabi and walked with her to the front porch. "Right now let's go inside and make a fire and some hot chocolate."

The wood that Cam had stacked on the back porch sat under an overhang and was dry and well seasoned, and caught right away. Ellie and Gabi decided it would be a great place to read, so they took their mugs of cocoa into the living room and curled up on the sofa, Gabi with *Anne*, Ellie with one of Lilly's journals. They'd barely gotten comfortable when Ellie's phone rang.

"Hi," she said after glancing at the caller ID.

"Hi yourself. How are you and Gabi getting along?" Cam asked.

"Just fine." She felt Gabi watching from the corner of her eyes and decided to leave it at "fine."

"Listen, my sister's on her way. We usually have Thanksgiving dinner together on the day after—because she's a chef and always works that day—but this year we had to skip it because of her move. She decided she wanted to do the dinner thing tonight. Any chance you and Gabi would want to join us?"

"How would your sister feel about that?"

"I already told her I'd like to invite a guest or two. She's okay with it. Actually, she's looking forward to meeting you."

Ellie looked out the window. The snow had stopped and none had stuck to the street.

"Sure. We'd love to. What time is good?"

"We're planning on six o'clock."

"Can I bring something?"

"She says she has it covered, so I'll say no. Just yourselves."

"We'll be there. Thanks, Cam." Ellie put the phone down and told Gabi, "Cam's invited us to dinner at his house tonight. His sister, who's a chef, is making a two-days-late Thanksgiving dinner."

"Well, you know, I already had Thanksgiving dinner. At the Foresters'." Gabi bit the inside of her lip. "Maybe the one at Cam's will be more fun ..."

It *was* fun. Wendy O'Connor was a petite dynamo who had put together a fabulous meal of all the traditional favorites and then some. In addition to the most delicious turkey Ellie had ever tasted ("It's organic," Wendy explained), there was zucchini au gratin, corn-bread stuffing with oysters, fresh cranberry sauce, and brandied carrots. For dessert there were cream puffs filled with pumpkin mousse.

Wendy was busy in the kitchen when Ellie and Gabi arrived, and there'd been little opportunity to engage in conversation with her until they sat down to eat at the beautiful table Cameron had made from reclaimed barn boards.

"So Cam tells me you're a new resident of St. Dennis, Ellie," Wendy had said pleasantly after Ellie had complimented the dinner.

"New resident, new homeowner."

"Bought a house?"

Ellie paused. Continue the lies, or take the first step

335

toward the truth? She glanced at Cam, whose expression told her, *You're on your own. But I'll back you either way.*

"Actually, no. I didn't buy a house." Ellie put her fork down. "I inherited one."

Cam looked up, his gaze flicking from her to his sister and back again.

"Really? Which one?" Wendy helped herself to the carrots, which had already made their way around the table.

"The house at the very end of Bay View."

Wendy looked up and frowned. "You don't mean the Cavanaugh house."

"I do. That's the house. I inherited it from my mother."

"Last I heard, Lynley Sebastian's estate owned that house."

Ellie nodded. "I'm Lynley's daughter."

"No shit." Wendy put her fork down on her plate and stared.

"None whatsoever," Ellie assured her.

Wendy turned to Cameron. "Did you know . . . ?"

He nodded. "Yes. I knew."

"You didn't say anything?" Wendy looked as if she were about to throw something at her brother.

"I've been a little sensitive about telling people who I am," Ellie said. "Don't blame Cam. He was only respecting my right to privacy. Because of my father."

"Lynley was married to . . . Your father isn't . . ." Wendy's eyes narrowed.

"Clifford Chapman, yes, he is."

Wendy's jaw clenched and she stared at her plate for a long time. Finally she said, "Clifford Chapman's shenanigans wiped out my pension. I lost every penny I'd scraped together to invest, thanks to him."

"I'm very sorry." Ellie's appetite left her, and she pushed away from the table. "Gabi, maybe we should—"

"No, no, of course you shouldn't leave." Wendy composed herself. "I'm sorry. It was just such a surprise. Cam, I really wish you'd given me a heads-up."

"I wanted Ellie to make that call," he told his sister. To Ellie, he said, "So is this your coming-out?"

"I guess it is. I hadn't given it much thought, except that I assumed that you'd told Wendy."

He shook his head. "It wasn't . . . "

" . . . your place. Thank you. I appreciate your giving me the option, but from now on, I think I need to own up. If Gabi can do it, I can do it." Ellie rubbed Gabi's back.

"You know there's probably people here in St. Dennis who invested through Chapman's firm and lost their shirts," Wendy said.

"Probably."

"I don't think anyone's going to hold it against Ellie or Gabi," Cam said. "I think everyone's going to think of Lynley and how good it is that her daughter has come back. The people who've already met Ellie like her. If anyone is bothered by it, well, there's not much we can do about that."

Wendy was lost in thought. "You know that Cam and I spent some time there when we were little?"

Ellie nodded.

"It was our sanctuary when we had nowhere else to go," Wendy told them.

"Me, too." Gabi piped up. "I didn't have anywhere to go, either, until Ellie said I could come to stay with her."

Gabi related her own story, embellished by her natural flair for the dramatic.

"Interesting, don't you think, that that house was a refuge for the three of us?" Wendy glanced from Cam to Gabi.

"All four of us, actually," Ellie noted. "I came here as a last resort. I didn't have anywhere else to go, either." She gave Wendy an abbreviated version of her own journey to St. Dennis.

"The house was a refuge for my mother, as well," Ellie said.

"Funny, but I can't help but feel that it's just Lilly looking out for everyone," Wendy said, "just like she always did. I'm not a superstitious person, but I can't tell you how many times over the years, when things were tough for me, I felt her arms around me. I know it sounds crazy, but I've never doubted for a minute that it was her, come to comfort me like she did that day when . . ." She paused and glanced at Gabi. "That day we came to stay with her . . ."

On the way home, Gabi asked, "Who is Lilly?"

"She was my great-great-aunt," Ellie explained. "She lived in my house a long time ago. When Cam and Wendy were little kids they stayed with her for a while after their parents . . . died." She thought it best not to go into detail on that incident.

338

"Does she have white hair?"

"I imagine she could have." Ellie turned from Charles Street onto Bay View. "Why do you ask?"

"Because when I woke up to go to the bathroom last night, there was a lady with white hair sitting in my reading chair."

"You must have been dreaming, Gabi. Lilly's been gone for a long time."

"I wasn't dreaming. She smiled at me when I walked past her to the bathroom."

"People smile in dreams." Ellie pulled into the driveway and turned off the engine.

"She was there," Gabi insisted as she got out of the car. "I was sleepy but she was there and I saw her."

Ellie slid out from the driver's side and locked the car. Gabi was already at the front door, waiting for her to unlock it.

"Maybe she'll come back tonight, and you'll see her, too." Gabi went inside when Ellie opened the door. "You'll see her and you'll know I'm not making her up."

"I don't think you're making her up, I just think you were dreaming and only thought there was someone there. Sometimes in the middle of the night, our dreams seem very real."

"She was real," Gabi grumbled.

"What was she doing?"

"Nothing. She was just sitting there, watching me."

"She didn't scare you?"

Gabi shook her head. "She's too nice to be scary. Like she's an angel or something."

Ellie watched Gabi chase Dune into the living room,

339

where the two flopped onto the floor, then went into the kitchen, where she tucked the leftovers she'd brought home into the refrigerator and thought about Gabi's midnight visitor, the white-haired old woman who sat silently, watching the girl sleep. Gabi was absolutely certain of what she'd seen, and well, who could say she hadn't?

It wouldn't really surprise me if Lilly did watch over her, Ellie concluded. *And it certainly wouldn't be the first time that someone described Lilly Cavanaugh as an angel . . .*

Chapter 20

SUNDAY morning was brisk and sunny, and after break-fast, Gabi set off for the beach with Dune. Ellie stood in the doorway and watched the girl and the dog run over the dune and disappear behind the tall grasses. She was just about to close the door when a white Toyota pulled into her driveway. She stepped out onto the porch and watched Wendy O'Connor exit the car and walk toward her.

"Good morning," Ellie called to her.

"Got a minute?" Wendy called back.

"Sure. Come on in. I was just going to have a cup of coffee." Ellie stood back to allow Wendy to enter the house. "May I offer you one?"

Wendy appeared not to have heard. She stood in the foyer and looked up the stairs, then from side to side, as if taking it all in. Finally, she said, "You haven't changed much in here."

Ellie shrugged. "I don't have any furniture of my own anymore—everything was confiscated by the feds when my father was arrested—and I haven't had time to do more than start painting the kitchen. So, no, not much has changed."

"You know that Cameron's always planned on buying this place."

"He and I have discussed that. He knows that when the time comes, I'll give him the opportunity to buy it before it officially goes on the market."

"I hope he can count on you to do that."

"I gave him my word, Wendy. Why wouldn't I keep it?"

"I hope you do. I mean, you probably will. It just means a lot to him, that's all. He'd be so disappointed if you went back on that."

"You don't have to worry. I wouldn't hurt him like that. I know what the house means to him. And frankly, I wouldn't want anyone else to have it. It should be his."

"Even if someone else could afford to pay a lot more?"

"We haven't discussed price or terms or anything else. But my intention is that he'll be the next owner."

"Good. Because it's going to be hard enough for him when you leave."

When Ellie didn't respond, Wendy said, "You have to know that he cares about you. Like, a lot."

"Cam and I have become . . . close."

Wendy snorted. "You don't know my brother. He's thirty-five and he's never brought a woman to have dinner with me. Ever. I've never met any of the women he's dated. He doesn't get involved and he walks anytime he thinks he's starting to care about someone. He's told you about our parents, so you can figure out why."

Ellie nodded. Their father had loved their mother deeply, and she'd killed him. It wasn't a stretch to figure out why Cam wasn't a believer.

"So for him to bring you to dinner last night—well, you can see that this is a big move on his part."

342

Ellie crossed her arms over her chest, not certain of the point Wendy was making.

"If you turn around and sell this place to someone else, he'll be angry. But if you leave St. Dennis, you'll break his heart."

"Wendy, I've already told you that I've committed to selling him the house." Ellie sighed. "And he knows I have no intention of staying here."

"I think he's hoping you'll change your mind about that."

Before Ellie could reply, Wendy glanced at the mantel.

"Mr. C.'s decoys. He let me play with them when I was little. I loved those ducks. I used to pretend they were real, and they were my pets. I'd sneak one or two upstairs with me at night to sleep on my bed." She smiled. "At least I thought I was sneaking them. Years later, Miss Lilly let on that she knew all along."

Ellie could tell that Wendy wanted to pick them up, so she went into the living room and took one from the mantel. "Cam said this was a pintail duck, I think."

"He did not. He knows better. That's an old-squaw. The one next to it is a pintail."

Ellie handed it to her.

"Mr. C. did the most amazing work. He'd spend hours working on these things." She stroked the wooden side of the duck, her finger tracing the painted feathers. "Cam said something about you giving some of these to him."

"No, he's earning them. The house needs a lot of work, some of which needs to be done by a professional. I can't afford to pay him in cash, so we agreed I'd pay him

343

in decoys. He's up to, I think, almost two whole ducks now."

"That's nice of you, but why don't you just sell the house now and be done with it. Move on now, before you and Cam take this thing any further." Wendy placed the duck back onto the mantel carefully. "You want to move on, then go. Go now."

"I'm afraid I can't do that, Wendy." Ellie was debating whether to share the terms of her mother's will with Wendy, when Gabi blew in through the front door.

"Ellie, guess what?" She ran breathlessly into the room. "We saw . . . oh, hi, Wendy. I didn't know you were coming. Thanks again for dinner last night. Everything was delicious. We're having turkey sandwiches for lunch today." She turned to Ellie. "The eagle is back. He's down by the old lighthouse. You need to come see! You can come, too, Wendy."

"Actually, I was just leaving," Wendy said, her gaze on Ellie. "Thanks for showing me the decoys, Ellie. It's good to know they're still here."

"They belong here. They'll always be here." Ellie grabbed her coat on the way to the door with Wendy. "Thanks for stopping by. I hope we'll see you at Christmas."

"Maybe you will."

They all walked outside and Wendy got into her car. She rolled down her window as if she were about to speak but merely waved instead.

"Bye, Wendy!" Gabi called as she ran to the beach. "Come on, Ellie. He'll have flown away by the time you get there . . ."

*

Cameron stopped over later in the afternoon, ostensibly to make sure they had enough dry wood for a fire.

"Want to stay for dinner? We're having leftovers from last night," Ellie said.

"Funny, that's what I'm having. Thanks, I'm going to have to pass. I have an estimate I need to go over with a client in the morning and it's nowhere near finished."

"I think I'll go upstairs and read for a while," Gabi told them.

"Sure." Ellie nodded and watched her go up the steps two at a time, Dune trailing along behind.

When they heard Gabi's bedroom door close, Cam asked, "How's she doing today?"

"She seems okay. Spending more time alone in her room, but maybe she needs some time alone right now. All things considered, she's doing remarkably well. I just hope it isn't an act, so that she falls apart one of these days."

"And how are you doing?" Cam drew her into his arms.

"I'm doing okay, too."

"No regrets?"

"No. At least, not yet"—Ellie tried to make a joke—"but it's still early."

"I really admire what you're doing. I don't think most people would do what you're doing."

Ellie shook her head. "I think anyone who thought about the situation would. Believe me, at first, I wasn't happy that I was being asked to do this. I didn't want to do it. But so far, it's better than I expected, and after getting to know Gabi a little, I'm glad I said yes."

He held her close, his chin resting on the top of her head.

"Her mother must have been a pretty good mom," Ellie said. "You can tell she's been raised well. And she reads a lot, hasn't asked for a TV, and doesn't have her face in a cell phone all day. Which makes me wonder if perhaps she isn't some sort of mutant child. Perhaps a form of alien life." She stopped and thought it over. "Of course, I haven't seen her with a cell phone, so maybe she doesn't have one. I mean, if she did, she'd be calling her friends back in New Jersey, wouldn't she?"

"Maybe she wasn't that close to anyone."

"Hard to believe. She's friendly and outgoing and she's smart." Ellie thought some more. "Maybe I should ask her if there's anyone she wants to call. If she doesn't have a phone, she can use mine."

"That would be nice." His arms were strong around her and she felt that if she dropped right there where she stood, he'd catch her. It had been a long time since she'd felt so sure of anything.

Cam sat on the sofa, pulled Ellie onto his lap, and kissed her.

"So what's the plan for Gabi?" he asked.

"Tomorrow I'll get her enrolled in the local middle school." She realized she had no idea where that might be. "Which would be where?"

"Out on the highway. About a mile past the Crab Claw on the same side of the road. It's a regional school now, Eastern Shore Regional."

"I'm not certain exactly what I need to do to get her registered. I thought I'd call first thing in the morning and see what I need to bring with me."

"What do you need to prove you're her guardian?"

346

"I don't know. That's one of the things I need to ask."

He began to massage her shoulders and she groaned.

"God, you're tense," he murmured.

"Can't figure out why."

His thumbs dug into her muscles and she yelped, but after several more minutes she was all but purring.

"Better?" he asked.

"Oh, yeah." She rotated her neck in a full circle. "Much."

He tapped her forehead. "Too much going on in there right now. Give yourself a break and put as much of it aside as you can."

"It's really tough right now."

"Name one thing in your life that was resolved by worrying about it."

She shook her head.

"Point proven." He kissed her again, helped her off his lap, then stood. "I'm going to get going or I'm not going to want to leave at all."

"I wish you could stay."

"So do I. But ... " He pointed toward the second floor.

"I know."

"However, we can have lunch together this week. I could meet you in town somewhere."

"Or we could have lunch here." She circled a button on his shirt with her finger.

"Or we could have lunch here." He grinned. "We could definitely have lunch here."

"Tuesday might be good." She walked him to the door. "Tomorrow might not be good because I don't know how long it will take me to get Gabi straightened out at school."

"Call me when you get back home and let me know how it went."

She walked out on the porch with him and shivered as the wind from the Bay picked up, but she stood with her arms wrapped around her middle while he drove away. She went back into the house, thinking that she was pretty lucky to have found him, and wondering what she was going to do about it.

"Does this look okay?" Gabi stood in the kitchen, her arms out to her side, an anxious expression on her face.

"Jeans and a cute top always looks okay," Ellie assured her.

"I have another top I wanted to wear but I can't find it. I think maybe I didn't pack it."

"I'll talk to Jesse today about contacting your mother's attorney and see what's what. In the meantime, eat some breakfast."

"I'm too nervous to eat."

"Then just have a piece of toast and an apple or a banana and a glass of milk." Ellie realized that she sounded just like Mrs. Timothy, their old housekeeper, who made her eat breakfast every morning. "Just toast, Ellis," and she'd hold out a plate with a slice of oat bread toasted with butter and strawberry jam. Or, "Just a few bites of this delicious oatmeal ..."

One of Ellie's first memories of boarding school was rejoicing that there was no one there to badger her to eat in the morning.

Ellie waited until nine before calling Jesse's office. After exchanging pleasantries with Violet Finneran, she was transferred to Jesse.

"How's it going?" he asked.

"Not bad at all," she replied, "but Gabi's going to enroll in school this morning and I don't know what to take with me besides the records from her old school. What do I have to take to show that I haven't kidnapped this kid?"

"Well, you're her sister and her mother is deceased— no death certificate yet but I'll see how quickly I can get my hands on one. Gabi's birth certificate is in the envelope I gave you—"

"Yes, found that."

"And we can probably get your father to sign something giving you custody of Gabi, so we'll start there."

"I have the name and number of Marilyn Hansen's attorney, the one who drew up her will." She read off the information to Jesse.

"We'll get a copy of the will, since Marilyn asked that Gabi be raised by her father should anything happen to her. Since he is unable to care for her, there should be no problem with you as an adult sibling."

"I hope not."

As it was, it took several hours, phone calls, and faxes, but before the day ended, Gabrielle Chapman was registered at Eastern Shore Regional Middle School. The following day she would undergo a series of placement tests, which, along with her grades from the school she'd attended the previous year, would determine her section.

To celebrate her successful enrollment, Ellie took her

for pizza at the acclaimed Dominic's, where they polished off an entire medium vegetable pie between the two of them.

"So tell me how it went today," Ellie asked over the salads she insisted they order along with their pizza.

"I guess okay. It'll be better tomorrow 'cause they said they'd score the tests right away so that I could go to my regular classes." Gabi sighed deeply. "I hope I get into the smartest group. I'm always in the smartest group."

Ellie bit back a smile.

"Then I would guess you'll be in the smartest group here, too."

And she was, much to her delight. She got into Ellie's car the next afternoon laden with her books. "I have a lot of homework to catch up on," she told Ellie. "My old school was further along in math and science, but the English class here is reading some stuff we didn't read, so I have to catch up on all that. Spanish is about the same, though, and history is, too."

Tuesday lunchtime brought Cameron with a ladder to help Ellie reach the high points on the kitchen cabinets, none of which were painted while he was there. They spent two hours together, mostly in her bed, and there was no talk of painting cabinets or homework or any of the other things that had filled Ellie's thoughts that morning.

By the end of the week, a routine had been set. Ellie drove Gabi to and from school, homework was done after a quick snack, dinner, then more homework, then bedtime. Cam stopped over again on Thursday, and met them for dinner at Captain Walt's on Friday night. Over the weekend, Ellie and Gabi went through the wardrobe that Gabi had brought with her, and they both decided that she needed to shop, which put Ellie in a bit of a bind, since she had little disposable income.

She thought of her options, and realized she only had one.

"Remember you said I could work for you stripping wallpaper?" she asked Cameron that night after Gabi had gone to bed. "Is that offer still good?"

"Anytime." He nodded. "Actually, I could use you this coming week. We're working over at Grant Wyler's place. He bought an old house a few years ago and is just now getting around to remodeling. Well, his wife—you met Dallas—has the remodeling bug. We've gotten a fair amount of the work completed, but there are several rooms and a long hallway that need to be scraped before we can paint. You interested?"

"I am."

"I'll see you at eight on Monday morning, then."

"Actually, that's about when I'm driving Gabi to school."

"Come by after you drop her off." He gave her directions to Grant's house. "Why the change of heart?"

"I need the cash. It's the only way I can think of to make some in a hurry. At some point, there will be money from those paintings that Carly took, but that's not going to be for quite a while, though. So it just makes sense that I find a job."

"Consider yourself employed."

"You're not just offering because you like me?"

"Nah. I'd find another way to let you know how much

I like you without putting my reputation on the line. You've proven to have a skill—"

"One I never would have suspected."

"And it happens to be one I need right now. So as of Monday morning, your time will be mine, from eight-something until four."

"That should leave me enough time to pick up Gabi."

"Can't she take the bus?" Cam asked. "There is a bus that picks up kids on Charles Street. I see them every morning."

"I don't know that she's ready for the bus. I can ask her, but that's a whole different social thing. Who sits where and with whom."

"I don't remember worrying about that as a kid."

"You're a guy. Maybe guys don't think about stuff as much."

"Or maybe I just knew everyone on the bus." He sat back in his seat and studied her face. "Did you ever ride a school bus?"

She shook her head, no. "I went to private school in New York when I was little. There was another girl in our building who went there, too, so we took a car together every morning and a car picked us up in the afternoon. After that, I went to boarding school, so no. No school bus. But I've read about bullying and stuff like that. As a new kid—especially one as serious as Gabi— she could become a target, and she doesn't need that crap right now."

"You've become very protective of her in a very short period of time."

"Someone needs to be."

"Well, you could ask her if she wants to take the bus."

"She'll say sure just because she'll think I'm asking because I don't want to drive her anymore. She's only been in school a week. She needs to get her feet on the ground."

"You're the boss."

A few moments later, Ellie said, "She hasn't mentioned making any friends or meeting anyone."

"Is she supposed to tell you if she's made a friend?"

"I don't know." She felt a prickle of annoyance. "I've never done this before."

"Did you tell your mother every time you made a friend in school?"

"I don't remember. Besides, my mother wasn't home a lot of the time." Ellie sat back and rested against his body on the sofa.

"Did you have a lot of friends when you were in school?"

She nodded. "A fair amount. And once I got to Rushton-Graves, I had Carly."

Ellie thought about what it had meant to her to have found the perfect friend on the day she'd arrived at boarding school. She'd been terrified and confused and she hadn't wanted to go, but her father had insisted that this was the place to be. She'd gone into her room on the second floor of the dorm, and there was Carly. She hadn't wanted to be at the school, either. She and Carly had been there for each other from that day on. She was hoping that Gabi would find a friend like that, too.

"There was a dance at school tonight that she didn't want to go to. A notice came home the other day but she didn't mention it."

"Maybe she didn't want to go. She'll find her way, El. Somehow, we all did . . . "

Ellie had made an appointment to take Dune to the vet's on Saturday morning for the rest of her shots.

"Want to come along?" she asked Gabi.

"Sure. Just give me a minute." Gabi ran upstairs for her shoes and ran back down a few minutes later. She got Dune's leash and snapped it on the dog's collar, then put on her own jacket. The girl and the dog were waiting for Ellie by the front door.

"You're going to have to hold her on your lap," Ellie told Gabi. "There's practically no room inside that little car."

"It's a very cool car, though," Gabi declared.

"No question there."

Grant Wyler's veterinary clinic was several blocks away on the other side of Charles Street. Ellie pulled into the lot between the clinic and the house and turned off the engine. They got out of the car and walked through the double doors that served as an entrance to the converted barn that housed the clinic. Another smaller barn in the back housed the shelter where Grant kept the dogs he and his staff helped rescue until he could find homes for them.

The receptionist's desk was right inside the door, and Ellie stopped to check in. The receptionist looked terribly young.

"I'm Ellie Ryder and I'm here with Dune."

"I'll let my dad know you're here." The girl went through a door and returned a few moments later.

"Dad ... ah, Dr. Wyler ... will be with you in a minute," she said as she started back to the desk. She stopped when she saw Gabi. "Hey, you're in my English class." A broad smile crossed the girl's face.

Gabi looked up and nodded. "Yeah. I am."

"You're new. You just started this week."

"Right again." To Ellie's eye, Gabi looked a bit uncomfortable.

"I'm Paige, Paige Wyler. My dad's the vet. Is this your dog?" Paige took the seat next to Gabi. "She is really cute. What's her name?"

"Dune."

"That's so cool."

The door opened and Grant stepped out.

"Ellie, hi. Bring her in." He looked across the room at his daughter. "Remember the dog that got away from the transport a few weeks ago?" He pointed down at Dune. "Fugitive."

"Dad, can I take Gabi over to the shelter to look at the puppies?" Paige asked. "Emmy just pulled into the parking lot, so she can take the desk."

"Sure, if Gabi wants to."

"Gabi, you have to see these puppies. Cutest ever."

"Okay." Gabi looked at Ellie.

"Sure," Ellie told her.

"How do you know my name?" Ellie heard Gabi ask Paige as they went through the double doors.

"Duh. I'm in your class ... "

Their voices faded away and Ellie followed Grant into the examining room.

Dune's vaccinations took less than ten minutes, but it took Ellie another twenty to find Gabi. She and Paige had decided to take some of the shelter dogs—two each—on a walk, and they were just coming back up the drive when Ellie came out of the barn for the third time.

"I'm sorry, Ellie," Gabi apologized. "We started walking the dogs, and one dog sort of led to another."

"I can see how that can happen." Ellie loaded Dune into the car yet again.

"I'll take these two back," she told Ellie. "I won't be long."

"It's okay, Gabi, I'll take them." Paige reached for the leashes. "Thanks for your help. I'll see you later."

"Did you make plans for later with Paige?" Ellie asked as she drove back to Charles Street.

"She's having a sleepover and she invited me. Could I go?"

"Sure, but you don't look too happy about the prospect. Do you not want to go?"

"I want to go. I like Paige. I just don't know about the other girls. I don't know any of them." Gabi looked worried.

"This could be an opportunity to get to know them."

"I have to think about it."

Later in the afternoon, Cameron stopped in, and Ellie assumed it was to pick up the ladder he'd left in the kitchen. She started to walk to the back of the house, but he sat on the steps in the foyer.

"Why didn't you tell me that my sister was here on Sunday?" he asked.

Ellie shrugged. "It didn't seem important."

"What did she say?"

Choosing her words carefully, Ellie replied, "She just wanted to make sure that I understood how much it would mean to you to buy this house."

"She shouldn't have said anything at all. That's between you and me."

"I'm sure she thought she was being helpful. And besides, I think she was looking for a reason to come inside, see the place again."

"She was meddling. She's one of those people who cannot leave well enough alone."

"It's okay, Cam. I didn't mind, and I assured her that come summer, you'll be the new owner."

"Have you thought any more about where you're going or what you're going to do?"

"Not really. I haven't really had much time. I've mostly been focused on the work I have to do to get the place in shape."

"You could just take it easy from here on in," he told her, "leave everything for me to do. I still don't really understand why you won't just sell it to me now."

"Trying to get rid of me?" she teased.

"No. I don't want to see you go. I just don't understand you."

"Here's the deal, Cam. Here's the part I left out the other day." Ellie sat on the step next to him. "My mother's will stipulated that I would inherit the house only if I lived here for six months. Which brings us to

357

May. So I have to stay until then, or the house is sold and the proceeds go to charity. I can't sell the house now, even if I wanted to, which frankly, I don't. I'm not ready. I can't even sell the paintings now, because the contents of the house are included in that stipulation. And besides, right now I can't afford to go anywhere else. Once Carly has sold a few paintings ... well, those paintings change everything. She says they're worth a lot of money."

"You're going to sell all of them?"

"Yes, when I can. She's certain she'll have buyers lined up for them. I can use the money to start fresh somewhere."

"So what exactly does 'starting fresh' mean?" he asked. "Just what is it you want to do, Ellie?"

A shuffle near the top of the stairs drew their attention upward.

"Is that true? What you said?" Gabi asked from the first landing. "You're going to sell this house? You're going to move away?"

"Yes," Ellie told her.

"Oh." Gabi appeared crestfallen.

"I've always planned on selling it, Gabi. I never meant to stay here in St. Dennis. But don't worry. You'll be going with me."

"Where?"

"Well, I don't know yet."

Gabi turned and went slowly back up the steps.

"Are you almost ready to go to Paige's? It's close to four," Ellie pointed out.

"I changed my mind. I'm not going."

"Why not? I thought you were looking forward to it."

"I was," Gabi said pointedly. "But what's the point in making friends if I'm going to be moving away soon and have to make friends all over again?"

"Not soon. Not till the summer."

"That's soon." Gabi went back up the hall and quietly closed her bedroom door.

"I should go talk to her. I guess the thought of another move has really upset her." Ellie avoided Cam's eyes. She knew their conversation wasn't over.

She stood, and looked anywhere but at Cameron.

"I'll talk to you later, then." He leaned over and kissed the side of her face. "I'll let myself out."

She nodded, and went upstairs to talk to Gabi.

From the hall, Ellie could hear Gabi crying. She knocked softly on the door and waited to be invited in.

"Come in," Gabi told her.

Ellie found Gabi lying across her bed, sobbing into her pillow.

"Gabi, want to tell me what's wrong?"

"Everything's wrong."

Ellie took a deep breath. Of course, for Gabi, everything was wrong. Her mother's dead, she's living in a strange town with a stranger, she just starts to make friends and finds out she'll be moving at the end of the school year. Again.

"I'm sorry, Gabi. It didn't occur to me to tell you about selling the house. It just isn't something I was thinking about." Ellie stood awkwardly next to the bed, then sat down cautiously on the edge of the mattress. "I know that all of this—everything that's happened to you over the past month—has been a nightmare. If I could change things back to the way they were for you, I would."

"I miss my mother," Gabi sobbed. "I want my mother back."

"I know, sweetie." Ellie rubbed Gabi's back and smoothed her hair back from her wet face. A few minutes later, Dune jumped up on the bed and licked the tears.

"I miss her so much, Ellie. I don't know why she had to die."

A few more sobs escaped her lips, then Gabi sat up, her face red and blotchy.

"I wake up sometimes at night and I cry because I miss her so much. I try to keep quiet because I don't want to wake you up. I don't want you to think I don't like living here with you."

"I wouldn't think that," Ellie said softly. "You can wake me up anytime. I don't want you lying awake, alone and sad."

"I'm sad but I'm not alone." Gabi sniffed. "The lady with the white hair is always here when I wake up."

"The lady with the white hair?"

"I told you about her. She just lets me talk, and she listens, and then I fall back to sleep." Gabi wiped her face with a tissue she pulled from a pocket of her jeans. "What would happen to the lady if we left? She wouldn't have anyone to keep her company."

"You know she's not real, right?"

"Not real like you and me, maybe, but she's real, Ellie. I see her every night."

"Does it scare you to see this . . . " What to call it? "This woman in your room at night?"

Gabi shook her head. "No. I like her. She makes me feel safe."

Great, Ellie thought. *I now have a thirteen-year-old child and a ghost of a woman who'd been near one hundred living with me. But at least the ghost is Lilly.*

Ellie shook her head. Had she really just thought that?

"The next time we see Cam, I want you to describe the white-haired lady to him, all right?"

Gabi nodded. "Has he seen her, too?"

"I think it's been a long time since he's seen her, but then again, not much would surprise me today." In spite of herself, Ellie was starting to think that maybe Gabi was seeing Lilly. It defied everything she believed, but still, the child was convincing. "So about tonight. I think you should go and have a good time. I think you'll have a lot of fun. You and Paige got along so well this morning. I think she'd be disappointed if you didn't go."

"Do you think so?"

"I do."

"Maybe . . ." Gabi scooched over to sit next to Ellie. "Why do you have to sell the house in the summer? Why can't you just decide to stay here?"

"For one thing, I'll need a job."

"You have a job. With Cameron."

"That's only temporary. I don't know that I could support us by scraping wallpaper."

"What's the other thing?"

"I already promised Cam I'd sell the house to him in May. I gave my word. I can't change my mind now."

"I bet he'd be okay if you wanted to stay. He likes you."

361

"Cam's waited a long, long time to live here. I can't tell him I'm not going to sell it to him."

"Even if you wanted to?"

"Even if I wanted to." Did she want to? She was starting to wonder.

"When I first got here I thought it was just an old house," Gabi confided, "but now I think it's the best place."

"Why's that?"

Gabi shrugged. "I don't know. It's just a happy place to be."

"Well, it *is* that." Ellie remembered something else she wanted to ask about. "Gabi, do you have a cell phone?"

"I did, but I don't have one now."

"Where is it?"

"It was in my book bag when my mom dropped me off for my dance lesson. It was in the car when . . . " Gabi swallowed hard. "When the truck hit it."

Instinctively, Ellie put her arm around Gabi's shoulders. "Look, if you ever want to call any of your friends in New Jersey, you can use my phone."

"I can?" she asked as if it hadn't occurred to her to ask.

"Sure." Ellie took it out of her pocket and handed it over. "Who was your best friend?"

"Laurie."

"I'll bet you miss her."

Gabi nodded. "Everything happened so fast . . . "

"Give her a call. Maybe after speaking with Laurie you'll feel more like socializing. I'll drive you to Paige's, if you decide to go. Otherwise, you'll have to call her and let her know that you're not coming."

"Thanks, Ellie." Gabi began to punch in the numbers.

Ellie stopped in her room to pick up the journal she'd been reading the night before, and heard Gabi laughing, a sound she hadn't heard since the girl arrived. She started toward the steps, Gabi's voice floating down the hallway.

"Oh, I'm living with my sister in Maryland. It's the coolest house, it's right on the Chesapeake Bay. And we have a dog. Her name is Dune. No, my sister is cool. She's the best . . ."

Ellie smiled. She'd met with one of the counselors at Gabi's school this week and discussed the situation. The psychologist warned Ellie that Gabi would most certainly have mood swings following the trauma she'd been through. Right now she might be happy, but an hour from now she might be sobbing and despondent. All to be expected, Ellie'd been told. It could all turn on a dime.

But right now Gabi was laughing with a friend, and Ellie was "cool." She'd take it. And if Gabi decided to go to the sleepover, Ellie would have a sleepover of her own.

Chapter 21

THE call to her old friend cheered up Gabi considerably. She was in a fine mood when Ellie drove her to Paige's for the sleepover.

"Paige said her stepmom is Dallas MacGregor. The movie star?" Gabi chatted happily in the car. "Have you met her? Is she really beautiful in person?"

"Yes, and yes," Ellie replied. *Mood swings, indeed. Let's hope there's no meltdown later tonight . . .*

"Paige said she's really nice, though. She said sometimes she likes Dallas more than she likes her real mom. She said her real mom mostly cares about her new baby brother. She said she's been wanting to live with her father ever since her parents got divorced but her mother just finally said okay so she came to live here in September. She likes it here better. She likes that her dad has all these dogs he takes care of. She gets to take care of them, too. She said I could help walk them sometimes."

Gabi continued her chatter all the way to the Wylers' house.

"Did Paige say what time I should pick you up in the morning?" Ellie asked as Gabi gathered her things before hopping out of the car.

"I think she said ten." Gabi paused in the open car door and blew Ellie a kiss. "Thanks, Ellie."

"You're welcome." Ellie blew the kiss back to her, then waited until the front door opened and Gabi was safely inside.

Sighing deeply, Ellie decided to stop at Cam's house instead of calling him once she got home. His pickup was in the drive, but there were no lights on in the house. She hesitated before getting out of the car. He could be taking a well-earned nap, or he could be out in the back. She rang the doorbell, waited a minute, then rang it again. If he didn't answer, she'd go quietly and call him later.

The door opened just as she turned to step off the porch.

"Hey. This is a surprise." His smile welcomed her.

"I hope you're not busy. I should have called, but I just dropped Gabi off at Wylers'—"

"She decided to go to the party? Good. I'm glad. The kid needs to be a kid."

Ellie nodded her agreement.

"Oh. Hey, come in. Sorry. I was so surprised to see you that I forgot my manners." He stepped back and she came inside. The house was warm and smelled of pine.

"I was just working on a table downstairs. Give me a minute to turn things off . . . "

"What are you doing to the table?"

"Making it. Out of old barn boards."

"May I see it?"

"Not much to see just yet, but sure . . . "

He led her down the basement steps and into a

workshop he had set up. The top of the table he was making was held in some sort of vise.

"I don't have a piece wide enough for the top, so I've had to glue several boards together to get the size I wanted," he explained.

"Will the glue hold?" She ran her hand across the smoothly polished boards.

"It'll hold pretty well, but I'll reinforce the bottom with brackets just to make sure." He looked up and grinned. "You don't want your soup to land in your lap because your table fell apart."

"Who's the table for?"

"It's for me, actually. I made it to fit that space near the windows in Lilly's kitchen." He looked mildly chagrined. "Yeah, I know, a little premature . . . "

"Good to plan ahead," she said. "I guess it takes awhile to make something like this."

"A couple of months, less if I'm not working."

"It's beautiful." And it was. He'd sanded and refinished the old oak boards in a way that restored the grain to its original beauty. "You could probably sell these if the remodeling business got slow."

"We were slow for a while last year, but this year, it's been tough to keep up. I have a waiting list of at least a month. Not a complaint, by any means. Just a fact."

He turned off the light over his worktable. "It'll have a better finish on it when it's done. I just couldn't wait to see what the grain was going to look like once it was sanded.

"Let's go upstairs and make a fire. We should take advantage of the fact that you have the night off . . . "

*

Ellie woke up in a strange bed, where a strange light played against shadows across the wall. She sat up with a start, then realized where she was. In Cam's bed, in his house, and the light was from the fireplace in his room. She settled back down next to him, and sighed.

"You okay?" he murmured.

"I just got disoriented for a moment." She rested her head on his chest. "I love that you have a fireplace in your bedroom."

"I love that you're getting to enjoy it." His fingers trailed lazily up and down her back. "You know, it's almost Christmas."

"It's the beginning of December," she corrected him. "That's hardly 'almost Christmas.'"

"Not if you're in St. Dennis. The holiday season begins early here. We'll be lighting the tree in Old St. Mary's Church Square next weekend. Weekend after that is the house tour . . . "

"Houses all dressed up for Christmas, open to the public?"

Cam nodded. "I think there are eight houses on the tour this year."

"I'd like that."

"The shops up on Charles Street all have special sales from the first right on through till the big day. Brings in a lot of tourist dollars."

"I noticed there was a lot of traffic and a lot of people milling around the shops when I drove Gabi over to Wylers' earlier."

"Some people in town complain about the week-enders and the day-trippers, but St. Dennis would have

367

died years ago without them. A few forward-thinking folks on the town council had a plan to attract people to come here to vacation. It took awhile, but slowly the economy has turned around. St. Dennis has become a real destination on the Bay. Everyone's profited from it. I sure have. Every time another old house changes hands, there's going to be work for me and my crew."

"Sounds like win/win. You keep working, someone gets a spiffed-up house."

He nodded. "You all set to go to work on Monday morning?"

"Looking forward to it. I'm going to need to earn a few bucks for Christmas shopping for Gabi." She wrapped the sheet around her torso and sat up. "She needs a cell phone."

"What thirteen-year-old kid doesn't have a cell?"

"She did have one. It was in her mother's car when it crashed. I let her use mine today to call one of her friends from her old school. It seemed to cheer her up a little." She pushed a pillow behind her head. "Christmas is going to be tough for her this year."

"It will be," Cam agreed. "So let's keep her busy. Take her to the old church tomorrow for their service and plan on the other stuff as we get closer to the holiday. It won't make it not hurt, but maybe you can help her to focus on other things."

"Is there somewhere I can go to get a list of what's going on each weekend?"

"You're looking at it." Cam grinned. "We'll do it all together. It's been a long time since I went caroling. It'll be fun . . ."

Over the next few weeks, it *was* fun. Ellie and Cam took Gabi to the living Nativity where the manger would lie empty until Christmas Eve and they went caroling three times, each time ending up at Cuppachino for what Cam had promised would be the best hot chocolate they'd ever tasted. There was a house tour that had left Ellie breathless. She'd seen a lot of professionally decorated houses, but nothing compared to the homes of St. Dennis, where each stop on the tour had been decked out by the owner and their family and friends.

Garlands of hand-tied pine boughs wound up stairwells and draped around polished newel posts where bunches of holly and ivy trailed. Vases filled with tall branches of winterberry holly graced mantels and sideboards, and silver bowls were piled high with colored satin Christmas balls. Mantels were festooned with arms of blue spruce holding pinecones and silver bells tied with red ribbon.

"I love St. Dennis at Christmas," Gabi declared one night when she arrived home from the middle school holiday musical.

"So do I," Ellie had agreed.

"I wish . . ." Gabi glanced at Ellie, then stopped in midsentence.

"You wish what?"

"Nothing." Gabi's eyes were downcast. "I guess I'll go up and look over my homework." She fled up the steps, two at a time.

Ellie's gaze followed her, knowing that Gabi must be wishing for so much this year, none of which were presents.

They picked out a tree at a lot on Charles Street, and

with the help of Cam and his pickup, got it home and set up in the front corner of the living room. Gabi and Paige searched the attic and found boxes of old ornaments, some of which looked as if they dated from the early 1900s. The china cupboard in the dining room was still empty, so Gabi and her friends set up displays of the oldest ornaments on the shelves, safely behind the glass doors. It was a Christmas unlike any Ellie had ever had, but it left her with a glow in her heart. She knew it would be an especially tough day for Gabi, but they managed to get through it.

And Gabi did seem to love her new iPhone on Christmas morning.

"It's exactly the phone I wanted!" she squealed. "How did you know . . . ?"

"I asked Paige what to buy."

"I can't wait to use it. Can I call someone right now?"

"Sure." Ellie glanced at the clock. "I'm guessing that most of your friends are awake by now."

"Are you kidding?" Gabi laughed. "It's Christmas. Everyone gets up early on Christmas."

As Ellie made her morning coffee, she could hear Gabi chattering away in the other room, and it pleased her enormously to have been able to buy the phone. It was the first time in her life—the only time in her life—that she had to work and save money to buy a gift for anyone. She'd put in a lot of hours with Cameron over the past four weeks, and had been pleased with the money she'd made. The compliments she'd gotten on her work had pleased her as well. The men on Cam's crew, while picking up right away on the relationship between Cameron and Ellie, may have been skeptical at first, but over the weeks they came to admire the quality of her work and her no-nonsense approach to the job. She came prepared to scrape paper every day, and she attacked every wall with skill and energy.

"You are really good," Cam told her when she'd called him in to look at a room she'd finished in a Colonial home in the center of town. "Want to learn how to hang paper?"

"Sure." She'd nodded. "That might be fun. When do we start?"

"No. It's not fun. But I appreciate your enthusiasm. And we start in your dining room. We'll do a trial run as soon as the holidays are over."

Later on Christmas morning, Cam had arrived with a stack of wallpaper books for Ellie to look through and a neatly wrapped present for Gabi.

"Your gift isn't finished yet," he told Ellie. "But it's coming."

Ellie had three duck decoys in one big box, wrapped in red paper and tied with white ribbon, sitting under the tree for Cameron. He'd not been expecting such a gift, and Ellie could tell he was truly moved.

"Thank you." He'd leaned over and kissed her, would have kissed her more if Gabi hadn't come into the room.

"I love my journal, Cam." She wrapped her arms around his neck for a hug. "Thank you so much."

"You're very welcome, Gabi." He glanced at Ellie. "I had to resort to asking Paige for a suggestion, too."

"She's my best friend here in St. Dennis. She knows what I like," Gabi said before scampering off to finish

371

making breakfast—bacon and French toast, her gift to Ellie and Cam.

"I was dreading today." Ellie leaned back against Cam on the sofa. "I was afraid it would be terrible for her."

"It still may be."

"She's been pretty good. Only had one or two melt-downs over the past week. We went to the midnight service at church last night, though, and she did cry most of the time we were there. But for some reason, I expected that. I have to admit, I cried a little myself."

"For her?"

"Partly." She turned in his arms. "But selfishly, for me, too."

"Well, this past year hasn't been easy for you, either."

"True, but it's funny, when you're focused so much on easing someone else's pain, you forget about your own. What made me sad in church was thinking about all the time my mother spent here in St. Dennis, here in this house, that I didn't get to spend with her. All the times I spent in places like Paris and London with people my dad thought were important but who I mostly didn't care about, I could have been here, in this house, with my mother. I'd have known Lilly, and . . ." She sat up straight. "I keep forgetting to ask you. Have you ever seen Lilly here, in this house?"

"Sure. I used to live here, remember?"

"No, no. I mean after. After she died."

"You mean, did I ever see her spirit?"

Ellie's eyes narrowed. "Why didn't you say 'ghost'? Most people would say 'ghost,' not 'spirit.'"

He twirled a strand of her hair between two fingers, a

gesture she'd learned was something he did while he was thinking of something to say.

"Because I never think of her as a ghost. It's her spirit that's still here."

"So you have seen her."

Cam nodded. "I take it you have, too?"

"No. But Gabi has. She says there's a white-haired lady who sits on the chair in her room and who watches over her while she sleeps and comforts her when she cries."

"That sounds like Lilly, all right."

"I'm her descendant. I don't understand why Gabi sees her and I don't."

"Maybe she thinks you don't need her." He dropped the strand of her hair and tucked it behind her ear. "Which room is Gabi in?"

"Back room on the left side," she told him. "The Bay side."

"That used to be Lynley's room," he told her. "After that, it was Wendy's when we stayed here."

"Little girls who needed to be comforted," Ellie murmured. "Little girls who missed their parents."

"That would be my guess."

Ellie got up, walked to the tree, and pretended to straighten an ornament.

"What?" Cam asked.

"I don't believe in ghosts," she said. "I never have. I'm surprised that you do."

"What can I tell you? It's not like I look out the window and say, 'Hey, look. I'll bet that's the ghost of one of André Bonfille's men.' I know that Lilly is still here. I've seen her, but more, I've sensed her. Felt her."

373

"When was the first time?"

"Right after she died. I couldn't believe she was gone. She'd been our rock, mine and Wendy's, and I couldn't imagine what life was going to be without her."

"You really loved her."

"She was more of a mother to us than our mother had been. And I still love her. She's here for me when I need her, El. I can't explain it any other way."

"Is she here now?"

He shook his head. "Maybe for Gabi, but Lilly knows I'm good now. I have you."

"You think she knows?"

"She knows. It makes her happy."

"Stop it. You're making that up."

"Maybe."

"Can't leave you two kids alone for ten minutes." Gabi stood in the doorway, one of Lilly's old aprons tied around her waist, trying to look stern, but she couldn't hold the pose. She giggled. "Come quick. The French toast is awesome!"

The French toast *was* awesome, made even better by Gabi's sheer joy in having prepared it for them. Sitting in her warm kitchen, the morning sun shining through the windows and spilling onto the table, with Gabi chattering away and Cameron's leg resting against hers, Ellie couldn't help but compare this Christmas with last year's, when she'd been engaged to a man who was so disastrously wrong for her. She and Henry had exchanged expensive presents—his to her had been an exorbitantly pricey watch that he'd probably sent his secretary to pick out, and that, in the end, had been confiscated to pay off those unfortunate people he had helped to defraud. This year the only presents under the tree had been the ones she'd bought for Gabi, Cam, and Carly, whose next visit wouldn't be for another two weeks. And yet she couldn't remember the last time she'd felt so contented, so happy in her heart, and she realized that for all the angst and all the shame and the emotional trauma of the past year, she had, as Carly had once pointed out, landed in a very good place. It was becoming harder and harder to think about leaving.

"What are you doing New Year's Eve?" Cam asked as he was getting ready to leave to meet Wendy in Baltimore for dinner, a yearly event.

"Nothing. You want to be my date?" Ellie fastened the top button of his jacket against the cold air.

"I want you to be my date for Lucy and Clay's wedding at the inn."

"I'd love to be your date. I heard it's going to be the Big Event."

"Lucy's a famous wedding planner. Wedding planner to the stars and other assorted celebrities. So yeah, it's going to be big."

"I think Paige is supposed to be doing something for that wedding. Like hand out programs or something. She asked Gabi if she wanted to do it with her."

"Then we'll make it a family affair." He kissed her, called good-bye to Gabi, who'd gone upstairs to write in her journal, and left.

A family affair.

Long after he drove away, those words were ringing in Ellie's ears, wonderful and terrifying at the same time.

Chapter 22

ELLIE wasn't sure exactly when the thought occurred to her, but once it did, she knew it was the right thing to do. It wasn't hard to figure out the best means of accomplishing it.

"I must say, I was happy that you called and gave me a good excuse to leave the inn," Grace said when she met Ellie at Cuppachino. "I'm nearing the breaking point with Lucy's wedding. Honestly, that girl is a whirlwind. You can't believe what she's doing in our ballroom for their reception. And with so little time to plan, so little time to make it happen. She makes my head spin."

"But you're happy about the wedding, right?" Ellie asked.

"Delighted. I love Clay like a son. It's exactly what I wanted for Lucy. He's the right man. I think they're going to be very happy together." Grace frowned. "It's just that the wedding preparations are making me crazy."

"Well, only a few more days, and it'll be over."

"And then I'll be crying in my tea that it all happened so fast."

Ellie sipped her coffee and tried to decide how to open the conversation. She'd tried memorizing a few lines but it sounded stilted and phony.

"Grace, I need your advice on something."

"Oh? A problem?"

"One I created for myself." Ellie told Grace the full story of Gabi's coming to live with her. "When I met with Jesse that first day I came to St. Dennis, I told him I was going to drop the Chapman from my name and go by Ryder. I was so afraid of the backlash against my father, so afraid that people would hate me if they knew who I was. Chapman's not such an unusual name, but if everyone knew I was Lynley's daughter, they'd know exactly who my father was."

Grace listened intently, stirring her tea.

"Jesse told me that I should keep an open mind and give people a chance to get to know me, that people here weren't as judgmental as I assumed they'd be. But I'd been so badly burned during and after the investigation, by people I'd known and worked with for years, that I couldn't believe that strangers would be any more kind to me than my so-called friends had been. He said that people here were warm and friendly." Ellie smiled weakly. "But I told him I wasn't here to make friends."

"And yet you have, in spite of yourself," Grace pointed out. "People here do like you, Ellie."

"I'm regretting those words. I regret that, right from the start, I didn't own up to who my mother was." Ellie's hands were folded on the table. "I don't want to hide who I am anymore. I'm embarrassed that, at thirteen, Gabi has been braver than I, that she hasn't made any effort to hide who her father is. I'm sorry that I started this charade, but I don't know how to set things right now. I was hoping you might have some suggestions."

"Well, dear, it's easy enough to get the word around. A 'By the way, were you aware ...' or a 'You know, of course ...'" Grace patted Ellie's arm. "And we could do that interview we suggested when we first chatted."

Ellie flinched. She did remember. Her reaction had been somewhere between "Over my dead body" and "Hell, no."

"We can focus on the fact that you've inherited the house from your mother and you're remodeling it. And there's the angle of how many generations of women in your family have lived there. We can mention Clifford or not." Grace paused as if to consider this option. "Everyone in town knows that Lynley was married to the scoundrel; I'm not sure we need to mention his name."

"But we probably should, if I'm going to go back to using Chapman." Ellie thought for a moment. "Do you think people will resent me for having lied?"

"Let's think of it as an omission more than a lie. Besides, how many people have you actually met as Ellie Ryder? Other than those people who have become your friends, of course."

"People at First Families Day. People at dinner on Thanksgiving at the inn. Mr. Enright, for one."

"People you meet once might tend to remember your first name more than your last." Grace waved her hand dismissively. "And for the record, Curtis knew exactly who you were."

"He did?"

"Of course. He wrote the wills for both Lilly and Lynley. He knew there'd been no sale of the house." She took another sip of her tea. "I think you'll find this will be all *much ado* as far as most people are concerned."

"Except for those people who invested in my father's company."

"There may be some of that. There were some who invested with him because he was Lynley's widower. So there may be some backlash, but you'll survive it."

"You're right. I will." Ellie nodded.

"Now, we have a little time." Grace pulled a notebook out of her bag. "Let's take care of that interview right now. I can run it in my paper on Thursday so it's done before the wedding. I hear you're coming with Cameron. Such a nice young man . . ."

Ellie could hardly believe that the room she entered was actually in Maryland and not a tropical place. The lobby and the ballroom of the inn sported a forest of palm trees, the trunks and branches of which had been wrapped in tiny white lights. Real orchids of every color, appearing to grow on the branches, delicately scented the air. Silver pitchers on each table held lush arrangements of orchids, stephanotis, pale pink roses, dusty miller, and ivy. The cloths covering the tables were silvery gray and the napkins were palest pink. Somehow, in the shortest possible time, the ballroom had been turned into a subtle fantasy of flowers and soft lights. It was the most romantic wedding Ellie had ever attended.

The ceremony itself was performed by Reverend Alston at the church in town that both Lucy and Clay's families had attended for many years. It, too, was handsomely draped with flowers and candlelight. Lucy had asked her business partner, Bonnie Shaefer, to be her maid of honor, and Brooke, Clay's sister, to be her lone bridesmaid, and Clay had tapped Cameron for his best man. Clay's business partner, Wade MacGregor, and his eight-year-old nephew, Logan, served as ushers. Because there'd been little time to prepare, Lucy opted out of having a slew of bridesmaids.

"I don't have time to deal with the drama of bridesmaids' dresses," Lucy had told Ellie when they ran into each other at one of the houses on the Christmas Tour. "This one doesn't like that color, that one likes the color but not the style. I only had a few weeks to put this all together. I didn't have time for dress drama. Brooke understood completely, and chose a dress that she and I both liked. So much easier when you're only dealing with one or two other people."

Lucy did have time to find a dramatic dress for herself: a pure white silk floor-length sheath with one shoulder and silk-covered buttons all the way down the back. There was a wide sparkly belt complemented by long sparkly earrings, and a long lace veil that both Grace and Grace's mother had worn. Escorted down the aisle by both her mother and her brother Daniel, Lucy carried an enormous bouquet of orchids and wore high silver shoes that added four inches to her petite height.

"Gorgeous." Steffie Wyler, seated behind Ellie and next to Vanessa and her husband, had sighed.

"Totally." Ellie had turned around to agree.

"I heard the ballroom is drop-dead magnificent," Vanessa whispered.

"It is. Wait till you see," a wide-eyed Steffie said. "I

peeked when I dropped off ice cream before we came to the church. It's gorgeous."

"Shhhhh ..." A woman at the end of Ellie's row hushed them.

Steffie mouthed the words "You'll see," and turned back to the program, which her niece Paige and Gabi had handed out at the door to the church. The two young girls wore white blouses and black straight skirts, and had carried out their duties in a mature manner that made Dallas, as stepmother of the former, and Ellie, as sister of the latter, quite proud.

The church was still dressed for the holidays, resplendent in white poinsettias, the altar marked with urns filled with evergreens and hollies, to which Lucy had added twinkling lights. The ceremony was brief but deeply personal, the minister having known both the bride and the groom from their preschool days. Lucy and Clay wrote their vows together, promising to be "best friends always, to celebrate the passing of the seasons together, to greet each new day with love, and to never be too busy to spend an afternoon crabbing on the Bay."

Ellie looked upon the cocktail hour at the inn as a sort of coming-out—the first time she was in a crowded public place since Grace's interview ran in the *St. Dennis Gazette*. While the paper had played up Ellie's relationship to Lynley, and had barely mentioned her father, there was no question that the cat was definitely out of the bag, just as Ellie had wanted it to be. For every person who made a comment about her father—polite or otherwise—there were ten who wanted to talk about Lynley. Before the reception was over, Ellie had compiled a list of older residents who remembered Lilly and who might be excellent sources of information for Carly's book.

"Are you having a good time?" Cameron's arms slid around her on the dance floor and they swayed to the band's rendition of "Wonderful Tonight."

"The best time ever." Ellie leaned back to look into his eyes. "I feel . . . I don't know . . . *free*, I guess is the right word."

"Free to be Ellie Chapman?"

"Yes, but more than that." She looked around the floor and saw several of her new friends dancing and chatting with their significant others. Steffie and Wade. Vanessa and Grady. Brooke and Jesse. "I feel like I've come home. I feel like I'm where I was meant to be all along." She grinned. "Do I sound like Dorothy from *The Wizard of Oz*?"

"I don't know, was that the clicking of heels I just heard?"

"Quite possibly."

They moved around the dance floor, cheek to cheek, and Ellie closed her eyes, just to savor the moment. She'd made a decision tonight, one she'd share with Cameron before the night was over, and she hoped he'd understand. She had only to find the right moment.

It came just before midnight. Cameron had gotten into a conversation about flavored beer with Clay and Wade and Ellie had wandered out onto the inn's lovely front porch. She'd been standing near one of the fireplaces and had absorbed more than her share of heat from the blaze. The air outside was cool but was welcome on her skin— for about the first two minutes. She wasn't dressed for the evening's chill, having splurged on a pretty but thin metallic tank top and wrap from Vanessa's shop. She turned to go back inside when she felt a warm jacket slip over her shoulders.

"You're shivering," Cameron said as he wrapped his arms around her from behind.

"Thanks. I was just thinking I should probably go inside. It's cooler than I thought."

"Pretty night," he said, making no effort to move.

"It's a beautiful night. It was a beautiful wedding. I can't remember ever attending a wedding where I felt so much love in the room. It really was extraordinary." Ellie sighed. The wedding she would have had with Henry would have been nothing like Clay and Lucy's. Thank God she'd not married that man. For one thing, she'd never have come here, never have met Cameron.

"It was that. Beautiful bride. Handsome groom." Cam kissed the tip of her ear. "Not to mention the best man."

Ellie turned to face him. "You are the best man, Cam. You're the best man I've ever known. It seems that the worst time in my life has brought me to the best. The best place and the best man." She touched the side of his face. "I have something to say to you, and I hope you understand."

"Uh-oh. Is this where you tell me that Carly sold all those paintings for millions and you don't need the money from the sale of the house, so you can just leave now?"

Ellie felt him tense in her arms.

"Because I need you to know that I'd give up buying the house if you'd stay."

"You love that house."

"I love you more."

"Do you?" Her eyes searched his face.

"I do."

"Then that makes this easier." She took a deep breath. "I have decided to stay in the house. I really feel that I'm meant to be there, that St. Dennis is where I'm meant to be. That house . . . it's been a sanctuary to so many troubled souls over the years. My mother. You and Wendy. Gabi. Me. We've all been affected by it. When I came here, I didn't expect to be healed of the pain of the last year, but I have been. I've realized that the past just doesn't hurt as much, it doesn't matter so much anymore. I don't want to leave."

"I'm so glad that you're staying." He lifted her in his arms and swung her around, his mouth finding hers in the process. When he set her down on her feet again, he said, "You know, I never believed that someone could sweep into your life and that you'd know that that person would change your life. That's what I felt when I first saw you. It scared the crap out of me—I saw what that kind of love did to my father—but there wasn't much I could do about it. I guess it happens that way sometimes. The fact that you were living in 'my house' did complicate things a bit. I wanted the house, but the more time we spent together, the more I realized that it was you I wanted most."

"Then you'll like the rest of it."

"The rest of what?"

A cheer went up from inside the inn as the countdown to midnight began.

Ten.

384

"The rest of what I have to say." Ellie took a deep breath. "I am planning on staying in St. Dennis, making this my home. But I feel a little guilty about having made a promise to you. I mean, I gave you my word, to sell the house to you."

Nine.

"So I tried to come up with some way to ease my conscience. So while I can't sell it to you, I am willing to share it with you."

"Share it? Share the house?"

Eight.

"Yes." She nodded. "But then it occurred to me that you moving in ... living with me ... would not send a very good message to Gabi. She's at an impressionable age ... "

Seven.

"As much as I hate to say it, you're right. You wouldn't be much of a role model for her."

"So I'm thinking if we're going to live together, we should get married."

Six.

"Do you realize what you just said?"

"I do." She laughed nervously. "Oh. I guess that's a line for another time, right? *I do?*"

Five.

"Ellie ... you just proposed to me." Cameron seemed stunned.

"I did, didn't I? I know it's a lot to take on, I mean, Gabi and I are a package deal now—and the house, too, of course." Ellie sighed. "I can't imagine my life without you, Cam. I can't imagine being with anyone but you, spending the rest of my life with anyone but you."

Four.

"I never expected to find a real home here, but I did. I never thought I'd find what I'd lost of my mother here, but I did."

Three.

"I never thought I'd find my heart, but ... " She gestured, hands up. "But here you are. You're the love of my life, Cam, pure and simple. So what do you say?"

Two.

"What do you think?" He swept her up in his arms and kissed her mouth as the cheers were raised inside.

One.

"Happy New Year!"

"The happiest year yet," Cam whispered in her ear.

"The happiest year ever," she agreed.

Diary ~

*Oh, my, what a week we have had here in St. Dennis!
First and most important, of course, was Lucy and Clay's
wedding. What a beautiful affair that was! I've seen Lucy's
work before, of course—the double wedding that we had here
last year for Dallas and Grant, Steffie and Wade, and then
Robert and Susanna Magellan's wedding last summer—but
oh, that anyone could pull off such a production in so short a
time! The church had already been decorated by the ladies
there, so other than adding some flowers to the end of the
pews, there was nothing much for her to do. Which was a
good thing, after all, because it gave her more time to focus on
the reception here at the inn. In anticipation of the wedding—
and her silver-and-pale-pink color scheme—we decorated the
inn's trees with a predominantly silver theme this year (Lucy's
idea, of course). Everything was sparkly and silvery and just
so festive and beautiful—"ethereal," my dear friend Trula
called it.*

*And it was. I can't imagine a more beautiful wedding or a
more beautiful bride . . . yes, I say that even though she is my
daughter. She looked so . . . so grown up and sophisticated, so
unlike my little Lucy and yet so perfectly her. I would have
given anything for her father to have seen her. Oh, I know he
was looking down from whatever cloud he was assigned to,
and he was probably as teary-eyed and proud as I was. But it
would have been so much better if he'd been here, flesh and
blood, to hold my hand and walk his girl down the aisle.
Though I have to say, Daniel did us proud. If only Ford had
been able to make it home. He did try, he said when he*

called, but the plane that was supposed to pick him up never arrived. Which, of course, has me worried about where that boy is and what he's really doing.

But back to the happy time . . . my daughter's wedding. We're so happy to welcome Clay to the family. He's always been the one for her. We've always known it, even when she fought against it—moved clear across the country to keep it from happening, but there it is. Lucy and Clay are married, and all's right in my world.

Except for Ford . . . but hopefully, his dad is watching over him, too.

And other big news! Ellie Ryder—Ellie Chapman, now that she's come to terms with her family issues—and Cameron O'Connor will be the next to walk down the aisle! I have it on very good authority that the wedding will take place at the house on Bay View Road—Lilly's house—this spring.

Ellie's hoping to have the entire first floor of the place painted and fixed up by then, though I don't know when she'll have time to do much work there since she's working full-time for Cameron now. I ran into her this morning at Cuppachino and she told me that Cam's teaching her how to use all sorts of power tools. She said that next she wants him to teach her how to build tables like the one he made her for Christmas out of reclaimed oak boards from the Madisons' old barn that came down last year. She said it's the most beautiful table she ever saw—and that she's never been happier. I'm betting that before long, the sign on the side of Cameron's truck will read O'CONNOR AND O'CONNOR.

I'm sure Lilly is dancing with delight, to have her boy—the boy she rescued—and her girl—the one who'd been kept from her for so long—together under her roof—and I'm sure she and Lynley are both proud as peacocks that Ellie took in Gabi and is being the big sister the girl needs. It was a tough situation to put Ellie in—only a fool as big as Clifford Chapman would ask his daughter to take in a child he fathered by his mistress—but Ellie has stepped up and seems to genuinely love Gabi.

I'm betting Lilly has plenty to say about all that—as a matter of fact, I'm off to pull out the Ouija board right now!

~ Grace ~

Manlutd.